Obsessed Fan

– A NOVEL BY –

Jill A. Nolan

Cover is designed by Harry Nolan and the photo is courtousy I photo smart.

Order this book online at www.trafford.com
or email orders@trafford.com

Most Trafford titles are also available at major online book retailers.

Printed in the United States of America.

ISBN: 978-1-4269-7539-4 (sc)
ISBN: 978-1-4269-7540-0 (e)

Trafford rev. 08/25/2011

www.trafford.com

North America & international
toll-free: 1 888 232 4444 (USA & Canada)
phone: 250 383 6864 • fax: 812 355 4082

INTRODUCTION

DO NOT ENTER, AUTHORIZED PERSONNAL ONLY.

I stood there contemplating this sign. I've been here before. I've seen this sign, on this same door before. If I go through this door, I'll be trespassing. If I don't go through it, I'll miss the greatest opportunity of my life…to meet Cam Konner.

I put my hand on the door knob, turn it and pull on the door. Its unlocked.

"Excuse me miss," I turn to see who is talking to me. A rather large man in a uniform, with a name tag on his shirt. I stand frozen, my hand glued to the door knob.

"You cant go in there," he says, huffing, trying to catch some air into his lungs. I make a face at him. I let go of the door knob.

"Sorry," I say, faking a smile at his bright red face. "I'm lost," I lie.

"You still cant go in there," he walks over to the door, sort of pushes me aside. A handful of keys in his hand. He finds the key that fits and locks the door. Gives me a lame smile and walks away.

My mouth hanging open, I realize, and I snap it shut. I wont cry. There has to be another way, backstage. I go back into the arena and look around.

Most of the fans have left. A few still linger. The stage. The black curtain that's covering the bottom of the stage. There's hardly any security guards now and the ones that are here are talking to the fans that have stayed.

The gate around the stage is open. No one sees me or seems to notice me, or cares. I walk to the fence and just stand there. Nonchalantly. Inch my way to the gate. Look around and in one swift move, duck under the curtain.

Its dark under here. I feel around. Criss crossed pipes are everywhere. I grab onto the closest pipe and climb over the ones that are in front of me. I hit my head, I bang the bone on my leg, try not to make a painful noise. I squeeze my eyes shut tightly until the pain passes. I nearly trip and fall. But its going to be worth getting hurt a little, just to get to Cam Konner.

I can see light through a crack in the curtain. I'm at the other side of the stage, the back stage. My throat is dry. My hands are sweaty. I crack open the curtain an inch and look through.

Someone grabs me by my jacket collar and yanks me out.

"There you are," a nasty smile on the red face security guard. He still has me in his grasp. "Hey Tom," he yells, "I got a stow away, here." He giggles. I give him a nasty look, and try to shake his hand off of me.

Tom, a man with a Mohawk haircut. Comes over, looks me up and down, shakes his head. "Come on, " he says. He grabs my other arm and both of them hoist me up and out the door. I'm mortified.

But before they throw me out the door, I spot Cam Konner. He's signing autographs, and taking pictures with fans. He briefly, looks up at me. I'm straining my neck to see him, "I love you, Cam." I yell to him. And Cam laughs at me.

They throw me out of the arena, slam the doors shut and lock it. I'm standing on an empty side walk in the dark of a balmy night. Damn.

The parking lot is just about empty, just a few cars left, probably the employees cars. Now I have a long ride home. And I'll probably cry, most of the way home, too….

CHAPTER ONE

"Mom? I'm leaving now," I yelled to my mom. "I'll be back late, don't worry...Mom...?"

I waited at the front door, until my mother answered me. I took stock, one last time of everything I was bringing with me. Didn't want to forget anything. Change of clothes, extra money, food, something to drink, my camera, extra batteries, extra memory card, cell phone, check. Plenty of gas in the car, all of my favorite CDs, GPS, E-Z pass for the tolls.

"Mom?" I call again. She came out of the kitchen, wiping her hands on a towel.

"Oh Janie, sorry I didn't hear you," she smiled. "Are you leaving now for your..." she made a face. "Concert?" she finished, her face lighting up, because she remembered.

"Yes...you know I'm going. I told you before, remember?"

"I guess," she said. "When will you be back?"

I exhaled, "probably very late, don't wait up for me, okay?" I kissed her on the cheek. Mom's memory isn't to good lately, since my dad died. She's always been a little flakey anyway. "Spent to much time at Woodstock," she used to say.

My friend April will check in on her while I am gone. I'm going by myself again, to another concert. I'm nervous about traveling alone, far from my home and excited that I am finally going to see my favorite band again.

Our last conversation wasn't so nice. April didn't want to come with me. "Your spending more money to see this band, again! I don't understand it. How you waste all of your money on some guy that doesn't even know your there. Your chasing him all over the eastern seaboard, your obsessed, Janie."

My best friend April, who's hearing is slowly going away, cant understand why I love this band and mostly the lead singer, Cam Konner, so much. She stands there with her arms folded across her chest, her tiny foot tapping on the floor, which is really annoying. Her left eyebrow arched upward, when ever she's pissed about something. And she's pissed at me.

"No I'm not obsessed about him…I just really like him…a lot. AND I'M GOING whether you like it or not. You were invited." I said indignantly.

"I just think your wasting your time. I don't want to see you get hurt. And spending all that money, so he can get richer."

"I'm not making him richer, look don't rain on my parade, April." I nearly screamed at her, so she could hear me, as she was leaving.

"More like a circus," she said as she walked away.

"I heard that," I said. Fine.

Did you ever want something or someone so badly, that it made you crazy?

That someone turns your insides into jello, and makes your knees go weak. Who occupies your thoughts night and day. I know it sounds crazy. To think that someone like him would be interested in someone like me.

He's so out of my reach, he might as well be on the other side of the moon. I dream that I could have someone like him. That someone like him would want someone like me.

He so famous, so unbelievably talented, so unbelievably gorgeous. I'm so out of his league, it isn't even funny. Besides…he wouldn't want someone like me. We all want what we cant have. Don't we?

Its only a dream of mine. A big giant fantasy. Something I think about all the time. To be loved by Cam Konner. I want to melt all over him, I want him to melt all over me. You have to have a dream. And this has been a dream of mine for such a long time. To meet Cam Konner.

"The Rock Star." The Mega Rock Star. I want to look into those beautiful blue eyes of his, and whisper, "I love you, Cam." And watch his face, as a grin slowly plays across his face. As he realizes, here is yet another adoring fan, melting all over him.

My head filled with anticipation, as I'm driving passed familiar sights, to things unfamiliar. Through towns that I really don't see. Over bridges, through tunnels, that turn dark. All the while listening to Cam's voice, coming out of the speakers, drawing me closer.

I leave early enough. Traffic is moving, my GPS talks to me, giving me some comfort. Keeping me on the right path, I hope. Its lonely traveling alone. Scary. I'm nervous, excited, wound up, stick a pin in me and I'll explode.

I rehearse in my head and then out loud, what I want to say to Cam Konner.

If I even get the opportunity to talk to him. "I love you Cam, I love you, I love you." No...I don't want to scare him. How about, "I love your music, I love the songs you write, I love the way you sing." I don't know, maybe just play it by ear. I want to tell him so many things, I want to say so many things to him.

I had to remind myself, though that I only had an orchestra seat ticket, and it was probably to far away from the stage. To far away for Cam to even see me. To even know that I am even there.. But I can dream about it, cant I ?

I remember my last conversation with April. I don't like to fight with my best friend. She's being unreasonable. I feel I'm spending my well earned money on something that makes me happy. And Cam Konner makes me happy. She said, "I'm obsessed," she called it, "a circus."

Humph. She can say whatever she wants, it still isn't going to change my mind, about any of this, about Cam Konner.

Someone cuts me off and I have to slam on the brakes. Idiot drivers, I have to avoid potholes, people trying to read signs, talking on their cell phones, not paying attention to the road. I take a deep breath and change lanes. Try to find a driver who looks like they know what their doing, someone you don't mind driving behind.

My mind goes back to Cam. His music is timeless, he reaches down to his very soul, where he pulls out those meaningful words. Deep, personal, its real, and I really relate to his music. My father dying for one thing. Sickness and death is not a fun thing.

I've kept his concert schedule by my bed. And wonder what he's doing right now? Is he with her? Is the concert over, did it go well? What is he doing at this very moment? I want to know, I have to know, I need to know. I guess I obsess about it.

I wake up every morning, at exactly 6:00 a.m. to one of Cam's songs playing on the radio. Its usually one of his love songs. I stretch, Cam is serenading me. And for that one moment, I'm so happy, and then the next moment, I'm so depressed, and sad. I only have a song on the radio from him. That's it, I don't have him at all. I get so depressed that sometimes I cant even listen to his music. Cause it just hurts to much to think about him.

I know I have an obsessive personality. I can obsess about anything. Whether its shopping for clothes, or shoes, or anything. If I like it and don't buy it, I go crazy.

I'm not sure how it happened. How I became obsessed about Cam Konner. At first it was definitely his music, and his voice. The beautiful words that make me cry. The way he moved, or just the way he looks.

I'll never give up, never, not if it takes my entire life time, for him to notice me.

April says, I'll get arrested and put in jail for stalking him. If I don't stop trying to get him to notice me. Notice me, please. That's all I ask. And I did try to get him to notice me. I go to as may concerts as I can afford. Even got my parents to pay for some of my tickets. Stood up front as close to the stage as the security guards would let me. Pushed and shoved my way passed the screaming girls, just to be closer to him.

Held up my signs that I wrote, telling him I loved him. And still he didn't notice me. And any time he would come over to where I was standing someone would get in my way. I jumped up and down, waving my arms, just like the other girls were doing. Screaming his name at the top of my lungs, like he could hear me.

Threw lacey thongs on stage, flowers at his feet, a few Mardi gras beads. And still he never even looked at me or winked at me, like he did to the other girls.

And this infuriated and upset me to no end. I have even thought about kidnapping him. Tying him up and gagging him. So that he would have to see me and listen to what I had to say. Telling him everything I wanted him to know, about the way I feel about him, the way he makes me feel.

But how would I pull that off? He's much bigger than me, and would probably fight me off. And…he has a bodyguard, who never leaves his side.

So I have to think of something else, that would be more feasible for me to do.

At some of the arena's, I would go down some corridors I wasn't suppose to be in, security would chase me. Or I'd crawl under the stage, in between and over the metal pipes that hold up the stage. Only to be met by some big burly guys, who would usher me out the doors. I'd flash them my best pretty, pouty smile, shrug my shoulders like I'm sorry, so they wouldn't lock me up.

Most times I'd hide in some utility closet, until they passed. April called my adventures, "antics." She says, its surprising I haven't ended up in jail." She stands there shaking her head at me. Scolding me for being so stupid.

I always make the mistake of giving her to many details. Every time I escape from being arrested or sent to jail for trespassing, I felt like I won a small victory. I was this much closer to Cam Konner. I'm sure he was told about some crazy woman trying to get to him, he never got an order of protection against me.

Was he ever mildly amused by me at all? I don't know. Did he ever once see me?

So at every concert I hold up my signs, he never looked my way, or made a comment about them like he did some other girls. You couldn't miss my signs, they were big and bold, creative. I asked him to marry me, or to take off his shirt, because he has an awesome body. No nothing.

Hey, I'm just a teen, and I've saved all of my money to go to as many concerts of theirs as I could afford. I have a job, its not the greatest of jobs. But it pays the bills and lets me buy things. I've saved up all of my money, five years, I think, worth of saving up, just to see you.

So when he winked at some girl who stood next to me. And smiled at another. Totally skipped right over me. I was so insulted and nearly in tears. What did I need to do to get this guys attention?

So I had a plan, my mind racing, the next concert I was going to do something, anything to get Cam Konners attention. And…the kidnapping sounded more and more like a possibility.

I could drug him, put something in his water bottle or food. Tie him up, hide him in a closet until everyone was gone. Some how get him to my car, and take him home. That made me laugh, yeah sure, like I could lift this 6 foot 1 guy and drag him out to my car. I'd need April's help. Which I doubt she'd give me. But I didn't totally forget the idea, I just stored it in the back of my head. If I was desperate enough. And I'm getting desperate.

The frustration building and making me crazy. I think I'm a pretty good looking girl, in my late teens, almost twenty. How I've wished I could be a Victoria Secret Angel. Walk around in sexy underwear. Walk down a runway in high heels and wings on my back. To have men dream about you and woman wish they were you. To be in magazines and on TV. To travel to exotic places around the world, for everyone to know your face and body. Or even to be in Sports Illustrated swimsuit magazine. Isn't that every girls dream? It used to be one of mine.

I had the chance once to be a model, but never did. Something about not eating. And I like to eat. And I remember something about no money to go to a modeling school. Mom had a friend that had a modeling agency a long time ago, when I was a baby I used to model baby clothes for Sears catalogs. Then for some reason when you get older they don't want you any more, told me to go to modeling school, because I was to awkward and clumsy.

I've been told I'm not that hot, anyway, by some jealous girls, anyway.

So why doesn't he see me? Every concert I go home crying. Every concert I've hidden on me, the beads, and the thongs, and flowers just so I could give them to Cam. I bribed one of the security guards to lift me over the fence, just to hand Cam a bouquet of flowers. I flash my pretty smile at him, how could he refuse. He lifts me up to the stage, my chin just above the stage floor. I hand Cam the roses, he says, "thanks," and continues singing. I don't know, I think I expected a little more than that. Like, "hey wow, I just got flowers from this pretty girl." He didn't even ask me my name.

The concerts are always good, beyond good, incredible, always exciting, because you never know what might happen, sometimes funny, intense, loud for sure, high energy, lots of piros. They want you to have a good time. And I just watch him, concentrate on every move, the way he walks from one side of the stage to the other. The way he drinks from his water bottle, the way he wiped the sweat off his face with a towel. The way he smiles, the way he sings. The way he moves his mouth, the way his eyebrows move when he sings something. The way his jeans fit on his sexy ass. The way I love to watch him play his guitar.

I absorbed his energy, I absorbed all of him. I wave, I jump, I sing every song. I scream his name. Nothing. I don't like to be ignored. No one likes to be ignored.

I was captain of the debate team, captain of the girls high school vollyball team, captain of the girls basket ball team, home coming queen. I'm not used to being ignored. Youngest girl to win the amateur go-kart racing championship. Youngest girl to race with the big dirt bikers.

Don't ignore me Cam Konner.

APRIL

Don't get me wrong, I love Janie dearly. She's been my best friend since kindergarten. She's defended me and stuck up for me when mean kids made fun of me, because I cant hear to good.

I worry about her. Ever since her father died, she's been obsessed about this rock star. I don't see it, what's so great about him. Its almost like she's trying to fill in this void, that her father has left. I can understand that. She was daddy's little girl. She was very close to her father. They had a special relationship. They did most everything together. She likes the kind of things men like to do. Like cars, she would help her father work on the family cars, racing cars, anything mechanical, or anything with tools, she was there.

So she's been lost without him. I didn't know what to do for her. Except just be there for her, if she ever needed me. I help out with her mom. Who's fallen apart too, except worse than Janie. Dementia and maybe alzheimers. And its happening fast. The deterioration of her mind is so sad to watch. I can see it in Janie's eyes how upsetting this is for her.

So when she found the music of Cam Konner and his band. I was glad she found something to take her mind off of all the sad things that have been happening in her life as of lately, like a bad marriage, and a not so nice divorce. I told her she was to young to get married. To a guy she hardly knew. After her father died. Trying to fill that void her father left. But then I don't know what happened.

She started doing some pretty bizarre things to get to meet Cam Konner. She talks about him all the time. She'd sit for hours at the computer, finding out everything she could about him. I'd call her on the phone, and she'd be so absorbed in what she was doing, that we didn't have much of a conversation, so I'd hang up. She bought everything she could find of theirs, CDS, posters, DVDs, T-shirts. But most of all she spent her money on concert tickets. The prices get higher and higher. Okay, its her money, but still…that's all she spends her money on, I even told her she's making him richer, yeah 9.7 million dollars richer.

I want to go out to the movies, or lunch, or go clothes shopping like we used to. She's so obsessed with this guy, all her spare time is his time. And I'm mad about that, I feel like I've lost my best friend. She seems happier in a weird way. How she lights up when she talks about him. Frankly, I still don't see it. He's okay looking. Not really my type. Don't really like his music, but she loves it. I have trouble hearing it anyway. Maybe that's a good thing, ah!

So I give Janie my opinion and she ignores it. Janie and I had a big fat fight. I was so mad at her for wasting her money. I guess someday I'll have to go to one of their concerts, just to appease her, and see what all the big deal is about. I've heard they do put on a good show, they like piros and things. Will see…

JANIE

I have to start at the very beginning of this story, in order for you, and me, to understand how I got so obsessed about this person.

The dictionary says that obsession is a persistent disturbing preoccupation with an often unreasonable idea or feeling. An emotion or idea causing obsession. To preoccupy intensely or abnormally.

Or was it infatuation? The dictionary says, that infatuation is foolish, completely carried away by foolish love or affection. I was once infatuated with this guy I met at one of the go-kart meets. That's what he said it was, "I was infatuated with him." The real reason was, he didn't exactly want my attention, or love, for that matter. But I wanted his. It was the chase, I think that I liked.

His name is Cam Konner. He's the lead singer/songwriter, incredible guitar player, in a popular band. They've been around for about thirteen years now. To me he is the band. He could go out on his own and be successful. He's written music for other bands as well. Songs for movies too. He's even helped launch new careers for other bands. I think he's incredible. And I've made him out to be something more, I think in my mind, than he really is. A god, maybe? So when I first actually met him, for the very first time, I got really stupid, and I couldn't even look at him.

I've tried to figure out, why this simple love for their music has turned into an obsession. My life as been crazy and chaotic, the past five years. With several family members passing away, my dad, my aunt, and dealing with my mothers dementia.... All I know is that his music, the bands music has saved my life, more than once. I listen to it every day, when I'm driving to work, or school or where ever. It gives me some sense of normalcy, in my rather crazy, chaotic life. They've helped me keep my sanity. Keep my brain in check, when I felt like I was losing it. When everything felt like it was spinning out of control. They kept me from going over the deep end or driving my truck off some bridge somewhere. Or drinking myself to death, even though I don't drink. And I wanted him to know this. I wanted to tell him, how he saved my life, so many times. His music soothed my nerves, and calmed me down, when I thought the world was caving in on me. They say that music, makes you feel good, it makes you feel happy, like chocolate does. Or like exercising, how good you feel afterwards. Like an endorphine. I know it lifts my mood, when I drive down the road, and I'm singing at the top of my lungs to the music in my CD player.

How he helped mend my broken heart, after my Dad died.

When I truly want something and believe its worth the fight, I will stop at nothing to get it. I can be very possessive about it and then it turns into obsession. I must own it, I must have it.

Like the bird who flies into the window over and over again, slamming into it because he sees his reflection and thinks its another bird. He's become obsessed with his reflection, he thinks its his mate. He'll slam into the window until he dies. That's the way I feel, like the bird. If I don't do something about my obsession, I'll become like the bird.

I've also begun to realize, I have an obsessive behavior thing. I was gonna say problem. But I don't think it's a problem, not yet anyway. I know I can be compulsive. I'm a compulsive buyer/shopper. Sometimes I just buy something, just to buy it. I really don't need it. It temporarily makes me happy, until I get it home. And then I say, "why did I buy this?" Sometimes I'll return whatever it is.

My very first concert ticket was non refundable, no way, no how, was I returning it. If I was sick and dying on the floor, I'd still go to the concert.

Even though in the back of my mind, I was aware of their music, it never really clicked for me, that I liked their music. In my subconscious, I must of like them, because I already have some of their music and music videos. I was really surprised when I finally realized this. It was a nice surprise.

But I'm a little ashamed to say, though, I really didn't grab onto them until about five years ago. Sad I know, all these years I could have grown with this band as they grew. So like I said, in my subconscious mind, I knew his voice, I loved his voice, but never put two and two together. I had been searching for years for a band that I could love, dedicate my devotion to, be the ultimate fan. But never found anyone, quite like this band. I bought countless Cds, and then ended up hating them.

I had a graduation to attend in North Carolina, in June. My father was suppose to go with me, but do to his passing of course he couldn't. So instead a friend went with me.

We fought the whole way down. We left later than I wanted to and traveled in the dark, which leaves me disoriented. Making things look weird and strange. Like mailboxes or garbage pails look like people standing in the road. Then your trying to focus your eyes on the object, and you cant because its so friggin dark out. Its scary.

I always have to use the bathroom a lot when I travel, I guess it's a mind thing. I'm always hungry. Which he's never hungry or he doesn't need to use the bathroom. So I have to make him stop, and he gets mad, and it makes me mad, and thus we have a fight. He can drive straight through from Long Island to North Carolina. He's done it before. I wanted to drive, I just got my license, my friend wouldn't let me drive his mustang. So that meant I had to rent a car, when I got there. Hey, I can drive, I watched every move my race car driver father made. Every move NASCAR drivers do. I'm a damn good driver. Hell yeah!

Hell, I even broke the crank shaft in my truck. Sheered it clean off. My mechanic friends said, "this was NASCAR stuff, this only happens in NASCAR. What the hell did I do? I said, "I just drove it." Sometimes I drive it, "like I stole it."

Not to mention the fact that we don't like the same music. He likes the head banging stuff, he likes it loud. And I don't. I like it loud but not deafening. I used to like music like Gun n Roses, Santana, I still listen to Santana. At the time Puddle of Mudd, who I don't like anymore, all of their music sounds the same. Van Halen, I still love Sammy Hagar, I still listen to him. And spent seven hours standing on line, in the rain to meet him and have him sign his new book he wrote. It wasn't really seven hours. It was on a Wednesday, a school and work day. Went to school, then to work, rushed home to take a shower and put on some nice clothes, just for Sammy. Something red. And he noticed, too. I was a nervous wreck, funny, rock stars seem to do that to me. I had called the book store three times to find out, if I could bring a gift, could I take pictures, what time to get there, and were there any more books left? They said, "people started to line up at 12 noon, get here before 5 o'clock to make sure you get a book, because that was all he was signing. Nothing else. No posing pictures. Which I thought was unfair, because he did pose with people. I left later than I wanted to, again with that friend I went to North Carolina with. He drove and was in a pissy mood, as usual, because he really didn't want to go with me. But I was never there before, didn't know where to park. When we found the bookstore on Main Street, I would jump out of the car and get on line. He would park the car, and come to the store. So we fought all the way there, because he was texting on his cell phone, and nearly rear ended several cars. He's a crazy driver. Has a lot of road rage. The store looked very small, and quaint outside, but was a very big two story building. I got on line to buy the book, when I'm nervous, I talk a lot, and just started talking to the guy in front of me. There was hardly a line yet, and I guess I got there at a good time. Because once I bought the book, I had to get onto another line to wait for Sammy to sign my book. It started at 7. They were even playing Sammy's music in the store, which I thought was so cool. While on line, every one swaps stories of who they have met, and who they've seen, what rock stars they like. Of course I bragged about meeting Cam, even showed my tattoo. The line moved very fast. Up to the second floor, and there was Sammy. Dressed in black. He had on sunglasses. His hair, more gray than it used to be, wild and curly. He's a grandfather! He's old enough to be my father, he's so hot, though. If he asked me to go to some room in back of the store, I would have gone with him. You have to read Sammy's new book, to understand why I would say such a thing, or why I would even do such a thing. I thought he was ageless. And there again, I put them, the rock star on a pedestal. Once I was on line, then people started lining up, and out the door. I tried to take a lot of pictures, but someone, I think a body guard, was always in the way. Those body guards, I don't know. And my camera is fairly new, I hadn't used it enough, so I didn't know how to use all of the features. I couldn't remember where the zoom button was, so I have a lot of far away pics. I try to be prepared as much as possible. They took your book, handed it to Sammy, who signed it, and then pushed you out of the way, really fast. People wanted to talk to him, he wanted to talk to the people who came to see him. When it was my turn, Sammy signed my book, even before I actually got there, and the guy in front of me was taking my book. I yell, "hey he has my book." Well, Sammy jumped up out of his seat, to make sure the guy gave me my book, then grabbed my hand, not like a hand shake, but like he was holding my hand, and I told him "I loved his music," and he said, "thank you, Sweetheart." I almost died. He called me, "Sweetheart." Then he hugged me, and I whispered in his ear, "I think your damn shittin sexy." He smiled at me and chuckled, and gave me another hug, and said," thanks." I had someone take a picture of me, with Sammy in it. Its not the greatest. But at least I wasn't making a dumb face. So as I was leaving I'm still taking pictures, walking down the stairs, someone said to me, "move it," I said, "yeah, yeah." I walked outside, called my friend, that I was ready to go home. And complained to someone that either worked at the store or was with Sammy. That we were pushed out of there to fast. God Sammy, couldn't even catch his breath, I was out of there a little after 7:30. And most of the line was done. I even took a picture of him through the window, outside the store. My friend still doesn't get the obsession thing, I have for rock stars. You have to be obsessed about something, you have to be passionate about something, other wise you have nothing.

And Boston, now there's another great band. I grew up listening to these bands, my parents always had their music on. Even Foreigner. Now there's another great band, too. Fleetwood Mac. Don't even compare

Cam's band to Puddle of Mudd, or any other band. Cause none can compare with them. They even criticize Cam, for his music, and make fun of him. Call him names. Because their jealous, that he's so talented. Millions of fans cant be wrong. And I mean millions and millions of fans. Everyone of their concerts are sold out. And sell out quickly.

I haven't listened to the radio in years. Cause they just play the same old crappy music. I'd listen to the classic rock, or the popular radio station, they play the same old stuff. So I got sick of listening to it, and listen only to my CDs. I'm not out of touch with new music or new artists, or even new songs. I read the newspaper, magazines, and watch TV. And I listen to friends music.

I watch VH1 and Fuse TV. I watch MTV too. I surround myself with music, all the time. It calms me, it inspires me, it gets me excited, its been a part of my life, since I could talk, even before then, when my mother would sing me to sleep, when I was a baby.

One thing I really hate is when you like a song and you buy the CD just for that one song, you spend fifteen dollars or more on the CD. And the rest of the CD sucks. So you just wasted all that money, cause you'll never listen to that CD again. I've done a lot of that. I have stacks of unwanted and unlistened to CDs.

But the one thing I found about Cam's CDs, is I liked, no loved, every single song. Then I'm a fan. A big fan. And for life.

When we finally arrived in North Carolina, my friend dumps me at a hotel, and leaves me there by myself, without a car. He stays with my friend who is graduating. And this is one of my best friends who moved down here. So with my friends all going off to college and my father passing away, my mother totally zoning out, I had no one, except, my one best friend, April.

I couldn't wait to see my friend. And he knew about my obsession. Always laughed about it. Said, "I was crazy, your a crazy bitch, Janie." He'd say. I was invited to graduation parties, but no one told me where or when they were.

My hotel was really nice. A big TV. A refrigerator. Even a microwave. The hotel had continental breakfast, so I gathered a lot of food and ate that all day. Went to Arby's for dinner. Which I walked to. I always consider any type of physical activity, such as walking a mile for dinner as exercise. So it really didn't bother me, only the excessive heat.

There was a nice pool. The weather was 95 degrees. It was June and our weather was cold and wet. I was still wearing pants and a jacket. I forgot my bathing suit, so it was a nice excuse to go shopping. And one thing I found was they have really great summer clothes, compared to what we have, I guess because their weather is so much warmer than ours.

My hotel was right across from the mall, and my favorite store, Kohls. I could walk across the four lane highway to the stores, even food, from the super market, if I wanted any. It was hot though to hot, all at once, especially from going from 50 to 95 degrees.

I did rent a car, only because I needed to get to the graduation. And know one had the time to pick me up, I have shitty friends sometimes, don't I? They really don't care. And they ignored all of my phone calls, too.

The car was nice. Fairly new, a red Chevy Impala. Cranked up the ac. Put on the radio and scanned the stations for something to listen to. Everything was country. I don't like country. Although I do know a lot about country music and country singers, Taylor Swift, Keith Urban, Carrie Underwood. My friend said that's all they have down here. I flipped through one end of the radio to the other end, and find nothing, I keep doing it until I find something. It seems to be an alternative radio station. So I leave it on. The song that is playing, is the most beautiful song I've ever heard. I drive down the road towards the school, saying "Oh my god, who are they?" I wait until the song is finished, and made sure I pay attention to the radio guy when he says who the band is. I think I lost a piece of my mind and a piece of my heart, that day that I found him. That voice, those words, that music. That might have been the moment I became obsessed.

I don't know I kind of feel that this was meant to be, that I was suppose to find this band and their music. I made a promise to myself to go to the store and get their CDs. I would go tomorrow.

The graduation was crowded and hot, the AC did little to relieve the heat. I had on gray dress pants and a lacey pink blouse, with braided sandals. My hair was up. I sat on the first tier in the gym. Sat with my friends, and their families. There was a seat next to me, which is where my Dad would have sat, if he was here with me. But an older gentlemen, asked if this seat was taken. I said "no I saved it for him." He was a handsome, southern gentlemen, looked like he might have been about the same age as my father might have been. He was missing an arm, I wondered how it happened. But didn't ask. He was so nice and polite, and for a few brief minutes, I felt like my Dad was sitting there beside me. Where everything, around me slowed down, and it was just this nice man and me, sitting there together. Frozen in time. Then it passed. And I waited for my friend to receive his diploma.

The graduation was over, we went out to eat, so I had plenty of time to do what I wanted, afterwards. I had a quest. I had to seek out and find this bands CDs.

The next day was just as hot as the day before.. I dressed in shorts and a tank top. At first I always feel funny putting on shorts and a tank top, I sort of feel naked. But everyone else was, even the fat woman, so why couldn't I? I'm very self conscience of my body, its rocking, and I make sure I take good care if it. I exercise and try to eat right. Although I'm a chocoholic.

I bought all the CDs the store had, which was three of them. There is a total of six so far. I would order some of the DVDs, of their concerts and videos.

I drove the car to the mall and that was it, oh yeah and Arby's. But no where else. I wanted to go to the beach, it was just over the bridge. The car rental place had me so scared, that if I messed up the car I would have to pay for it. I even had to fill it up with gas. You should see them, when I returned the car, they circled it like vultures, looking at every single scratch and ding that was on the car. I kept saying "that was there, that was there." I guess they were a little concerned and didn't trust me, because I was a knew driver. But I never told them that. So how would they have known? But I've been racing go-karts and dirt bikes, since I was a little kid. I know I didn't damage the car. So I basically hung out at the hotel.

I was suppose to go back home in three days, and my friend tells me he's staying for a couple more days. I freak out because I was suppose to be back at work. I had to call my boss and tell her my ride, didn't want to come home. So we had another fight about that. I was going to fly back home, that would have cost me about 300 dollars, or more. Wouldn't be to good for my budget. But he reluctantly drove home, neither one of us talking.

So with my very nice, new bathing suit on, a couple of magazines, a box of fresh strawberries, and my new CDs I went to the pool. It was really nice too, cause I had the pool all to myself. I went for a swim, and sat in the sun, at a table with my CD player.

I was absolutely and utterly blown away by what I heard on the new CDs. I certainly didn't know what to expect, I always listen to the whole thing, even if I don't like the music. But this, oh my god. The music was beautiful, edgy and sometimes very naughty. I loved it. Finally music that I loved, finally the music I've been looking for. I could have kicked myself for never listening to them. But at least now I found them, and I was going to learn everything I could about them.

As I listened I focused on his voice. Damn, the sexiest voice I ever heard. Sexy, deep, but not to deep, but yet not to high either, its just right. The kind that doesn't irritate you, or grates on your nerves. Not like he's singing through his nose.

The kind that makes you feel really sexy and naughty. I went through all the CD covers, looked at their pictures. Read what they said, on the CDs. And read the words to the songs. I loved it all. I wanted to know more, so when I went home I was going on the computer and find out everything I could.

There is like a million websites for his band. Millions of fans too. There are also some nasty people that go on their websites, and trash them. I hate you people that do that. Your just jealous.

And stupid.

I copied everything and printed their bios, pictures, and whatever I could find. I've had a lot of fun doing it. I have enough info on them I could write a book. Mostly just on Cam, though, cause he's the only one I care about.

CHAPTER 2

One day I said out loud, as if there was a higher power listening to me, "I wish they would come to New York for a concert." I think it was a week or two, maybe less. And in the newspaper, was the announcement that they were coming to Nikon Jones Beach Theater, in July. In Wantagh, New York. I've never been there.

I also asked some friends if anyone wanted to go with me. No one wanted to go, so I went alone. Asked April too, of course she said no.

Its kind of spooky though, that sometimes when I say something…. it comes true. And this was one of those times when it came true.

I went to the computer and ordered my ticket. I got the orchestra seat. It wasn't a bad seat. But it wasn't the one I really wanted. I wanted the VIP ticket with the meet and greet, where you become part of the show. But it was a lot of money. And most of the seats were sold already. Man if you want to go to their concert you better jump at it. But I got it, I got my ticket.

It was still about a month away. I couldn't wait. This was my very first concert, of Cam's, that I went to. Money permitting. Five years I waited for their return to the United States, after traveling in Europe for who knows how many years. And finally they were going to be here, up and down the eastern seaboard. Where I lived. I could even drive myself there. I saved up all of my money, in those five years, holding my breath, waiting. And finally, here it was, they were finally here…

It was a Wednesday. I prayed that it wouldn't rain, because lately we were having a lot of rain. But it was a nice day, and turned into a nice night. A little cool, being we were right on the water. I bought a jacket with me.

I got to the theater really early, about four o'clock in the afternoon. I wasn't sure how long it would take me to get there, so I wanted to make sure I was on time. There were people there already. Having tailgate parties, and listening to the bands music. I wanted to talk to every single person and ask them what their favorite song was, but I didn't have the nerve to go up to complete strangers and start talking to them. I did do a lot of smiling though.

I was really excited, and nervous at the same time. A little sad too, because I was by myself. Everyone else seemed to have someone they came with. Mostly guys with girls. I don't have a boyfriend right now. I'm not depressed about it or anything, just a little lonely.

I looked really good. I'm thin, but not anorexia's. I've got meat on my bones, and a nice ass. Cause I walk a lot, and use the elliptical exercise machine. And I run when I have the time to.

I had on my Gloria Van der built jeans on, a pretty soft gray shirt with white ruffles on the low cut neckline, and a black leather jacket. I had on my skechers, so I was a little taller. I'm tall anyway for a girl. I also had on a new pretty pink lacy bra. I was told by my friends, and especially April, not to flash my boobs at the band. I said I wouldn't, but I didn't say I wouldn't flash my pink bra at them. I was to far away from the stage anyway, for them to have even a clue that I was here.

There were three opening bands. They started to play almost as soon as I took my seat. The theater was pretty empty, compared to the size of the place it looked like it was empty. But there were plenty of people there. The first band came out when it was still light out, I cant remember the time. Saving Abel, a new Southern band, they were pretty good, and I did go and buy their cd.

The second band was Hinder, I really didn't like them, they were scary. The lead singer came up into the audience. The security guys come racing up behind him, to protect him. From all the adoring fans. Ha…

The third band was Papa Roach, who I like a lot. I bought all of their CDs too. Jacoby the lead singer is scary too, except its kind of a sexy scary. He's got the bluest eyes. He also came up into the audience to sing, the security guys were all over him. No one tried to maul or even touch any of these guys. In fact he went up to people further up the tiers behind me. He was pretty funny too, after they were done playing, he jumped off of the stage into the water, twice. I guess he was hot, after all he was dressed in leather pants, and a leather vest. He looked pretty hot too. Sexy wise, I mean. They had security cops in boats too, to rescue him. If he drowned in a foot of water. There was a pile of sand there.

All these bands are ones that Cam has helped to get started. I think. He's really an unselfish guy. Maybe that's part of what appeals to me about him. Maybe someone helped them out, when they first started their band. Its nice to give back. No its not, it's the bad boy image he has, that I'm attracted to.

So each band plays a set for about thirty minutes to forty five minutes each. It wasn't until 9:45 that Cam and the band came on.

Everyone thanked us for being there to listen to them. I couldn't understand why people wouldn't want to hear the other bands too, I want to get my monies worth. I couldn't believe how empty the theater still was. My row was empty right up until the main attraction came on. Once Cam and the band came on, then people started to fill in. And it was annoying too, because they had to crawl past me to get to their seats.

I think a lot of people were drinking somewhere. I had two woman sit next to me. They were drunk, and bought their beer bottles with them. Which I thought was unfair, because they made me throw out my water bottle. The security guards said the band requested that no one be allowed to bring in any kind of bottles. Because they went to Amsterdam, and were pelted with bottles from the audience, and they walked off stage because of it.

So the annoying woman who were sitting next to me started to light up a cigarette. Which I absolutely hate, so the smoke is blowing in my face. I gave the woman such a dirty look that she put it out. I think she got scared of me. I'm a pretty scary person when I want to be. I'll beat the crap out of you. They left before the concert was over, so did a lot of other people too. I couldn't understand that either. Oh well, good riddance.

I have to say the theater was humongous. The light things that hung from the rafters of the stage, looked like UFOs. It is outdoors, so if it rained to bad. And I don't think they cancel either.

A soft breeze was blowing in from the water. Seagulls were flying overhead. Not a cloud in the sky.

When the band finally came on it was pitched black outside. A few stars dotted the sky. They come out playing, and piros go off. Everyone stands, and screams, I'm not a screamer. I could feel the heat from the piros, I felt sorry for the drummer, because the ashes from the piros were falling all over him. The music is very loud, the bass, if its measured in G-forces, I 'd have to say on a scale of 1 to 10, it was a 11.

It felt hard to breath, like my breath was being sucked out of me. I wondered how the people standing up front right by the stage, how they felt. A lot of people had ear plugs. I've never experienced that kind of force before, not even on a roller coaster.

I had brought my Canon power shot with me, bought the biggest memory card. That cost a small fortune. I filmed almost the entire concert. I had two annoying girls in front of me, who kept waving their hands in the air to the music, like they were at some Gospel church thing. So on my memory card you see their stupid hands on it. I wanted to hit them over the head with my pocketbook, but I didn't. Lucky for me I am tall. So I just angled the camera another way.

I smelled pot too. Always somebody in the crowd, who likes to party. I have to say, this group wasn't a wild group of people. We were very well behaved. No one flashed their boobs at the band, like they do. I wonder if the band was disappointed, cause Cam is a boob man.

I told everyone "that nothing was going to stop me from going to this concert, no matter who died or what ever happened." I made it perfectly clear to everyone not to bother me on this day or they would die. I wanted to focus all of my attention on getting ready and getting there.

Cam is a great front man. He's got a lot of energy. He yells, at the fans to get up out of their seats. "Come on." He says. "Do you want to rock? Lets punch a whole in the sky, or do you want to get naughty?" I guess if they don't act like they like what their doing then people aren't going to like them. The sweats pour down his face and by the time he's done he's soaked. I think they like what their doing. They give 110 percent. But I've found a lot of it is acting, their playing a part. Because really most of them are quiet, when their not on stage. Even his right hand man, Rob could be the lead singer, he's that good too, has a nice friendly personality, and he's cute too. Little… did I know.

Cam stops in-between songs to talk to the people up by the stage. Lucky. Some girls have signs, that say I love you. He says, "I love you," back. I was jealous, just a little, I wanted to be upfront, I wanted to be that girl that he talked to. But I wasn't.

I made another promise to myself, that the next concerts, I went to, I would get the VIP ticket. And I've made a big promise to myself, that I would always keep my promises. Because over the years people that have made me promises have never kept them, thus breaking my heart every time.

The first time I met Cam, the thing was a total flop. It was my second concert, of his, theirs. The band. It was at the Prudential Center, in New Jersey. Every promise that I made to myself, I broke, at that concert. When I was waiting outside, in the corridor, with the rest of the meet and greeters. I was fourth in line, my new friends went first. I was so nervous, hadn't eaten or drank anything all day. Was feeling rather lightheaded, that here was this moment, that I built up in my head. I flirted with Cam's body guard, Hawk. I wanted his autograph and picture with him, but didn't. Next time, I said I would. Promised myself. I had shorts on, because it was still hot out. And I was doing a lot of walking. When it came time for the meet and greet, I changed into some dressy black capris. But this covered up my tattoo. The one I got for Cam, especially for Cam. When it was my time to go in, I crept around the corner, and I mean crept, that the guy who was in charge of the whole thing, had to practically drag me in. When I finally did, come around the corner, there they were, four gorgeous guys, standing there smiling at me. Smiling at me!…….

Rob was the first one to greet me, grabbed my hand and pulled me in, because I was hesitating there. He said his name, he seemed like he was the team captain. Then Cam, who I could barely look at, and I wanted to look at him, I wanted to stare into those blue eyes, and Dale, then Matt. I was so scared and nervous. I wanted to hug them, and tell them, how much I loved them, but I clammed up. I forgot to say my name, I forgot to show them my tattoo. I forgot to say, "thank you, or even "good-bye." Then some how, I ended up in between Cam and Dale, with their arms around me. I remember leaning into Cam, and you can see it in the photo. They put their arms around my waist, and I said, "okay, oh my god, Cam Konner is touching me. Oh my god!" And I had my arms around Cam and Dale. They both had strong arms, I could feel it. And they just grabbed right onto me. Weren't shy, about it, that's for sure. I made the worse face ever, and the photographer took me that way. Now its on the internet, for all the world to see. I cried when I saw it. I looked so pale, and washed out. I had a good tan, even had makeup on. She did a close up, and it was the flash, they all looked good. That's her job, to make Cam look good.

When we were done, I never looked back, and ran out of there. I heard someone snicker at me, when I was leaving. Probably saying, "what the hell was that all about?" I was so rude. They probably thought I was the nastiest bitch ever. But that was far from the case, I was star struck. When I left the room, and went out into the corridor, with the rest of my new friends, I leaned on the wall, and sank to the floor.

They asked me if I showed Cam my tattoo? "NO," I said, "I forgot!" I wanted to go back, but security wouldn't let me. There I blew another chance to get Cam's attention.

But that was okay, because the night was still young.

We were herded to the area by the stage. Towards the end of the show, they bring out the camera. Cause Cam wants to make a video.

One of the camera guys, who I later learned was Eric. He was standing on the stage right next to me. I grabbed his pants leg and gave it a tug, to get his attention. He turned to look at me, and gave me a big grin. I pointed to my tattoo. I held up my leg to show him. He smiled again at me, and pointed the camera on my leg, the tattoo was up on the big screen, Cam came over to see it. My tattoo has the bands name, and a line from one of Cam's dirty little songs. He took a picture of it on his cell phone, but just of my leg, not of me. Okay at least of my tattoo. Said, "it was nice." And went on with the concert. Wow. How could he not notice me? I'm dumbfounded. So the promise that I made to myself, to get Cam to notice me, no matter how hard it might be, or how ever long it took. He was going to notice me.

So after the concert was over, it was around 11 o'clock, it was still early, and I did take the next day off from work. I was following them to their next concert in Connecticut, at the Mohegan Sun. So I could stay all night if I wanted to, and I wanted to. I was planning on getting a hotel room, but didn't. I had one last chance, tonight to get Cam's attention. Before the concert, I walked around the outside of the arena.

The arena is like in the middle of the city, and there's streets circling the entire arena. I walked to the back of the arena, where I could see the tour buses parked. Behind a very high fenced in a gated lot. I stood there, and contemplated the whole scene. Could I get in there, with out anyone seeing me? There was a guard, who looked very stern and who wasn't very friendly. He was being teased by another fan, who basically had the same idea I had. We talked a little bit, I asked her if she saw anyone? She said 'no,' and she didn't know which tour bus was Cam's. I walked back and forth, from the front to the back of the arena, because when I'm nervous, I cant sit still. Like all the other people, that were waiting in line. I had a sure way in, anyway, so I wasn't worried about where I was going to stand for the entire night. I made some friends with some other girls, who were waiting on the general admission line. While I continued to walk around the outside of the arena, Stevie D. from Buckcherry, rides by me on his skateboard. I talked to him. He was cute. He plays the guitar, and is back up singer for Josh. He was very nice, and signed my CD, and took a picture with him. No one even saw him. And they were like, oh my god, I cant believe we didn't see him. Because he skated right by all the girls that were standing on line. So after my disastrous meet and greet with the band, I stood at the gate until 3:00 am. I knew it was about the time that the bands departed for their next destination. I had another bouquet of flowers, with a note, to the band. A thank you note.

I was getting tired. I have been there, since early morning. I sat at the back entrance, sitting on the sidewalk. Trying to keep my eyes open. And waiting to see someone. Anyone from one of the bands. That maybe I could talk to, and give them the flowers. Even tell them how much I loved them too. Even Three Days Grace, god if Adam came over I would die. I sat with my camera ready. Took some more pictures. Hey you never know, I might have taken something, I didn't see. I was really starting to nod off, when I heard the roar of all, six tour buses start up, and they were leaving, headed out the opposite direction. The front of the arena, instead of the back. Will it only made sense, they were pointed in that direction. Of course, I couldn't run through the guarded fenced in lot, so I had to run around it. I ran the fastest, I think I've ever run, in shoes with a three inch heel. In fact, I almost lost them. I slipped out of one of the shoes, and had to make an about face to get it. I finally got to the front, of the arena, two buses had already pulled out, were they Cam's bus? I was panicking, I was so desperate, that I got in front of the third bus, before it left. The driver had to come to a complete stop, just inches away from my face. I begged and pleaded with him, to please tell me who was inside. He opened up his window, and I handed him the flowers. I flashed my pretty little pouty face smile at him and batted my eyes at him. Twisted my hair in my fingers. He said it wasn't Cam's bus. It was Buckcherrys bus. Josh's bus as a matter of fact, because he came to the window. I almost died, then too. Josh is so hot. He's got blue eyes, too. A different color blue than Cam's. But blue. Every rocker I have a crush on has blue eyes. I don't know what it is, but blue eyes do it for me. Even my ex, had blue eyes, except they weren't a pretty blue, more like a gray blue. Josh smiled at me and even came out of the bus, to take a picture, with me, hell the whole band did. Josh has more colorful tattoos, then I've ever seen on anyone. Even I was jealous. But still no Cam, and no one was saying, which bus was his. Still it was a good night. Thanks, Josh.

I'm left standing there, on the sidewalk, watching the last four buses pull out. I feel like I want to cry, I probably look like I'm going to cry, I want to cry. My arms down at my side, holding my belongings. I see someone in the last tour bus look out the window, could it have been Cam? I watch the buses disappear around the corner, and there gone. I should follow them, I'll be going to the next concert. I'm tired, I want to sleep. I just stand there, for a long time. I feel so deflated, so sad, so upset, so in the twilight zone. So depressed. I drag myself back to my car, parked on the third level, of the parking garage. And sit in it for an even longer time, my eyelids getting heavy, its getting light out now. Its already the morning. I bet Cam is sound asleep in his tour bus, I wonder if he's alone. I was tired, I needed to sleep too. I have plenty of time to sleep, drive to Connecticut, go to my hotel room, which I already reserved, take a shower and get dressed, before I go to my second meet and greet. This will be it, money has run out. So here was the other promise, to go to as many concerts as I could afford. The two concerts, for two meet and greets are costing me over a thousand dollars. It took me a few years of diligent saving up, just to meet Cam. So after this I only have money for a general admissions ticket.

Well I gave it my very best, I tried to keep the promises that I made to myself. I did everything in my power to keep those promises. I should go to the Mohegan Sun and be happy, be satisfied, but somehow, I don't feel anything, but deflated, I guess I'm just tired.

Before I went to sleep, I needed to use the bathroom and went to the Starbucks, that was around the corner. I bought a water, and on the counter they had this five hour energy drink. I've never tried it, but I needed something to get me wound up. But I'll take it at the Mohegan. So I bought four of them. Went to sleep, set the traveling alarm clock for around noon. That should give me plenty of time.

Got a fine in the mail a couple of weeks later, that I passed through an e-z pass without paying the toll on the New Jersey turnpike. Don't remember doing that.

The alarm going off at noon, jolted me awake. Startled me actually. Forgot where I was for just that one second. Drank one of the five energy drinks. Drove out of Newark towards Connecticut. About twenty minutes later I had a slight buzz. Whoa! didn't expect that, I never know how I'm going to react to things I take. I was overly excited. Happy, I was on my way to see Cam again. I popped Buckcherry in the Cd player, and was dancing in the car to, "Crazy bitch." Hey, yo crazy bitch, I'm singing, and people are looking at me from other cars. Like my seat was on fire, or maybe I was having an orgasm.

I made it to the Mohegan Sun in good time, had about two hours to take a shower and get dressed. The tour buses were already parked by the arena. So I knew they made it safely here.

This time I was changing my strategy. Cam seems to responsed to people who are obnoxious, flirtatious, loud. I've got to be that way, I cant clam up, like the last time. I've got to make this work. I was also getting dressed up to the nines. I bought this very sexy, little black dress with me. Very low cut, no sleeves, lots of flowy fabric, just above the knee, and my red patent leather four inch pumps, with a little ruffly red bow, made by Carlos Santana. A teardrop necklace. Put on a little bit more eye makeup then I normally do. Smokey eyes. My hair up, with some curls. Kind of crazy.

The meet and greet was for four oclock. I waited with the rest of the people. Who looked at me, over dressed for the occasion. I didn't care, I felt great and looked fabulous. I drank the other two five hour energy drinks, felt like I was bouncing off the walls. I was goofy, silly, I talked to everyone. Flirted with every guy, I met. I bought a change of clothes with me. Security searched through that. I even met Chris who was at the NJ show. He remembered me. He looked tired. I wondered if he got any sleep. He was one of my new friends.

I found one of those stickers, that says, Hello my name is, I put on it, 'Janie.' And slapped it on my chest. So I wouldn't forget to tell the guys my name. I had no panty hose on, so I could show them my tattoo, this time up close. And I wont forget. I told Chris to remind me. We lined up, just like the last time.

Hawk-Tom, was there, Cam's body guard. This time I flirted with him. Begged him for a picture with him, which he reluctantly did. I put my arms around his waist, he's just as tall as Cam is. But like bigger. He wasn't exactly dressed up either, looked like he had on his PJs. Had on flip flop sandals. Gave him a kiss, and asked him to sign one of the pictures, I took of him the last time. I bought my mini photo printer with me. He really didn't want to do that either, but I flirted and teased him, and wouldn't leave him alone. Until he did sign it. I must of pissed him off or annoyed him or something, because the next thing I knew, he picked me up and threw me over his shoulder. I screamed, and not because I was scared, I kind of liked it. I screamed with glee. But pretended I was appalled. His hand on my butt. My legs crossed, behind me. It was my turn to meet the band. I guess Hawk was well aware of that. He dropped me unceremonisly down on my feet. And huffed away. I stood there with my hands on my hips. Watching him leave. I forgot I had an audience behind me. When I heard them laughing. I bet they were going to tease Hawk about that for a long time. Rob cleared his throat, and I had to straighten myself out, and realized my boobs were just about to spill out of my dress. Hum, looked down at my chest, I have cleavage! So I left it that way. Rob cleared his throat again, and I turned to see those four gorgeous guys smiling at me. And they were grinning at me. I smiled a big grin myself, back at them and pointed to the name tag, I put on my chest. And pointed to it every time I met each band member. They introduced themselves, I think they recognized me. I remembered to show them my tattoo, I put one of those tags on my leg too, to remind me, cause it was annoyingly scratching my skin, now they remembered me. I had such a buzz going, that I asked Rob if I could hug him, he said yes, and I squeezed myself close to him, felt every part of him against me. He was nothing but muscle, then to Cam, who I sauntered over to, he looked me up and down. And grinned an even wider grin, when I pointed to my name, his eyes right on my cleavage. I asked him the same thing, if I could hug him, he said, "he would be disappointed if I didn't." I jumped into his arms. I whispered in his ear, that same line I said to him before, " I wish I was Melissa." He looked at me then, like really? I hugged him against me, and felt every muscle. I held onto him for just a little longer, closed my eyes. He returned my hug. He let me go. He looks at my cleavage again, and I ask him if he wants to touch them? He's confused at first, like what kind of a question is that to ask. And I say to him, "just say yeah." Play along Cam, as if he gets the idea, he says "Yeah." I turn my back to him, and I know that this is mean, but he deserves this, for all the woman he insulted by talking about their boobs at his concerts. Its pay back. I pull out the falsies that I have tucked in my bra, and turn around, and hand them to him. He looks at them, and the face he makes, is the funniest thing I've ever seen, he's not to sure what to do, the nipples are pointing up, staring at him, and he breaks out in hysterical laughter, that tears are rolling down his face, he's laughing so hard, he has to sit down on the floor. The rest of the guys are laughing too. I think the photographer, got some good pictures of us. Cam pulled me down to the floor to sit next to him. He hugs me, and gives me a kiss on my cheek, tell me, "that was awesome, can I keep them?" I tell him yes. Of course he can.

We're still all laughing. And I giggled and flirted so much that I thought it wasn't even me talking. I still have to introduce myself to Dale, hugged him too, and then Matt. I know Matt is a devoted family man. So I respect that. But I asked for a hug anyway. I got another picture. In fact I know that photographer took more than one and I made sure they came out good. This time I went to her camera, and made her show me what she took, and what she would put on the internet. I was happy with the pictures. I looked hot, and absolutely happy. Then went to the concert, with Chris. Chris was at the New Jersey concert, last night too, I had hung out with him. Changed my clothes, into jeans and a T.

This meet and greet went so much better, then yesterday. And this made me happy.

CHAPTER 3

My next concert, all the money was gone and I had to settle for just a general admissions ticket. The concert was again at the Jones Beach Theater. I had the orchestra section, like the first time I went, I almost was sitting in the same seat. But I was so disappointed that I was sitting here, no more money, no more meet and greets, with the band. While on stage, Cam's cell phone rings, he forgot it was in his pocket. He takes it out and says it was probably his mother, I don't think he looked to see who it was but handed it to someone a crew member, tells them to throw it out or better yet break it to pieces. I wondered who it was? Was it his girlfriend?

There were big TV screens that had some of the fans on, and you could see the band better. I have some of those pictures too. I really loved the concert, and it seemed over really fast. They did an encore, one of their naughtiest songs they sing. That was awesome. The concert generally runs the same, the same play list. Even the crowd seems the same. I still loved it though.

I decided this was an okay present, I gave myself, it was for my birthday, I treat myself with the very best of everything, if money is available.

Everyone was really friendly, no head bangers, I was really surprised that it wasn't a younger audience. We were slightly older teens, more like the twenty set. I thought it was a little inappropriate that parents brought their young children with them, in fact Cam even mentioned it. Teased them about not getting a babysitter, or that they were trying to tell him something, like the kid was his. The contents of his songs aren't appropriate for young children, but oh well its their decision. He also drops the f-bomb quite a bit. And his songs are very sexual. He didn't mention not one single time about boobs. In fact I've read on some websites, that a lot of fans are pissed off at him, for mentioning boobs so many times at concerts.

I think we have to much class here in New York to flash our boobs. Three of the band members are married and have children, only Cam has a girlfriend as far as I know. If I was there better halves, I don't think I'd be to happy about woman showing my husband their boobs.

By the time the concert was over I was hoarse, I sang every single song and I sang it like I was the only one singing. Most people pour out of the theater as soon as the concert is over. So they can get to their cars and be first in line so they can sit in their cars, sit in a long line of cars trying to leave the parking lot. To me that's stupid. I'm the kind that lingers. Sometimes good things come to those who are last.

I went up to the stage, just to see what it looked like up close. Most of them look the same too. Lots of metal, and steel beams, big speakers, big lights. I was hoping that maybe one of the band members would come out. But no one did. The crew was already packing up the equipment. Each band has their own stuff, and there's a lot of equipment to pack away.

I noticed to the left of the stage, that a lot of people, are going in and out of the side door that leads to the backstage. I wanted so badly to go back there. I want to meet Cam, again. I dream about me meeting him, again. I know they paid to get back there. That's the only way to get in there, unless….. The VIP ticket. The one I couldn't afford anymore, until I saved up enough funds for it. The VIP package includes a whole bunch of stuff they get, meet and greet with the band members. Autographs and pictures. Included like I said in the concert. Maybe included in a DVD if they were making one that night. Well I came all this way and dreamed about this day for a month. I had to do something before this moment slipped away. Anything to try and get back there, so I could see Cam, again. I wondered if he would remember me from the other two meet and greets.

If I didn't do something now, I would hate myself for a long time. Letting this moment slip away like the night was slipping away. One last time to see Cam.

Since I had gotten there so early, it gave me a chance to explore the theater, I remembered from the last time, I was here, how to get around. Where all those doors were that I saw. I had to use the bathroom several times. I remembered all those doors along the outside of the theater.

Doors with signs that said DO NOT ENTER, or AUTHORIZED PERSONNAL ONLY. I've stood here before, in front of this very door. It sends chills through me. So I figured that possibly one of these doors led to the backstage. Was it a dream that I was here before? In front of this very door, and was Cam going to laugh at me again? I was so hurt that he had laughed at me. I have to make this work.

Because there was no way, I was getting in with that big guy guarding the door. I stood there and studied him for a few minutes. He looked mean, and would probably break both of your arms if he had a reason to. And no way was I giving him a reason. He looked at everyone's ticket that they had around their necks in their neat little case. A souvenir given by the band as part of the VIP package. I didn't have a new one, I had old ones from the other concerts. I should have brought them with me. Maybe they would have passed for a ticket. All I had was a legal size piece of paper with the ticket printed on it, with the bar code, which every time you left the theater, the staff would scan it again, to let you back into the theater.

The theater was pretty empty now, except for a few lingering people who were standing around talking, probably hoping for the same thing I was hoping for, that one of the band members would come out.

I looked to see who might be a threat to the plan I was hatching in my head. The only one seemed to be that big galoot standing by the stage door. I made my way outside of the main part of the theater into the outer corridor of the theater. I passed several of those doors I had seen earlier. I passed the ones with the demanding warnings on them. I look around again to see if anyone is watching me. No one is around.

So I try the first door, the door is locked tight. There are plenty more doors to try, so I go down the line, trying each doorknob. I'll try them until I find one that some stupid person forgot to lock.

The next couple of doors are locked. I'm getting a tiny bit upset, but I wont give up. I keep going. The next door has a DANGER sign on it. And its unlocked. I look again to see if anyone followed me or if anyone is watching. No one, I cant believe my luck, its as if I'm the only one left in the theater. I turn the knob and push open the door.

Except I hear some guy calling to me, I turned to look, it's some fat, sweaty security guard, trying to catch up to me.

"Excuse me miss," he's calling to me, "you cant go in there." But I don't care. Nothing is going to stop me from doing what I have planned. He's got a big gut hanging over his belt, his face is bright red, he could have a heart attack, any moment. I close the door, and stick a broom handle in the lock, so he cant open the door. Even if he goes to the other end of the tunnel, I'll be long gone, by the time he even gets there. The tunnel or passageway, goes downhill and then up again towards a set of stairs and a door, that says backstage door. I run down the tunnel, so I beat the fat guy. I put my hands out in front of me, incase I bump into something. Then I stop, about half way down.

I'm a little scared and a lot excited. I'm this much closer to Cam, I'm dying to see him, again.

By the dim light bulb, on the wall is a map. It says "you are here". With an arrow showing me where I am in the theater.

This tunnel takes me under the theater and directly to the backstage. There's one of those safety vest hanging on a hook and some garbage bags. I grab those, remember I'm improvising here, I still haven't a clue what I'm going to do. It's the same kind of vest the theater staff wears. So I put it on. In my purse I have my work ID, it might pass for a work ID in the theater.

I put that around my neck. I make my way a little slower than a run, down the rest of the tunnel, towards the other dim light. I keep my hands out in front of me, feeling my way down, towards the end. I'd die if there was a mouse down here. Or worse yet a big damn hairy spider.

I'm at the end of the tunnel, I stub my toe on the first step of the stairs. I climb the stairs to the door. I swallow and take a deep breath, put my ear to the door, to see if I can hear anything. I hear some muffled sounds, people talking and laughing. I try the doorknob. Its open. My heart pounds in my chest, and my hands are sweaty.

I push open the door, just a tiny bit, to see if anyone is standing by the door. There are people milling about. I hear laughter again, its Cam's laugh. I'd know it anywhere. He must be standing close by.

I open it just a little bit more, and I can see bodies. I see an arm with someone holding a beer bottle, a pair of ripped jeans, a t-shirt. I know its him, I'd know that cute ass anywhere. And it's a nice cute ass too. I've put my hands on it.

I have to wait for everyone to move. If I get caught, I'd be in a lot of trouble.

So I wait. I close the door almost all the way, but leave it opened just a crack. It seems like it took forever for everyone to move away from the door. Someone called Cam, and I heard him reply "that he was coming."

I open the door and peek around it, everyone is gone, all clear. I step into a brightly lit room, there's tables and chairs, food on a table and drinks. I sure could use a drink. Do I dare take one? I dare, cause my mouth is so dry right now. I take a Snapple ice tea. Open it and take a big long drink.

Now to find Cam. I follow the voices, I hear down the hallway. To another room, where there are a lot of people with the band members, signing autographs and taking pictures. Talking to their fans. I'm one of your fans, I want to say. I'm your number one fan, I'm your biggest fan ever. Do you remember me? But I don't. I walk in, a few people look at me, but no one really pays attention to me. They probably notice the stupid bright green vest I'm wearing, its like its own beacon in the dark.

I see a garbage pail, and head for it. That's my plan as lame as it is, is to pretend I work here.

The garbage pail is full. And its heavy. I manage to pull the big bag out of the can and replace it with a new one.

Now I have to drag it some place to get rid of it. I'm thinking to myself that this is one of the stupidest ideas I've ever had.

I'm so close to him, he moves out of my way as I pass. I never look directly at him. Because wonder if he recognizes me? Then what? Will he think I'm chasing after him? Well of course I am. I can sense everything about him. How he smells so good. How tall he is. He looks at me for a second, and at that exact second is when I look at him. His eyes are the bluest, sky blue. He's taller than me too, which is nice. His hair is curly again and dirty blonde. I want to touch him, I want to run my hands through his hair. And look into his blue eyes. But I don't.

He smiles at me, and I turn away, really quickly, which gets me a tiny bit dizzy. I can feel my face blushing. I hide my face with my hair as it falls down over my eyes. I make a beeline for the opposite door on the other side of the room.

It leads to another hallway, and I don't know where that leads to. I'm still dragging the heavy smelly garbage bag behind me.

He smiled at me. He saw me. Did a light bulb go off in his head? I hope it didn't, I really don't want to get into trouble, tonight. I feel really lightheaded. I have to stop for a minute to catch my breath. Breath…. I say to myself. I wish I had my inhaler with me.

I'm dragging the garbage bag, I'm going to turn this corner and leave it there. I hear this really weird sound coming behind me. All noises sound weird here because of the echo. But this noise sounded out of place here. Its like a plop, plop sound, click, click sound.

The bag is being uncooperative and feels even heavier. I turn around to find a big puppy, barreling towards me. Wheezing, like he's been chasing me for a long time. He starts ripping the garbage bag open. He thinks it's a game. He thinks its a tug of war game. And any minute I'm gonna have a big shit load of garbage all over the floor. I try to shoo him away. But he thinks I'm playing with him. He might bite me, and a bite by puppy baby teeth really hurts. I want to kick him, cause now he's pissing me off. He finally rips the bag open and the garbage spills out all over the floor. Someone calls him. But he doesn't obey, of course not, he's a puppy. He starts to eat the garbage. Someone comes and pulls him away from the garbage. I'm already starting to pick it up and trying to put it in another bag. My head is down, I'm gonna cry any minute. I'm looking at a big mess and I have to clean it up. I could just leave it and run away. But that's not the kind of person I am. I made the mess I should clean it up. Actually the stupid puppy, or better yet the owner of the puppy should clean it up.

I'm squatting down, so I don't see who sends the dog away. The dog runs away towards whoever it is that called him.

Luckily I grabbed more than one garbage bag. I'm trying unsuccessfully to get the garbage in the bag. I'm getting frustrated. Cause this is taking to long and I want to go home now. A hand reaches out to help me. I'm so wrapped up in cleaning up the damn garbage, that I don't even noticed anyone approaching me. I'm damn shit scared that someone is going to find out I don't belong here, that I'm not an employee of the theater.

The dog was eating the garbage and dragged some of it down the corridor. I tried to shoo him away, what a pain in the ass. I still haven't look up to see who the hand belongs to. I'm trying frantically to hurry up and pick it up.

"Here let me help you clean that up," I look up at the person, into the bluest eyes, it's Cam Konner. I suck in my breath. And fall backwards landing on my butt. And for a second, it looks like he recognizes me. But then the look disappears.

"No, I have it, thanks," even though I don't and he can tell I'm having a hard time getting it into the bag. And that I'm getting flustered.

"Please I want to help, I want to, I'm sorry about the dog, its one of the other band members dog." He says. His voice makes my skin tingle. Just being near him makes me tingle.

I've decided that this is the worst idea ever in my entire life. I'm working fast and my breathing is getting faster, I'm embarrassed, sweaty, and probably smell like the garbage.

"Hey," he says. "Are you okay?" My hair is covering my face and he gently pushes my hair out of my face, behind my ear. I shudder from his touch. Like I did, the very first time he put his arm around me.

He touched me, again. I can hardly breath, I bit my bottom lip, to keep it from trembling. I feel like I want to pass out. Not because of the garbage, but because of who is touching me, he's got me so unnerved, that I'm falling slowly apart. He has no idea what his touch is doing to me. How being so near to him is making me crazy. I'm feeling lightheaded. I cant think, hell, every thought I had falling out of my head. I cant even talk.

CHAPTER 4

I look at his hand. I have a thing about men's hands. I love them, cause there so strong, and can be so gentle. I guess I have a faddish about hands. His hands are thin and nicely shaped. I bet their strong too. Cause he plays that guitar like he owns it. He's still holding a beer bottle in his other hand which he never puts down. I slowly look up at him. Its my friggin fantasy, my obsession. He's smiling at me. He smiles a lot. He's looking very concerned and he's looking very intently at me. I love his blue eyes, sky blue eyes, that's what I'm gonna call them. He has a gorgeous smile too. His hair was straight when he first came on stage tonight, now its curly again. Like it is now. And I love it that way, its so damn sexy that way.

He smells really good, he must of taken a shower. He changed his clothes too. I don't know what to say to him. I've suddenly lost the ability to think. I think my mouth hangs open.

His eyes sparkle when he smiles. And he's smiling at me now and it takes my breath away.

I look at his mouth and I know I've done it more than once. I've licked my lips more than once too. I had glossy lip gloss on before, but I know its all gone.

I look at his hand again then back up into his eyes. He's really looking at me. Studying me intently, what do I have something stuck in my teeth, or something on my face, oh god there's something on my face. Oh no! he knows who I am. He knows I shouldn't be back here. He's going to get security. I try to wipe whatever it is off. I'm so friggin nervous. Embarrassed. I want to leave fast.

" Are you okay?" He asks again.

"Wha?" I say. Inside my head, I'm screaming at myself to say something more intelligent than wha. What's the matter with you? Say something witty or cute or smart. Don't say something stupid.

"I really liked your concert," I say, barely above a whisper, that he has to move closer just to hear me.

"Thank you, what's your favorite song?" He asks me, all the garbage is just about picked up. He helps me put the ripped bag into the new one. Our hands keep brushing each other, I don't think he notices, but I do. Every little touch by him is driving me insane, sending a burning sensation up my arm.

"I liked them all," I whisper, stupid you should have said, "you loved all of them," because you love him. I'm blinking a lot, I know I am cause I might cry after all. And I'm thinking, does he know me, or is he playing dumb. Is he pretending he doesn't remember me?

The garbage is picked up the bag is tied up. I stand up and so does he. He is taller than me, I think he's 6'1. I love tall guys, not to tall but just right for me, cause I'm 5'8. He's lean too, not one single piece of fat on him. He's got a six-pack too. I know cause I've seen it. He's so hot, and making me feel even hotter. My mind wanders a lot. He'd be the right height to grab him by the neck and pull him down to kiss me. Which if I was a more gutsier person I would do it, but I don't, cause I'm a big chicken. I could use a couple of energy drinks, right about now. I just keep on staring at him. My mouth is so dry, my lips are sticking to my teeth, and my lips feel dry and cracked. Someone calls him and he turns around to see who it is. "I'm sorry I have to go," he says.

"Thank you," I say, "For your help."

"Sure no problem," he smiles. And winks at me, he knows, I've got to get out of here fast.

"Hey man where have you been?" Its Rob, his guitar player/backup singer. He looks at me and makes a face. Does he remember me, too?

"Bye," he says over his shoulder to me.

'Bye," I say back to him.

He nods and gives me a quick smile as Rob is practically pushing him along. Gees. But then he stops and says something to Rob. And Rob leaves. He's watching me drag the bag down the corridor. I get behind one of those huge cement pillars, and leave the bag up against the wall. Someone else can put it in the right garbage bin. I want to go home, my big adventure has left me exhausted.

I peek around the pillar to see if he's still there. He is, it look's like he's thinking about something. Then he starts to walk in my direction, oh shit, I want to run, but I don't, I want to see what he's gonna do next. I'm so fascinated by him. The good half of me wants to go, the bad half wants to watch him, after all I'm a stalker. He's so hot looking, he's got the hottest walk, and he's got the cutest ass too, so why wouldn't I want to watch him.

I see what it is that's caught his attention. What's making him walk over in my direction. I dropped my name tag, my ID tag from work. I look down, and its gone. Oh no… it must of pulled off of the chain it was on. Its only a piece of plastic. I'm mortified.

He bends down to pick it up. It has my name on it, where I work, and it has a horrible picture of me. Its not the most flattering picture either, I look tired. Cause it was early in the morning when it was taken. My hair is tied back, so it looks like I have no hair. I have puffy eyes, and dark circles probably from my allergies. I'm not even smiling.

He smiles at it and puts it in his pants pocket. He walks the other way. I should run after him and demand my ID back. But I don't. I think I'm gonna die.

The stage, the theater, the whole complex is like a labyrinth puzzle. I walked down more hallways, and more corridors, then I can remember going through. Ended up at more locked doors and dead ends, that I was getting scared I'd be lost in here for ever, they'd find my dried up bones in a pile in some tunnel somewhere. Holding onto my concert ticket and a picture of Cam still in my boney hand. Or worse yet, I'd be locked inside the theater unable to get out because its locked up tight. I'd have to wait until the next concert to get out. I had know idea when the next concert was.

I threw away the vest. I saw a ramp and trucks being loaded with large boxes on wheels. Thank God…it was the outside. I could see the dark blue of the night sky.

But where was I exactly? And where exactly was the parking lot with my car parked in it?

I see the tour buses. There plain brown. Used to be Kid Rocks tour bus. No names on it. No markings at all telling you hey, this is your favorite band. Nothing.

I was on the opposite side of the theater. I remember seeing the tour buses when I first entered the theater. I didn't want to go back the way I just came, no way, that was a nightmare. So I'll have to walk around the whole place, there's a big cement wall in front of me, and impossible to climb over, so I'll have to walk around that.

Cars are still leaving the parking lot, not to many are left. Except my car. That made it easier to find. And I was so happy to see it. Cause it was the only one left, parked in the front row.

I couldn't believe how this night ended. I had the opportunity of a life time to talk to him and ask him all those questions I have, and I said nothing. I blew it…I'll never have that kind of chance again to talk to him, ever, ever again………cause at the meet and greets, they don't want you to talk to them, no personal questions, not enough time, was the arenas excuse, or maybe securities excuse.

I leaned against my car and slid down to sit on the pavement. My head hurt. Well there was nothing I could do to change anything.

A cool breeze was blowing in off the water. It shook me out of my reverie. Time for the long ride home.

My CD player turns on. His music is always in it. His words and the bands music fills the inside of my car with electricity. And sends goose bumps up and down my arms. His face, his devilish smile and his sky blue eyes flash in my head like a replay of the whole night. I wanted to reach out and touch him. But I didn't. I wanted to tell him how much I loved him, but I didn't. I want to remember this night forever, and I will. Along with all my other memories, of Cam.

My ride home seemed like it was shorter, then the ride it took to get there. Before I knew it, I was home safely. It was after one in the morning. Don't really remember looking at the clock to see what time it was. Didn't matter. I had a wonderful feeling all over me. I have a secret.

A big secret, a secret nobody else knows. A secret no one else can take away from me.

I went to work on Monday. Everyone asked me how the concert was. I said it was loud and really good. I had good seats.

I didn't dare say, "I stalked the lead singer of the band, I roamed underneath the theater, I trespassed in places I shouldn't have. To find him. I acted like a jerk, posing as a worker just to get close to him, pretending I worked there. Then when I did. I acted like a star struck teenager.

I didn't tell them I dragged a garbage bag around the theater with me and had a tug of war with a puppy. That I met Cam Konner, again, but it went a little crazy, and he helped me clean it up. Or that I dropped my work ID and he picked it up and he now has it. No I didn't tell them any of it.

Three days later, my boss hands me a package. Really strange I never get packages here, no one does.

I don't recognize the hand writing. No return address. I open it in my car. Its my ID tag, the one I dropped at the theater. The one Cam picked up.

Inside the envelope is a note, " you dropped this, I thought you might need it, "FOR YOUR JOB." PS…I thought you were cute. Janie, I remembered you. I remember your green eyes." He signs his name.

I have his autograph on this piece of paper. Because at the meet and greets, they weren't signing autographs, their excuse was there wasn't enough time, for everyone to get personal with the band. I have something he touched. I smell it. I smell everything, I'm a smeller. I can smell a faint scent on it, it smells like him. Ah…He smelled so yummy. I add it to the rest of my Cam collection.

I hold everything close to my heart. He noticed me…he remembered me. He noticed my green eyes.

And this is totally the wrong thing for him to do. It just added fuel to my fire.

I printed out the schedule of their concerts and the next one is in Atlantic City, New Jersey. At the end of August. Its really odd how they figure out where they're going for the next concert. Sometimes to me it doesn't make sense how they scatter around all over the states. In stead of doing the same state but do different cities. So it was a little over a month away. I decided I would go to every concert on the Eastern seaboard, with in reason. And what I could afford.

It gives me enough time to do the next thing on my get to know Cam list.

I bought the general admission ticket again. If I couldn't get Cam's attention at this concert, then I needed a back up plan. Whenever I work inside my house, like painting or cleaning I always put on my CDs and dance to them. There's one song that's so naughty, but it's the best song to dance to. That's what gave me my idea.

First thing I had to do was enroll in dance class. I enrolled in Arthur Murray school of dance.

I cant dance to save my life. When I was younger, about 9 or 10, my mother enrolled me in dance class, I hated it. Couldn't dance to save my life, even back than. So after much whining and complaining, to my mother, about how much I hated dancing, she took me out of the class. Now I wish I had stayed. I wish she had forced me to continue. But when your young, you never realize what might be important to you later on in life. And now as I stand here remembering all of that, I'm suppose to dance. Like a graceful swan. More like a drowned rat. Have you ever seen how a swan tries to fly. That aren't graceful at all. I feel, all arms and legs, twisting in every direction, out of control.

I bought the music with me, and told the teacher I needed a seductive dance to go with this song, and I had only about a month to learn it. She didn't ask me why, just said it was a great band and a great song to dance to. She started me on the basic steps. I have to say, I suck at dancing. I have two left feet. I'm so uncoordinated it isn't even funny. She thought that maybe I'm to self conscience, do ya think? I don't like being the center of attention, I'm the person that hides in the back of the room. She said I have to let go, pretend there is no one in the room except me. Let the music move and take me to another place. The place I want to go to with the person, I'm going to dance for. Its always so easy at home, when I'm alone. The teacher was patient with me, when I fumbled and fell, or stepped on her toes. She showed me ways to tame my wild feet. "It takes practice," she said, "and plenty of it."

She said practicing at least three times a week, would more than help me reach my goal by the end of the month.

She wanted to know what I was dancing in. I said some kind of sexy dress, I guess. I hadn't picked one out yet. No, no, she wanted to know the shoes I was dancing in. I told her it wasn't shoes, its boots. The ones that go up to your thigh. With about a 4 inch heel. She made a frown, and I said, "what?"

"You'd better practice walking in them, and then your gonna have to practice dancing in them."

I hadn't even thought about that. So the next dance lesson I bought the boots with me. She just look at me and sighed. Said "Put them on."

I had been practicing at home with them on. But every time I put them on it was a whole new experience. I wobbled a bit, twisted my ankles a couple of times. "Now," she said, "let me see you walk in them." She was holding back a laugh, I could tell. Because the studio is nothing but mirrors, and I looked hysterical. She put her hand over her mouth to hide the smile. "Good, now walk around, wiggle your ass a little bit more, act like you own those pair of boots."

"Well I do," I said.

"I'll put the music on, and see how you walk to the beat." She put on my song. I started to walk up and down, passed the mirrors. I didn't want to look at myself. I always think I look so stupid.

"Good, good," she said. "You've got the beat, swing your hips more, good, throw your shoulders out behind you, stand up straight, good extend your legs more and sort of angle your feet when you land, good, that looks perfect." She looked like she was thinking. "Now lets see the dance part." I did the steps, that I learned and used the dance pole. Not that there will be a dance pole on stage, but maybe I can use Cam as one. No scratch that.

"Excellent," she says. "Now start from the beginning, do the whole routine and don't stop until the music is over. Remember to position yourself where you need to be to do the slide." I nodded.

She started the music again. I did the whole routine from the start to finish without messing up to bad. I was a little nervous.

"Practice again, and again, practice at home when you can. Practice, practice, practice." She says.

"I will," I say, "even in my dreams."

CHAPTER 5

It's close to a month now. One thing I didn't like when I looked in the studio mirrors was the jiggle, that was going on. To much jiggle. So I got on the elliptical and exercised every day. Did some running and the Zumba dance fitness. It was just enough to get the jigglies under control. Plus I could wear spanks if I need to.

I got another tattoo of the band on my leg, not to big just in script, and above it "A diamond in the rough." Cause that's what I think Cam is, "a diamond in the rough."

The teacher wanted to know how my dance routine went, so I'll let her know.

I ordered a pink sequined dress. It had a lot of beaded fringe on the bottom. Spaghetti straps, it was high above my knees, for the boots. I was kind of trying to decide if I should get rid of the boots and opt for some shoes instead. But changed my mind when I show how awesome the two looked together.

I let my hair grown longer, and went blonder, after all blondes have more fun. Tried some new makeup at the makeup counter at Macy's.

As the days ticked off one by one, and I checked them off the calendar every day. I practiced every day. And felt confident enough that I could pull this off.

It was finally the day before the concert, I packed everything up in my car. Had my precious ticket. Made sure the car was in driving order. Had my GPS set to Atlantic City, NJ. Money for tolls, gas and food in my pocket. A better camera with the biggest memory card in it. I was sure I had everything I need. I had my jewelry on already. Three holes in each ear. My CDs in the CD player. I hate that feeling you have like you forgot something, and I always have that feeling. I always forget my bathing suit.

It was time to go, I couldn't really sleep the night before, but I think I did a little bit. I was to excited to sleep. I made signs too. One said "I love you," another said, "do the slide." Which is something he does with the guitar strings. I also had a pink thong. Its in the song. I got them from Fredericks of Hollywood.

The ride was slow at times, that traffic going over the bridge with all the potholes. All the trucks, and all the confused people, trying to figure out what line they should be in. Including me. Even though I had the GPS, it still didn't tell me what the best lane would be.

I panic sometimes when I think I'm lost. The stupid GPS, can lead you on a wild goose chase, like it did to me in Washington, DC. But all went well. I arrived in plenty of time to get familiar with the arena. I was searched before I was allowed in. They wanted to know why I was bringing in so much stuff with me? I told them I wanted to get dressed up for the meet and greet with the band. Did they understand that? I was okayed with some suspicious looks from the security guards. They looked at everything. Even my posters.

I found a seat right up front, I got here so early I was first on line. I picked a seat to the right of the stage.

Around 7 o'clock, those who had a VIP ticket came out from backstage after meeting the band. So I knew I didn't have much time left to get ready for what I was going to do. I had to run to the bathroom to change into my dress. I wore my nice jeans, and a cute top, over my dress.

There was a lot of people in the bathroom. I missed the opening acts, that was okay because I've seen them before. It took me a long time to find a stall. As I was changing, I was remembering my meet and greets, I remember how Dale seemed to be the most enthusiastic about the meet and greet, I've heard they get nervous before they go out. That's understandable. How Matt never smiles, how Rob leads you in.

How delicious Cam looked.. When I get very nervous, I cant breath, so I took out my inhaler, and took a puff. I was sure no one was looking. I feel embarrassed when I do it.

I wasn't paying to much attention to anyone around me. But someone touched my arm, I turned to see who it was.

"Are you alright? I noticed you were using an inhaler."

It was Cam, I nodded. My eyes went wide, I could use another puff.

"I'm okay, just nervous," I choked.

"Nervous about what?" He asks me.

"About meeting you." I say.

"I'm just a regular guy, like everyone else." He says.

I swallow, "No you aren't, you're a god." I say. And he laughs and smiles one of those gorgeous smiles at me.

"No I'm not," he smiles again, his blue eyes sparkle. "Would you like an autograph and picture?"

"Yes, can I pretend for a couple of minutes to be Melissa?" I ask him. I hand him one of the CDs. I had asked him that once before, I wonder if he remembered that.

"Why do you want to be Melissa?" He asks me. And I hand him my camera cause his arm is longer than mine, he takes a picture of us together. He put his arm around my waist. I had mine around his. I grab his hand and put it on my ass.

"That's why I want to pretend to be Melissa," I say. He laughs, doesn't pull his hand off of my ass either. I actually got to hug him and to touch him, again. I thought maybe his bodyguard, Hawk would be all over me. Did this really all happen? Sometimes I wonder if I embellish my meeting. Every time I think of it, the whole thing seems to change. My imagination I suppose. After I change into my dress, I go back to the arena.

They let the band collect themselves before the show. Even though I met Cam, several times. I was still going to follow through with my plan. And that was to dance on stage for him, when he played my song.

He noticed me for sure. And I was happy about that. I put on my makeup. Made sure I had all the things I needed. I find my seat. I needed to make some friends. So I started to talk to the guy and the girl who sat next to me. They had friends with them. So I told them I would need their help once the show started and I would tell them when. I told them vaguely what I was going to do. They looked surprised. And could I pull it off? I hoped so, without getting thrown out, or worse yet, get arrested. Which is like one of my worsed fears, getting arrested and sent to jail.

I had their play list and my song was the second song they were going to play. So if I didn't get in trouble, I could enjoy the rest of the show. I was so nervous, when they first came out, I felt like I was in a fog. But then I focused. I told the two new guy friends that I needed them to lift me up onto the stage as soon as they hit the first note of the song.

I peeled off my clothes. Put on the boots, and zipped them up. "Okay, I'm ready," I yelled to the guys."

"Whoa look at you," they said. The piros were still going off, and when Cam comes out he's already playing the song. So as soon as their done playing the first song, they go right into the second song. He gets the audience up and on their feet. Well it was now or never. And I planned this for months, there was no going back now. I wasn't going to break the promise I made to myself, and that was to get Cam's attention.

When he hit the first note of the song, I told the guys to lift me up onto the stage. They did and I strutted and did the walk over to Cam. At first he didn't see me. The other band member's did. But no one stopped playing, though. So that was good. They didn't lose the beat or the rhythm of the song. I walked over to Cam, I didn't touch him, then I went over to Rob, who gave me a nasty face, then I danced over to Dale and danced in front of the drum deck. Then I went over to Matt, didn't touch him either. He gave me a nasty look too. I never touch any of them and never invade their space. I have my back most of the time to the audience, and my hair is covering my face. I could hear the audience whistling and clapping, so I knew it must have been good. I wasn't sure if security was waiting for me. I didn't want them to feel threatened by me. The sweat was trickling down my back, the song was almost over. I was in the right place for the end of the song, for the slide that I was going to do. I put the thong on Cam's guitar. When he sings the words, "pretty pink thong." I know he was surprised. I know he smiled. He kept playing and singing. I could feel his eyes, following me.

I hope this works. I made sure I swung my hips like the teacher told me, strutted like I owned the stage. Swung my hair around from side to side. Put on perfume, the scent of every flower in the desert. And hoped this worked.

The stage was slick, I take out the lollipop I have stuck between my boobs. Put it in my mouth, because, "you look better with something in your mouth." I take a running start and land on my knees and slide across the stage, and stop right at Cam's feet. I never look at him while I dance.

It was the longest 3 minutes and 36 seconds of my life. I'm breathing very heavily, its hard to catch my breath. I'm laying on my side with my head propped up on my hand. With my back to the audience. Everyone is screaming. The place goes ballistic. Okay, now I'll be taken away.

I was afraid to look up at him, afraid he was mad at me for messing up his show. Afraid that he has devil horns, he's breathing fire out of his nose, his face beet red, and his voice is an evil demonic low grinding his fanged teeth together, cause he going to eat me, and he going to yell at me in front of the whole audience. I try to calm my breathing down, so I can get up and run off the stage. I see a hand reach down to me. Cam was giving me his hand. I hesitate to take it. He kinds of shakes it, like come on take it.

"Take my hand." He says. I do and he pulls me up off of the floor. "That was incredible," he says.

" Um, what's your name?" He asks me. And then there's that look, the one he gave me before, the one that says, I know you. And he smiles at me, gives me a big wide grin.

"It's Janie," I yell in his ear.

"Give it up for Janie," he says. "I've met you before, haven't I ?" He says.

I just nod, I want to get off the stage as quickly as I can. I'm not sure if security, is about to come out and get me. I'm sure his body guard Hawk, is already on his way out. I can see them gathering at the back of the stage, probably waiting for Cam's signal to come and haul me away. But he never gives them the signal, at least that I can see.

I run off the stage, back to the side I jumped up on to, into the arms of my new waiting friends. Everyone surrounds me like a human shield. I take off the dress and put my pants and t-shirt back on. Put on a hoodie, put the hood over my head. Take off the boots, when I sit in my seat.

Everyone separate's. When I was leaning on the wall of the stage, there was a panel, that pushed in. The security guards did come, they saw the panel moved and thought I went in there. They went to go catch me at the other end. Ha. I'm hoping I got away with this. So far so good. But I'm still holding my breath, I don't want to be to smug, because it always backfires on me.

CAM

"Cant you find that girl?" I asked my security guy, Hawk. "I want you to find her."

"I cant, she's disappeared, the panels under the stage were opened, I think she went under the stage, man she simply disappeared." Hawk says.

"Look again, she has to be out there, and don't come back until you have her." I m so pissed, she jumped off the stage, before I could say anything else to her. It was Janie, the girl with the green eyes. The one I have met several times at my concerts. The one with the puppy and the garbage bag, I found her ID badge. I had hoped I would some day meet her again.

I tried to watch where she was going when she jumped, there were a couple of big guys that helped her. Maybe her boyfriend. I saw someone with a hoodie on that wasn't there before, I almost think it was her. She was probably scared shit.

JANIE

Someone held up my signs. And I put a bouquet of flowers on the stage. I think guys should get flowers too. I gathered all of my things, stuffed everything into the bag I bought with me. I still wanted to linger. I had sunglasses on to cover my eyes so no one would see the heavy makeup I had on my eyes. I tried to wiped most of it off.

The security guys were still roaming around and seriously looking at all the woman that were still in the arena. Hawk was in the lead. I quickly walked around and far enough away from them, hoping they wouldn't get a good look at me. I thanked my new friends for helping me out. "We recorded the whole thing," They say.

My new friends say. "They'll send me a copy, and where you'd learn to do that?" The guys ask.

"It was so awesome." They say.

"Thanks, I practiced a lot, and I had a good dance teacher help me out." We exchanged e-mail addresses and said good-bye. We walked out to the parking lot together. I waved goodbye, and found my car, when I realized I forgot my pocketbook in the theater. Under my seat. Oh shit.

The cleaners were probably starting to clean the place up. I put the bag with my dress and boots, under the car and ran back in to the arena.

Went to my seat and my pocketbook was still there, thank god. I noticed the bouquet of flowers were gone. I hope someone gave them to Cam. I wrote a note and attached it to the flowers. I said " Thank you for the best show ever, I hoped you liked my dancing I did it for you, because I love you guys." J.

As I walked out of the arena, I felt kind of sad. I don't know why? Everything went exactly as I had hoped it would, exactly as I had pictured it, I should be happy. But this incredible let down feeling hit me. I walked to my car and opened the door, put my stuff in the back seat and sat there for a long time, thinking.

He noticed me again, and seemed pleased with my dancing, he didn't have me arrested, or thrown out of the arena. And I got to enjoy the rest of the concert. I even got a big applause after the song was over. So why was I so miserable? I know I was hoping Cam would ask me to stay or something. And I had been working for weeks for this day, anticipating this day, and now it was here and now it was over.

Something that made me smile though, when I hung the pink thong on his guitar, I remembered that he stuffed it in his pocket. I also put a tag on that with a note too.

CHAPTER 6

Four days later, I get a letter in the mail. Don't recognize the handwriting, no return address. This is a familiar feeling. I open it. It's a simple, plain envelope, a scrap of torn paper inside.

"I knew it was you, Janie." It said. "Are we going to have a problem?" And his name scribbled on the bottom. It looked angry. So sloppy, it was hard to read.

So I guess he was mad. Now he'll have me arrested or a restraining order put out on me.

I was planning on going to Hershey park, Pennsylvania. Where their next concert is going to be.

April my hard of hearing friend has been trying to get me to learn sign language. When we used to go to church, I always pointed to the words in the song book for her, so she could follow the song. But never learned to sign. So.....

It was being offered at one of the local schools at night in one of the adult classes. Okay I agreed to go, and try to learn. She made a joke about signing one of the songs on the CDs I always listen to. She can feel the bass when it plays, that's how she can feel music. When she said that I just laughed it off, laughed along with her. I know it was hard to learn, that there is a lot of things you need to know to sign language. But it gave me an idea. The concert was in a few months. In the meantime they were still going around the country giving concerts. They'd be back here again.

So we signed up together. She would go with me to the class and help me out. The teacher didn't think I could learn all that I needed to learn in such a short amount of time. I brought the words to one of the songs I wanted to learn to sign. I told her just teach me this. It was one of the love songs that Cam wrote.

The teacher said that number l, learn the alphabet A to Z. Number 2, don't call a deaf person, mute or deaf and dumb. Just say deaf or hard of hearing. Which in my friends case she's hard of hearing. She can hear some noises, and she has hearing aids. But her hearing is slowly going away. So she learned sign language.

The teacher also said, "Don't assume that a deaf person wants to teach you to sign, they aren't going to drop everything to teach you." I smiled at my friend when she said that. My friend did try to teach me, I wasn't a willing student at the time. Although I did learn some simple things like thank you, please, yes and no. And the teacher also said that "don't think that you can help out in a life threatening situation. If it involves a deaf person. You could say something wrong. A police officer would wait for a certified sign language person."

She said the whole body is involved in sign language. Not just the hands. Facial expressions are important, that's why a deaf person will look at your face. Like raising your eyebrows would mean you are asking a question.

I took lots of notes. Numbers by hand shapes. Never make up a sign. Get a good dictionary.

And practice, practice, practice. So with my friends help I was going to learn this song.

I learned the easiest words first. This was a basic class anyway.

I would focus on just the words in the romantic song. April was coming with me to the concert. I know she would be able to feel the music, especially up front. And we had VIP tickets. April's parents paid for the tickets. As a present, for the two of us. Just because. I wanted her to meet the band. She couldn't understand what I was so obsessed about.

I practiced, every night, and went to the class two times a week. April, helped me out with the words I couldn't get.

By the end of four weeks, she was impressed that I had learned the entire song, and she understood what I was signing.

She wanted to know what I was up to. " Me... up to something?" I looked innocently at her.

The night before the concert, I had a stupid dream. I was at the concert, and I was signing. I was doing the song, only I was messing it up and making an idiot out of myself. Everyone was laughing at me, I ran away crying. I woke up, trying to shake off that awful foreboding feeling it gave me.

APRIL

I'm finally going to appease Janie. Why I don't know, only that she finally went to sign language classes with me, and she's learning, sign language. So we sort of made an even trade. That's the way its always been with us, she does something for me, and I do something for her. And visa versa. We give and take, but never to much.

JANIE

We left early in the morning for Pennsylvania. It was hard to talk to her while I was driving. We got there early again. Put our VIP tickets around our necks. There was that big galoot standing in front of the stage door. With his big tattooed arms folded across his chest. This time he wasn't going to scare me. I gave him a nice smile.

We packed a picnic lunch, and something for dinner. We had our own tailgate party. Then we went into the arena. Searched. I grabbed April's hand and pulled her up the stairs to the backstage. As soon as I saw the crowd that waited for the band, it occurred to me that maybe Cam would remember me. I was hoping that he didn't, sort of. Just in case, he decided to file charges or something.

I had our pictures taken with the band members, and autographs. She thought Rob was cute, and Dale. Then when she saw Cam, standing there, his tall lean body, his curly blonde hair, his gorgeous smile and those sky blue eyes, she knew what I was talking about. I signed to her see...

And she nodded. Cam was sweet, to her and kept looking at me, like he knew me but wasn't sure, then he would give me that look, again. How could he be sure. I changed my hair color, slightly, and got a new hair style. He must meet thousands of fans, and everyone must look the same after awhile.

When he was talking to some other fans, and we were talking to Matt. He kept looking at me. His forehead furrowed. I could tell he was thinking about it, like he knew I was the one who danced on stage. Or the one who had the garbage spilled out all the floor. Did he know? No way he could remember me. Could he? And that got me scared, I wanted to run.

Besides tonight I wanted my friend to have fun, this was her birthday present from her parents.

I had to warn her about the piros. Sometimes when she didn't expect something it left her a nervous wreck. So I had to tell her about them. We would feel the heat, because we were right up front. She was okay with it.

Right before we left the meet and greet, I shyly gave Cam a glance, he caught me looking. Oops…

We missed the first two opening acts, I wanted her to see Three Days Grace, which we did. We caught the end of their concert. She liked their music, and thought Adam and Brad, and Neil were cute.

The show is about to start and I tell her to brace herself for the piros. She feels the explosion.

And the heat. The bright lights, and the band comes out. The music is so loud, I have earplugs in my ears. I learn from the other times. How my ears rang all the way home.

I'm a little nervous. I tell April, she waves me off like you have to be kidding, you've been practicing. You know the song. They pull up stools and sit on the stools when they play the slow, romantic songs. I tell April the song is coming up. She nods.

When Cam starts to play the guitar. And starts to sing, I start to sign. April is watching me, and her eyes are smiling at me, cause I'm doing a good job. April is singing along with me.

The song is over and she hugs me. Cam gets up and comes over to where we are. He motions for me to come to the stage. Or course there is security guys all along the stage. But he tells the security guy to let me over.

"That was really good," Cam yells at me. "Can you do any other songs?" He asks. I shake my head no. Then he gets back to the concert.

Damn, why didn't I learn another song.

They take a short break, and I drag April to the bathroom with me. She knows when I'm nervous

I always have to go. The line is out the door and around the corner. The men's room never has a line. We finally get in and run back to the concert. They have a couple of romantic songs to play so their still sitting on the stools. Couples everywhere cuddling. Yuck, it makes me want to puke. Well at least, this concert I didn't come alone.

We stand back in the spot where we were for the entire night. The band comes out again. They all changed their shirts. Cam asks everyone" if there having a good time?" Everyone roars, their approval. Then he says "I have an unusual request, I hope you guys don't mind, but I'd like to do the last song over again, and I have a special guest." He points to me, and wiggles his finger to motion me over to the stage. He bends down and asks me if I will sign the song on stage for him, "it was very interesting to watch," he says. I look at April, and she says, "yes do it." "Okay," I tell him.

"Come over to the stairs," he meets me over there and offers me his hand and leads me over to the stool that someone put there for me. He sits down and offers me the chair next to him. I see April grinning at me and waving. I roll my eyes at her. I am so nervous, if the stool was any smaller I would fall off of it. The sweat is trickling down my back. It's so incredibly hot on stage.

I can smell Cam's aftershave cologne, he smells so good. The sweat is rolling down his face. Cant someone get him a towel. He asks me if I'm ready and I nod. He says to the audience, "I usually never do this, but Janie was signing to her friend…. the song we just sang and it was so beautiful to watch her hands, that I thought maybe you would like to see it." Everyone starts whistling, and yelling. But they all quiet down enough so that I can concentrate. Once they turn down the lights, you cant even see the audience. So I can just block them out. I turn a little to look at Cam, he starts to play the beautiful cords of the song and starts to sing. It's like he's singing to me. I sign the words, he singing a little slower than the song is played normally, but I'm not having any problems keeping up.

As I'm signing I realize he remembered my name. He must not think I'm a threat to him. He seems very comfortable around me. So I guess

I wont be arrested this time either. The song ends, and everyone goes wild. April is jumping up and down, clapping and waving her hands.

I have a big grin on my face. I nailed it, I didn't miss a word or mess up any of the signing.

Cam gets up off the stool, and says "give it up for Janie, she did a fantastic job." He takes my hand and kisses the top of it. And looks into my eyes, like I want you to remember me and you tonight on this stage. 'I will never forget its embedded in every brain cell I have.' I say to myself.

He says "thank you " to me and walks me back over to the stairs. He's such a gentlemen. He's made me feel so special. I walk back over to April and she give me a big giant hug. "You did great," she said, "the teacher would be so proud of you, what did Cam say to you?"

"I'll tell you later," I told her. We watched the rest of the concert, and sang every song. Its kind of hard for April, she had to watch Cam's lips, which in my opinion is not a bad thing to do.

The concert ended again with the piros. We got covered in the ashes from them, just like Dale does. The band says good-night. And leaves the stage. Well I tell April, I guess its time to leave.

She likes to linger too. So we hang around for a while. Some of the fans come over to me, and tells me the sign language song was really great, and different. I say thanks.

Someone, a very scary guy, someone I haven't seen before, grabs the back of my arm. I turn to see who it is. Someone scarier than his body guard, Hawk. He says in my ear "Cam would like to talk to you backstage, will you come with me, please?" I look at April and she nods, yes.

We follow him backstage. He shows us into one of the dressing rooms. "Wait here, Cam will be here in a few minutes."

April sees that I'm nervous. Cause I pace. She's calm. She sits on one of the couches. "I have to use the bathroom," I tell her, she shrugs her shoulders and points to the door and says, "go."

"I'll be right back," I tell her, "If Cam comes in tell him, I will be right back, okay?"

She laughs at me cause she always thinks I'm so funny when I'm nervous. I run out into the hallway to find a bathroom. I find one and open the door. I hear water running and see steam coming from a shower. Oh crap, someone is taking a shower, and I have to go so badly, I'm about ready to wet my pants.

I can sneak in and no one will know I was there. There's a pile of clothes on the floor. "Hawk is that you, man can you give me a towel, I forgot to get one." He says. Its Cam. He thinks I'm his body guard. "So what did you think of that girl?" He asks, Hawk, who isn't here. And how come no one was guarding the door. And here I am in the bathroom with him, and he doesn't know its me.

"Hawk did you hear me?" I grunt like I'm the guy, isn't that what guys do, grunt. I have to look around to find a towel. There is a closet, up on a shelf. I grab one. His hand is sticking out of the shower curtain. I close my eyes and hand him the towel, "thanks," he says. I trip over his clothes, souvenir, I pick up his shirt and stuff it in my pocketbook. I could take everything laying on the floor. But I don't.

I go to one of the stalls to use the bathroom. I wash my hands, when I round the corner, he's standing there with the towel wrapped around him and nothing more. I gasp. He looks up at me, cause he was looking through his pants pocket for something. And gives me a big wide grin. I blush, my knees get weak. I've been caught.

"Hiiiii, Janie," he grins at me.

"Yeah, I'm sorry…I didn't know anyone was in here, and I really needed to use the bathroom. I hope your not mad?" I say. I cant help but look at his body, his six-pack abs. His tall, lean body. He is smiling at me so devilishly, he knows what I'm looking at. I swallow a couple of times.

" Um, no I'm not mad, I usually don't have an audience when I take a shower." He leans up against the wall. God, I hope he has that towel wrapped around him tightly. Cause I would die if it fell off.

My hand is on the door knob cause I want to go. "I'll be in the dressing room," I tell him.

"Wait a second, lets talk privately for a minute, your friend is in the dressing room?" He asks.

"Yes." I whisper.

"Are you stalking me?" He asks. He just… out right… asks me.

I don't answer him right away. I'm thinking of the best answer I can give him with out condemning myself. If he doesn't like my answer he'll tell me to leave him alone.

I look at his wet hair, its curly again, the way I like it, I used to have a boyfriend who liked his hair pulled, funny what you think of. He's waiting for an answer. I must look like the deer caught in the headlights of the car. Because he says to me, "I really liked the sign language thing, I guess you learned it for your friend?" He smiles.

"Uh yeah, I did learn it for her, her hearing is getting worse, and soon she wont be able to hear at all."

"I'm sorry about that." He says. He's thinking about the next question, I wish he would let me leave and I wish he would get dressed.

"You were the one that danced on the stage too, weren't you?" He asks me rather nicely.

"Yes." I say again.

"So are you going to answer my question?" He says.

"I'm pleading the fifth." I say. Holding up my hand, as if taking an oath. He laughs.

"No you cant do that, I want to know, do I have to protect myself from you, are you a stalker, are you out to harm me?" He asks. I'm not sure if he's kidding or if he's serious. But his questioning is getting me upset and I can feel the tears behind my eyes. I don't want to cry in front of him.

"No," I say. "I don't want to hurt you, I'm just a really big fan, and I just wanted to show you how much you mean to me, and that was the only way I could think of to show you. I love you, I would never hurt you, I love you guys. I would never, ever think of anything so awful……." I hiccup and turn my head towards the door so he cant see my face.

I babbled enough. I have nothing else to say, if he doesn't believe me, well…, then I don't know what he'll do.

He knows, I'm upset, "Please can I go now, I wont bother you anymore." He sees that I'm turning the door knob.

"You know your dancing was incredible," he says, I stop moving, and stand still. "I couldn't stop thinking about it. You must of practiced a lot. I liked what you were wearing too, and you smelled really good. I tried to find you, but you disappeared. I lost your address, and I didn't have your phone number. I wanted to tell you how much I liked it."

My eyes are closed as I'm listening to him, his voice sends chills all over me, he's not mad at me. He actually liked what I did.

I'm not sure what he wants me to say "thanks," I say.

I open the door a little, but before I leave I ask him, “are you going to have me arrested?” I wont look at him. I feel him move up close behind me. And he softly says “No,“ in my ear.

I nod and leave as quick as I can. I catch my ankle on the corner of the door, ouch shit, that’s gonna leave a mark. I limp down the hallway towards the dressing room where I left April. I open the door and she sees me, she stands up. She sees my eyes, and she knows something is wrong.

“Come on,” I motion to her that I want to go.

“What’s wrong?” She asks.

“We have to go,” I grab her hand and yank her out the door and make a beeline for the nearest exit.

“Janie what’s wrong? Tell me,” she pulls me to a stop and turns me around to face her. By now the tears are coming down my face. And all is it takes is one look at my friends sweet face and I’m sobbing like a baby.

“Aw Janie, what happened? Come on lets go to the car.” She pulls me now towards the exit sign.

Just as we are about to walk through the door, Cam comes out of the bathroom, he’s dressed.

I hear him call me. “Janie, wait, I want to talk to you….”

But I don’t hear anything else, because we are running down the stairs of the arena to the parking lot. “Janie, wait.” Its Cam he’s chasing us.

April turns around and says to him “what did you say to her?” She gives him such a dirty look that he stops coming towards us.

He puts his hands out like I don’t know, I didn’t do anything. But April doesn’t believe him. And she pushes me through the door and slams the door shut.

CHAPTER 7

I cant see where I'm going so she's holding my hand and were practically falling down the stairs. We run past crew members, past security personnel, past the fans who have lingered. Everyone turns to see the hysterical woman being dragged by another woman. But no one stops us to ask what's the matter.

We make it to the parking lot and find the car, I fumble with the keys. My hand is shaking so badly, April takes the keys from me. She gets it open , pushes me in and gets in on the other side.

She calms down her breathing, before she talks to me. I'm still breathing heavy, but at least I've stopped crying. She turns me to face her. "Now tell me what happened, you were gone an awfully long time."

I take a deep breath, and wipe my eyes. Blow my nose. She's waiting patiently, she always does. "He asked me if I was stalking him." I finally say.

"Oh...well you sort of are." She laughs a little. "If all truth be told, you have done some pretty bizarre things to get to meet him, haven't you?"

"Yeah," I sniffle, "I guess I have been doing some pretty ridiculous things, to get to meet him." I laugh too and sniffle, blow my nose again.

"So why are you crying?" She asks, she takes my hand in hers.

"I don't know, I accidentally went into the bathroom, where he was taking a shower, I didn't know he was in there. He thought I was someone else and asked me for a towel. Which I got for him and handed it to him. I used the bathroom, and when I came out he was standing there in only the towel. I was so embarrassed, and scared. He came right out and asked me if I was stalking him. I was so scared that he was mad and he was going to have me arrested."

"Oh….." She says again. "So you saw him practically naked?" She smiles.

"April !"

"How did he look?" Her eyes are big and wide.

"Oh my god, gorgeous, I saw his six-pack, and he is so hot. I couldn't stop looking at his chest. I was sort of hoping that his towel would fall off."

"And then if the towel did come off what would you have done?" She laughs.

"Probably, either fainted or screamed."

"So can we go home now?" April asks. "It's been a long day for both of us."

"I agree, to much drama."

"Before I forget," I say, I reach for my pocketbook and pull out the t-shirt. "Look what I have."

I hold up Cam's t-shirt.

"You have a souvenir," April laughs. Then we both start laughing. At least I got something out of it. I lay it out on the seat to dry, "it's wet, from his sweat. I have his DNA, all over this thing, I'm never gonna wash it. I think I'll put it in a frame and hang it in my room." April nods, it's a good idea.

"I cant believe you took that," she says. "You are getting crazy Janie, what are you going to do next? Kidnap him?"

"You know that's not a bad idea," I laugh, I look serious for a minute.

"Are you kidding?" April says. "Of course," we both giggle, "can you imagine the look on Cam's face if you did?"

I start the car and pull out of the parking lot and head for the exit. The bands music is playing in the CD player. I turn it off. " I think I'll listen to Daughtry, for now." April agrees.

The ride home was long, and bumpy. Seemed like a lot of traffic for such a late hour of the night.

We're both quiet for most of the ride home. Both lost in our own thoughts. Mine kept going back to my conversation with Cam. How could something so innocent go so wrong? How could he take anything I did as a threat, or anything I said, he made something out of nothing. I was glad the concerts for the eastern part of the country were over until next year, when they were scheduled to come back to New York next year in July. The rest of the year they were out west and in Canada. Good, maybe he would forget everything. Even though my last meeting with Cam sort of turned out as a disaster, I still wanted to see him again. I will always want to see him.

There was a contest to win five different vacations in Canada. So I entered as many times as they would allow. I never win anything, so I didn't expect to win this one.

The contest was over in June, of next year. So after a while I completely forgot about it. Until I received an e-mail, a letter in the mail, and a phone call saying I won, one of the Canada vacation getaways. I had won the one at a ski resort, even though it would be the summer. But that was okay, an all paid vacation. Besides I knew Cam lived in the mountains, somewhere in Vancouver. I had to pick my own time I wanted to go. I had two weeks in the summer. The band would be in Canada at that time. Before they went back to touring. I was hoping I could find his house. Normally I would think that this contest was some kind of a scam, but it's the only way I could be in the same country as Cam, and it was the only reason, I responded to it. The only way I could afford to go to Canada. Besides the Vancouver Canucks were in the Stanley Cup play offs. Maybe I could catch a game. It's Cam's favorite hockey team. If they lose again like they did in 94, to the Rangers and this year, to the Boston Bruins then there will be riots, I'll make sure I'm not anywhere near that. Canadians are suppose to be so non-violent.

When they sent me the tickets, for the plane ride and the lodge I would stay at, I knew it had to be the real thing. Funny, but it was for only one person, usually it's a trip for two. But I really didn't think that anything was wrong with that. I would have invited April to come with me.

I took off the two weeks from work. Packed my bags. April's mom, drove me to the airport.

I even get a rented car to drive around. Everything is paid for. Even my meals.

So I was going to make this the best vacation, the best adventure ever. I bought extra money with me. My GPS, tons of maps of Vancouver. I was going to find his mansion, if it took me all the two weeks to do it.

April said she didn't think it was a good idea to do this. She said she'd be visiting me in a prison somewhere, for trespassing, or worse yet, like Cam asked, for stalking him.

His tour ended in Vancouver, in June. Then they had off for a month and would start the new tour. So I made my vacation for the middle of June.

All is I had to do was phone the lodge house I was going to stay at and tell them the dates.

I packed everything I thought I needed including my cameras. I am a photographer too. I take excellent pictures. It's a hobby of mine. I probably packed to much. All the pretty, sexy clothes I owned were in those bags.

I was so excited, I couldn't contain myself and babbled on and on about it to April. She kept telling me to "Be careful".

"Yeah, yeah," I said to her.

"Well good luck and happy hunting," she wished me.

"Thanks," I said, "I'll call you when I get there. And I'll let you know how it goes, especially if I find Cam."

A car came for me instead of Aprils mother driving me. A chauffeured limo. Someone has thought of everything.

CAM

Janie was on her way. I made sure my limo guy kept me informed. I set this whole vacation/contest winner thing up. Its just a coincidence that she entered a Canada contest. Besides I have people who can find out things for me. It wasn't difficult, to find out she entered a contest to go to Canada. I had her work address, when I sent her back her ID. But I lost that. She once gave me a bouquet of flowers. I found them dumped in the trash can in the tour bus, Melissa. I remember seeing a pink tag attached to the flowers. I pick the now wilted, dried out, two dozen, different colored roses out of the pail and find the tag. It's pink, of course, with fancy cut edges, on card stock paper. Folded with fancy looking hand writing, with her e-mail address, her phone number to her house and cell phone. Even her house address. That's how I could contact her for this make believe contest, of mine. Even though my people had found all of that info for me and more, even her school records. She was on the honor roll. Impressive.

The way we left and the last concert, really upset me. Not to mention the fact that she was just as upset about it and I made her cry. Which is something I hate to do, ever since I was a little boy I hated it when girls cried.

So I had to make it up to her in some way. This was the only way I could think of. Besides I didn't know if she would ever come to one of our concerts ever again.

In all honesty, I couldn't stop thinking about her. Her dancing was the most incredible, sexiest thing I've ever seen except in a strip club. She used me like a dance pole. I could feel the heat and her passion coming off of her in bucketfuls. She really had me going. Then when she did the sign language thing for her friend. I thought that was the most beautiful thing I ever saw.

I was glad I had asked her and her friend to come back stage and talk. But after that everything seemed to go wrong.

I had no idea it was her in the bathroom. I thought it was my personal body guard, Hawk. He always grunts when you ask him something. She seems nervous around me, she needed to use the bathroom. It was an innocent mistake. I can understand that. But when she was sort of caught. Like a deer caught in the car headlights, she got really upset.

I could tell though she was very interested in my body and what was underneath the towel. I bet she even hoped it fell off. Hey I worked hard for these abs, you want people, especially woman to see them.

I have a girlfriend, her name is Melissa. I look, hey I'm not dead.

So my limo guy said "she is hot," I know she is.

I arranged every little detail, of her vacation, the best of everything. But then I'm going to arrange an accidental meeting with her. Make it seem like she's the one who found me.

I haven't stopped thinking about that dance she did to one of my songs. I knew I wrote a raunchy song, but to actually see someone dance to it, just blew me away. To know that someone really likes, no really loves your work, is the best compliment you could ever get.

Janie's dancing just blew me away. I made a really slutty video, recently, with practically naked girls. Except Janie wasn't half naked, like these girls were. Melissa wasn't to happy about the video either. Some one on the internet thinks its Melissa who is dancing all over me, it's not. It was only for the video. It didn't mean anything.

My driver, got on the plane with her, and explained to her that he was sort of like her body guard to make sure she arrived safely at the lodge in Vancouver. He said she bought it. She was all dressed in pink, he said. Must be her favorite color. So I had pink roses put in her room.

I want to have dinner with her and take her out somewhere special, maybe a play or a movie. But I cant do it right away, I don't want to scare her away. Besides I have a proposition for her.

My driver calls me to tell me they've landed. He'll be driving her to the lodge within the hour, as soon as he gets all of her luggage. And he emphasized 'HER LUGGAGE,' meaning she had a lot. I laughed. He never did get woman. I guess that's why he's still single.

He said she was very quiet, but looked at everything, and seemed very interested in the landscape. The only thing she asked him was how long it was going to take to get to the lodge.

He called me again when they arrived at the lodge, when she signed in. He helped carry her luggage up to her room, it was the VIP room. Hey, I'm no cheap skate. He said she was very pleased with the room. And couldn't believe that she had won a fabulous vacation. She never won anything before. She loved all the pink flowers that were in her room, I ordered some tulips, roses, and anything else that they had that was pink.

I asked him what she was wearing? He said some kind of pink velour type of suit thing. It showed every curve, every line of her body. I could picture her in my head. The pink thong she hung on my guitar, the one I stuffed in my jeans pocket, was a frilly lacey girlie little thing. I wondered if she wore this. I didn't show it to Melissa. In fact I have a secret box with little mementoes that fans have thrown up on stage over the years. I think the pink thong is my favorite.

I tell him to show her around, before he leaves. He can go home for now. I ask him how many flowers are in the room. He says a whole ton of them. She thinks there from the Canadian tourist bureau, but its not. Its from me.

I wanted to know what her face looked like when she saw the flowers. He said she closed her eyes and smelled almost everyone of them. She had a cute little smile on her face and her eyes lit up when she saw them.

I have a lot of making up to do. I want her to be happy.

I went to sleep anticipating tomorrow, when I let her find me.

JANIE

"This place is so beautiful. I even have the VIP suite." I tell April. She has a machine that is hooked up to her phone that displays the words I say to her so she can read them.

"How was the plane ride?" She asks. She knows I'm not that crazy about flying, but I will if I have to.

"It was okay, I had a guy drive me in a limo and he said he was my body guard until I got to the lodge. Then he showed me around, and it's a big beautiful place. They have a big heated pool, and a sauna, Jacuzzi and everything else you could think of."

"Sounds really nice, Janie I'm really happy for you. Have a lot of fun, okay, and remember don't get into trouble." She warns me.

"I'll try not to April, but you know me, trouble seems to follow me." I laugh. "Wish you were here," I say.

"I know, me too. So when are you going to go searching for Cam?"

"I think maybe I'll start tomorrow, or maybe the day after, I'm a little jet lagged."

"Yeah enjoy the lodge for a day or two. Get a massage and a spa treatment." She says.

"That sounds really good. I think I will do that, thanks for reminding me." There was a knock on the door. "I gotta go April, someone is knocking on the door, I'll call you tomorrow, okay?"

"Okay, love ya."

"Love ya, too." I hang up and go to the door. Its room service. I didn't order room service. I let the kid in with a cart filled with all kinds of food.

"Compliments of the lodge, ma'am." He says.

"Thank you," I fumble in my purse for a couple of dollars to give to him.

"No thank you, its been taken care of." He tells me.

"Oh okay."

He leaves, I hadn't realized just how hungry I am. I hadn't eaten since I left my house. I dive into the food, a little bit of everything, and its not cheap stuff either. Lobster, steak, shrimp, even a big hamburger. Dessert, champagne, strawberries dipped in chocolate. Man, I feel like a queen.

I stuffed myself, and felt sleepy. I laid down in the big king size bed and fell asleep. Don't know how long I slept but was awakened by the phone in the room ringing.

"Hello?" I groggily answered.

"Hello, this is the front desk, is everything to your liking?" The man asks me.

"Oh, yes," I tell him.

"There is a jeep, waiting for you. When you would like to use it, just come to the front desk, you also have a scheduled massage and spa treatment in an hour if you would like one. Or we can make it for another time."

"Oh no that will be fine, where do I go?"

"Come to the front desk and someone will show you. Anything else I can help you with?"

"No, I think that's it, thank you." I hang up.

'Let my vacation begin.' I say. I take one of the flowers and put it in my hair. I freshen up, before I go downstairs to my spa treatment.

The phone rings again, before I head downstairs, I pick it up and say hello. Hello I say again, "Is anyone there? That's strange, will its your quarter, nice to talk to you." And I hang up. Normally a phone call, would have me freaking out about it, like I have a stalker, or I'm being watched. Or someone is in the house with me, yeah I watch to many horror movies. But I was in such a good mood that it didn't bother me.

I went down to the front desk, and told them I was here for my spa treatment. A nice lady led me down the hallway to a spa room, and introduced me to the massage person. I had to change into a bathrobe, and lay on a comfortable table. Then just relax and let the lady do her magic. I had my nails done, my hair done a little, because I already had it just done. My toes too. When I left I felt so relaxed I could have melted all over the place.

CAM

I called her room, who's stalking who. She's my stalker, I have my very own stalker! That thought makes me laugh. I write a couple of songs about stalking. Except I'm the one who is the stalker.

I wanted to hear her voice, if she sounded like she was happy. I arranged the spa treatment for her. I hope she enjoys it. I want her to be in a really good mood, when I meet her.

JANIE

I had the best time at the spa, everyone was so nice to me. I woke up this morning ready to start my big adventure. I call it, "Search for my fantasy." I have a big breakfast in the dining room, and meet some nice tourist from NY. We sit and talk for a while. But I want to get going as soon as I'm done. I say good-bye, it was nice to meet you.

The front desk gives me the keys to the jeep, its new. And they don't tell me to be careful with it and scare me into not going anywhere with it. Just have a good time the guy says.

I take some of my clothes with me and my carry-on bag with every essential thing I have.

Hey you never know.

The jeep has plenty of gas, and I program my GPS with the lodges address, just in case I get lost. Which I do on occasion. I have a paper map too. My sunglasses, cause it's a nice day out.

I ask the desk clerk which way is Abbots Ville, and he points me in the direction.

Its fairly early, but not to early in the morning. I feel really good about today. I'll call April later. She's probably sleeping still. I kind of wish she could have come with me. But it was only a ticket for one. Usually at least two people get a trip, I never thought of that before, and its kind of bugging me. That's kind of strange. But I forget about it quickly.

I pull out of the lodge parking lot. And head towards the mountains. Everything is so beautiful up here, and I'm going to stop when ever I see something I want to take a picture of. I have my cameras. I pop Cams CD in the CD player. "I'm coming to get you, Cam." I say out loud, like its going to send him a message through the air and he's going to hear it.

I go up and up the roads taking in all the beautiful scenery. I stop several times to take pictures of waterfalls and the beautiful majestic mountains. The colors are incredible. I stop to eat lunch in a small café. When ever I eat in a place I always look at all the people, just in case there might be someone famous there. I've never met anyone famous, except Cam. Oh no, yes I have, I met some of the cast of "Twilight, New Moon, and Eclipse, Breaking Dawn." So sorry Cam, but you're the only one I want. You're the only one I'm stalking.

I should stop saying that, that I'm stalking him, because if someone asks me, it may slip out. And I don't want anyone to think I'm a lunatic.

I finish eating and pay my bill, use the bathroom, take one look at myself in the mirror. I look hot, I have to say, my blonde hair wavy down my back, my green eyes looking very sultry, as they stare back at me. I put on a little lip gloss and off I go. I always wondered why I get looks from people, all the time no matter where I go, and my friend, who is a guy, said, "it's the blonde hair."

There's something about being a blonde that attracts people to you. And I'm not the dumb blonde either, even though I've gotten those stupid jokes about dumb blondes.

I'm running low on gas so I better stop at the next gas station. Although this jeep gets pretty good gas mileage.

I look on the map to see where the next gas station is. I'm getting a little nervous, I don't want to run out of gas, out here, in the mountains, few and far between people and stores.

The next one should be a few miles up the road, and there it is. I pull in relieved that I wont run out.

I pay inside for the gas. I start to pump the gas. When I notice a guy in a hoodie, with sunglasses on, jeans that make his ass look really good. And if it isn't obvious, he's trying to hide. He goes to his car, which is a Corvette. Nice car. And then it dawns on me, I think its Cam. Is it possible?. Cam has a corvette, I remember reading about it. I watch him out of the corner of my eye. Because if I can watch how he moves I might be able to see if its him or not.

He's pumping gas into his car too. He standing there, and he catches me looking at him. I turn quickly away. Then I sneak another look and he gives me a grin. That smile, its got to be him. I'd know his smile anywhere. I smile shyly back at him. The pump clicks off, and I put the nozzle back in the cradle, I slam the gas door shut.

"Don't forget the cap," he says to me.

Oh yeah, I almost forget that, "Thanks," I say. And feel embarrassed that I forgot to put the cap back on. He's got me a little flabbergasted. I know its him, its got to be. Oh please, let it be him, I'm getting tired of riding around. I should follow him, just in case.

He's done pumping gas, and gets in his car. But he doesn't start it right away, he doing something inside. I hurry up and get back into the jeep. Put my seatbelt on and start the jeep up. He starts his car up and it roars to life. I love that sound. The roar of a big powerful engine.

I put it into gear and pretend to pull out, but I stop just before the exit to the main road. He follows behind, sees that I've stopped then, goes around me giving me a nod. I wish I could be sure its him. Still I'm going to follow him.

He's driving on the slow side and I've already caught up to him. If I had that car I'd be flooring it. I love speed, the feel of it, the power under you and you have control of it, your in command and it does what you tell it to do. I give him a space cushion and let my jeep fall back a little. In case he stops short and I wont rear end him. I notice he's looking in his rearview mirror quite a lot. I wonder if he's playing a game with me?

That's okay. Because I can play. I'm a damn good driver. I'll tell you a little story, my dad was a race car driver. It was a short career, but none the less it didn't curb his need for speed. He always drove like he stole it. The car. So I grew up watching my dad drive. And I almost think you inherit driving skills, either you're a good driver or you're a bad one. I can drive anything, land or sea. Big or small. Two wheels, four wheels, six wheels. Eight wheels. I haven't driven an eighteen wheeler though.

CHAPTER 8

One day I was going to the store, I wasn't in any rush, I think I had the day off from work. I think I was going food shopping. I made a right hand turn, and actually it was a stop then go, with a green arrow so I wasn't sitting there for no more than a second or two. But some little dufus, in a little station wagon car, decided I was in his way and I wasn't going fast enough. I made the turn and he passed me, there was no reason, and he certainly wasn't fast enough. He had a little 4 cylinder car and I have a big six cylinder truck. Well it pissed me off that he passed me, especially that there was no passing lane, and it was only a one lane road. But it really did piss me off. No one passes me, for no reason, I'm the one that passes people. So I drive for a while right on his tail, and I mean close. He stomps on his brakes a couple of times, and I almost rear end him the first time, but now I know what he trying to do. And I have really bad grinding brakes, I'm waiting for my friend to put new brakes on for me. So they are really, really bad. There's some traffic. But not that much. So when I see a clear opening, I pass him and give him the finger. So he tries to get up on my bumper only he cant keep up with me. But he does catch up and he passes me, then I pass him and give him such a look, like you loser, I do the loser sign on my forehead to him. Stupid piece of shit. He passes me one more time, only cause I let him. Then I make the final pass. And get back in line with the other motorists. There's a traffic light up ahead. But right before that he tries to make another pass. But he cant get back in line with the traffic. And has to drive on the wrong side of the road, heading straight into on coming traffic. I laughed so hard. He had a woman in the car with him. Either his wife or girl friend. I bet she was yelling shit at him. I wondered if there was a kid in the car too. I bet she beat the crap out of him for being such a jerk. I couldn't believe what an idiot he was, and I don't think I've ever seen anyone ever do that before. So I know I'm a fantastic driver.

But I'm giving this driver plenty of room. Then I hear him put it into second gear and he takes off. Leaving me in the dust. I step on the gas, the speedometer is going up to seventy, seventy five, eighty. He's up ahead. And makes a turn onto a side road. I slow down so I can make the turn without flipping the jeep over. I can see his trail of dust up ahead of me. But I cant see his car. Its up a hill. Were heading up the mountain.

I go up further and further. I still see the dust, and want to get to where ever he is before the dust settles, and then I wont know where he went.

I slow down a little because its getting to dusty to see. He's turned into a gated driveway, and the gate has just closed when I get there.

Okay at least I know where he went. If my mother knew what I was doing she'd yell at me. She always told me never pick up hitch hikers, she never said don't, 'chase after someone that you don't know.'

There's no name or anything on the mailbox only a number. That's helpful! Sarcastic humor always helps. I turn around so I can sit in front of the gate, but as I do that I hear a loud pop. I wonder what that is, and then I think I know. I hear a hissing noise too. Great I have a flat tire.

I get out to see, sure enough it's the left rear tire, its getting flat and flatter as the air escapes through a nice hole from a piece of rock, that I pull out of the tire. Great, what am I going to do now?

I look at my cell phone, no service up here, I have no bars.

I look at the tire. These are some massive truck tires made for going in the mud. Big knobby tires. I take out the jack, and try to get the spare off of the back. I cant even budge the bolt that's holding it onto the back of the jeep.

I try to loosen the lug nuts on the deflated tire, but I cant get that either. They put it on with a impact drill. It's a hydraulic wrench. How do they expect you to get it off by hand. I need help.

So I go over to the gate, and search all over for a button or something to call the house. I find the intercom button. I take a deep breath, and try to calm myself down so I don't sound so hysterical.

I press the button. I have to press it several times, before I hear a click like someone turned it on. "Hello?" I say.

I hear a click, "hello?" It's a man voice, I cant tell if its Cam's, cause its kind of crackly.

"Hello, yes I'm sorry to bother you but I have a flat and I have no service on my cell phone," I pause, " Could you call a tow truck for me, please I would really appreciate it." I hear empty air. I'm not sure if he's still there or not. "Hello?"

"Sure, hang on." He says.

"Thank you," I say, before he hangs up.

"Sure," I hear a click, I guess now he turned it off.

I get the jack under the jeep and start to jack it up. Its gotten really cold, the sun has gone down behind the mountain, I grab my jacket and put it on. I could ride on the tire back down the mountain until the tire shreds. But that would probably ruin the rim, and I'm sure I'd have to pay for that. I'm not staying here all night. I'll try to change the tire. I could walk, I look down the hill, no that's not a good idea either. I try the lug nuts and I'm struggling with them, wrestling with the five of them, I haven't budge them at all. As I'm wrestling with the tire, I see the headlights of a car coming down the driveway, it stops at the closed gates. The gates open and the driver gets out of the car. He leaves the car lights on. It makes it difficult to see the man. I only can see his silhouette. He tall and lean. Has a sexy walk, he has his hands in his pockets. His hair is curly and a little below his ears.

"Its gonna be a while before the tow truck comes," he says.

My teeth are chattering by now, instead of summer, it feels like the fall. "Sure is cold up here." I say.

"Yeah when the sun goes down it gets cooler. I see you have a flat." He notices.

"I was going to see if I could change it, but I cant budge the lug nuts, I need a pipe and a hammer."

"Well let me see if I can loosen them," he takes the lug wrench and gives them a big tug. He gets one or two of the loosened, but the other ones are on tight. He tries another one and slips off of the tire, smashing his hand on the ground.

He stops moving, like the pain is too much.

"Oh your hand," I take it in mine. Its bloodied. I notice he has nice hands. And a couple of rings on his fingers. Do guys really wear that many rings anymore?

"Ouch, damn," he says.

"Oh I'm so sorry, I made you hurt yourself, its bleeding, I hope you didn't brake it. I feel so bad, please can I do something for you?" I do feel awful, because he just messed up his hand really bad.

"No I don't think I broke it," he moves it and flexes his fingers. "See I can move everything. Its just a cut. I'll live." He says. I like his voice, it has a musical quality about it. He smells good too. And I know that smell, its very familiar.

"Stupid tire," I say and kick it with my toe, I do it a little harder than I intended to, I kick it so hard that the jeep falls off the jack. And…I think I broke my big toe. I bit my upper lip to keep from crying.

'OUH!"

"What?" He looks at me. I still haven't gotten a look at his face yet, because of the lights from his car, are shining right in my eyes.

"I think I just broke my toe," I sit on the ground and pull off my sneaker. I have tears in my eyes, cause damn does it hurt like hell. I'm afraid to look at it.

"Here let me look at it," he says. He slips my sock off, very gently and I forget all about the pain, and I get a good look at him. Its Cam, I'm almost positive.

"Um, I'm not sure, but it looks like it might be broken, its swelling up pretty good." He says.

"Oh great, how long did the tow truck guy say it would take to get here?" I ask.

"Maybe tomorrow," he says. He's looking down at me.

"Great."

He looks around like he's trying to decide something. "Listen, you cant stay here by yourself. Why don't you come up to the house. Will leave a note on the jeep. When he comes he can call the house. Then you can leave with him."

I looked around like I had another option. “Are you sure? I don’t want to inconvenience you.”

“Its no inconvenience, I’m alone at the house. It’ll be nice to have some company.” He smiles, that gorgeous smile at me, and I melt all over.

Well great I’ll be alone in a house with a sort of stranger. “Let me get my stuff.”

I hobble over to the drivers side of the jeep, turn on the auxiliary for the lights, and the CD player starts playing. Its loud like I always play it. I turn it down and pop it out. “Sorry,” I say.

He nods and acts as though he doesn’t know its his music, cause we are both playing dumb.

I cant leave my CDS behind, I put them in my special box, which is a shoe box. So that people only think that its shoes. Its my prized possession. I hold it to my chest, and I grab my pocketbook. And try to pick up my travel bag too. Lock the jeep. He puts a note on the windshield under the windshield wiper. He takes my over night bag from my shoulder.

“Ready?” He asks.

“Yes,” my shoe is off, he puts his arm around my waist and swings my arm around his neck. Oh my god, oh my god, he has his arm around me, and I have mine around him. Déjà vu, I’ve had my arm around him once or twice before, I’m standing here with you. Keeps popping into my head. I’m sort of mesmerized by him, and feel like I’m having an outer body experience. He helps me to his car and opens the passenger side door.

“Nice car,” I manage to say.

“Thanks, its not new.” He says. He closes the door for me and walks to the driver side and gets in.

“It’s still nice.” I say.

Leather seats, smells like a man. God, it smells like him. And that’s a good thing.

He starts the car, pulls out into the road to turn around. Then pulls back into the driveway. Closes the gate.

I feel really funny sitting next to him, in the small confines of the car. The driveway is very long and windy. I see lights up ahead on top of the hill. And a big house. More like a mansion.

All the bells and whistles are going off. Mama's voice is in my head. "Not good, Janie, you shouldn't be here, alone with a man. Something bad could happen." I quickly tell her to leave.

He pulls up front of the hugemongus house. "Wow," is the first thing I say about it, "Oh my god," is the second thing I say.

"Your wife isn't home?" I don't know why I asked that, but I did.

"No, no wife," he says.

"Oh," I say. And I smile to myself. YES!

He helps me out, I still haven't gotten a good look at him yet. I feel so shy. I'm really not shy at all. His voice is deep, but not to deep. Its very appealing to me. He helps me out of the car and to the front door. He grabs my stuff. It's a good thing I didn't bring more.

"I think I can walk, if I walk on my heel," I tell him.

"Its no problem," he says.

He opens the front door and shows me in. Its nice and warm. I smell a fire. He puts my stuff down by the door, and closes it, I notice he locks it too. "Cant be to careful around here," he says.

He puts everything down except my shoe box. "You like this band?" He asks me.

"Oh my god, yes, I love these guys. Why?"

"Oh nothing," he says.

Its dim inside, but very cozy, even though its so big. My toe is really throbbing and I'd like to sit down, his hand is still bleeding and it looks horrible. "Where is your kitchen? We need to clean your hand."

"In there," he points up ahead. It's the biggest kitchen I've ever since.

"Do you have some bandages, and some antibacterial cleaner?"

"Yeah, I'll go get it." He says and leaves me in the kitchen, so I can look around. Its beautiful, I wonder who designed it, a man or a woman. Its white with splashes of color all over. And it has all chrome appliances, like my house does. There is a huge picture window above the sink and I can see out the back, where its all light up with lights scattered here and there. Looks like a pool.

In my whole life time, I'd never be able to afford anything like this.

I see a guitar on the table and papers spread out across the top.

He comes back with everything I asked for, and dumps it on the table. Its quite a pile of stuff.

"Is this enough?" He asks me.

"Yeah, I think so." I laugh. "Here let me look at your hand." He puts his hand over the sink. "This might sting," I say, cause I'm going to pour some hydrogen peroxide over the cut.

He flinches a little, it bubbles and I rinse it off with water.

I look at his hand closely. His knuckles are all cut up. "Can you still move your fingers?"

He moves them again, "Yeah feels okay." He says.

"I see you play the guitar, will it interfere with your playing?"

He picks up the guitar and plays a few cords, from one of his songs. "No, I'm good." He says.

"Let me finish your hand, it needs a bandage on it , otherwise your gonna bleed all over the place."

He comes back over to the sank and gives me his hand, and I put some medicine on a gauze bandage and wrap it up with surgical tape. I'm holding his hand in mine, looking down at his hand, and he's looking down too, it reminded me of a picture I once had of my now ex-husband and me when we were married. The picture was of us holding each others hand while putting on the wedding bands. I think every person that's been married has this same exact picture. It was a short marriage. Isn't it funny what you think of?

When I finish with his hand he doesn't pull his hand out of mine right away. He leaves it there, letting it linger in mine. I'd like to caress it and turn it over and trace the lines in his palm. And work my way up his arm, then to his chest, to his neck and to his face. Then I'd like to.........

I'd better stop. Or before I know it I just may do what I'm thinking.

"Janie?" He says. He knows its me.

"Cam?" I say back, "You know its me?"

"Yeah, I have a confession to make, and I wasn't going to tell you until years from now, but I guess I better tell you now." He says.

"What is it?" I look up at him, were still holding hands.

"Well, you know your contest? I shake my head, how would he know about that?

"I was the one that arranged it," he smiles.

I guess I look really surprised, cause he hurries with his explanation. "I know I got you really upset, the last time we met, so I wanted to make it up to you, and I have a proposition for you, which was the thing I wanted to talk to you about, but you ran away." He takes a long breath.

"Oh," I say, "I really thought I won the "Canada see it now.com, contest. How did you know I entered a contest or even that one?"

"I didn't, it's a coincidence, I swear." He says.

"Well before we get into this, lets take care of your toe, maybe I should drive you to the hospital."

"No, I think it'll be okay, it doesn't hurt so much now. As long as I don't bang it. I'll let you know if its to painful, okay?"

"Sure, here sit down and I'll get you some ice." He offers me one of the kitchen chairs. It really is throbbing, but I'm afraid that if he takes me to the hospital, he'll leave me there, and I'll never see him again. So I want to stay here with him. He's looking around for something, he comes back with a big pot, and starts pouring ice into it. When its full he puts it on the floor by my feet.

"Here put your foot in there and see if the ice helps any."

It's a little hard to put my toe into the ice. "Could you put some water in there, its hard to put my toe in there." I tell him.

He puts some warm water in and it makes it easier for me to put my toe in. He's very gentle, and pours the water slowly over my foot, he holds my foot like it's a precious jewel. I like that. I watch him intently, I cant help staring at him. I study him and want to absorb everything about him, to store it away in my mental library, so I wont ever forget anything about him.

He feels me watching him. And looks up at me, "how does that feel?" He asks me.

"Not to bad, feels a little better actually," and it does. The coldness is numbing my toe.

"I have some aspirins, I can give you for the pain, or even a strong drink, if you want one?"

"Oh no thanks, I don't drink, but the aspirins sound good. I could use a couple of those."

He goes somewhere, I guess to the bathroom, its far away, to get the aspirins. It gives me another chance to look around, and I pull his notebook over to me to see what he's writing.

Its his book with all his songs and notes. It looks like he writing new songs. I try to read some of the words, but I hear him coming back so I push it back to where it was.

He hands me some aspirins, and I touch his hand again, you know when you touch someone and your so aware of the feeling, and you wonder if the other person can feel it too. That's the feeling I got when I took the aspirins out of his hand. Little sparks tingling on my fingertips. He gets me a glass of water. I swallow the pills. They better be aspirins, I heard he used to deal drugs when he was a teenager, for extra money.

"Are you hungry?" He asks me. I hadn't even thought about food, and I haven't eaten since I stopped at lunchtime.

"Yeah I am." I say, "I think my stomach is grumbling."

"I can make you something, I not really a good cook, but I could make you a sandwich or something."

"Well... how about I cook for you, so do you have food?" I ask.

"Yeah the freezer is loaded with stuff, steak, lobster, what ever you want. Just look around, you'll find whatever you need, I have a lady come and stock the kitchen for me when I come back from touring." He says.

"What would you like?" I ask him, I hobble over to the fridge, looking inside.

"I was going to try a steak," he says. "There's one in the fridge thawing."

"Okay, I'll make that, you have potatoes, and stuff?"

"Yeah, just look around."

"I will, let me surprise you, you go ahead and do whatever it was you were doing before I disturbed you."

"You didn't disturb me," he says, "It was all planned, you were suppose to find me, at the gas station, that was no coincidence." He smiles at me and sits down at the table and picks up his guitar. He starts to play softly. I recognize the song.

I start looking through the cabinets and the fridge. I feel funny at first, like I'm invading his privacy, but it doesn't seem to bother him, I find everything I need and start to cook. He's playing, his guitar..

I am being serenaded by Cam Konner. I close my eyes to store this in my mental library, too. Hopefully by the time the tow truck comes, I'll have a whole library full of memories stored.

Then I can die a happy old lady with memories of a guy I used to know.

I hobble around, its not to difficult to walk as long as I don't hit my toe. As he's playing, I wonder if he knows how obsessed I am about him? Or if he even knows that I'm obsessed about him? I'm trying to act so cool about it, when I really want to jump all over him, touch him everywhere and kiss him every other place.

"You play really beautifully," I tell him.

"Thanks, I try," he says. God he's perfect, he taught himself how to play the guitar. How perfect can that be? I've tried to teach myself things and failed.

"Smells good, I'm hungry too," he says. "I bet you're a good cook."

"Its almost done, you'll see." I find some dishes, and put them out. "What are you drinking?" I ask him.

"I'll get it. I usually have a beer. What do you want?" He asks. What I want is him. Forget the food, forget the drink, I WANT YOU, CAM, ON THE TABLE, ON THE FLOOR, ANYWHERE AT ALL. I don't say that though. That's my over active brain, that's screaming at me.

"I'll just have some juice or what ever you have. But not alcohol."

I put the food on the plates and bring them to the table, he got the drinks. " Well I hope you like it," I say.

"I'll like it cause, I didn't cook it," he laughs. "Let's eat in the den, I have a nice cozy fire going."

I follow him, with the plates, into a dark wood room with a fire place, and a cheerful fire in it. Big brown leather chairs face the fireplace. He sits on the floor in front of it, I've forgotten about my toe until I hit it on the chair. I almost fall over.

"Whoa," he says and steadies me from falling over.

"Oh that hurt," I cant even rub it, its throbbing all over again.

"I bet," he says.

"How's your hand?" I ask.

"Its okay," he flexes it a little, I watch him, I like the way his hands look in the light of the fire.

We eat, thank god the fire is crackling so we don't have to listen to each other chewing. I'm very self-conscience when I eat in front of a stranger.

"That was excellent," he says, he leans back against the couch. "You're a good cook, thanks for doing that."

"Your welcome, and thanks for rescuing me," I smile shyly.

"By the way, I want to talk to you about something. Since were both in a good mood." He says.

"Wait will be in an even better mood once we've had dessert," I say. "Let me go make something, okay."

"Sure, Janie," he says. "Let me help you with the dishes." He helps me up. God every time he touches me, it makes me dizzy.

He washes the dishes, while I make the dessert. He's got everything I need to make this delicious apple bread dessert. "Who is the woman who stocks your kitchen?" I ask him, "I have to know, she has thought of everything." I say.

"My mom," he says.

"She must be an incredible woman," I say.

"Well when I was growing up she worked in a diner, so I guess she knew all the food that they needed to run the place. So I guess that's where she gets her experience."

I remember all of the ingredients, because I've made so many of these breads, and it really isn't a bread, its just the kind of pan I put it in. It has to cook for about an hour. So in the meantime I guess we can talk. And honestly I'm not sure if I want to hear what I think he's going to say to me. Like I have a restraining order against you, and right now I could have you arrested, because your in my house. But he invited me here.......

I set the timer on the oven, so I'll know when its done. "Lets go back to the den," Cam says.

I hobble along, behind him, those jeans, I let my eyes wander to his butt.

"I know your looking at my ass," he says. I feel myself turning red.

"And what makes you think that?" I ask trying to sound like that's not the truth.

"Cause I can feel you looking," he says.

"Yeah but, I have to look cause your in front of me, and your leading the way into the room. So....? What do you want me to do? Close my eyes, and feel my way to the room?"

He laughs, "Then you might touch me," he says. He turns to look at me, I almost crash into him.

"See I knew you were, your beet red," he teases.

"I'm beet red because, my toe hurts." I lie.

"Oh, sure, maybe I should take you to the hospital," he looks down at my toe, and frowns.

"No, its okay. So what is it you want to talk to me about?" I need to change the subject, so he wont insist on taking me to the hospital.

CHAPTER 9

"Sit down," he offers me one of the big chairs.

I must look a little scared, cause he says, "you aren't in trouble, if that's what you think I want to talk to you about, far from it." He says. I nod.

"I loved your dancing, the night that you did it, I was thinking to myself how boring and mundane the concerts were getting. Why doesn't something interesting happen. I didn't see you at first, I think my brother did, and the rest of them, before I did. It like blew me away, you looked so sexy, that's why I didn't stop the music, I wanted you to continue. So after the song was over, I was going to talk to you, but you dove off of the stage so fast, and then my body guard couldn't find you. The sign language thing, was awesome, and was something different. But we sort of had a misunderstanding. After our short meeting. So that's why I made up this vacation for you." I nod again, still not sure where this is going.

I can smell the apples baking in the dessert, it smells good. It should be done soon.

"Well my proposition is, how would you like to join the tour, with us and do this every night, the dancing and the sign language thing you did, you'd be paid of course, and you'd travel with the band." He's looking at me to see my reaction.

I hadn't expected this at all, it's a lot to swallow. But I love the idea, I would get to be with him every single day.......

"I think that would be a great idea," I finally say. "I would have to take care of some personal business before I could join you, but I can take a leave of absence from work, and have someone look after my house and mail," I say. "I'm sure there's other things I'd need to take care of, I just don't know what. But I love the idea." I want to jump into his arms. But I remain cool, I don't want him to know what an obsessed, fanatic, lunatic, person I can be.

I hear the buzzer for the oven go off, "I'll get the dessert," I say. I want to go jump up and down for joy, without him seeing me do my little dance. I cant believe what he just asked me, I cant wait to tell April.

When I come back to the room, with the dessert on a plate. He's got his guitar and his note book. "I've been writing some new songs," he says. "Would you like to hear a new song? You'd be the first one to hear it."

"Oh...yes, I'd love that," I hand him a piece of the apple bread.

He starts to play a beautiful love song, the words are from his heart. He must be a really deep person, cause where ever he gets these beautiful words from, I could never do that.

"That was the most beautiful song I've ever heard yet, besides all the other ones you've written," I say. "Beautiful."

"Thanks, that dessert was delicious. Thanks again. Are you tired?"

"Yes I am, the food, the warm fire and you playing, is putting me all to sleep," I yawn.

"Oh so what are you saying my singing is boring?" He says.

"No...your voice is very soothing, that's all I've had a big day."

"I know, I'm only kidding."

"Oh." I don't know him well enough to know when he's kidding or not.

"You can sleep in one of the guest rooms, there's plenty of them," he says.

"I think I'll stay here, if you don't mind, its nice and cozy in here."

"Suit yourself, good-night, Janie."

"Good-night, Cam." He gives me a nod, he hesitates at the door, like he wants to say something else, but then changes his mind and leaves. There's a fluffy blanket draped over one of the chairs and some over sized pillows on the couch. I poke the fire and add a couple of more logs. Find my over night bag and change into my nightgown. Its not the sexiest thing, but it'll have to do. I lay down on the couch, my toe is throbbing, but I'm so tired that I don't care. What an incredible day this has been, I look at my cell phone, its late, to late to call April now. I'll call her tomorrow. Besides I still have no bars.

CAM

Well I took care of it, like I said I would. I hope I've made her feel better. I wonder what the rest of the band is going to say? Probably something like, "not a good idea, Cam, or what about Melissa?" I'll deal with them later. She's right down stairs, I could invite her to my room. I guess I better behave myself.

JANIE

Early in the morning I needed to use the bathroom. I searched all over for the damn thing and couldn't find it. Where the hell did they hide it?

I have to go so badly I was dreaming about water. I woke up confused for just a minute or two, until I remembered where I was. So this wasn't a dream. I look down at my toe, its big and swollen, and blue. Nope it hasn't been a dream.

The fire has died down, but the room is still warm, I need to go so badly, I stand at the bottom of the stairs. "Cam?" I yell. "Cam?" I yell again. I hear him stirring, he banged something and I hear him curse.

"What's wrong, are you okay?" He rubs his knee, he has no shirt on, and he's wearing a loose pair of PJ bottoms.

"I'm sorry to bother you, but I need to use the bathroom and I cant find it."

His hair is tousled, look at those abs, I'd never get tired of looking at those, he's so hot. Holy shit.

He's rubbing his eyes, and yawning. "Go straight, to the left open the door and then through the next door."

"Thanks," I say, "What time do you get up?"

"Around 12, I guess, why?"

"I'll make you breakfast."

"Sounds good, you better be careful I may get used to this, or I might keep you here as my favorable slave." He smiles a wicked smile at me.

"I wouldn't mind being your slave," I smile back. He turns to leave.

"Oh by the way, nice sleepwear."

I look down, my nightgowns buttons are wide open so he had a nice view. How embarrassing. I give him a smug smile, okay you can have that one, a free look. Something to keep you thinking about me.

I find the bathroom. I start to button up my nightgown, then I stop, eh I'll leave it open. I smile a mischievous grin to myself. Janie you're a bad girl, I say to myself.

CAM

I find the number of the tow truck company and call them, back. A sleepy voice answers and I tell them not to come until I call them up. They say why? I say because. Its none of their business.

So now she can stay longer. Or until she has to leave to go back home.

JANIE

No wonder I couldn't find the bathroom, it was hidden behind door number two. Its huge too, like everything else in the house. I could fit my whole house in here.

Its got a steam shower with tons of different nozzles, beautiful tile all over, marble or granite. Something expensive. A Jacuzzi tub, looks like a small pool. I'm hoping I can use it. I shouldn't be to pushy.

I go back to sleep for a while longer. I make sure I wake up before Cam does. I want to make him a really big breakfast.

I limp to the kitchen, find everything I need. I'd like to met his mother. I make him everything, because I don't know what he likes. I'll just make him the usual breakfast stuff.

Pancakes, eggs, bacon, toast, coffee, juice, some fruit. I finish with it all and put it on a makeshift tray. I balance it, precariously, I hobble about, to the stairs and look up. Now how am I going to do this?

I look at the clock, its 12:30 and I don't hear Cam. So he must still be sleeping. I put my good foot on the stairs and hoist myself up. This is going to take a few minutes. I heel my injured foot up. I make it to the second floor, which door is Cam's bedroom?

There's so many doors, at the end of the hall way is double doors, I figure its probably his room. I go to the door, and put my ear to the door to listen. I hear no noise. I tap lightly on the door, no answer, so I open it. It's a huge room, nicely decorated, not to feminine, but not to, to manly. I wonder who decorated this, Melissa? I haven't even met her, and I hate her already. "Cam," I whisper. "Are you awake?" I whisper again.

"Uh?" He mumbles.

"I bought you breakfast." I stand next to his bed, maybe the smell will wake him up.

He rolls over and sits up, rubbing his face and running his hand through his hair. "Oh, what time is it?" He asks. He's got some facial hair growing beside his signature mustache and goatee. I like the rugged look.

"It's a little after 12:30," I say. "I made breakfast, are you hungry?"

"Yeah smells great," I put the tray across his lap. He grabs my hand, "come sit and eat with me. There's enough for the two of us." I limp over to the other side of the bed. It's a king size bed. I hobble around it. I sit down, he looks at my toe.

"Whoa that looks awful, I think you did break it. You probably should go to the doctor, we have one here in town, I'll take you after breakfast, okay?"

"Sure," I say.

"I hope you like it, I didn't know what you like so I made a little of everything."

"It looks good." His chest is bare, I'm trying not to look at him, he looks so yummy I would like to lick every part of him.

I forgot napkins, I should go and get some. He's made me sweat. I'm sweating cause I'm so close to him. This is way to intimate. But he doesn't seem bothered by it. So I'll try not to let him effect me this way. His nearness is intoxicating. I think… I'm gonna die!

I need to get away from him for a few minutes to calm myself down, just being near him sparks this flame in me, this desire to devour him. It would be so wrong of me. "I have to get napkins," I say. "I forgot them," I run before he can stop me, I close the door behind me and take a deep breath. If he ever had any idea how he makes me feel, or what he does to me, he might throw me out of his house.

I hobble back down the stairs and into the kitchen, where I notice a message on his answering machine. I shouldn't be so noisy, but I press it any way. "Hey babe, you aren't answering your cell phone, you must still be sleeping, just calling to say "I love you. Bye, I'll call you later, love ya." Must be Melissa.

I find the napkins, and hobble back upstairs. Knock on the door to let Cam know I'm back. He's waited for me. "Why aren't you eating?"

"I'm waiting for you," he smiles.

"Well hurry up and eat before it gets cold."

So we eat, like I said before, its hard for me to eat in front of a stranger, even though Cam is very easy to be around. He asks me about the proposition, he offered me? Have I thought of anything else I need to do, or anything I want?

I don't think there's anything else, except maybe some more costumes, shoes, I'm not wearing the same thing every night.

After eating, I clean up and get dressed. Cam insists he takes me to the doctor, I mind as well. I agree. He helps me into his hummer. The drive isn't long, it's a nice day out. I really feel like I belong here. I don't want this feeling to end. We get to the doctors office, he's closed, but Cam makes a phone call. The doctor will be right down. He's only upstairs. I expect that everyone jumps for Cam.

He opens the door and lets us in. He x-rays my toe. "Yup," the doctor says, "Your toe is broken," he gives me some pain pills. Tells me to put it in ice, and wraps it up for me. That's about all you can do for a broken toe. I get crutches.

"Do you want to go any place else?" Cam asks me.

"No, I don't think so, I have enough pain pills, until the tow truck comes," I spot one but I don't say anything, hoping Cam doesn't see it. He doesn't say anything either. So we head back to his mansion.

"What do you want to do today?" He asks me.

"What were you going to do?" I say.

"I was going to go dirt bike riding," he says. "But you probably don't want to do that."

"Are you kidding I ride all the time, I have a Kawasaki 125 at home, come on lets go."

We go to his garage, where he has all kinds of toys to play with, there's different dirt bikes, different sizes and makes. "What do you want to ride?" He asks me.

"Something small," I say. I spot a Yamaha 110. "There that one," I point to the blue bike.

"Good choice," he says. "Its fast." He says.

"I know, I'm not intimidated by a little speed." I can feel the adrenaline starting to rise, especially when competing with a man. Even more so that its Cam.

"Where do we ride?" I asked.

"Behind the house, up the mountain I have dirt trails all over up there." He points.

"Lots of trees?" I ask.

"Yeah of course, why?"

"I'm not used to riding around trees to much, I mostly rode in clearings."

"Backing out?" He teases.

"No, I'm sure I can keep up."

We have to get the proper gear for dirt biking, he has gloves, helmet, glasses, jackets, knee guards, chest protector, elbow guards, and most important, the dirt bike boots.

"Oh crap what about my toe?"

"Still trying to get out of this?"

"No…!"

We suit up with all the necessary stuff, except I don't wear the guards, any of them, "You wear these things?" I ask him.

"Yeah why?"

"Whimp." I tease.

"Will see who the whimp is, get your big fat toe in the boot."

I push my foot inside the boot, ouch it hurts like hell, but I'm not going to admit it to him. He piles the rest of the equipment in my arms. "Thanks." I say.

Cam picked out a KTM 450. It's a big bike, I couldn't even lift it. I put on the rest of the gear. And I'm ready to go. We push the bikes outside and start them up. It gives me goose bumps to hear the roar of the engines. I haven't ridden in a while. So this feels exhilarating. The clean air of the mountain, and a really hot guy next to me. I ask Cam which way, he points up. "You go first," I tell him. I'll follow behind him, besides I'd rather look at his cute ass, bouncing all around. The way his back and arm muscles flex.

The trail is cleared of rocks and ruts, but not of trees. Its windy, and gonna take a lot of maneuvering on my part, and a lot of physical effort to keep it in control. I'm concentrating on the ground ahead of me, I keep plenty of space between us. Cam has stopped up ahead. He's waiting for me. "How are you doing?" He asks me he has to yell over the engine.

"I'm doing good, lets keep going." Our faces are close, so that we can hear each other, I could just plant a kiss on him, except the helmets are in the way, I really have to stop thinking of him that way, because its making me stupid. I can smell the soap he used to wash this morning.

He goes to the left and I follow, the ground levels out. Makes it a little easier for me to ride.

He stops again and points, in the distance is a water fall. I forgot my camera. "Wow, that's incredible, its so beautiful, can we go there?" I yell.

"No its to far, it would take all day to get there and its getting late now." I'm disappointed, but oh well.

We head back down the trail to the house…mansion.

He's got a dirt track behind the garage. I point to it. "Go-karts." He says. He raises his eyebrows at me. I nod my head up and down.

"Lets race go-karts," I say.

"Yeah what'd ya have a lot of brothers?" He teased.

"No, just one, I just wanted to be one of the boys." I lie again, sorry, I don't like to lie, but telling guys that I used to race these things, kind of gives them an attitude. And then they get all obnoxious about trying to beat me.

We put the bikes away, and pull out the go-karts. Electric start. They cost about 6,000 dollars a piece, I know I had a couple of friends that used to race them, in professional races. I used to race them too. We only owned one. I take off the dirt bike gear, just leave on the helmet and gloves. We start them up. Ah… the smell of racing fuel. You never forget that smell.

I love speed. I'll race anything with wheels, the faster the better I like it. And I like to win. I like to beat and bang. Step on the gas, go fast and turn left.

We take a few warm-up laps, "this is the starting line," Cam says. "Lets go around about 20 times. Go ahead take the pole." He says.

"Okay you'll be sorry," I yell over my shoulder. Were both grinning. He's a competitor too.

"Get ready, get set, go," he yells. We sped around the track. The fumes bring back a lot of memories. I used to spend every Friday night at the race track in Medford. With my friend, and some new friends, racing against them. Fierce competition. Tuesday nights were practice night. Sometimes we raced at other tracks, on Long Island or Upstate. How strange, that smells triggers memories.

We're banging into each other, skidding sideways around the turns. I'm laughing the whole time, so is Cam. I hope he's counting, cause I'm not. He holds up two fingers, two laps to go. I gun it for the finish line. We're even around the turn for the last lap, I'm gonna try a dirty move and push him from behind and push him out of the way.

I try it but he knows what I'm thinking. He dodges my move and both of us cross the finish line at the same time. I think my nose is first over the finish line. He thinks he's first.

We're arguing about it. We have our helmets off.

"I won," I say.

"No you didn't, I did." He says.

"Your wrong. I was a nose ahead of you, and you know it." Our faces inches from each other.

"No way, I was the one out in front, and you know it." He pokes me in the chest, and I'm so aware of his touch that I stop talking. He realizes what he did. I get my wits back, and say.

"Do you have pictures?"

"No."

"So then I won," I laugh. I push him and run away. "I won," I yell over my shoulder at him.

He runs after me. He grabs my jacket. I cant run to fast because of my big toe. I fall, he falls.

We're laughing. Then he kisses me. Whoa…I stop moving and look at him. He kisses me again. Longer and harder this time. "I won." He says. He gets up. Pulls me up into his chest. Kisses me again. I'm really surprised. And speechless. Damn he's a good kisser. He lets go of me. Walks to the go-karts, as if nothing happened. Leaving me there breathless. I cant move from the spot I was in, I'm all flustered, to say the least. More like bowled over. I have to stop letting him paralyze me like he does, I cant seem to move when he touches me. I take a deep breath, I push my go-kart into the garage.

He's cleaning the go-kart, and puttering around, he seems unaffected by the kiss. Doesn't he have a girlfriend? He must be awfully lonely.

CHAPTER 10

"Could I use your Jacuzzi the one in your bathroom?" I ask him. "I've used muscles I haven't used in a while." I tell him rubbing my sore muscles.

"Sure," he says, "I'll join you, I haven't used the Jacuzzi since the last party I had here." It wasn't what I had in mind, but its his house.

"I don't have a bathing suit." I frown. I left it at the hotel.

"There's a couple of spare suits in the draw in the bathroom, just pick one out." He offers.

I really wanted to be alone, and I have to ask, "You'll wear a suit, right?"

He laughs, "Yeah if you want me to." He laughs again. I feel myself turning red.

I find the draw with the suits, all bikinis, which I hate. I like tankinis, better, they hide a little bit more then the little strings that they call a bathing suit. Oh well its better than nothing. I find the one that looks like it'll cover the most. A little pink polka dot two piece. Don't get me wrong, I have a great body, and I look hot in it. I'm just a little conservative that's all. I look through the entire draw, at all the suits, there all the same size, I wonder if there the girlfriends. She is really irritating me, and I don't even know her. I wonder what she would think of this little situation?

He's got the water in the tub and its bubbling, he even put bubbles in the water. I have a towel wrapped around me. He's already in the water and he's watching me. He's bare-chested, and he better have something on down below. I feel so self conscience, that it makes me feel clumsy.

I wish for just one second, he would turn his head, so I could take off the towel, and get into the water, without him seeing me. But he has his eyes on me.

I stick my toe in the water, its hot. I don't know if my big toe could stand the heat. But the rest of me is begging me to go in. I suddenly feel achy all over. Oh the hell with it, I let the towel fall to the floor. I don't care if he's staring at me. And he is, a slow smile is playing on his lips. "WHAT", I say.

"Nicce…." He says.

"Hrumph" I say. "I know I have a smoking hot body," I tease. "I get this all the time." I brag.

"I bet you do," he says. I sink into the water, "Ahhhh…Oh that feels so good," I moan. "I cant believe how achy the bike made me feel, it usually doesn't do that to me."

"Out of shape, maybe?" He grins. I splash him with the water.

"I don't think so, I mean look at me," I scan my body, and his eyes follow. I love this bantering that we are starting to do with each other, its like we've been doing it for years. He's just a regular kind of guy. I always had him up on a pedestal, like a god, or a superhuman being, well the way he plays that guitar, I think he is.

"Where were you just now?" He asks me.

"Oh no where, just thinking about superhuman strength, how I don't have any."

"The suit looks nice on you," he says.

"Thanks, it was the best one I could find, who's are they?"

"A friends," he says.

"Like a girlfriends?"

"Yeah something like that."

"I know you have one."

"Do you have one?" He asks.

"No, I'm through with boyfriends, they all seem to be jerks or losers. I'm better off alone."

"Oh well, uh getting back to the bathing suit, you seem to like the color pink?" He says.

"Yeah its one of my favorite colors, I do like other colors though. I hope your wearing one?"

"And wonder if I'm not?" The corner of his mouth goes up a little, not quite a smile but a devilish half grin.

"I'd close my eyes." I say.

"No, you wouldn't," he laughs. "Well I'm not wearing one," he says.

"What!" My eyes bug out. And I'm ready to jump out of the Jacuzzi.

"Just kidding," he teases.

"Oh, okay." I make a face at him, he laughs again. A big bellowy laugh.

"Okay laugh at my expense." I say. And splash him again.

Our legs are touching each other, neither one of us moves away. He's staring at me intently, and making me feel uneasy. "Do you have to do that?" I ask him.

"Do what?" He asks.

"Stare at me, like that?"

"I didn't know I was staring," he says, nonchalantly.

"Well you do that a lot, like I have something funny on my face or something."

"You have a very pretty face, and beautiful green eyes, and pouty lips, and you always smell so good." He says matter of fact.

"You've really been studying me, uh?"

"No just observing, that's where I get a lot of my ideas for songs by observing what's around me."

"Sure," I say, I'm not buying it. He just wants to ogle my body.

I bet he can get any girl he wanted. After all didn't he pick Melissa out of a crowd of thousands of fans? She apparently claims that she didn't know who he was. I don't buy that either. Come on you were at his concert. How could you not know it was him, when he asked you to come back stage.

"Where were you, you keep disappearing?" He asks.

"You should check your answering machine, and see if the tow truck guy called." I say. I'm not telling him, where I keep disappearing to. My thoughts are my own, its where I escape to.

"Later," he says.

If I stay any longer I'll have to call my boss and tell her I wont be coming back to soon. I'd stay the rest of my life if I could. If he'd let me, if he wanted me. I wonder how serious he is with his girlfriend? And who made the first move, he probably did, cause he picked her out, so……..and he's kind of an aggressive guy.

"I wish I could get into your mind," he says. "I keep losing you, like your taking a walk some place else." He says.

"Oh I'm sorry, I was just thinking, that if the tow truck doesn't come soon, I'll have to call my boss and tell her I wont be coming back when I expected I would. She'll be pissed."

"She'll be pissed when you tell her you quit?" He says.

"I think I'll just take a leave of absence, just incase this thing doesn't work out." I say.

"It'll work out, you'll see." He says confidently.

"We should cook something for dinner, what would you like to eat?" I ask him. Changing the subject for a second.

"Anything, we could cook together." He suggests.

"Lobster, I think I saw some in the freezer, I'd really like to met your mother, she thought of everything." He's got a funny look on his face. "Stop looking at me like that, your making me nervous, why are you doing that?"

"I was just imagining this every night, you know what it might be like?"

"Really? With me or with the girlfriend?"

"With you, of course." He smiles.

"Be careful what you say, Cam."

"Whys that?" He asks.

"Because I'm a psycho fan, be careful what you wish for, I had a friend who always used to say that to me."

"You don't seem like you're a psycho fan, your very in control."

"Only on the outside, on the inside, I'm this boiling pot of emotions and I'm almost ready to explode. So be careful what you wish for." I smile.

He swims over to be, pinning me against the wall of the tub. His arms on either side of me.

His face is inches away from mine. His blue eyes, the sky blue eyes are thunderous looking.

His eyes travel down to my lips and then back again to look into my eyes.

He moves in closer, I can feel his breath on my face. I hold my breath. And its getting really hot in here. I remember my toe, is throbbing from the hot water. I push the pain out of my mind.

Cam is trying to decide something. He's hesitating inches from my lips. Kiss me already. I want you to, what is wrong. I'm not pushing you away. Maybe that's a good idea. So I put my hands up on his chest and push, he grabs my wrists, and pins them to the top of the tub. He leans in and kisses me, gently at first, then more intensely. He lets go of my hands and I wrap my arms around his neck. He unties my top and throws it over his shoulder. He sits on the seat in the tub and pulls me into his lap, my hands are in his hair and I pull it, he moans. Oh, he likes that, I used to have a boyfriend that liked hair pulling, isn't it funny what you think of.

"Come with me, Janie," he says in a seductive voice. He holds out his hand to me. I put my hand in his and he pulls me out of the Jacuzzi. I was a little self conscious of my missing top. And tried to make an attempt to get it, but he pulled me towards the shower, opens the door and pulled me in, against him. The water washing over us. The steam filling the air around us. Our bodies pressed together. "Cam, I…." I started to say. When his mouth came down on mine. And that was the end of my resolve. I have my hands all over him, his all over me. "One time in the shower, with me." He says. And then he whispers in my ear, the water splashing over our faces, "Please take all of me, Janie, take all of me." He moans. I'll take everything from you, Cam, everything, I think to myself.

I've spent almost two weeks with Cam. Its been really fun, I saw how he made a CD, a video to one of his songs, done some hiking into the mountains, to that waterfall, I saw. One thing I was concerned about was the girlfriend stopping by. He listened to the answering machine message. Before I could ask the question, he told me she was visiting her grandmother.

But almost the last day of my vacation, she stopped by the house. I was up stairs, changing the sheets on Cam's bed. I know you say why? Because it's the least I can do for his hospitality. Like I said, 'favorable slavery.'

I heard her come in, she has a key. She calls Cam. He was somewhere in the house. The first thing she asks, out loud is, "who's jeep is parked down by the gate?"

I hear her plodding up the stairs towards Cam's bedroom, where I'm just finishing up making Cam's bed. She pushes open the door, "Oh hello," she says. I had picked up the pile of bed linens so they covered my face, and I was kicking a pile of his clothes out of the room. "Do you know where Cam is?" She asks.

"No, ma'am," I say, "he might be in his studio."

"Oh yeah right," she says, " and you are?" She's fishing around. I think she wants to know who I am. So I make something up to appease her.

"I'm the temporary house keeper, the other lady couldn't make it. So I'm subbing."

"Oh I see," she says. She lets out an exasperated breath, and leaves the room.

Actually, he fired her. For stealing some clothes, of his girlfriends. So why would she be suspicious of me? I laugh. You're the one who got all bent out of shape, because the woman was stealing some old clothes of yours, that you were discarding anyway.

I have everything in a clothes basket that I found in one of the extra rooms upstairs, and carried the load down to the laundry room. Cam and Melissa come out from the kitchen arms wrapped around each other, laughing. They both stop when they see me. She ignores me as they pass by, Cam gives me a 'thanks for playing along,' look over his shoulder at me.

"Who is she anyway?" I hear her say. "Is that her jeep outside the gate?"

"I guess it is, hon. The agency sent her. She's very good." He knows I'm very good.

It's a good thing my vacation is almost over, cause if Melissa is staying, then I'm going. She has big brown doe eyes. Petite features, little perfect mouth, little perfect nose, little rosy cheeks, isn't to tall, fits right into the curve of Cam's side. Has lighter blonde hair then mine. And she seems very suspicious, of me. If she only knew.

The buzzer for the washing machine goes off the laundry is done, I'll put it in the dryer for Cam. Cam is playing his guitar and singing one of his new songs for Melissa. God what I wouldn't give to hear him every night, singing to our kids, or singing to me. I want to be his girlfriend. I want to be her. I wanna be that someone that your with. I stand outside the door of the den. He's singing something about you'll never be alone. That's the way I feel right now, alone. I'll go home, and he'll probably marry her. I'm alone all the time. I could cry. I suck it in, take a deep breath, and knock on the door.

"Excuse me Mr. Konner," I say, I see Cam raise an eyebrow at me. "Would you and your lady friend like something to eat? I could make you some lunch if you would like."

"Oh yes, that sounds good, hon what about you? I'm sorry, your name is?" He asks me.

"Its, Joan, Joan Collins," I tell him, that was the first name I could think of.

"Joan, this is my girlfriend, Melissa," I nod. And my heart pounds in my chest, when he said Melissa is his girlfriend.

She barely looks, at me, god what a snob. I should poison her food, and bury her body in the woods out back on the dirt trail, and he can ride over her body every day.

That's pretty stupid of me, I laugh, and walk to the kitchen to make them something to eat. I should find out if she has any food allergies. Wouldn't it be funny if it was something like pepper.

Or something, and I could put it in her sandwich. Like Mrs. Doubtfire. I know I'm normally not the jealous type, but what do I have really of Cam? 'Nothing,' I say. I slop together her sandwich, with as little love as possible. Hope she chokes on it. I put it all on a tray, with a beer for Cam, and a soda for her. Carry it into them. Their laughing, "Oh Cam, that's such a beautiful song," she coos. I stand just outside the door and want to puke.

"Knock, knock," I say. Cam stands up and takes the tray from me, with his back turn towards Melissa, he looks into my eyes, I'm not sure what he's trying to say to me, but it looks like a desperate plea for me to play along. "Thank you, Joan." he says, emphasizing, my fake name.

"Your welcome, Mr. Konner." I leave the room. I really hope she's leaving soon. I only have one more night with him and then I have to leave. The silver lining though, I get to come back, and join his tour, and she hasn't a clue.

She leaves really late at night. The Jeep is parked in the garage. He must of put it in there. The tire is fixed. I can pack all of my stuff in there tonight. I've hidden away all this time, waiting for her to go. "I'll see you tomorrow," she says as she's sucking his face.

I make sure I have everything in my bag. I find a pink lacy thong, that I'm going to leave Cam in the bathroom on the floor, like I accidentally dropped it there. My perfume is all over it. Just to tease and entice him. So he will remember, me. The wonderful days we spent together. What is yet to come…..

CHAPTER 11

"Why so quiet?" Cam asks me as I crawl into his bed.

"I'm leaving tomorrow, I don't want to go, but I have to. And I feel a little funny about deceiving your girlfriend today." I snuggle next to him. He puts his arm around me.

"Yeah, thanks for doing that, she's a little on the jealous side, suspicious type, if you know what I mean."

"I do, she didn't like the fact that I was here with you. What is she going to do when she finds out I'm part of the tour, now?"

"Oh she'll have a fit I imagine, but she'll get used to the idea, she'll have to." He sighs.

The morning came all to quick. I left the pink thong where Cam could find it, pack everything into the jeep. Cam gave me his cell phone number and I'm suppose to call him when I get home safely. Call him when I'm leaving my house to get the plane, which he says he'll arrange, call when I land and call him when I get to the arena their playing in.

I left in the morning, not early, but not to late that it was noon already, I had to return the jeep, pick up the rest of my luggage and get to the airport before my flight.

The good-bye was awkward. I didn't want to let him go, when he grabbed me and gave me a big bear hug. I smelled him, and tried to memorize his smell. He laughed cause he knew what I was doing. “Here,” he said, “My aftershave lotion, so you remember what I smell like.” I took it without hesitation. I didn’t care I wasn’t denying it, I was in love with him. Not just obsessed, but seriously, whole-heartily in love with him.

“Come on,” he said as he helped me in the jeep, “I’ll see you soon, and then we’ll see each other all the time, and get sick of each other, don’t cry, okay.” He knew I was on the verge of tears, I tried to keep it together. When I drove down the road, I’d ball my eyes out. But for now, “I know, I cant wait, its going to be exciting. I’ll call you when I get to the hotel, and the airport, and home, and then when I’m leaving, okay?” I barely choke out.

“That’ll work,” he closes the door, leans his head in the window and gives me a kiss good-bye.

“Bye,” he says.

“Bye,” I say, I start the jeep, and put it into gear, I drive slowly away watching him in the rearview mirror. He’s getting smaller and smaller. I want to turn around and go back. He’s still standing in the road, waving to me until neither one of us can see each other.

I put his CD in the CD player. I start to cry, this isn’t going to work, so I take it out and put in Chris Daughtry, no something stronger, Buckcherry. Sorry Cam, but hearing your voice is going to make me hysterical.

But my mind cant help thinking about him. Cam is just a regular guy. Quiet and easy going. Which is shocking, considering how he acts on stage. And that’s just it, its an act, he’s an actor.

We went to dinner and a movie, a couple of times. I watched Cam record a song in his recording studio. Lots of buttons and gadgets. I kept my hands tucked under my legs, so I wouldn’t be tempted to touch anything. Took a drive around town and to some of Cam’s favortie places, not that there really was any great place to go. Mostly mountains. Rode the dirt bikes a couple more times. After I finally got accustomed to riding around the trees and rocks. I was really feeling comfortable riding and opted for a bigger bike, which was a big mistake. It started to rain and we were far up the trail, far from the house. We were getting soaked. It was blinding, the rain hitting me in the face so hard that it was making it hard to see the trail. Cam was up ahead, turned around and said, we better head back. I was all for that. I was soaked and chilled to the bone, my teeth chattering, keeping time to the bumps I kept hitting.

The trail was getting muddy and slick. I had to slow down to a crawl, the bike was getting hard to handle, because of its weight. I should have stuck with the smaller bike, but you know me, I always have to have the biggest and best.

We made it down the trail safe enough, until Cam slowed way down, to go through a very large puddle. Only I didn't see him or the puddle in time. My bike slipped out from under me and I landed in the middle of the biggest mud puddle I've ever seen.

I thought I was going to drown. Face first, mouth full of mud. I was covered from head to boots. Cam laughing his head off at me. I spit out the mud, it crunches between my teeth, I spit some more, and glare at Cam.

Cam is still sitting on his bike, looking down at me. I wipe my mouth off with my sleeve. I'm very insulted to say the least, that he's laughing at me and that he totally missed getting dumped in the mud. I'm not to happy. Sat looking up at him, when he offered me his hand to pull me up.

But I pulled harder and pulled him into the mud. Now both of us laughing and covered in mud,

"Why did you stop?" I yelled at him. And threw a handful of mud at him.

"Hey…I didn't want to go in the puddle," and he threw a handful of mud back at me. We ended up throwing mud at each other, laughing hysterically. Until we were both exhausted and cold.

Time for another shower and definitely the hot tub. We hosed off the bikes, but would clean them better later.

Peeling off the wet caked on mud clothes was a lot trickier then it looked, trying not to make to much of a mess all over the bathroom floor. We helped each other peel off our clothes. Our faces and hair caked in mud. The laughter stopped and Cam becomes quiet. Watching my face as he lifts my shirt up over my head. Another shower together. Its hard to get the gritty sand out of your hair and other places. I feel like I was at the beach being tossed by the waves, unable to get up out of the water, because I have a ton of sand in my bathing suit. Ahhhh, I miss Cam already.

CHAPTER 12

I get to the hotel safely and return the jeep. Everything is paid for. I get a ride to the airport. I finally have cell phone service. April has called me a number of times. I have to call her and tell her everything that's happened. She isn't going to believe it.

I call Cam and tell him I'm on the plane and headed for home. "Oh by the way, where am I going to meet you?"

"When you are ready to leave I'll tell you where we are. I'll have a ticket waiting for you at the airport, a driver, so you wont have to worry about anything, okay? You just take care of all the things you need to do, I'll see you soon." He reassures me.

"I will..." See you in my dreams, I think to myself. As soon as I hit the pillow.

I called April while on the plane. I gave her a brief story, told her I give her all the juicy details when we see each other.

Back to work on Monday, filled out all the necessary papers, took a leave of absence, just in case...

There's always someone to take your place. I make sure my Mom was all taken care of. My house would be taken care of by my traveling friend. I told him no wild parties. Send my bills e-mail.

I pack more than I probably need. I bought new dance dresses, some new big heeled shoes, some other necessities. My bags are by the front door and I'm waiting for the limo, of course.

I go through the mental list. Everything was crossed off the list, all the T-s were crossed, all the I-s dotted.

The car arrives. How many times should I call Cam. It's the same driver I had the last time, when I went to Canada. He's on the phone. He's probably talking to Cam. He keeps looking at me, and shaking his head. Which makes me nervous.

CAM

I call my driver, he's at the house. "How does she look?" I ask my driver. He says she looks hot. Even better than the last time. I tell him to keep his hand off. He laughs. "You know Cam, you cant have every woman you see," he jokes. Why cant I? Is it wrong to want more than one?

"What is she wearing?" I ask him.

"A see through white dress," he breaths heavy.

"Keep your eyes on the road." I tell him, "other wise it'll be your neck."

"Aye, boss." He laughs.

She's on her way. I haven't told any of the band guys. I know Matt and Rob will have a problem with her, Dale he's cool, nothing ever bothers him.

I haven't been able to stop thinking about her since she left my house. I love Melissa, don't get me wrong, but there's something about Janie. That drives me wild. Crazy. Obsessed. Wild, animal attraction.

JANIE

In a few hours I'll be in Raleigh, North Carolina. That's where I'm to meet the band. We left from MacArthur Airport. Small planes. And my body guard is sitting by me. He kind of makes me nervous. He doesn't talk to much. He seems very gruff. He looks me over quite a lot. Like I have three eyes or something. All though I've caught him looking at my chest, one to many times.

April and I spent a couple of days shopping for new dance clothes, and I told her everything that happened while I was in Vancouver. She couldn't wait to hear more. But warned me again to be careful. I said I would.

I start to fall asleep in the plane and play my dance routine in my head. The first night when I did it, I landed on my knee. I thought my knee exploded. I'd have to change that. I fall into a deeper sleep and have this weird dream.

I'm back at my old house where I grew up. I'm in the basement, with my brother. I have a big beautiful dog that looks like a wolf. Its not, it's a Siberian Husky, he's a sweet and gentle dog. Outside are real wolves, and their trying to get through the basement window. There's four of them. Their vicious, with big long snarling teeth. And yellow eyes. I think their trying to get to my dog. One breaks through the screen on the window and he's just about to get in.

The one that's almost in, is biting my hand, because I'm trying to push him back out. I tell my brother to get the dog out of here, I cant hold the wolf back any longer, he's to strong. The other three are passing the other windows and can see in. Pacing, snarling and yipping. I can feel the pain in my hand. As the wolf continues to bite me. I wake up with a start. The other passengers look at me, as well as the body guard.

"Sorry bad dream," I shrug. I use the bathroom. I wonder what the dream meant. Usually they don't mean anything. Like the four wolves, are the four band members? That would be scary, and the wolf that's biting me is, Cam?

I'm sure its just my vivid imagination.

The plane lands in a couple of hours. The body guard is on the phone again. There's a car with my name on it. I have all of my luggage. He puts it in the car. It shouldn't be to long to the arena.

I wonder if Cam wants me to dance tonight? I feel a little jet lagged. And stiff, my legs and back are achy from sitting so still for a couple of hours, I was so afraid to move with that body guard next to me. Every time I did move he stared at me. Like I was doing something wrong. Its still hours away. I'm sure he'll let me know.

We arrive at the arena, late in the afternoon. There's tons of people around, all working to set up the stage for the concert. The limo/ bodyguard stops in front of the arena doors, takes out my luggage, and leaves me there on the sidewalk alone. "Good luck," he laughs. "Call Cam, he's waiting for your call." And drives off.

I have four big luggage bags with wheels on them, but that's doesn't help me out. I call Cam, but he doesn't pick it up the first time I call. I call him again, this time he answers.

"Hi, Cam, its me, Janie, I'm here at the arena, outside with my luggage." I say. I can hear so much noise in the background.

"Janie, oh good, you're here. I'll send someone out for you," I hear him yell to a guy named Jeff.

"Someone will be right out, Janie." He breaths into the phone.

"Jeff, go out and help the new crew member, she's out front." I hear some gruffy guy, answer him.

"Sure boss." He says.

"Okay someone will be out in a minute. See you soon," he says. And hangs up the phone, before I can say, hey I cant wait to see you again, cause its almost been a month.

But the guy is taking to long, its already been ten minutes. So I start to drag my luggage through the doors and into the arena. Why is it you can never find someone to help you when you need help.

I follow all the noise. I'll find Cam sooner or later. I walk down the tunnel and into the vast expanse of the arena.

"Janie," I hear my name being called. I turn to see Cam waving at me over the heads of all the workers. When I spot him, I suck in my breath. It always surprises me how he takes my breath away. There he is. He moves towards me, weaving through the crowd. His dirty blonde hair is curly and wild, his blue eyes are sparkling as he looks at me. His smile is big and welcoming, his teeth are white and perfect. How and when did they get that way?

"Hi, Cam," I wave back. I want to run to him and jump into his arms, but I hold myself back. Every ones attention is on us right now. I can feel the heat in my face as he gets closer. I suddenly feel very nervous and shy. With an audience watching us, yeah.

I'm standing on a landing, the top of stairs that go down to the main floor of the arena. Cam walks up the stairs to me. "You made it," he yells, " I'm glad you're here."

He looks at all of my luggage. "Didn't Jeff come out to meet you?"

"No, no one came out, I got tired of waiting, its okay." I apologize for Jeff's lack of help.

"No that's no good, where is Jeff," he yells over his shoulder.

"Over here," he says, "I went out there she was gone," he gives me a smug look.

"Is that all yours?" Cam asks me.

"Yeah." My red luggage looks formidable. Cam looks at me, looks at the luggage.

"Jeff," he says, "Take Janie's luggage to the tour bus."

"Sure, Cam," Now Jeff is a big burly guy, with tattoos and a ponytail, he picks up all four bags and walks off with them. I shake my head, if only it was that easy for me. Thank god for strong men.

The arena is huge, like most of them. Its intimidating at first, until you learn which way to go. Most of them are built the same way. Tunnels, corridors, and hallways.

"Come with me," Cam takes my arm and pulls me with him. "Come to the stage, I want to show you where you'll come in." He gives me a program. "This is how the concert will run." He sees my face. " What's the matter?" He asks me.

"I wasn't sure if you wanted me to start tonight," I say, "Its all so overwhelming." I look at the program.

"Well if you think your not up to it tonight, you can ditch the dance for tonight," he says but sounds disappointed, and a little sarcastic.

"No, I can do it, I just need some time to get organized, that's all, I'll be fine." I smile a forced smile, cause the truth is I'm scared shit to do this.

"Good, the show starts at 9:45. Your dance will be the second song of the night. You can come in over here at the right of the stage," he points to the side of the stage. There's no stairs. I frown.

"How will I get up there, onto the stage? I had some help the last time I did it."

"Oh yeah those two guys you were with," he says. "I can have someone help you, that isn't a problem."

"Good," I sigh. "This place is incredible." I say, as I look around the whole place. Its so overwhelming, intimidating. Scary.

"Yeah they all are. Holds thousands of people." Cam says.

I went pale, the color all drained out of my face, I had to sit down, "Thousands?" I say.

"Yeah, thousands, don't worry you'll get used to it. They just become a blur." He laughs.

"Oh good." I say.

I look at my watch, there is a couple of hours before the show, time for me to unwind, exercise a little. Eat something. Take a tour of the arena. Get myself together.

"Where can I go to get changed?" I ask him.

"Come on I'll show you." He grabs my arm again, his touch, tingling on my arm, sends shivers to my entire body. I have to remember to breath.

Cam yells, "Hey Rob, I'm going to show Janie the dressing rooms, I'll be back soon."

Rob looks up from the sound broad, gives me that face that he gave me when I was dancing around him on stage. And its not a nice face either.

"Cam we have sound check to finish." He says.

"Yeah, I said I'll be back. Come on," he says, "Before they tie me up."

I laugh nervously, I bet Rob and Matt would do that to keep him away from me. They don't even know me and already we've started off on the wrong foot.

He takes my arm again and turns me around to go back the way I just came. He walks very close to me. The people we pass, are curious, some say hi, others nod. Others just stare. I don't know if anyone knows about me, yet.

Its another labyrinth of passageways, stairs and doors. He opens the door and lets me go in first. His arm touches mine, skin against skin. It send chills all over me, again. Is this how its going to be, he touches me, and my body goes chaotic? I'll never let him know what effect he has on me, not yet anyway, that even someone calling his name makes my heart skip a beat.

"This is your dressing room, the guys have one next door. In case you need something." He pushes open the door.

"My luggage, I need my luggage, my dress, and my stuff are in it." I'm a little panicky.

"In my tour bus, I guess will go and get it, then I can show you where the bus is." He closes the door and we walk through the passageway to the parking lot where the tour buses are parked.

I cant believe it, I'm going to go inside of the bands tour bus. I saw this bus when I went to the concert at Jones Beach Theater, it was a plain brown bus with no markings. Nothing on the outside that says, this is a famous band inside. Cause if it did. I guess people would follow them, and that would be me. I'd follow them, well, Cam to the ends of the earth.

Its new and has all the modern things a house would have. Its beautiful inside. His guitar is on the table, along with his notebook. I hope he's working on a new CD. I love the six I have and the DVD's, but I'd really like some new music.

Its not to messy inside. He sees me looking around. My luggage is just inside the door.

"If you want, you can get ready in here," he says. "Then you don't have to lug your suitcase around."

"That's a good idea, thanks." This feels so strange. Being here, in his tour bus. In such a small space. So close to him. I feel like I've just met him for the first time, I feel so awkward, I wonder if he feels that way too. Probably not, Cam is always cool.

"I have to go back to the arena, my cell phones been vibrating in my pocket for a couple of minutes now, their getting impatient, I guess. I'll see you later, okay, we have food in the dressing rooms before the concert, so come and get something to eat." He smiles, one of those adorable smiles at me. He closes the door of the bus, he opens it again, " lock the door behind me, never can be to safe." He closes it again. I walk over and lock it. Kind of looks like anyone could break the lock on the door.

I walk around and look at everything. This is his guitar, the one he was playing at his house. I touch it, his worn guitar, his fingers lovingly play the strings, this is the guitar all those beautiful songs came from. The notebook on the table in his handwriting. There's words and music on those pages. Some new songs. "I love the way she walks, I love the way she smiles at me. I love the way she does it to me.." Okay another naughty song, from Cam. Cant wait. Just how nosy should I be?

I go into the bathroom. His soap, his shampoo. Toothpaste, razor, well why am I so fascinated about this stuff. I spent two weeks at his house. But its like rediscovering him all over again. I didn't really pay to much attention to his personal stuff at his house. I go into the bedroom, the one that's in the back of the bus. I guess its his. There are bunk beds along the sides of the bus.

I sit down on the bed, I wonder if she's been in here? Melissa…his girlfriend. Has she slept here?

I'm so jealous. I want to be the one to sleep here with him. I'm not generally a jealous person, but when it comes to him, I guess I am. I have no right to want him, she had him first. I look back at the bed. I want his arms wrapped around me at night, like they were at his house. Every night of my life. I want to lay my head on his shoulder and listen to his breathing, or ask him to sing me to sleep. I want him to kiss me good-night, and whisper in my ear that he loves me. Oh god….I better stop this, I'm going to make myself very unhappy, and very horny.

I groan….

I open up his closet, a dress shirt, a dress jacket, a pair of dress pants. I know he looks good in a suit, I've seen him in a black suit, looking like the funeral director. I bet he looks really fine in this silk shirt. I feel the fabric and smell it. His smell is embedded in my brain. Plus the fact that I smelled the cologne he gave me every day, and sometimes I even put it on. Especially if I was having a bad day.

I open up the draws. T-shirts, jeans, underwear. There's a picture of him and Melissa on the dresser. I want to know what hold she has over him. I want to know what it is that he loves about you, what made him pick you out of a crowd of thousands. Its not fair. I sigh.

I look at the clock, I've wasted so much time being nosy. I open my suitcase and find my exercise gear. I put it on, I'll go for a nice run and get all of this pent up foolishness out of my system. I cant screw this up, I better be careful. Otherwise he'll fire me.

I run around the big parking lot, several times. Until I'm good and sweaty. And I feel all that tension gone. I feel excited now about tonight's show. I can do this, I know I can. I go back to the tour bus and take a shower. Take a shower so I can get all sweaty all over again. I want that beach crumpled look in my hair, so I wash with some kind of wavy shampoo I bought. It smells like the desert flowers. I want to smell breath taking to Cam, so he remembers what I smell like, and then he'll have déjà vu and he'll remember the days we spent together at his house.

Get dress in a red sparkly dress, with sequins and beads, a fringe at the short bottom, that when I move its going to swing all over the place, emphasizing the movement of my ass. I made sure it did that when I tried it on for April. She said, "It shakes and shimmys all over the place, what man will be able to resist that?"

I put on my pantyhose and shoes, the 5 inch heels, I wobble in, sure I can just see this. I put on my makeup, I don't want to look to gaudy, so I'll ease off on the black eyeliner. I put on Jasmine Perfume. Another pink thong for Cam's guitar, a lollipop. I feel like I'm forgetting something. But I cant think of what it could possibly be.

I take one final look at myself, damn I am hot….I close the door, and lock it. I should wear sneakers instead of my shoes, but I need to walk in them. I haven't worn them in a long time.

Besides I feel sexy when I walk in them. At first the shoes feel good on my feet, but as I walk to the arena, they start to hurt. Brand new shoes, and I'm going to dance in them. WHAT WAS I THINKING?

I walk into the arena, the song, 'don't you wish your girlfriend was hot like me?' Kept playing in my mind, as some of the crew members whistled and stop what they were doing to look at me.

I smiled my sweetest smile at them, tossed my hair from side to side, wiggled my ass and made my stride longer like I was walking the cat walk. I got the response I wanted from them. I walk to the main part of the arena, every guy I pass gives me the same reaction, appreciation of the fine female body. Mine….

I hear the band practicing. There playing one of my favorite songs, 'Mistake,' its not in their play list, I'll have to ask Cam to play it. Even though he didn't write it, he still sings it so beautifully. I follow the corridor to the main arena and step into the light, and it hits me. My dream has finally come true, I'm really here, Cam has finally seen me?

CHAPTER 13

You know the Cinderella story? When she stands at the top of the stairs and everyone turns to look at her. That's what it felt like when I stepped out of the shadows in to the light of the arena. All eyes were on me. Well only for a minute. I was only looking for one set of eyes.

Then I remembered what I forgot, another outfit for the sign language song. I didn't want the audience to know that I'm the dancer, the one who's trying to seduce the lead singer. Except I don't know what Cam wants me to wear. I dial his cell phone. I hope he has it on vibrator, because its so noisy in here. He looks up and I wave. I hold up my cell phone. He takes his cell phone out of his pants pocket, I wish I was that cell phone.

He says, "Hello."

"Hi Cam, its Janie," I yell.

"Hey, everything okay?"

"Yeah, I want to know what you want me to wear for the sign language songs?"

He takes a minute to answer, and looks my way, "Do you have a school girl outfit?"

"Yeah, I do, cause you asked me to bring one, are you sure?" I ask him.

He laughs, " Um, yeah!"

"Okay, I have to go back to the tour bus to get it, I'll be back soon." I hang up, he waves to me, now I have to trek back to the bus through the arena out to the parking lot to the bus. My feet are screaming at me to stop and take the damn shoes off.

There's a crew member in a golf cart, I wave at him to stop. He stops next to me. Gives me a big smile after he looks me up and down.

"Can you give me a ride back to Cam's bus?" I ask him, gees he looks awfully familiar.

"Sure," he says. "Hop in." He's cute too. And very fit, really good looking, damn, so many men so little time.

"Your Janie, aren't you?" He asks me.

"Yes , how did you know who I am?" I tilt my head in his direction, trying to get a better look at him.

"Cam has been talking about you all week. Your pretty good," he says and smiles at me again, he almost hit's a garbage pail.

"Hey watch where your going!" Someone yells at him. "Sorry," he yells back. I'm nervous enough as it is, I don't need an accident.

"I saw you dance at one of the concerts, I thought you were fantastic." He blushes. How cute.

He has dimples too. He looks tall too. He seems really sweet.

He keeps his eyes on the corridor, and exit's the arena, out into the parking lot, its getting dusky out. The sky is a pretty dark blue, a few wispy clouds are dotty the night. The air feels warm. He parks in front of the tour bus.

"You want me to wait?" He asks.

"Yes, please, I might be a few minutes, I have to look through some suitcases." I say apologetically.

"I'll wait," he says. He watches me walk up the stairs to the door. "I locked the door," I turn to tell him.

"Cam hides an extra key under the mat," he says.

I bend down to retrieve it, I know he just got a big view of my ass. I turn to show him the key and he's grinning from ear to ear. Oh gees, guys!

Everything I dumped into my luggage was done with little thought, I didn't organize anything, so I have no idea which bag the outfit is in, I'll have to look through all of them.

I find the skirt, the socks, the white shirt. I need the sneakers, glasses and some bands for the pigtails. I have to look like a school girl. I take off my shoes, and put the sneakers on. Oh thank you, my feet sigh. I look at them and my toes are all red. My once broken toe is still sore.

I put everything into a bag. He's still waiting for me. He's leaning against the seat, relaxed, his leg hanging over the side of the cart. He turned off the engine of the cart. So its fairly quiet outside, you can hear fans on the other side of the arena. That makes me nervous again.

I close and lock the door, hide the key back under the mat. He looks at my sneakers and makes a face.

"My feet hurt," I say. He nods and starts the cart back up. He turns the cart around and heads towards the arena.

He heads to the door we came out of. And drops me off. "Thanks for the lift," I say, I never even asked him his name. "What's your name?" I ask him.

"Eric," he says. With the cutest smile I've ever seen, that lights up his whole face, his whole being.

"Thank you, Eric, you are a lifesaver, I really appreciate it, I guess I'll see you around?"

"Your welcome," he says, "You will see me around, I'm part of the crew." Now I recognize him, he was the camera guy, the one who filmed my tattoo, and put it up on the big screen.

"Oh great, I look forward to seeing you again, soon…" I smile at him, he's got blue eyes too, except their a different color blue than Cam's. But still very sexy. And he has the longest lashes. That's so unfair, why guys always have the nicest lashes.

"Bye," I say.

"Bye," he says, and he drives off, I watch him go. I stand there until I cant see him anymore. Wow, he kind of made an impression on me. Damn he was cute. And hot.

Its still a long walk back to the main part of the arena. I have to dodge workers and equipment to get over to where Cam is. He's talking to the band members. They stop talking when they see me.

"Hi," I wave. I put on a brave and nonchalant face, like I don't care if your unhappy that I'm here, when I'm shaking like an earthquake inside. I'm not a pushy person, unless I want something. I try not to intrude or invade their space. I can wait my turn. I feel the animosity coming from the other band members. Fine they don't like me. Including his brother and his right hand man, Rob. I don't think its fair, I didn't do anything to them. I try to play it cool, like I don't care. But it's really hurting my feelings. I'll probably cry about it later. Right now I bite my lip to keep myself from crying. Their like mean little girls.

Cam was the one who invited me, didn't he tell them that. It's not like I just showed up and barged in.

Maybe the animosity towards me, is for Melissa. Since she's not here, they'll stand in for her.

How nice of them.

This will make it a little harder for me to dance around them, but it might actually be fun, for me. I could really tease them and make them feel really uncomfortable.

Cam pulls me aside. Shows me the stage again, to make sure I know what he wants me to do.

He wants me to climb up on the drum deck with Dale, Dale grins at me.

"That's pretty high up," I say, "Is there enough room for me to dance?"

"Go and take a look," he says, "Dale take Janie over to the drums."

Dale walks over to me and winks. "Hi," he says. And holds out his hand to shake mine.

"Hello," I say holding out my hand, he takes it and pulls me towards the drums.

" It looks awfully small, " I have a scowl on my face, I can feel it puckering my lips and that's not an attractive look.

"Naw, there's enough room for you and me, just hold on to me," he smiles a devilish smile at me.

Right now the drum deck is low on the floor, when their playing it gets raised. Heights scare me.

Dale sits behind his drum, he's cute. He's the only one who is some what friendly towards me.

I walk around the deck, there isn't much room, this is going to make me very nervous, but I'll try it. If I happen to slip and I grab onto him, I'll pull him down with me. Then they can hate me even more.

I guess one day I'll have it out with the band members, not right now. Hey, look your front man hired me, get over it. I'm gonna be around for a long time.

I climb down from the deck, I still have a scowl on my face. "Well can you do it?" Cam asks.

"I don't know, its awfully small for the two of us. Especially if I'm wearing my 5 inch heels, but…I mean I'll do it." I don't want to be disagreeable and I haven't even started yet.

"Okay, well I'm sure the music will tell you what to do, if you feel like it… then go for it."

"I will," I frown. Dale comes over to me, says in my ear. "Cant wait."

I hope he's teasing me, cause if I go down, he goes down with me.

The opening acts start the show, a couple of hours before Cam goes on. I know I make it like its just Cam, but it's a band. Its their band, its not like its his name, like Chris Daughtry. In Daughtry.

The arena has filled up with screaming fans, I used to be one of them. It looks so much different back stage then it does sitting out in the audience. I'm getting apprehensive. Maybe I should run, I should bolt, run and hide. No….. get it together. I cant back out now, I've dreamed about this forever. I need to see Cam, if I can see his blue, sky blue eyes, I know I'll calm down.

Sick puppies go on, for about thirty minutes. Then Hinder, and Papa Roach. I haven't seen any of the band members in a while now.

I'm so nervous, I'm sweating. I modified the dance routine a little, I rehearse it in my mind.

I feel nauseous, and light-headed. I'd be so embarrassed if I passed out.

"Hey Janie, where have you been?" I hear my name, and turn to see Cam and the rest of the band members following behind him.

"You were suppose to come to the dressing rooms, for the before the show meeting. Didn't anyone tell you?" Cam yells in my ear, the noise is so loud.

"No, no one told me." I look suspiciously behind Cam, at Matt and Rob. I wonder who was suppose to tell me?

Rob walks past me with a self satisfied smile, so does Matt. Fine I get it, I got it a long time ago, that this will be an on going thing between us. Hate Janie club.

Dale flashes me the evil Dale grin.

"Are you ready?" Cam asks me. I must look like a frightened rabbit caught in a trap.

"Relax you'll do fine, just keep your eyes on me," he says.

"I will, I hope I'll do fine," I take a deep breath.

"Hey were nervous before we go out too," he reassures me.

"You are? I didn't know that," I say.

"Yeah sometimes, I'm not sure if I remember the words to the songs, or how to play the music, but then it all comes back to me, and I'm playing, and singing, I remember everything, it amazes me sometimes. You'll do fine." He whispers in my ear, his hot breath tickling my ear. He pats me on the shoulder.

He gives me a smile before he goes out, the piros go off, and they run on to the stage already playing their first song. My song is the second one and I have to make my way down in front of the stage. I weave in and out around other fans, I push passed them and get some dirty looks. I have a jacket over my dress, so no one knows what I'm about to do. There's a lot of woman, of course by the stage. No men at all. I need someone to help me up on to the stage. I could ask the security guards. But that's not a good idea, cause their the ones that are suppose to chase me. I call Eric, he gave me his cell phone number in case I ever needed his help, I guess I need it now.

"Hello," he answers.

"Eric, its Janie, I need your help, I need you to lift me up onto the stage for my dance. There isn't anyone here to help me, do you think you can?" I have to yell of course.

"Yeah I can, where are you?" He yells back.

"I'm in front of the stage on the floor, on the right hand side if your looking at the stage."

"I'll be right there," he says and hangs up.

The first song is almost over, it got all of the fans up out of their seats, everyone is jumping up and down to the music, Cam looks at me, and I shake my head no. He needs to talk to the audience, or something, until Eric can get here. Cam takes the mic and strolls from one end of the stage to the other and talks to the audience, he asks everyone how their doing, are they having a good time? Everyone roars. And the girls scream.

Eric comes up behind me and touches my arm. I jump slightly. Relief floods my face. I wave to Cam, that he can continue. I show him that Eric is there behind me.

He plays the first cord of the song and that's my cue to jump up on the stage. Eric makes a path for me and pushes some of the people out of the way. He's a big guy, so no one protests. I shed the coat and hand it to him. He lifts me easy enough up onto the stage. His hand on my butt, which I'm very much aware of his touch.

Cam gives me an encouraging smile. I focus on him and the music. I feel the music, I let the beat move my body. Its such a naughty song, I want to feel as naughty as the song. I strut across the stage towards Cam, past Matt.

The shoes, the 5 inch heels give me that extra sexy walk. The dress makes me feel sexy and sensuous. I walk over to Cam and lightly run my fingers over his chest, around his shoulders and back. Then I stroll over to Rob, I dance around him, but never touch him, he ignores me. I can ignore you too. I dance my way over to the drum deck and dance in front of it wiggling my ass, and tossing my hair all around me, then, I look up at Dale. He nods to me to come join him, the deck has already been lifted up off of the floor by some kind of hydraulic lifts. I hate heights, I really do. I push the thought out of my head, and walk up the stairs that lead up to the deck.

The lights are really bright, almost blinding. I don't want to TWIST my ankle or worse yet fall off. I dance on each step, and then grab onto Dale. I wrap my arms around him and wiggle my ass some more. Putting my face on either side of his and I kiss his cheek, he turns his head and grins at me. I laugh. Sweat is pouring off of him, he's beating the drum wildly. He's got muscles, that's for sure and I get to feel them. I put my hands on his shoulders and dance seductively. Then I make my way back down to the stage. As I'm getting off the drum deck, my heel catches on something and I go down. Dale sees me and misses a beat, but continues, the audience doesn't have a clue. I make it look like its part of the dance. I landed on my knees. So I crawl sexy panther like over to Cam. I climb up his leg, he gives me one eye, like what are you doing, but I like it. But I cant get up any other way because of the 5 inch heels. After I get up and slither all over Cam, I walk over to Matt. It's the end of the song, I get a running start and slid on my knees to Cam. I hit my knee so hard, that little dots flash in front of my eyes. I blink them away.

I'm gonna have bad knees when I get older. Its gonna leave a mark that's for sure. I was suppose to leave the knee slamming jump and slid out of the dance, but like Cam said, I let the music tell me what to do, and it told me to do the slid. My lollipop is in my mouth and I'm laying under Cam by his feet. The song is over, the longest 3: 36 minutes of my life, like it was the first time I did it. I'm breathing heavily. The sweat is pouring down my face into my eyes. I'm sweating profusely, I never knew it was this hot up on stage. I did it, I cant believe I actually did it. Everything comes back into focus, and I hear the audience, whistling and clapping. Cam gives me his hand, he pulls me up and were faced to face with each other, he has a weird look on his face, I smile at him. And look into his blue eyes, down to his lips and back again. He says to me, "that was incredible." Then the look vanishes, and he's the front man again. He remembers that there's several thousand eyes watching.

"Thanks, Cam." I mouth to him. I'm so out of breath, I can't find my voice.

"Hey give it up for?" He says.

"Janie," I say. I barely squeak out my name.

"Give it up for Janie." He yells into the mic.

Everyone goes wild, and then I run and dive off the stage into Eric's waiting arms. He covers me with the coat and pushes past the fans. The security guys pretend to chase after me. Which makes everyone boo them.

I have to change for the sign language songs. "Wow, that crawling thing you did was so damn sexy." Eric says to me. "I really liked it."

"Thanks…I.. didn't plan that… " I say. "I kind of fell, my heel got caught on something."

"It worked." He says. "I have to go back to work, I'll see you later, okay." He smiles shyly at me. A little bit of a blush creeps up his neck to his face. He's so cute.

"Eric? I yell to him. He turns to look at me. "Thanks for your help."

"No problem." He yells back, and runs back stage.

I wave bye. I hope I do see him later. I find one of the dressing rooms to change in. Change out of my dress and put on the school girl outfit, I'm not really happy with the get-up. It looks to Britney Spears. And its to slutty looking, its worse then my dance outfit. But this is what Cam asked for. I'm not suppose to distract from the sign language. I put on the Ked's sneakers and my hair up in pigtails. I haven't worn pigtails since I was a little girl and then I never really liked them, anyway.

I've got a while before the end of the concert. When the slow songs are played. Eric passes me several times, lets out a slow whistle at me. And shakes his head, "Damn." Is all he says. I laugh. The other crew members notice too, hopefully this will wear off soon and I'll just be one of the guys. I hope… the only attention I want is Cam's.

I have to get down to the floor again. Cam is suppose to ask me to come up on stage.

They sit on stools, and Cam starts to play on his acoustic guitar. I start to sign, it would be so much more believable if April was here. Who I'm I signing for? Some people are looking at me, like I'm nuts.

Cam stops playing, and asks me to come up. People are confused and getting pissed off that they stopped playing. He tells me to come on stage and walks over to the stairs to the left of the stage. He offers me his hand and I take it, he offers me the stool next to him, which he makes Rob move over to another stool. His hand is strong in mine as he helps me sit on the stool. He pulls the mic closer to him, and begins the song again. I do three slow songs, all romantic songs. I learned two new ones, over the past month.

CHAPTER 14

He asks, me my name after the songs are over, "Hey give it up for?"… "Melissa," I say. He raises his eyebrows at me.

"Hey wasn't that great… give it up for Melissa," and he hisses the S's in the name like a snake with a lisp. I give him a mischievous smile, give a curtsy and skip off the stage.

They play a couple of more songs and an encore. The show is over. Fans who paid come back stage.

I changed out of my school girl outfit, I don't want to wear it again, in fact I think I'll lose it. I throw it out in one of the garbage pails. If Cam asks for it again I'll tell him I cant find it.

All the usual people are back stage, the giggly girls, the ones with the fake boobs, and to much makeup. They try desperately to get the guys attention, makes me kind of want to puke, kind of reminds me of myself. Didn't I do something like that? I'm such a hypocrite. There so phony.

Is that what men really want?

I cant answer that, I'm not a man, maybe its their fantasy. But in reality they rather have someone that mom would approve of.

Its been a long night, they've sign autographs and taken more pictures. I wonder if they ever get tired of it?

People walk passed me and around me. No one pays attention to me, good. I like being invisible. I'm outa here. I need some night air. The crew guys are packing up, already. Loading the trucks for the next concert. I put my clothes in the tour bus. I walk around the arena parking lot. The parking lot is almost empty. The night air feels good on my skin. I jog and run around the parking lot to unwind. My knee hurts. I look down at it. Black and blue already, and its swollen. That's the knee I fall on when I do the slid to Cam. I think I'll eliminate that part of the dance routine. In fact I better.

This is my favorite part of the night, I enjoy the most. I am a night person. I think better at night. When all of the noise is gone, all of the people are gone, everything went well tonight, wait until the next show.

I grab a bag of ice from the tour bus. I sit down on one of the concrete planter's. Put the ice on my swollen knee. I love the quietness, the only sound is the bugs. A lonely cricket calling for a mate.

I close my eyes and take a big long cleansing breath. I love the quiet time alone. Don't get me wrong, this touring thing is going to be fun, I've only just begun. This has been my dream, my fantasy, my obsession. All of my new friends I've made, I get to be around Cam 24/7.

My reverie is interrupted by someone calling my name. "Janie, are you out here?" Janie where are you?" I hear a worried voice. "It's time to go," It's Eric. He spots me. "Oh there you are," he says. "It's time to go, were ready to go. Otherwise their going to leave us behind." He looks at the bag of ice on my knee.

"Bad, uh?" He asks.

"Yeah, its swollen and black and blue…" I take off the ice to show him.

"Oh gees, that looks pretty bad, can you walk?"

"I could before I sat down, I don't know about now." I try to stand but my knee buckles under me.

"Ow, it really hurts." I bend down to grab my knee, the pain is making me whoozy.

"Here let me help you," Eric offers. Before I can protest he scoops me up in his arms to carry me to the arena. I put my arm around his neck, I can feel every muscle in his chest, in his neck and arms. I study his face for a second. He has nice skin, and rosy cheeks. He has beautiful blue eyes. He smells so earthy, like fresh air, and clean water. He's smiling the whole time he's carrying me.

"We gotta go, I have to tell Cam I found you."

So I let him carry me into the arena. The last of the boxes have been loaded into the trucks and their pulling out along with the other tour buses. Everyone turns to look at us coming in. I turn red and so does Eric.

Cam looks at us and tells Eric to put me in the tour bus. "Sure," he says. He gets me to the tour bus, and puts me in the chair by the door.

"Thanks, but I think I could have walked," I tell Eric. "Did you see all the looks we got?"

"Well your welcome, and I did notice, especially Cam." He smiles. He hangs around, hesitating.

"Did you want something, Eric?"

"No, I guess I better catch my ride, I'll see you at the next arena." He smiles at me and ducks out of the bus.

"What's that all about?" Cam asks me as everyone comes piling into the tour bus. Rob and Matt see me sitting in the chair by the door, and frown.

"Nothing, my knee hurts," he looks at it.

"That's pretty messed up, when did that happen?" He asks.

"It happened when I landed on my knee to do the slid, I think I'm going to eliminate it from the dance routine. I landed so hard on it, I felt it crack."

"Um," he says. He touches my knee and examines it. Touching my skin ever so slightly by his hands sends chills all over me, and not bad chills, excited chills. I'm biting my lip, he has no idea what his touch does to me. He's concentrating on my knee, but over his shoulder, I can see the looks the guys are giving each other. Like Cam knows what he's looking at, like he's a doctor. Plus the fact that he's touching me, and the reaction I have on my face.

"Well I've had a knee injury or two, and this doesn't look good, you better go to a doctor for this, it could be really bad, maybe even an operation."

Cam is only inches from my face, his blue eyes are blue, sky blue, his dirty blonde hair smells really good. The hair on his face, I want to touch his face, I want to caress his cheek in my hands. I almost forget that we have an audience, I let my hand fall back into my lap.

I want to touch his lips, and run my fingers around them, trace the outline of them. I want to run my finger along the line of his nose. And put my hands in the hair on his chin. I love the way his hair falls over his forehead when he leans forward to look at my knee. I swallow hard, and he can feel my gaze on him, he looks up to meet my eyes. He's smiling that little playful way he does, I think he knows what it does to me. I think he knows what I'm thinking.

"I don't need a doctor Cam, I'll just ice it, it'll be okay." I finally say.

He shakes his head at me, "well okay, but if it gets worse, you better go."

"Okay," I say. If I go to the doctor, he'll tell me I cant dance anymore, and I need an operation, then I wont be able to dance and I'll have to leave the tour. I just got here. And that makes me a little depressed. So I push it out of my head.

The tour bus pulls out. Everyone goes to their respected places, everyone is sleepy, the gently rocking of the bus, lulls me to sleep in the chair. Cam is sitting at the table with his guitar, playing something on it. Someone put a blanket on me. And a bag of ice on my knee. I hope I don't snore and I hope I don't drool.

I dream of weird things. Eric on a white horse, Cam on a black horse. In knight armor. Swords drawn on each other. Me in a beautiful flowing white gown. Fighting over little ole me.

Then it went into weird over drive, bits and pieces of other dreams I've dreamed, stuff I couldn't remember. My mind working over time, as I slept, probably cause I'm in a ton of pain. Cam gave me a pain killer, wonder what he had this for. I usually hallucinate when I take pain pills. And I feel like I'm flying around the room.

The bag of ice has turned to water and I need to use the bathroom, the bus is still traveling. I get up and my knee buckles under me, so I crawl to the bathroom, I can see Cam sleeping in his big bed. Everyone else sleeps in bunk beds that line each side of the bus. I guess I have one too but I don't know what one it is. So I'll just sleep in the chair.

I would love to stand there and watch him sleep, but my knee is throbbing. I find some extra strength aspirin, don't want any pain pills, they make me feel to weird.

When I come out of the bathroom, I stop and watch Cam, for a minute. Couldn't I pretend that I was sleep walking and climb into his bed, I could be really quiet, the bed is big enough that he probably wouldn't even feel me climb in. The chair is making me ache all over.

I could try it for a few minutes. If he wakes up, I could pretend to be mortified. Maybe he would think I was Melissa… I wonder if she's ever been in his bed here?

The shades are down, but there's enough light that I can see where I'm going. I walk around to the other side of the bed. I gingerly sit down. He doesn't move. So I slide in under the covers. He has silk sheets on the bed and there cool to the touch and so soft. The pillow is extra fluffy. The sheets are warmer by Cam's body. It feels so nice and comfortable. I'll only stay a few minutes, pretending that I'm his wife and I'm suppose to be here.

I fall asleep, my back turned to him. The bed is so big I never felt him move. Until he put his arm around me, at first it startled me, then got me scared. Because I thought I woke him up. I didn't, I can hear his gentle breathing on my back, so I go back to sleep. He's so warm against me. I could do this every night. I want to entwine my fingers with his. He still has his rings on. If I touch his hand he might wake up. So I slid my hand under his. I love a man's hands, their so strong and rough, but can be gentle. I have a faddish about men's hands, I love them. I think I said that already. Its also probably another thing I obsess about. Oh and a guys ass, especially if he has jeans on.

Then I start to think, wonder if he's not to happy I'm in his bed with him? Especially in front of the other band members, and his brother. I'm not so happy about my decision. He might be mad, and then he'll fire me. I don't want to move. This is to soon to be aggressive towards him and to let him know my intentions. Remember I'm suppose to be cool about this. I get up very quietly and hobble out the door back to my uncomfortable chair. Fill the ice bag back up with ice, put the ice back on my knee, and the blanket over me. He wont ever know.

What is the next city were going to? What state? The next one we go to Cam makes Eric take me to the hospital to get my knee x-rayed. I protest the entire way there, and insist Eric turn the truck around. But he wont. I was pretty mad by the time we got to the hospital. Neither one of us were talking.

Eric carries me inside and puts me in a chair, while he goes to sign me in. He talks to one of the nurses. She's nodding her head a lot. And looking in my direction. Eric walks over with a wheel chair, "get in," he says.

The emergency room is crowded and there's people a head of us. They take me next. The doctor sees me. I have a cracked knee cap, there's some kind of medical term for it. He gives me some pills for the swelling and pain, tells me to ice it and rest. And no dancing for at least two weeks. NO...... Possible surgery. I tell him not now.

He says he loves the band, I'll pass it on. Eric gives him a free ticket.

As were driving back to the arena, I have a talk with Eric. "Oh your talking to me now?" He says.

"Yeah, please don't tell Cam I'm not suppose to dance, he'll send me home." I plead.

"Sure, my mouth is sealed," he says. Steps on the gas, and gets us rather recklessly back to the tour buses. So he's a little angry with me. About what? I don't care.

"So how'd it go?" Cam asks me.

"Okay, I got some pills, I need to ice it, rest. Maybe surgery some day." I say nonchalantly as I can. "I just need to change the routine, that's all. I hope you don't mind?"

"No, don't mind, what ever you need to do," he says, " just make it good."

"I will," Eric looks at me sideways.

I figure if I crawl, like I did when I fell, might be a good way to get to Cam. But that's still on my knees, unless I put all my weight on the other knee, I'll figure something out.

Even though my knee hurts I still need to exercise, and keep fit. Its important that I keep my stamina up. Even though the song is only 3 minutes 36 seconds long. It takes a lot out of me. I am so winded after I'm done. Can you imagine if I was out of shape? I probably have a heart attack. The dance routine is a work out in itself.

While the crew is setting up the equipment, the towers for the PA system, the lights, the instruments, and the piros, I like to run around the arena. I'm fascinated by the piros. There is a special guy who just does that. He's methodical, and he knows every thing there is about them. I like to watch him work.

I change into my favorite workout clothes. Pink of course. The arena is big, so I can exercise without getting in their way. There is a ton of stairs and tiers, walkways, corridors, and hallways to run around in. I put my shape-ups on. Do some warm up stretching, I'll take it slow and see how the knee feels.

The stairs are a good cardio workout. Great for the legs and butt. I run to the top of the stairs and back down again. I run into each section of the arena, starting with A and so on through the alphabet. I run in each section around and around. I work up a good sweat. So far my knee is feeling pretty good, so I push on. I've got my favorite band playing on my CD player in my ears. So it blocks out most of the noise in the arena, there's a lot of shouting and banging. The annoying microphone noises that blast around the arena until they have the speakers set to their liking. I pass several crew members, we smile at each other. I'm serious about my workout. I drink from my water bottle, take a minute to catch my breath. The band is on the arena floor, I can see them from way up here.

I drink some more water and it gives me a chance to watch Cam. He feels my gaze on him and looks up at me. He looks a little longer then maybe he should, then goes back to the mics he's testing. Eric sees me and waves, comes over to me to say hi. I'm always happy to see him. He always makes me laugh, our little spat that we had is long forgotten. He tells me something funny about his work, and I laugh, were laughing together. He's facing me with his back towards the stage, I can look over his shoulder at Cam. Who's looking again up at me. I wonder what he's thinking? Is he thinking there's something between Eric and me? I put my hand on his shoulder, as we are still talking and laughing. He has to go back to work. I have to finish my workout. I'm starting to feel the burn as they say. I'll have to quit soon. I haven't reached the feeling of gratification yet, when I feel like I've burned off all the junk I've ate in the past week.

CAM

"Hey man, pay attention, before we get electrocuted. Will you!" My backup singer and my right hand man Rob says to me. He hits me on the arm to get my attention.

"Stop looking at her," my brother says to me. Their both getting annoyed with me. I'm paying way to much attention to Janie, then I am my work.

Yeah, yeah I wasn't aware that I was watching her. Its sort of become a habit. I seek her out no matter where I am. My brother Matt, smacks the back of my head. "You know you shouldn't be looking, Cam. What about Melissa?" He says.

"Yeah, I know, I'm not dead man," I say in my defense.

"Well if its driving you crazy, then go and talk to her." Dale says. The other two give him a I'm gonna kill you look.

"What?" He says, and shrugs his shoulders.

Dale likes her. Matt and Rob don't. They feel she's intruded on us somehow. That she's going to interfere with me and Melissa.

"Don't go, you'll be sorry," big brother says. "You'll be hurting Melissa, man and you wont feel good about yourself."

"Shut up, Matt, she's here and Melissa isn't. I'm just talking to her, that's all." I look up at her, she was talking to Eric, one of my childhood friends, brother. I make sure, he's gone. Janie is alone.

I take off running towards her, up the stairs. She's up on the second tier of the arena. Its high up. I get a little winded. I get a good view of what some of the fans see from up here, and its far away from the stage, boy this sucks. I feel sorry for the fans who have to sit up here. That's why we have those big screens on either side of the stage. So they can see us.

I can just make out my brother shaking his head as he looks up at me. Fine, I'm a grown man, I don't need my brother telling me what to do. He's married, I'm not. So is Rob, I can hear the two of them tsk, tsking me. Hypocrites, I know they enjoy a little ass now and then.

She's wearing a nice form fitting jogging suit, her favorite color pink. It molds to her damn sexy shapely ass. I'd love to grab. She'd probably beat the crap out of me if I did. So I'll keep my hands in my pockets. The zipper is down just enough to see a little cleavage. Every night I imagine what she looks like without the dress. I relive those two nights in the shower, at my house long ago, over and over again in my mind. That thought makes me sweat. She's cute. And sexy, hot, and I'm drawn to her, like bees to honey.

I gravitate towards her, I cant help it.

She has a slight smile on the corners of her mouth as she drinks from her water bottle. Her long dirty blonde hair is in a ponytail, and when she runs it sways from side to side. She runs like a dancer, delicate steps. I know she hurt her knee, I feel bad about it. But she doesn't complain.

She said that she would postpone the surgery, she's probably afraid she'd have to leave the tour, I wont let her go. She still could sign the songs she does. She even offered to drive the tour bus. Give Carl a break if he needed it. She's qualified. She drove when Carl was ill. That's a good excuse.

Her pretty green eyes, are watching me with an intensity as if she's trying to see inside my soul, it makes her eyes look very dark. They burn into me. Like fire running threw my veins.

The smile is still there. She has no make-up on and looks like the girl next door. If she was the girl who lived next to me… I would have been in trouble a long time ago.

She always smells so good, even when she sweats. Like every flower in the desert.

Don't get me wrong I love Melissa, I've been with her for seven years now. I just… she's not here. And Janie is.

My mouth is salivating. I reach her just as she comes down to the landing of the second tier.

"Hi, Cam," she purrs. I swallow the extra saliva that's in my mouth.

"Hi, Janie," I croon back at her. Awkward silence for a minute. "How is your knee?" A lame question, but legitimate.

"Oh, its not bad, at all," she smiles coyly at me.

She takes another drink of water, I wish her mouth was around any part of my body. I know she has a thing for men's hands, she often hangs onto mine just a little longer than necessary. I notice how much smaller her hands are, they feel soft too. In fact I know their soft, what I wouldn't give to have her put them on me, now.

"I was wondering, Janie," I enunciated her name. "What were you going to change in your dance routine? And will it require anything different from me?"

She thinks a minute, before answering me. She makes a sucking noise on the water bottle, and that's driving me wild.

"Well…" She says. "Since my knee is messed up, instead of sliding like I was originally doing, I like the crawling, so I'll crawl over to you and all over you… if that's alright with you?" She looks at me from behind half hidden eyes.

"Yeah that sounds good, I liked it the first time you did it." I sound pathetic.

"It was an accident, I caught my heel on something and fell. Its hard to get up with the 5 inch heels." She smiles.

"Well I'm sure what ever you do will be exciting." I'm trying desperately to think of something else to say to her so I can stay here by her. I look at the guys on the main floor, they look up at me every so often. Their probably ripping me apart. She wipes her face on a towel.

"You look hot, Janie… you know sweaty." Ugh I cant believe I just said that, she's got me all tongue tied, like I'm some stupid teenage boy.

"Oh you think so Cam?' She smiles, a little mischief in her voice. She starts to take off her pants. At first I'm about to have a heart attack, cause I don't know if she has anything on under them.

She has tiny shorts on, I think they call them boy cut. And she unzips her jacket very slowly, biting her bottom lip and watching my reaction. She has on a white, tank top that you can see through. Its clingy. She puts her clothes over my shoulder.

"Put them in the bus for me Cam, will you." She says over her shoulder as she starts to run away. "Thanks."

Those shorts, holy shit. Oh my god, she just tortured me to death, and she knows she got to me. She even has the bands logo on the back of them. Sweet…. Could she tell how uncomfortable she was making me feel? and not in a bad way uncomfortable. A sexual uncomfortable. That funny feeling I get every time we touch. That little twisting knot in my stomach, that tingling sensation, every time I'm near her. Winding me up inside. The way my heart beats faster, my breathing faster, the way my mouth goes dry. The excited feeling I get, just knowing that there might be something between us. Sometimes she is all I think about. She knows she can tease me to no end and I cant do anything about it.

Or can I?

CHAPTER 15

I need a cold shower, she's laughing, she's running further away from me. I want to chase her. I'm the hunter, she's my prey. She knows I'm putty in her hands. From the first time I met her. At the meet and greets. And the time with the garbage, and when she jumped onto the stage. I watched in awe, that someone would want to dance to my song, in such a seductive manner. I hadn't even seen her at first when she was there, dancing. I was focused on some girls in the audience. Who I was trying to encourage to flash me their boobs. No takers though. I caught her shiny dress out of the corner of my eye. The way it swished back and forth. Her long blonde hair flying all around her. Her long legs in those thigh high boots. She hung a pink thong on my guitar. She hid her face from me most of the time.

We never missed a beat of the song. She never touched any of us, and stayed out of our space. I think she was scared. She smelled good, too, I remember. Like her clothes do now.

She did this amazing slid that ended up with her right under my feet. She had a lollipop in her mouth, where she got that from I have no idea. But it was in her mouth, and she was sucking on it. I remember licking my lips. She never looked up at me, until I offered her my hand. Which she took, her hand fit nicely in my hand, it was soft and warm.

I helped her up and we were faced to faced, god she was beautiful. I asked her, her name.

She said "Janie," Like it floated on the breeze. "Janieee……"

Then something scared her and she ran off and disappeared. Isn't it funny what you think of?

I think it was her who was picking up the garbage, still not sure about that, I should ask her about that. I'm pretty sure it was her, though. The sign language thing. She did this all to meet me. I think.

I start walking after her, in the direction she went. I don't see her, so I pick up my speed, until I'm running at full speed.

She stopped to tie her sneakers. She sees me coming. Gives me a wicked smile, and a giggle, and takes off running. Squealing with pleasure that I've followed her. Okay then, its on, I'll chase her for all it worth.

I have to work off all of this tension, she makes me feel. Sexual, animal tension. I knew she was in my bed last night. I'm a light sleeper and when your not used to someone being there it kind of makes you aware of your surroundings more. I wanted her to stay. I even threw my arm around her to hold her captive. But she must of got scared, because she left. She must think I'm a guy who gets mad a lot. I hide a lot of my feelings from people. My facial expressions look mean.

Hey I'm cool… I wasn't going to have her arrested or anything. She said it to me "she wanted to give back to us what we gave to her." That's the biggest compliment anyone could give us. Except for awards, of course.

She runs pretty fast, she's in better shape than I am. She's still giggling the whole time, she's running. It's become a game to her. I like games too. If I catch her then what? What am I going to do with her? Id like to take her into a private room, throw her on the floor and do what ever the hell I want to her.

Everyone looks at her as she runs by, then at me running after her. With her clothes over my shoulder, no less. I get a lot of dirty smiles, from the crew.

I probably look like an idiot. So I stop running. There's less people here in this section of the arena she ran into. In fact there's no people. She's lead me down a dark and dangerous place. Yeah me. It depends on who is doing the pursuing. Is it her, or is it me?

She's definitely, playing with me. Toying with the lust I feel for her, yeah that's it, the word I was looking for, LUST. A strong sexual and uncontrolled desire for someone I shouldn't even be thinking about. But everything about her drives me insane. She has the power to draw me in, I cant fight it any longer.

"Janieeeee....Where are you?" I say a little above a whisper the echo bounces back to me. I hear her giggle. It echoes down the corridor.

"Janieeee.....," I call again.

I hear her giggle again, she's right around the next corner. I'm gonna get her. I try to make no noise as I creep around the corner. She's standing there with her finger in her mouth. Smiling, a devious smile at me. She looks like a doe caught in the headlights of my car. But she's far from an innocent doe. Isnt she?

She's gonna run, she's trying to decide which way to run and when. She takes a step, but I block her. She takes a step the other way. I block her again. She's pouting. Then she smiles.

She laughs, a nervous laugh, I laugh. She's driving me wild. She's making my mouth water with anticipation.

She's standing with her hands on her hips. I'm waiting for her move. Its all up to her. But what ever way she goes I'll grab her. She makes a face, and then dives right into my arms, I wasn't ready for that, and the two of us go down. She's on top of me. I've got my arms around her. She runs her finger along my nose, around my lips, I bite her finger, then she sticks it in my mouth and I suck on it.

We haven't said one word to each other, there's no need to, she's gotten serious, she's searching my face. She's not sure what to do.... She wants to kiss me. Its okay, do it already.

So I grab the back of her head and pull her down to my face, our lips are barely touching, I can feel her breath on me. She's breathing in short little gasps, then she leans in and our lips are touching. Its tender and gentle, at first. She sucks on my bottom lip. That is erotic. I flip her on her back. And start kissing her hard, she returns it back. I bite her tongue, she does the same to me. Another thing that drives me wild, with desire. She's moaning, or is that me?

She's trying to rip my clothes off. I've got my hand under her tank top. God she's so soft.

She's got her hand on my belt, she's trying to unbuckle it. She's trying to get her hand down my pants. I put my hands on her ass. It fits perfectly in my hands, its so firm and tight. I've finally grabbed it.

I pull her tight to me. How much further do we go? She wants to go all the way. So do I.

Someone is calling me. I think its my imagination. I hear it again, but I don't stop. She hears it to, but doesn't want to stop either. Their still far enough away. Maybe they wont find us and give up. There's more than one voice. One is my brother, the other is Eric. We stop. And both take an exasperating breath.

We both look at each other. Like we've been caught. I get off of her and get up. I give her my hand and pull her to her feet.

"I guess we should go," she whispers. She smiles shyly up at me. She turns to go. I grab her hand. "Hey," I say, she looks back at me. "Next time stay, okay."

She nods, and says, "Okay." We hold each others hand. We have to part. She runs the other way. She picked up her clothes before she left.

I straighten myself out. I'm walking back towards the arena. I go to the door that leads outside. And pretend I'm walking back in. Matt is there and so is Eric.

"Where have you been?" Matt is pissed. "We needed your final okay on everything."

"Okay, I'm coming," I pick up my speed, so they cant see how I really look.

"Where's Janie?" Eric asks me.

"I don't know where she went," I say.

"You don't have her clothes anymore," my brother noted.

"I dropped them off in the bus," I tell him, I'm getting pissed myself with all the questions.

I know they don't believe me. I don't care. Eric however is starting to become very protective of her. He obviously has a thing for her. Join the club.

"You smell like her," my brother says. "Why?"

I'm getting really pissed now and I'm going to wail off on them. I stop abruptly and turn to look at him. "Because Matt I was holding her clothes, remember?" I don't wait for his response. I'm so pissed I could spit nails. Don't accuse me of something you know nothing about.

I go to the main floor. I finalize the set up for the show tonight. I gotta go and take a cold shower, and call Melissa.

JANIE

I'm taking a warm shower, I'm not the one to take a cold shower. Even though it was getting hot and heavy with Cam. It wasn't the greatest place for sex. I would have liked some place romantic. Not some cold, hard concrete floor. We were acting like animals.

Eric was looking for me. I've noticed he's become very protective of me. That's going to be a problem. I haven't proclaimed anything to him. He's just a friend.

I find one of the private dressing rooms to take a shower, I lock the door behind me. I have to get ready for the concert. I hadn't realized how much time has gone by. My knee is so, so tonight. The doctor said its MCL… Medical Collateral Ligament. It's a tear in the knee ligaments. Not a cracked knee cap like I was originally told. Ice, rest, elevate it. Maybe surgery.

I have so much sexual tension, I cant think straight. I'm trying to do forty million things at once. Focus, take a shower first. And I doubt my knee will bother me at all tonight.

As I take my shower my mind wanders, I think our next stop is Washington, DC. I would love to tour the capital. But there's never enough time. My mind is wandering all over the place. I forget my shampoo and soap. Where is the stupid towel? The clothes I took off smelled like Cam all over. I close my eyes and breath in. I almost… we were almost…. Oh damn. I don't know if I'll ever have that chance again.

I feel disappointed, sad, mostly disappointed. I take a long shower and drown my sorrows. Warm at first, then a nice steamy shower to get all the kinks out. By the time I come out I'm a prune. I take extra care of my hair, I don't comb it out. Let it look like the beachy look. Which is wavy. Add some curls to it with the curling iron. I burn my neck with the iron, it looks like a hickey. My hair is normally straight as a board, it looks super sexy when its curled.

I want to absolutely torture Cam, tonight. He left my insides all tied up in knots. My dance is going to be over the top. Parents might have to cover their children's eyes. And yes, stupid parents bring their children to an adult show. Cause Cam curses, and his songs are sexually explicit. Oh well, its not my problem.

I'm pulling out all the stops, as they say. I have a new dress, purple with sequins and beads. Sheer from the shoulders to the waist except the bead and sequins cover the right places, so it looks like its hanging by air. I have new purple heels, too. A teeny tiny pink thong for Cam's guitar. A new perfume, Eternity. So I'll smell like every flower in the desert. I practically wash my hair in it.

I put on silk stockings. Lace up the dress. Strap on the shoes. Make up my eyes, so that they stand out and are very expressive, smoky hot. The purple color of the dress make my eyes a darker green. Some sparkly jewelry. A big lollipop, for something in my mouth. Stuck between my boobs. Actually I hate lollipops, they give me a stomach ache. And leave my cleavage sticky.

Eric has been lifting me up onto the stage. I don't know if I want to see him. But I have no one else to help me. He comes and stands behind me without saying anything to me. He just gives me a lame smile. He looks me up and down, "Nice," he says.

"Thanks," I say. His touch is always gentle but firm. He'd make a good father someday. Plus he has the patience of a saint.

Before I go on stage he says to me, " Watch out for Cam?"

"Why?" I say, I want to know what he means by that.

"I'll tell you later," he says.

He lifts me up onto the stage with the first guitar note of the song.

This time my steps are slow and seductive. I make my way across the stage, towards Cam. As he's singing, he's trying not to look at me. But he loses. He cant help but look. I walk over to him, I'm in his space, I run my fingers along his arms and his back. I'm so close I can smell his breath, he was drinking beer. I put my fingers lightly, along his shoulders, and down his back. I feel him shudder. Rob and Matt are watching me with malicious contempt. I'll just do the usual with them, which is nothing. I never touch them. I go to the drum deck, and dance first in front of it, then make my way up to Dale.

Dale is a whole lot more fun. I climb up on the drum deck and it raises up off the floor, this is something new for me. The stairs were a little hard to climb in 5 inch heels. So they would leave the deck on the floor until I climb on. I put my hands all over him, he's loving it. He kisses my cheek. I run my hands through his hair.

The deck lowers again and I climb off. Dale can control it with a button. He raises it again, up to the highest it will go.

I crawl like a panther next to Rob, and rub my body against him like a cat. I can feel him freeze. Then I crawl over to Cam. Matt I didn't even bother with tonight. I'll get him the next time. He's just a spectator this time.

While I crawl I feel my knee pop. Its not hurting. But now it feels funny. I only have one thing on my mind. Making Cam feel the way, he left me feeling. The song is almost over. I'm over by Cam, and I slowly crawl up his leg. The song is over and I fall to the floor, under his feet, where I usually end up if I did the slide. I have the lollipop in my mouth.

Cam has more sweat on him then he normally does. Everyone is screaming, fans are whistling, and clapping. It's the longest minute ever, before Cam offers me his hand. He pulls me up a little harder than he usually does. We're looking eye to eye. He says, "I'll talk to you later."
"Fine," I say.

"Let's here is for?" He wants to know the name I'm using tonight.

"Melissa," I hiss the ssss.

"Melissa," he says. Everyone screams again, whistles, and applauds. I run off the stage, jump into Eric's waiting arms. He puts me down on the floor, we make our way off the main floor to the back stage. People are touching me and patting me, Eric is pushing their hands out of the way. I think people are beginning to realize that I'm part of the show.

CHAPTER 16

Eric has his arm behind my back, pushing me forward, away from the probing hands. Everyone wants to touch you. I'm happy for Eric's over protectiveness right now. He puts himself in between me and the audience. My own personal body guard. I steal a look at him, he's very serious looking. He takes this very seriously. I'm glad to have him next to me.

When we get back stage he says to me, "What did you do out there tonight, I think Cam is mad. That was like x-rated."

"Eric, I didn't take off my clothes." I huff.

"Yeah, but your ass was hanging out the whole time. And the way you were touching Cam and Dale, Whew! It even made me blush and all hot and bothered." He clears his throat.

"I told him I changed the routine, he knew." I say a little louder then I intended.

"Not like that I don't think, I don't think he was expecting anything like that." Erik adds.

"OKAY! Eric I get it I was naughty, I get it. I'll be fired now, okay are you happy?" We were walking to my dressing room.

"Thanks, Eric, for all your help, I really appreciate it," I gave him a kiss on the cheek, pushed open the door, and walked in, closed the door behind me. I leaned against the door. I have a knot in my stomach, I guess I went over the limit. He's always talking about woman's tits and everything and gets away with it. MY DANCE MADE HIM MAD? TO BAD…………………………

I change out of my clothes. I'm not in the mood for another stupid costume. I put on jeans and a t-shirt. Take off all the make-up, rather roughly too, as I wipe it off my face. Take off all the jewelry, except my earrings that I always wear.

I stayed in the dressing room until someone comes and gets me. Or maybe Cam wont send anyone. Eric taps on the door, "Your up, Janie." He says.

When I open the door he's gone. I'm in a bad mood, so now everyone has bad feelings. Yipee. All because of me.

Cam is talking to the audience as he often does. He talks about the songs sometimes their meaning, the CDS. He's sitting on the stool his guitar across his lap. Rob is beside him, one stool set there for me, too.

I really don't want to do this, I walk down to the main floor in front of the stage, in front of Cam. I cant look at him and I don't want to. I want to cry. Burying my head under my blankets.

Rob starts to play the guitar softly. Cam calls my name. He puts his hand over the mic. I still wont look up at him. I'm like the stubborn little child, who knows they've done something wrong.

The crowd is getting pissed because their stalling. Cam gets on his stomach, holds out his hand towards me, "Janie," he says. I look up at him. His blue eyes look so kind, not mad. He can do the show without me, he's the show, not me.

"Janie, are you ready?"

"Yeah sure," I yell.

I walk over to the stairs where he meets me, I offers me the stool next to him. He starts to play with Rob, he nods to me.

I start to sign. He sings with emotion I haven't heard from him before. The songs always make me cry because there so beautiful. Now he's singing with his heart on his sleeve. I don't want to cry, but I can feel the tears escaping my eyes. His eyes are closed. Rob is looking down at his guitar. He looks at Cam and then at me. Matt is looking every where else. Now I know why they don't like me. I add unnecessary emotions, they don't need to deal with, this trivial shit.

The three songs are over. The crowd is silent for a second, then they roar. They appreciate the intensity of Cam's singing. I wipe the tears from my eyes. Cam puts his arm around me.

"Thanks, Janie," he says. He kisses me on the cheek. I walk off stage, the audience fades away.

I want to have a good cry. Alone. I go find a secluded place, a place no one will find me. I don't care if they leave. I'm mad at myself. Why did I think I could get away with it, every time I try to get back at someone it always backfires, and I end up in trouble. I thought I'd be funny. I think I'll go home. I made an ass out of myself. I made Cam mad at me. The band hates me. Their wives and girlfriends can kill me. I cry until I get tired. I want to go to sleep. I wish I had my car, I'd sleep in there.

I avoid everyone, including Eric. I feel most embarrassed in front of him. I think he thought I was really cool, now I'm just some dumb blond bimbo.

I sneak back to the tour bus, making sure no one sees me. I crawl into one of the bunk beds and close the curtain, I fall asleep.

I've been asleep for a couple of hours now. By the time the meet and greet is over, the equipment is packed it might be 3 in the morning.

I hear the guys come in, they aren't their usual chatty, laughing selves. Thanks to me. Their talking about me, Cam is worried, on one can find me. They cant wait any longer, they have to leave, they have to get on the road.

Next stop is Atlanta, Georgia.

Rob says the show was amazing. That really surprises me, but doesn't make me feel any better, cause I really don't care what he has to say, it isn't important to me.

Dale says, "She really can dance." Matt agrees.

"So what do we do?" Rob asks.

"I don't want to leave her, I guess we find her." Cam says.

"People were asking for her, they want her autograph." Dale says.

The driver, Carl, asks Cam if he should leave now. "I don't know, we cant leave her behind, I could stay behind and try to find her."

"No you cant," Rob says. "Tell Eric to stay behind."

"Okay, I'll call him, Carl you can leave." Cam tells him.

I feel the bus engine fire up, and we pull out. I'm to tired to care if they know I'm here or not.

Everyone goes to there respectful places.

Someone notices the curtain pulled across the bunk bed. I make believe I'm asleep.

"Cam," Dale whispers. "Look," I feel all of them peeking in.

"She's been here the whole time, better call Eric and tell him we found her." Cam says. Rob makes the call to Eric.

"Should we wake her?" Dale asks.

"No leave her sleep, she was pretty upset with me."

"What did you say to her after the dance number?" Dale wants to know.

"I only said to her, I'd talk to her later. That's it. I wasn't mad at her or anything." Cam whispers.

"Yeah well, she must of took it the wrong way."

There still talking about me. Standing there, making me feel uncomfortable. I decide to move, I stretch and yawn. I open my eyes. I see eight pair of eyes looking at me. I rub my eyes.

"Hi," I say.

"Hi, where have you been?" Cam asks.

"I've been right here the whole time, why?" I yawn.

"We've been looking all over for you," he says.

"Oh, I'm sorry, I didn't know you cared," I say back at him. And stare into his blue eyes.

"Of course we care," he exhales in my face.

Since the mystery is solved the others leave me alone with Cam. "Come to the back room, with me, to talk."

I really don't want to. He's going to tell me I'm fired.

I reluctantly get up and follow him in the bedroom. He closes the door behind him. I feel like a little kid about to be punished. He sits on the bed and pats the bed beside him, "Sit down."

I feel so stupid right now, but I'm not going to say anything until he says something. He looks somber.

"I liked your dance routine tonight, it was….. Very interesting." He smiles.

I'm surprised. But I still don't say anything. "Your dress was really sexy. The shoes too. I know the audience certainly liked it."

"Yes…. But did you? You seemed like you were mad at me?"

"No way, I…. uh was blown away." He shakes his head as if he's remembering it.

"Oh, cause you said, "I'll talk to you later, and it wasn't nice the way you said it either."

"It was incredible, I'm sorry if you thought I was mad."

"Yeah but Eric said you were mad."

"Oh he did, did he?"

"Yeah, he said he could tell by your face, that you were."

"No, I wasn't, and I'm not, its suppose to look like it wasn't planned remember? I was just playing the part."

"Sure." I frown, cause I don't believe him.

"And don't listen to Eric, I think he has a thing for you. He might be jealous."

"No were just friends."

"Uh ah, not the way he looks at you, I don't think that's what he has in mind."

"I think your imagining things, Cam, he knows we are just friends. Nothing more. Funny, but Eric said to watch out for you."

He laughs, and shakes his head, "Yeah that is funny," he pats my leg, "So are we good now? It was all a misunderstanding."

"Yeah were good, I guess it was just a misunderstanding." I put my hand over his, the one that's still on my leg.

"Good night, Cam, I should leave."

"No stay, there's enough room, besides we could talk some more."

"I don't think that's a good idea, what will they say out there." I point my thumb at the door.

"I don't care what they say," he looks at the door and makes a face. "They don't run my life."

I want to stay more than anything else in the world. But it isn't right, just like I stayed at his house. Yes I was his guest, yes it was his house. And yes he did invite me. But him and me alone together. My mama would say "that was just wrong."

"Okay, I'll stay, you stay on that side of the bed and I'll stay on this side, deal?" I point to his side and to my side.

"Deal, don't make such a big deal about this Janie. Its like a slumber party. Only its just us."

"I'll be right back," I say. He gives me a wink. Oh gees, I have some idea of what he plans on doing. Right under the noses of this band members, and his brother. I close the door quietly so no one hears me.

I go get my PJ'S on. Brush my teeth. I look pretty awful, my eyes are red and swollen from crying. I put my bathrobe on. Its not the sexist look, I look like a house wife. The lights are out in the bus, everyone is sleeping, the driver is playing some music, softly. I look around, I have no idea what I'm looking for, Cam's guitar. I grab it off the table. Maybe he'll play me something.

I go back to his room and close the door. He's already under the covers. I hand him the guitar, "Would you play me something?" I ask him.

"What would you like?" He asks me.

"Something romantic, soft, what ever you want." I sit on the bed, and he starts to play softly, I recognize the song. Its one of the best songs he's ever written, so far.

I lean against the pillows and get comfortable. Cam is in the middle of the bed, so were laying close to each other. I love to watch his hands play, I wish I could play. I used to play the clarinet, the electric organ, the tuba, for a week, that thing was the hardest instrument to play. I even tried the guitar, I got a B in class for it. I remember how my fingers hurt from the strings. I had blisters and callous on the ends of my fingers. But I wasn't very good at it, in fact I sucked at it. That's why it always amazes me when someone can play with out music, and even write music. I cant. Isn't it amazing what you think of.

"Any other song you want to hear?" He asks me.

"Anything new?" I ask.

"Yeah, I have lots, I'll play you the one I wrote yesterday."

"You wrote one yesterday?" I'm amazed, he just comes up with this stuff. "How do you do it, you know think of a song to write?"

"Sometimes it's a word, or a sentence, or a phase, or an idea for a story, then I have a melody in my head and I start to play that, then the words usually come. Then whalla, a song is born."

"I wish I could do that, I never can put two words together." I sigh.

"Don't under estimate yourself, it isn't that hard to do. Its like telling a story, if you have a story you can write a song. Maybe someday we can write something together."

"Cam, I would love that, could I have my name on the CD?"

"Sure, if you wrote it." He says.

"Yeah well, I sort of did write a song for you. It was kind of when I was, uh… stalking you. And I was kind of mad at you, because you weren't paying any attention to me." He raises his eyebrows at me. "Well do you want to hear it?" I ask him.

"Yes." He says, and then adds, "so you were stalking me?"

"No of course not, just sort of following you." I smile.

"It's called, "I wanted you." So I sing him, the song. I really don't have any music for it. So I just kind of say the words. {words at the end of the book.} So after I'm done sort of singing it. I wait for his response.

"Interesting," he says. "You must of really been mad at me." He laughs, a little.

"I guess, I was." I guess it isn't recording worthy though. Maybe someday he'll use it.

I nestle down into the bed, I watch him play the cords. I understand that, it's the rest I don't.

I, as usual over analyze everything.

"Anything you'd like to talk about?" He asks me. As he gently picks at the strings.

Yeah I'd like to ask him how would Melissa like the two of us in bed together. But lets leave her out of the night tonight. She's, who knows where, who cares. She isn't here.

He throws the covers over my legs, its nice and warm under here. I sink down, sure feels better than that stupid, hard recliner.

"So what's on your mind?" He looks at me, his eyes look dreamy. I bite my bottom lip.

I stare up at the ceiling, my hands folded across my stomach. He still plays the strings softly.

"What does it feel like to be you?" I ask him.

"What do you mean?"

"Well woman throw themselves at you, {I think I'm on that list, guilty}. To everyone it probably seems like a fairy tale life, they want to be near you, they want to know you, they want to be you.

You make lots of money, you get to travel all over the world, you meet lots of famous people, you get to go to special events, like a NASCAR race, or the closing ceremonies of the OLYMPICS."

I turn on my side to face him. "So what does it feel like to be Cam Konner?"

"Wow, that's some question, what are you writing a book?" He kids.

"Yeah something like that. Can you answer my question?"

"Well, yeah its fun.... Most of the time. Its far from a fairy tale though. Your gone from your family, most of the time. Its especially hard on Rob and Matt, their wives and kids. They miss a lot of their kids growing up. You sleep in different places every night. You live out of a suitcase.

You really don't get to sight see. Because your sleeping during the day and up at night. Everything is usually closed. You meet so many people that after a while they all start to look the same. You could have any woman you wanted, but were very careful, you know with std's, so most of the time we don't. We have to get immunized all the time. Especially if we go over seas. Sometimes I feel like a pin cushion," he laughs. "And they always want to give it to you in your ass," he laughs again. "I have had some sore asses, from it that I couldn't sit down for a week."

I laugh, I could just picture it. Cam rubbing his ass. I've had them in my ass too, so I know what he's talking about.

"Its exciting to see all the fans fill up the arenas, to know that all these people like what you do, that's a real big ego booster. And then when the show goes well you feel like you accomplished something big. You feel really good, until the next concert, then you get nervous all over again.

But its rewarding. To know you make so many people happy. That maybe you made some small part of their lives a little exciting. You have to surround yourself with dedicated people, because without them..... The show doesn't go on." I watch his face change from thoughtful to reminiscing. Like he was remembering something he'd forgotten.

Some how as he was talking to me, I ended up snuggled up to him, my hand on his chest, I can feel his heartbeat. He puts his guitar on the floor and puts his arm around me, and pulls me tighter to him. My head resting in the hollow of his shoulder.

"So that's what it feels like to be Cam Konner. Anything else?" He squeezes me tighter.

"No I don't think so." I would like to ask him about Melissa, but if I bring her here, it'll ruin this moment, so I kick her out of my head. What's wrong with this? Two lonely people trying to get through the night.

"I want to live like I was a piece of history, I want people to remember me, us, the band, and say, yeah they weren't just some band that made some records. I want them to remember us as the band that made the best music for all time." He takes a deep breath.

"But you are, you were named the band of the decade. I think people would remember that."

"Maybe, your only as good as your current CD.. Then they forget about you. I once heard a race driver say that, your only as good as the last race you won, the next race they forget about it."

So it's really bugging me, and yes I am a little nosey about Cam's relationship with Melissa, so I have to ask.

"Anything else?" He looks at me.

"Well yeah, and I really don't want to ask, because it might spoil this moment, but I'm so nosy I have to know," I gasped it all out in one breath.

"Breath," he says. "What is it, you can ask me anything."

"You and Melissa, are you going to marry her?"

"I don't know, she's put up with a lot of my crap. I don't think I'm marrying material."

"Are you afraid? You aren't getting any younger and neither is she. Your what 35 now?

You know your biological clock is ticking too." I say.

"And how old are you?" He asks.

"Twenty four, why?"

"Just wondering, I never did ask you, maybe I am afraid, she deserves better." He sighs.

"Does she think that?"

"I don't know," he lets out an even longer sigh, this time.

CHAPTER 17

"Okay see I'm sorry I asked, I just want to know what your relationship with her is like. If I was her, I'd never let you out of my sight. Cause there are woman, who wouldn't stop at nothing to get you." I think, yeah me. "And the saying," being apart draws you closer. It's a bunch of bullshit. The further apart you are, the further apart it drives you away." I say.

"You sound like you speak from experience?" He says.

"Something like that." This time I let out a big sigh.

"Care to spill." He asks.

"Well, I was married once," I take a peek at his reaction, his face is thoughtful. " I got married at nineteen, to young. I wished I never did. It was horrible from the start. I should have divorced him days later. He would work all day, or so he said. Work overtime, or so he said, go to the gym, so he said. Where he met some fat bimbo, who knew how to butter him up. He'd come home really late, and expect me to be happy about it, I got tired of waiting for him night after night." I sigh. I'm telling Cam way to much information about my past, then I really want him to know, but why stop now. It still hurts. It molded me into the person I've become. "He never kept his promises, broke my heart all the time. Disappointed me all the time. Even forgot my birthday. Said he didn't have any money. But I found a receipt from Sears that he bought her a gold locket for two hundred dollars. That hurt so much." I gasp.

"I'm so sorry, Janie" he kisses my head.

"It's okay, because I got rid of him. Then when we divorced, he made my life even more miserable. He tried to get me in trouble with the law. I hate him."

"I'm really sorry, I didn't know, I promise Janie I'll be a good friend to you, no matter what. I'll never forget your birthday, Janie, I promise that too." He says.

Friend wasn't what I had in mind. But I would rather have Cam as a friend than not in my life at all.

"Thank's Cam, it's in the past now, I've moved on. I'm doing things for me. I make myself happy. I never break a promise I've made to myself. The dance thing was one of the promises I made, no matter how hard it was for me to get on stage I was going to do it." I say proudly.

"I'm glad you did, cause we never would have met, you sound like you have things together."

"Sometimes, I do…. Other times I fall completely apart." I say.

"You mean like tonight?" He grins at me.

"Yeah like tonight, sometimes I get paranoid, especially if I think I've done something wrong." I sigh. "I'm sorry Cam, I didn't mean for it to end up the way it did. You know you guys looking for me. I really thought you were mad at me."

"It's forgotten Janie, and your forgiven for feeling the way you felt, that I'm a big idiot." He laughs. And I give him a little punch in his stomach.

"You aren't a big idiot, maybe just a little one," he squeezes me tight again. And laughs.

I turn my face up to his. I bit my lower lip. I hold my breath. I want him to kiss me so badly.

He looks at me searching my face. And leans over to kiss me. Its so tender, slow, exploring and savoring. I crawl up closer to him, and trace his lips with my tongue. He kisses it. "I want you Cam." I say with as much sexual tension in my voice, that I feel like I'm going to explode. He moans.

"Ssssshhh, they'll hear us."

"There probably listening at the door." He teases.

"You can laugh, I don't like an audience." It makes me a whole lot of nervous.

"You really want me?" He whispers.

"All over me," I put my hand under his shirt.

"I can do that," he nuzzles my neck, kissing my neck down my shoulder. That drives me wild.

"Bit my neck," I tell him. "I love that, it makes me crazy."

"Well then, that's what I want to do….. Is make you crazy," he bites my neck, and I moan.

"Oh that feels so good," he's got his hand under my shirt. We start to explore each other. The clothes start to come off. He just about has my night shirt off when the bus starts to shake violently.

"Oh my god what's happening?" We're being tossed about.

"What the hell?" Cam says. Gets up out of the bed, to go to the door. He opens it, "What the hell is going on?" He yells to Carl.

Everyone is up, hanging on, and looking out the windows, "Did we hit something? Rob asks.

"No, I think we have a blow out." Carl says. There was a noise but we weren't paying to much attention to it.

"Hang on," Carl yells back. I crawl out of the bed to the door, I should be up there with him to help him stop the bus. But I cant because it's tossing me all over the place.

"Don't brake," I yell to him. "Shift into a lower gear, let the engine slow the bus down."

"I know," he yells over his shoulder, I can see the sweat on his forehead. Were slowing gradually.

The trucks up ahead have slowed down too. Carl gets it safely on to the shoulder, were we come to a stop.

My heart feels like its pounded out of my chest. I think Carl left his somewhere back behind us.

Everyone takes a big breath. Cam sees if Carl is okay. He's taking a moment to calm down. His hands are white knuckled on the steering wheel. He's frozen there.

"Carl are you okay? You did a fantastic job," he nods, and kind of makes a squeak noise.

I'm laying on the floor, catching my breath, I've had vehicles that have lost there brakes, it's a frightening feeling, and even worse with something that weights a couple of tons.

Cam sees me on the floor and helps me up, I get my bathrobe on. All of us, take a moment to calm ourselves.

"Its okay," he puts his arms around me.

"I know, how is Carl?" I ask.

"Shaken," he says. The bus starts to fill up with smoke. Its one thing that terrifies me, is smoke, cause where there's smoke, there's fire.

Someone opens the door from the outside. Fresh air comes flooding in. We jump out as fast as we can. We all get out to see what happened.

Carl, has the fire extinguisher, and sprayed the tires, that are now smoldering in the dirt. He's surveying the damage. And it did a lot. "Were gonna need a tow truck," he says.

The tire is completely shredded. The other tire that's next to it which is called a dual. Is messed up too. The side of the bus is ripped apart. Carl is on his cell phone with emergency. The crew from the other trucks all come running back. Everyone is looking at the damage. Will have to travel with the other trucks. I get dressed and grab my bags. The guys grab their stuff too. It's a good thing we live out of suitcases.

Eric is at my side already waiting to help me to the truck he's riding in. He's happy to see me.

"You can ride with me," he says. And he's already pulling me towards the truck he was in. He gives Cam this very smug look, I'm not sure what the look is for. But it doesn't look nice. Sort of like contempt. Its gone as fast as it appears on his face, so I'm not sure if Cam even sees it. He's got his hand on my back, pushing me towards the truck. His hand is annoying me, I don't need to be herded. I know which way to go. The guys are going in the other trucks, all of us separating.

I look over my shoulder at Cam, before I get into the truck, he waves at me. I wave back. Another intimate moment gone forever, again........ Eric makes a harump, noise. If I had an inkling I'd think Eric is jealous.

Eric is chatty tonight. I'm not in the mood to talk. I say the first thing that comes into my head. "Are you mad at Cam, or something?"

"What, why?" He sounds surprised.

"Are you mad at Cam? I saw you give him a dirty look, what was that all about? The look was not very pleasant."

"Yeah cause he always looks at you like he wants to eat you. I don't like the way he looks at you, that's all." Eric huffs.

"Oh I hadn't noticed." I say, like I really don't notice, but in fact I do.

"Yeah, I bet you don't." He huffs, again, as he looks out the window.

"What's that suppose to mean?" I give him a sideways look.

"Nothing." He says.

"Fine."

"Fine."

The guy sitting next to me, the driver, laughs a little, "Oh shut up." I tell him. He laughs a little again, but then stops, when he sees my stormy face.

We're all silent, as we drive towards our next arena. I want to be with Cam. No matter where we go or what we do, I want to be with him. And Eric isn't my father.

"I warned you about Cam," he says through gritted teeth, low enough so that only I hear him.

"You never said about what," I whisper.

"His womanizing," he says. Whispering in my ear.

"I've never seen him do that," I whisper back and hit my head against his. "Ow." We both say. Then we start laughing. It's stupid really.

"I just don't want to see you get hurt, that's all." He whispers, and kisses my cheek.

"I know and thanks." I snuggle down into the seat, my arms folded across my chest.

He has his arm over the back seat. I lean against him and fall asleep. He's like a big stuffed teddy bear. He could easily beat the crap out of Cam. Cam is very thin and lean, were Eric is bigger and muscles everywhere. Eric is like a big linebacker. I think he said he was in high school.

"Where are we going?" I cant seem to remember, cant seem to remember anything at the moment, except Cam.

"Atlanta, Georgia." Eric says, he's still looking out the window at the passing landscape.

"Oh yeah, that's right. I hear people talking. In between waking and sleeping. I think I'm dreaming. I don't want to wake, I'm so warm and comfortable. I remember that I'm sitting next to Eric and he has his arm around me. I feel safe.

But sometimes I wake up confused, for just a minute or two, I don't remember what day it is or what time it is, or even where I am. Then my head clears, and I remember.

"Were stopping for breakfast Janie," Eric gently shakes me. "At one of the rest stops, you want to wake up?" He says.

Every one is out of the trucks, stretching, aching from sitting so long. I wake up and yawn, stretch too, I think I feel worse then I did when I first fell asleep. I need to run or something. Eric helps me out of the semi. I need a bathroom. Grab my suitcase to change my clothes. I'm headed towards that way, "How's the ride?" Cam is behind me.

"I slept most of the way," I grin, "So I've missed most of the fun."

"Dream about anyone?" He smiles.

"No Cam…. To frustrated to dream, if you know what I mean. How about you?"

"Frustrated about what?" He asks innocently. I walk away shaking my head at him, he's got his hands shoved in his pants pockets. Wonder if he wants to grab me? Cause I want to grab him.

I smile at him as we walk to our separate bathrooms, its early in the morning, you'd be surprised how many people are up traveling at this hour. The rest area isn't to crowded, but everyone that's there looks at the big crowd that's piling inside. If I was a fan of the band and I recognized them, I would go ballistic.

As a fan I'm crazy about them, especially the lead singer, did I tell you that?

Someone has a football and their throwing it around. I want my breakfast. I sit down outside at the tables, Eric brings me something from MAC D's. The pancake breakfast.

At this very moment I feel so happy, blissful even, this is my dream. And I'm living my dream. I look at all the guys around me, I try to see if I know all of their names. Some of them I don't know, but I've seen. Others I know.

When I'm old will I remember this moment? I embed it in my brain, to be in love with someone you only dreamed about, I don't know what's going to happen down the road, but I want to live it like the best is yet to come.

I do a little stretching, and jog around the parking lot. Climb the stairs up and down. Why do they all watch me? Am I that interesting to look at?

My knees get really stiff from not moving, I don't know how truck drivers do it, all those hours behind the wheel. Once I start moving I feel better, the sleepiness has gone from me. I increase my speed around the parking lot, even go backwards. Up and down the stairs, until its time to leave.

I want to go with Cam now. But Eric has other ideas. "There's no room in his truck," he says to me, as if he's read my mind. Probably because I keep looking in Cam's direction.

I'm the kind of person the more I cant have something, the more I want it. So the more he pressures me, the further he's taking me away from Cam, the more I want to fight him. And if I have to I'll avoid him. Except when I need him. There are plenty of other guys who would jump at the chance to lift me up on to the stage. And have me jump into their waiting arms after the dance routine. He's nothing special.

After today, I'm going to distance myself from Eric.

We arrive in Atlanta, Georgia, two days before the concert. Which is nice because it gives us some time to have fun. There's nothing I really want to do here. Maybe sight see some civil war stuff.

I'm in the mood for a home cooked meal. Everyone else has something to do. I call a cab. "Take me to the super market." I haven't been in a super market in such a long time. How strange it feels, but yet familiar. I find everything I need to make my favorite meal. Dessert too.

Lasagna, homemade sauce, the works. Even a decadent dessert, chocolate brownie cheesecake.

On my way back to the arena, I spot a little dress shop in between the big shops. It's a cute little shop tucked a ways back from the main road. And its got the prettiest pink dress in the window.

I tell the driver to stop, wait for me.

The dress is a little pricey, but its gorgeous, and it looks incredible on me. I wiggle my ass and it swishes from side to side. It's the effect I'm looking for. I've got the perfect shoes that would go with it. It even has a matching wrap. Its pink, chiffon with a halter top, its short just above my knees and it has lots of folds of fabric for the skirt, it's a great little dancing dress. A few sequins and crystals dot the dress, not to much just enough to make it sparkle. It's the perfect date dress.

And I do have a date. I know I said I'd avoid him at all costs. But he came, after not seeing me for two days and apologized for his possessive behavior and for bad mouthing Cam. Apology accepted. He looked like a sad little puppy dog. He wanted to take me on a real date, before the show. I accepted. Hey I always give people a second chance. After all look at how many second chances I've had. You cant condemn a person for caring about you.

CHAPTER 18

All morning I cooked in the tour bus. Its got everything a regular kitchen has, but on a smaller scale. I've done this so may times, that I know it by heart. I make it like an assembly line. Make two huge pans of Lasagna. The dessert smells really good, and looks mouth watering. I hope it tastes as good as it smells. It's the first time I've made it, but brownies are a no brainier, anyway.

Its like lunch time-dinnertime, you can smell it outside the bus. And it brings the guys back. Like someone had a hook in their noses and was pulling.

They were pretty excited that they were getting a home cooked meal. I told them don't get used to it. They sit around the table. "I know you like meat and potatoes, but this is what I like to eat, my favorite Italian, I could eat it every day." I say as I handed them each a plateful of food, salad, and garlic bread There's plenty left over for seconds.

They noticed I wasn't eating. Cam asks me why. "Aren't you eating Janie, this is so good." He says in between bites.

"No I have other plans, but save me some. The dessert is in the fridge." I say.

While they eat, I get dressed. I do my hair in those curls I love so much. Delicate, frames my face. Light makeup. The beautiful pink dress and pink sandals with the big heels. Some jewelry, a pink pearl necklace, and three sets of earrings cause that's how many holes I have in each ear.

I take one last look at myself before I walk out. Happy with the way I look. Put the wrap around my bare shoulders. I do have soft shoulders. Walk out of Cam's bedroom. They all stop eating and look up at me. Mouths drop open.

I smile, "How's the food?"

"Delicious," they all agree.

"Where are you going?" Cam asks.

"I have a date," I say while I put on some pink lip gloss, smack my lips together.

"With who?" Cam asks.

"With Eric," I say nonchalantly, cause I can see its bothering Cam.

"I thought you were staying away from him?" Dale says,as he shoves a piece of garlic bread in his mouth. They all cant seem to get the food in their mouths fast enough.

"I was, he apologized." I say.

"Oh…. You'll be back in time for the show? Right?" Cam gets up out of his chair, to look out the window.

"Yes, Dad, I'll be back in time." Cam follows me to the door. He looks me up and down.

"I don't think I should let you go, you look to beautiful for Eric." He puckers his lips. "Damn you look good enough to eat." He says.

"Yeah I've heard that before, good night Cam, I'll see you later. Goodnight guys. And don't forget the dessert is in the fridge." I yell over my shoulder as I walk out. "Its chocolate brownie cheesecake."

"Goodnight," everyone except Cam, yells back.

Eric is waiting with a black limo, wow. "Impressive," I say to him. He shrugs.

He's all dressed up in a black suit. He looks handsome, he kind of takes my breath away.

He's got the door open for me.

"Wow you look beautiful," he says and kisses me on the cheek. He sees Cam standing in the doorway of the tour bus. Watching us.

"Your father let you out tonight." He says sarcastically. Jokingly?

I look at Cam, he's got his arms folded over his chest. I wave before I duck inside the limo.

"Yeah," I laugh, "dad let me go, but I have to be back before the show starts. Otherwise, I'll turn into a pumpkin." I giggle.

He gets in and closes the door. We drive off, I take a quick look out the rear window, Cam is still standing there until he cant see us, any more, we've left the arena parking lot.

We go to a cozy restaurant. Very posh. And probably expensive. I think about Cam the whole way there. Its unfair to Eric, so I push Cam to the back of my mind. I have the rest of my life to think about him.

I laugh at all of Eric's jokes, and he is funny. I smile at him, a lot. He says "order what ever I want." I order stuffed flounder. He gets a big steak. The food is good. The lighting is dim, but its makes everything look romantic. Makes even the food look good. Makes us look good.

There's music playing softly.

Eric gets up out of his chair, and offers me his hand. "May I?"

"Really?" I say.

"Yes, really."

"I never new you were the type," I say.

"I, am and I'll tell you why. But first lets dance."

We are the only ones dancing, maybe they don't even do it here. But no one seems to mind, in fact several couples get up too.

"I think we started something."

"Yeah, I guess we have."

He really is a good dancer and hasn't stepped on my toes yet.

"So..... Tell me your dancing story. I want to know how come you don't have two left feet."

He laughs. "Well, when I was in middle school and high school, I played football...."

No guess there.

"Our coach made the whole team take ballet lessons." He laughs again as he remembers it.

I smile, I can just picture him in a tutu. I choke down the hysterical laugh that's trying to escape from my lips.

"Yeah I know what your thinking... no we did not wear tutus."

He's got his hand in mine and the other one at the small of my back. He still hasn't stepped on my toes yet.

"So?".... I say.

"So the coach took us two times a week to a dance studio for lessons. No one knew about it, not even our families. We kept it very hush, hush. The coach said it would help with our jumping in mid-air, when we caught the ball. To land correctly, so that we didn't hurt ourselves. And just to look graceful while we played. Coordination, speed, agility, it all made us look good. And we definitely played better, because of it. And people noticed. Won the championship, too. But the coach wasn't telling our secret to anyone."

"We all objected and bitched and moaned and groaned about it. When we saw that it was actually working, we continued doing it. Most of us who played in middle school, played in high school, so we just continued taking ballet lessons."

"Wow.... You know I've heard of athletes doing that. You know pro football guys."

"Yeah its true. I went on to play collage football. I got hurt in one of the final games. My knee." He smiles.

"Oh?"

"Yeah that why I can sympathize with you, with your knee." He says.

"I guess you can," No wonder Eric has been so caring. He understands exactly how it feels.

His alarm on his watch goes off. Its time for us to go. The **limo is waiting.** We drive back to the arena.

"Eric I had such a nice time. Thank you." I glance over at him, taking a peek at him, how good he looks.

"Your welcome, we should do this again, it was fun."

"I'd like that," I say and I give him a peck on the cheek.

"I'll see you in a few," he says, "I got to get out of these clothes."

"You look handsome in them," I tell him, he waves at me, as he runs into the arena.

There's no time for me to change my clothes, so I'll have to wear the pink dress I went on my date in. I love this dress anyway, I'd like to wear it a little longer. I have just enough time to run to the tour bus and freshen up before I go on stage.

The guys cleaned up, there's a little bit of food left. They devoured the brownies. There's a thank you card and some flowers. How sweet, I guess they really did like my dinner. I freshen up and run back to the arena. Everyone is running around backstage, the arena is full again tonight. I make my way down to the floor, front and center. Its really funny, people don't want to move out of the way for you. One time I said, pregnant woman coming through, they reluctantly moved aside.

Eric is behind me, on cue. He's always got my back. He puts his arm around my waist, this time I don't mind. I lean against him, and wait for the show to start. My song is second. Like always. The piros are lit, and going off. The band comes running out, playing their first song. The sound is so incredibly loud, I usually have ear plugs in my ears. Besides my knee being messed up, I don't want to loose my hearing too.

I wonder how many G's are pounding against my chest, if there is such a thing as G force in music. It always makes me feel like its sucking the breath out of me. It makes it hard to breath.

The heat from the piro's make me feel like I'm on fire and burning up.

Cam spots me. I forgot the lollipop and the thong. I'll have to use my finger, and some how get my underwear off. Or not…..

Cam hits that cord I know so well, the one I've memorized in my dreams. He turns his head to watch me get on stage. Which he shouldn't be doing, cause this is unplanned, right. His eyes light up, and a slow smile starts at the corners of his mouth. He notices the dress. I look like a lady instead of the usual slut.

I change my dance steps just a little. A little more dignified. There's a line in the song, that says, she smells so good, like every flower in the desert. I put my arm in front of Cam's face so he can smell the perfume I put on. He rolls his eyes, at me.

I go over to Rob, put my arm around him, he doesn't tense up like he always does. I go to Matt and do the same thing to him, he's okay with it to. Maybe my dinner smoothed things over.

I'm still shaking my ass, the dress twirling around my legs to the beat of the music. But its different.

Dale has a part in the song where its heavy on the drum beat, that's where I always am when he's playing that, standing on the drum deck with him. I wrap my arms around his shoulders, and he's still pounding the drums, he always gives me a kiss on the cheek. This time he stops playing grabs me, pulls me onto his lap and kisses my mouth so hard, he's taken me by surprise and sucks the air out of me. The audience goes wild. He stands me up, slaps my butt and continues playing again. He's got a big stupid grin on his face, I cant help but smile myself, I toss my hair all over my shoulders. I have this little hop, I do when I walk off the deck, its more like a skip step. As I make my way over to Cam.

Everyone in the band is having a good time tonight. The song is almost over. I slid down his leg.

I can feel every muscle in his leg, tense up. I hope its because he likes it. He pushes his guitar out of the way. He touches my cheek, then my shoulder. The audience is clapping and whistling. I look up at him, he's looking at me with a look I've never seen before in his sky blue eyes. He takes my hand and gently, slowly pulls me up against him. He looks at me for one long minute. He's just staring at me. "Say something Cam." I say to him. He blinks his eyes, and snaps out of whatever it was he was in. A trance?

"Hey give it up for… Janie," he says.

I curtsy, give Cam a kiss and run off the stage, into Eric's waiting arms.

Dale starts the next song, and Cam snaps out of it. What ever happened to him? I don't know.

"Cam wants Janie to come sign autographs for the fans," Eric says to one of the crew members. "Have you seen her?"

I hear him, near the door of the dressing room. "I'm in here, Eric."

I like to dress up, but after a while it starts to get uncomfortable. My feet start to hurt from the shoes, I'm really a jeans and sneaker girl. The most uncomfortable thing is the stupid pantyhose, they dig into my thighs.

"Oh, Cam wants you to wear the dress," he says through the door.

"Sorry, its already off."

"Oh….. Okay." He says.

Well usually they've been doing the meet and greet before the show, I'm usually dressed. And I'm not hot and sweaty. Eric is outside waiting.

"Well hurry up anyway. People are asking for you." He says, through the door.

I open the door, he's standing there with his arms folded across his chest leaning against the door frame. "Jeans and a t-shirt," I say. "Sorry."

We walk to the conference room. The guys are lined up behind a table, there's a line of fans out the door. Signing autographs, and taking pictures. Cam sees me, "Janie come sit next to me."

He says. Rob is sitting next to him. I take the empty seat at the end of the table. I wave at all of them, and sit down. "Move," he says to Rob.

"Let Janie have your seat." Rob looks at him, like what the hell, you've got to be kidding.

"No, I'm good, Cam," I say, I don't want a fight between the two of them because of me, another reason for Rob to hate me.

I do a lot of autographing, my hand is starting to hurt. By now most of the fans have figured it out that I'm part of the show, I think its on the internet, face book, and twitter. I haven't been on a computer since I left home. So I don't know what's going around.

Some guy has a whole bunch of pictures of me, dancing and signing. There really good too.

He wants to sell them to me.

Cam hears him, "NO," he tells the guy through gritted teeth, " we have our own photographer." he says. "We don't buy pictures," he says to the guy.

He get's the attention of one of the security guys, and he pushes the guy out. He moves him along and out the door. I look at Cam and frown, I don't have any pictures of myself dancing, or in any of my pretty dresses. It would be nice to have some, to make a scrap book.

He's pissed at the guy for even asking, and even angrier that security let him in. I sign some more autographs, its fun. My hand is cramping. Who would have thought that anyone would want my autograph. I've gotten autographs from the stars of Twilight and New Moon, and Eclipse, and Breaking Dawn, even the director, Catherine Hardwick. I even have Cam's. Now I know how Catherine must of felt after signing something like five hundred or a thousand books, by the time she was done I remember seeing her hands covered in sharpie ink. She was nice too, and spoke to each person as if she knew them, I liked her a lot.

Having someone ask me for my autograph, makes me feel special and very flattered. Everyone walks away as if they have a prize. I remember feeling that way when I got the wolf pack guys to sign their pictures. Even cute, Boo Boo Stewart. He even gave me a hug.

Before we leave Georgia, everyone wants to go to the beach, its on the way to our next city.

We have a day or two before we have to go to Tulsa, Oklahoma.

We take all of the trucks, and the tour buses. To the beach. We gather firewood, and make a big bonfire. We have hotdogs and hamburgers to cook. Someone got salads, and stuff to drink. Someone bought marsh mellows, and stuff to make smores.

We roasted the hotdogs, and hamburgers, everyone got their own plates. And we sat around the fire eating and talking. Its chilly out, there's a breeze blowing off the water. But sitting by the bonfire is keeping me warm. There's large bleached trees laying on the beach, washed up from storms. The guys drag them over around the fire and we sit on them. Its so relaxing, and the food tastes extra good.

The fire is hypnotic. The flames leap into the air are blue and red. The sky is dark, but its clear and you can see a billion stars. I even see a shooting star and make a wish. I hope it comes true, and no I cant tell you, cause if I do tell you, it wont come true. So sorry. But I bet you can guess.

CHAPTER 19

Cam and Rob have their guitars out. They start playing. I want to sing one of their fun songs. The one about the weeds in the back yard are ten feet tall, and Harold and Kumer want to smoke them all. Beer bottles all over the living room floor.

Everyone sings along, its fun. We all have fun. And yes, there are other woman there besides me. Some are the wives of the crew guys.

Those that want to go to bed, leave. Some still stay by the fire. I could fall asleep here, myself. The equipment trucks leave, to get a head start.

"Care to go for a walk, on the beach?" I look up with sleepy eyes, to see Cam standing there with the wind blowing his hair in his eyes. His blue eyes sparkling from the fire, god he looks so hot. He standing over me with his hand in his pocket and the other one held out to me. The fire has made me very sleepy. I'm wondering where Eric is?

I have on his big sweatshirt, I can smell him all over it. I look at Cam, and lick my lips, the wind has blown my hair in my eyes. I brush it away. "Sure," I say, and take his hand, its warm.

I wipe the sand off of my butt, and stuff my hands in the pockets of the sweatshirt, cause I want to reach out for Cam. Which is an automatic thing I want to do. But people are watching. So I don't.

We walk without saying anything for a while, listening to the surf pound the shore.

"I liked your dress tonight, it was very pretty... you looked very pretty in it. I'm glad you wore it on stage. I really didn't get to have a good look at you when you went with Eric." He's looking out at the water. I cant see his face, but I can hear something in his voice. It almost sounds like he's upset about something.

"Thanks," I say.

"How was your date with Eric?" He tried to sound nonchalant about the question, but I can tell its eating him up.

"It was nice," I smile, I remember how he held me as we danced.

"Where did you go?"

"We went to a little café restaurant, had a nice dinner and even danced."

"Oh yeah! Eric dances?"

"Yes he does, and quite well." I say.

"Hrumph," he says.

"Why?" I ask him. "Why don't you believe me?"

"Yeah I believe you, I just cant picture him dancing, you know as big as he is."

"He's very graceful, better than me actually."

"Really? "Your pretty graceful, and quite sexy, too." He adds.

"Okay, Cam what is it you really want to ask me?"

His hands were still in his pants pocket, he isn't looking at me. But he's walking close to me, our shoulders touch as we walked further down the beach.

"What Cam?"

"Have you done it with him yet?"

"You mean Eric?"

"Yeah Eric."

"Done what with Eric, Cam?" I knew exactly what he was asking me, but I wanted him to say it.

"Sex, Janie, have you had sex with Eric?"

"And what if I had? Would you be upset?"

"HAVE YOU?" He snaps. He's getting mad cause I wont give him an answer. I make a face at him, which I doubt he sees cause its dark.

I ask him again, "Would you be upset?"

"YES!" I smile to myself, so he admits it he has feelings for me. He's jealous? One point for me. I wonder, does he feel like he's competing with Eric? Hum? I smile to myself.

"No Cam, I haven't, were just friends right now. Why?"

"Just wondering, that's all."

"Well we haven't yet either, so….." But we have, we just don't want to admit it, "you know in the shower, twice." If we don't admit it, then it isn't true. We can deny it, just to justify it. He cheated on Melissa, and I let him use me…but I wanted him to?

"Yes I know that, gees I was there remember?"

"Just wondering? Well you know Cam you have a girlfriend as I recall. I have no one. It gets lonely, you know."

"I know, I'm lonely too. Melissa isn't here. I'm away from her a lot."

"I know," I say, should I feel sorry for him? But I don't, I feel sorry for me. Cause I'm the one he should be with.

We continue walking down the beach, further from the warmth of the fire. I turn around, and look how far we did walk. The fire on the beach looks like a dot on the horizon.

"We'd better go back, its cold here. I'm tired. Its been a long day." We turn around, and start walking back to the fire.

"It has gotten cold…hey um, your lasagna was the best I've ever tasted, and that brownie cheesecake was decadent, just thinking about it is making my mouth water. I remembered you were a good cook….. When you were at my house. Anything else your good at?" He looks at me sideways. And smiles. Wiggles his eyebrows, at me. Oh gees.

"I'm good at a lot of things, you should remember, do you want to find out what other things I'm good at?"

"Yeah actually I would, how about Sex again? Those two times in the shower, it was over to quick. It was just, I don't know, not very fulfilling, I'd like something that maybe lasted all day."

"Sex? Sex is always the answer for you right? Never a question, right?" I say. "Not very fulfilling? I seem to remember you moaning and groaning a lot." I tease.

"Yes, exactly right, sex is always the answer, we've come so close you and me, we always get interrupted. I feel a lot of tension between us, don't you? Maybe if we get it over with, we could you know see how things go between us." Cam says.

"You mean like an affair?" I say.

"I wouldn't call it that, maybe just some maintenance." Cam says.

"I would say there's a little bit of tension, { and here's where I play with him, I know its mean, but he deserves it.} "Wonder if we do, and it turns out lousy, I mean in the shower was good, but it was to quick, like you said. And the second time was to gritty, with all the mud and stuff. So I wouldn't go by that. I mean wonder if its really bad? And then we cant stand each other, or be in the same room with each other, then what? Then you wont like me and fire me? I would be devastated if that happened." And why do guys always think its better, than you think it was? I can just make out his facial expression from the light of the fire. He really thinks I'm serious, he's thinking of a good answer.

"There's only one way to find out, we have to have sex." I knew that was his answer. It always is with guys, don't they say that guys think about sex like every other second of the day. Although Eric hasn't said anything to me about it. I'm sure he thinks about it too. And he's warned me about Cam.

"We've tried a couple of times, remember? We always get interrupted, its almost like someone is trying to stop us from finding out. Like a higher power." I tease some more.

"I don't believe that, besides when it does happen, it'll be incredible, you'll see." He says.

We're back to the fire, people are sleeping by the fire. Me, I want my bunk bed. No sand fleas for me, thank you.

"I'm going to bed, Cam, good night."

"Me too, come to my room."

"I think I'll sleep in my bunk, tonight."

"Sure, sweet dreams." He says a little disappointed.

"You, too."

Horny little boys, just aren't happy are they? Maybe he should call Melissa.

Everyone was sleeping, Cam came in a few minutes later. I was already in my bunk bed, under the covers and almost asleep. I could feel him standing outside my bunk. He hesitated there for a moment and then went to his room. I held my breath until he left, I didn't realize I was holding my breath, until I heard him close the door. I let out a big breath and breathed in an even bigger breath. It's a good thing I'm not the driver, cause I'd be a zoombie in the morning. Carl has been asleep for hours now.

I can hear the pounding of the surf on the shore. It has a hypnotizing sound. I drift off to sleep. And dream about absolutely nothing. Not even a dumb twisted nightmare, not even about Cam or Eric.

By the time any of us wake up, were on the road already. Tulsa, Oklahoma. I've never been there. Doubt I'll see any of it. I wanted to see the beach in the daylight. I miss the beach, I grew up at the beach.

I once met some people who were from Missouri, they never saw the ocean before. They stood in the freezing water and stared out at the water. I thought it was weird. They talked about it the rest of the day. Isn't it funny what you think of?

When I finally got up out of bed, I had a pukey taste in my mouth, and felt like I was something that the cat dragged in. I feel like I've been wrestling with the devil all night. My bed blankets look like it, there all twisted up.

I make breakfast. I stocked the kitchen in the tour bus. Pancakes, bacon, eggs, sausage. Canadian bacon. Cause their Canadian. The smell got everyone up. Carl pulled off the road and he ate too. You get tired of eating out all the time, all that greasy food.

Everyone looked like something the cat dragged in, besides me. It was kind of scary.

The guys are all raggedy, unshaven, which they usually are normally, but this is messy. I looked like the old house wife, that thought sends chills up my spine, I never want to look like that. When I'm older, I do right now, I don't care.

When we stop, I put on my skechers shape-ups, and walk around the rest stop parking lot. I also do the DVD's, the Brazilian butt lift, and the Zumba Latin fitness workout. I can do the dance steps outside with my CD playing the music in my ears. Again the guys all watch me. "Why don't you join me," I ask them. "You know some of you guys could use it." They all look down at their guts. When the guys stop looking at me, then I'll start to worry.

Eric joins me, "Hey, how was your sleep, last night?"

"It was good, I was so tired. How about yours?"

"I was tired too, I think I fell asleep in front of the fire."

"You did." I laugh, he looked so cute curled up in a ball in front of the fire.

I wake up the next morning with my throat feeling very dry. I cook breakfast again, it becomes a tickle in the back of my throat. A few hours later I have a slight cough. I'll work it out exercising, probably from being on the beach the night before. It was damp on the beach, the wind blowing the cold water off the ocean.

I feel chilled, and cant get warm. My chest starts to feel heavy and congested. Probably just a cold. I shook so many hands the other night, I'm germaphobic, I usually have the anti-bacterial wipes with me. But I didn't have any with me that night.

We travel to Oklahoma. Cam writes another new song. I read a book. The guys are playing video games on the x-box. I look out at the landscape, farms, cows, horses, tractors, and old cars.

My throat hurts really bad. It hurts more and more as the day goes on. I really feel like crap.

I try all the old remedies. Chicken soup, hot honey tea. Lots of cold pills. Hot shower. Nothing makes me feel better, if it does, its temporary. Sleep, when I'm sick, I usually cant sleep. But this time I zonk out. I cant seem to wake up and when I do, I want to go back to sleep, Cam is watching me, "You okay?" He asks.

"Not really, I feel like crap, I have a cold I guess. I'll be better tomorrow." I curl up in the big comforter off of Cam's bed. How can I be hot one minute, cold the next. I close my eyes, my head hurts too. My mind is racing all over the place. Thoughts race through my head. Stupid thoughts from years ago, things I haven't thought of in years. And have nothing to do with my life now. My head feels dizzy. My nose is runny. I've already used a big box of tissues.

We're almost to Tulsa, and the next arena. Cam is watching me, his forehead is furrowed, he has a worried look on his face. My head feels hot. Cam puts a cool hand on my forehead, "your burning up." I know I can feel it, we have no thermometer to tell me how much I'm burning up.

I stay in bed the rest of the day. No one is in the bus, everyone is at the arena. I'm alone for the whole day, I put the TV on. It blocks out the rushing water sound that's in my head.

There's no show tonight, thank god. I don't think I can move. The crew is setting up the equipment, the band is making the final touches.

I don't have much of an appetite, although soup has been on the menu all day.

My cell phone rings, it was Cam, "How are you feeling?" He asks.

"Lousy," I sniffle.

"Well were going to stay in a hotel tonight, so you can have some peace and quiet."

"Sure, its lonely by myself. Yeah, I know you don't want what I have, right?"

"Yeah, something like that, if any of us have it yet, I'll call you tomorrow. If your to sick, you don't have to do the show, okay, I don't want you to get sicker and I don't want you to worry about it, just get better, okay?"

"Okay, I'll see how I feel, I let you know, thanks Cam."

"Alright feel better, have a good night sleep, bye..." he hangs up, I wanted to talk more, I'm lonely, Cam. I miss you.

"Bye..." I put my phone down.

Gees, I've done everything I can possibly do by myself. There's nothing on TV. With how many channels to choose from, I cant find anything I like. My head hurts to much to even focus on reading a book.

I shiver from the chills that keep racking my body. It hard to breath, it hurts to take a deep breath. I have coughing fits, that wakes me up, when I finally fall asleep.

Its dark outside. I call Eric. I get his voice mail. I guess he's still working. I haven't heard from him all day, this is torture.

I go outside in my PJ's. It uses up all of my energy, just to walk down the stairs and climb back up again, I fall into the chair, gasping for air. I don't think I've ever felt this bad in my life. I had bronchitis once, that was pretty bad.

So I guess I'll stay in the recliner, tonight. It takes a while for my breathing to get back to a slow breath.

Eric calls me back. "Heard your sick."

"Yeah, I am," I wheeze.

"Wow you sound terrible, want me to bring you anything?"

I think for a minute, "Is there a Chinese place around somewhere?"

"I think so, what do you want?"

"I could use some chicken wonton soup, and maybe some shrimp chow mein.."

"Sure I think they deliver, I'll call for you. I'll have them deliver it to me, I'll bring it by." He says.

"Thanks, I'll leave the door open, I keep falling asleep, just come in, okay."

About a half hour later Eric comes with the food. I was just dozing off, and woke with a jolt. Confused where I was, for a second. My head hurts so bad.

Eric knocks lightly, "Come in Eric," I rasp, and start coughing.

He steps in and takes one look at me, his face turns red a little, "Janie you look awful, why didn't Cam take you to the hospital?" He asks. He's mad.

"I'm not that bad, its just a cold or something, I'll be better in a day or two."

"Did he do anything for you, did he give you anything? What did he do for you?" He huffs.

"Calm down, he gave me some pills, and he's gone to a hotel so I can have peace and quiet."

"Peace and quiet," he grunts. "That sounds like he abandoned you."

"Never mind, what did you bring me to eat, and don't get to close, I don't want you to get sick too."

He looks through the cabinets, and finds a plate and coffee mug. Gives me the food, and soup.

The soup feels good going down. He's standing over me, watching me. The same look Cam had on his face.

"You better go Eric, thank you for the food, I don't want you to get sick," I sip the soup some more.

He hesitates in leaving. "I don't want to leave you, Janie."

"I'll be okay, I promise, just check in on me tomorrow."

"I will, let me know if you need anything else, okay, no matter what time, no matter what hour, anything." He runs his hand through his hair, he looks worried. He opens the door and stands there. "Anything!" He says.

"I will. Bye."

"Bye...." he closes the door, and I hear him walk down the stairs slowly.

Poor guy, I know he cares. The soup is soothing going down, I take a steamy hot shower, and eat the chow mein. But everything is only temporary, the throat pain comes back as well as the aching pain in my bones and my head.

After the shower I go to Cam's bed. Why not use it, he's not here. I curl up in all the blankets, lay my head on his pillow. I can smell him all over it. I close my eyes, and fall asleep.

I have vivid nightmares, bizarre to say the least. My hair falling out, my teeth falling out. Cam telling me he hates me and to go away. Leave him alone. Swimming in black water, where I know there are creepy things just below the surface, but I cant see them. Trying to keep my head above the water, trying not to drown.

I wake up drowning in sweat and throw off the covers, I don't remember where I am and panic for an instance, until I turn on the light in the bathroom, oh yeah, Cam's tour bus. His new tour bus.

I bump and flounder my way from the bathroom, back to Cam's bed and fall down in it. I'm so worn out to even roll over and get comfortable. So I stay that way, for the rest of the night, my face smooshed into the pillow. Its gonna leave wrinkles and creases on my face.

Eric calls me to see if I'm still alive. "Yeah barely," I have just about no voice.

"How are you feeling?" He asks me, I can tell he's worried.

"Like crap, I don't think I've ever felt this bad ever."

"That's not good, Janie, is there anything you want, or I can do for you?"

"No, I'm good for now, I still have a little bit of the food you bought me, I'll heat that up, I just want to sleep."

"Are you sure?" He breaths heavily into the phone.

"Yes, just come and get me before the show starts."

"Cam said you don't have to do the show if you don't want to," he says.

"I'll be alright, I still have the rest of the day to get better, I'll be fine."

"Okay, I'll come around nine."

"Okay, thanks, bye."

"Bye..." He breaths into the phone again, and hangs up. I can tell he's not to happy.

I have the rest of the day to get better. Cam never calls me. And that upsets me more than being sick.

It took me a long time, a lot longer than normal to get ready for the show, everything is an effort. It exhausts me to move. I take another steamy shower, I look in the mirror. I have dark circles under my eyes. My nose is red, all the makeup in the world isn't going to help me.

I'm just putting the finishing touches on myself, when Eric knocks on the door, "Use the key," I tell him. He opens the door. He surprised to see me dressed and ready to go.

"Hi," I say.

"Hey, you feeling okay?" He asks, he walks over to me and touches my head. Makes a face.

"Not really, I'm dizzy, my head hurts, and I'm really hot, but yeah just great."

"Then you shouldn't go tonight, I can tell Cam, I should make you stay, Janie, you don't look good at all."

"Thanks...... Have you seen Cam?"

"Yeah, his girlfriend is here, Melissa isn't that her name?"

I freeze, that sinking feeling in the pit of my stomach. I get dizzy and nauseous, and not from being sick either. My back is turned away from Eric, so he cant see my face. Tears well up in my eyes. Don't cry. I tell myself. I sit down on the bed, hiding my face from Eric. I'm trying to put my boots on, I'm having a lot of trouble getting them on.

"Here let me help you," Eric offers, I hold out my foot, he can see I'm frustrated and upset.

"Okay don't get so upset, its just boots," he puts them on my feet and zips the first one up so easily, it makes me look ridiculous. He has no idea just how upset I am that Cam didn't call me today, when he said he would, and that the bitch Melissa is here. And he totally forgets about me, like I don't exist in his life.

He has no idea how much I want Cam, how in love I am with him, how I eat, breath, sleep and dream about Cam everyday, all day. No one has any idea, not even Cam.

Eric zips up the other boot, he's very gentle and very sure about himself. "There," he says, and looks at me with sympathetic eyes. I touch his face with my fingers.

"Thank you," I wheeze and have another coughing fit.

"Janie you don't have to do this, Cam will understand. You look terrible. Your hot. And I don't mean you know sexy hot, will you are, wait... let me start over again," He takes a deep breath, I have to smile at him, he's so cute when he flounders. "You are sexy, your feverish. That's what I meant to say."

I give him another half smile. “That’s okay, Eric, I know what you meant.”

“Look I’m gonna call Cam and tell him your not coming for the show.”

“Noooo.....” I jump up and grab his phone, “I’ll just do the dance, see how I feel, then I’ll leave if I feel really bad, okay, I want to do this, I’ve been cooped up here, all day.”

“Okay, but I’m gonna keep my eyes on you all night.” He says.

“You always do.”

He wraps me in a sweater, even though its warm out, I shiver. It still feels cold to me. My teeth chatter. I clinch my teeth together, to stop them but I still shake. We walk silently to the arena. He’s got his arm around me. By the time we get back stage I have to sit down, I wheeze and cough. It makes my head hurt more.

I completely forget about Melissa, until I see Cam. He barely looks at me, just nods as he acknowledges that I’m here. Wow, that really hurt, like a dagger in my heart. Rob and Matt pass by and nod also. Dale is his usual friendly self and says “Hi, how are you feeling?” He deserves a medal.

Tonight I wont kiss any of them, and make sure I’m not to close to them. Although I would love to infect Rob. Maybe I’ll cough in his face. He’ll hate me for the rest of his life. I laugh at that thought. Dale, I wont be wrapping my arms around him, or kissing him either.

The show starts. I’m not sure if I see Melissa at all. Everything is kind of foggy, I might have walked right passed her, nothing is registering in my head. I might of even bumped into her, I don’t know, I don’t care.

Eric is walking me to the floor and my spot in front of the stage. People near me give me a big space when they hear me cough.

“You don’t have to do this,” he says in my ear.

“Yeah I do.” I say, I hope Melissa sees me. I want her to see me.

CHAPTER 20

Cam doesn't look at me, but for a brief moment, what do I have the mumps or measles, with dots all over my face? He's being so rude to me. So mean, maybe I'll make him sick. He drives the dagger deeper into my heart. His guitar sounds off and so does his singing. Eric helps me up on the stage. I walk across the stage at the first note. I feel better then I have felt all day. I pass Cam, I don't make eye contact with him, but run my hand along his butt. He jumps. Go to Rob, you ass. Matt I usually ignore.

Dale heavy on the drums looks at me between the sweat drops. I get up on the deck with him. The swaying and tossing of my head from side to side, left me dizzy and my equilibrium off balance. My eyesight goes black and I try to grab the rail, I try to grab onto Dale. But the dizziness is to much for my balance. I take one step backwards, and I go down. I'm falling, falling off the deck. I'm not scared, I feel like I'm flying. Dale is the first one to stop playing, cause I don't hear the drums anymore. Cam stops singing, the music stops. I hear Cam say "Will take a short break." I hear booing. Sick puppies fill in, I think.

I'm lying on my stomach, my face smooshed into the floor. The floor is cold. I wish someone would pick me up. People are around me, someone touches my face.

Some one says, "Cam don't move her, she might have broken bones." Someone picked me up off of the cold floor. And their holding me in their arms, I remember the smell, its Cam. He's warm, against my cold, damp skin.

"The paramedics are on their way," someone says. Oh good, then maybe I can get warmed up. Slowly everything turns black, I fade away. I feel nothing, I don't feel, cold or hot, my head doesn't hurt, all the aches are gone, my throat doesn't hurt either. I feel free. And light. I can see the whole stage below me, like I'm in a helicopter riding over the arena. Except there's no noise, its so quiet. I see Eric and Cam, some of the crew, the rest of the band, the paramedics are putting someone on the stretcher.

CAM

I guess I'm feeling guilty. Guilty of the feelings I have for Janie. Melissa came to visit. I didn't know she was coming to visit. Is it possible for someone to love two woman at once? I never told Melissa about Janie.

When I heard Dale suddenly stop playing, I had no idea what happened. Until I saw him jump up from behind his drums, off the drum deck. He disappeared. I knew what happened. Janie wasn't there, it was my worst fear ever, since she started dancing up on the drum deck.

My heart pounded in my chest, I didn't care about the audience, I didn't care that they were booing. Felt like my dinner was going to come up. I dropped my guitar on the floor and ran back stage.

I stopped short when I saw her lying on the floor all twisted up, laying on her stomach I wasn't sure if she was breathing. Dale was touching her face and feeling if she had a pulse, I held my breath, when he nodded yes. I breathed again.

Someone told me not to pick her up. But I had to. I gently pick her up in to my arms, I sit on the floor holding her. She's burning up. Her dress is soaked.

Eric is standing over me, he looks like he going to cry. And then I realize, he loves her too. I hear some commotion, that gets my attention, I look up to see Melissa, looking at me, then at Janie. She looks shocked, and very unhappy. Disbelief in her big brown eyes. I tell Eric to take Janie, I don't want her lying on the cold floor.

The minute I get up off the floor, Melissa takes off. I didn't know which way she went, but its got to be only one way out. We still have a show to finish. People are starting to leave, one of my crew members tell me.

Sick puppies filled in, I owe them big time. I run after Melissa, but can't find her, Rob followed. "Cam we have to finish the show, he grabs my arm to turn me around. "We have to go back."

"I'll be right there," I take one look around outside the building. I don't see her, I'll have to deal with her later. I come back to the stage, they have Janie on the stretcher, and she has oxygen over her nose, and an IV in her arm. Their taking her to the ambulance. I make sure that Eric is going with her.

Her face is wet with sweat and she has dark circles under her eyes. She turned white as a ghost. How can I get through the rest of the night not knowing if she's died or alive? How can I get through the night without her? God if ever I needed a favor its now, I say. Help me get through the night, help Janie, I didn't know she was so sick. Help me with Melissa, I don't know how I'm going to explain this to her, I screwed everything up. I should never have allowed Janie to go on stage. I never called her to find out how she was. Now Melissa saw me holding her.

I'm a compassionate person, I care about my crew members. She has to understand, she knows me better then that, she knows all of my deep dark secrets, well most of them, not about Janie though. She's seen a side of me that no one else has or ever will. So she has to understand.

Rob, Matt and Dale are back on stage and their playing something, I join them. I have to talk to the audience, I apologize for the interruption and tell them that the dancer had an accident, so I hope they understand. Some of the fans come back. I ask them what songs they would like for us to sing. Some one yells out, "Mistake," that's one of Janie's favorite songs. I can sing that. I'll sing it for her. I sing the song like I've never song it before, tears are trying to escape my eyes, luckily I sweat. So no one can tell. Everyone whistles and applauds, when I finish. I tell them I'll sing them a brand new song that we haven't even recorded yet, everyone cheers.

The guys are really good musicians and can follow me with any song. I hoped we made it up to the audience.

I don't know how I made it through the rest of the night, but I did. Its all a blur. It was if I was on auto pilot. I hurried with the last two songs the crowd picked out and played a few lines from the new song. The piros go off, I say goodnight. And I run off stage. Find Melissa first, take care of Melissa first. I search every where for her. I call her on her cell phone.

"What!…. Cam," she answers.

"We have to talk, where are you?"

"I don't know, some room, somewhere, has a soda and snack machine in it." I know where she is.

I run up the stairs two at a time, I know the room she's in. I open the door. She's sitting at one of the tables, in the conference room. She's been crying, I hate that. I hate it when I make someone cry. Even when I was little, it always upset me. Especially when I did it…..

"Melissa," I say to her, she wont look at me. "Melissa," I say again, she turns and looks at me, I've never seen that look on her face before. Its pure hatred. Disbelief, shock, sadness.

"Who is she Cam?"

"She's one of the crew, she's part of the show, she's the new dancer." I tell her.

"Is that all?" I know she doesn't believe me.

"Yeah, that's all, she's been sick, she shouldn't have worked tonight, I was concerned for her."

"Yeah, sure…."

"Babe come on, you know me, I care about everyone." I plead.

"I know you do and that's the problem." She says, with a biting tone.

"Okay listen I have some things to take care of, will talk later okay?"

"Sure, if I'm still here, I'm glad you don't think that this is worth talking about." She says, with that biting tone of hers.

"Stay okay. I love you. You know that. Look at that ring on your finger." I point, to that big rock I gave her.

She looks down at it. It could have been a lump of coal the way she looked at it and made a face.

I call Eric's cell. Have one of the drivers, drive me to the hospital. People try to stop me for autographs, sorry but I have no time for this. I meet Eric in the emergency room.

"I told them I was her brother," he says, "You should say the same. That's the only way they'd let me stay, with her."

He pushes the curtain aside. Janie is in a hospital gown. She has some machines hooked up to her, an IV bag, needles in her arm. Things beeping. It makes me gasp, I guess I hadn't expected all of this. She must be worse than I thought.

The doctor comes in. "Well, well, Cam Konner, big fan," he says and shakes my hand. "She's your sister too?" He smiles as he writes something in her chart.

"Yeah," I say. "Something like that."

"Seems to have a lot of brothers. You two don't look alike. "The doctor says, I know he was teasing us, which I was in no mood for.

"Different fathers," I tell him, god he's a doctor shouldn't he know stuff like that?

"How's Janie?" He looks at her chart again, eyebrows scrunched together.

"We've done tests, were waiting for the results. But from what I can tell, and from the symptoms, she has some kind of a virus. But what kind we don't know yet. From what your brother Eric," and he emphasizes, 'your brother, Eric,' "tells me your in contact with a lot of people. She probably picked up something from one of the fans."

I tried to think, everyone I came in contacted with, so did she, so did the rest of us. Everyone I touched, she touched. But none of us were sick. I racked my brain to remember every face that passed through the line at the meet and greet at our last concert.

Then it hit me like a slap in my face, that guy that was trying to sell her the pictures. He never came over to me or the rest of the band members. He just went to her, seemed infatuated with her, and why not? She's a beautiful woman. When I ordered him away from her, he shot me a poisonous look. He looked feverish, I remember the way his eyes looked. Haunting, deathly. I didn't like the fact that he was so close to her.

I can find out who he is, we have a list of every person that passes our way for all the meet and greets. Everyone has to sign in, they all have tickets.

I call Tim, he's the guy who takes care of all the meet and greets. He should have the list.

He says he remembers the guy, because he was such a pain in the ass. Kept complaining that the line wasn't moving fast enough. He was an arrogant bastard, and annoying, he was bothering Janie, making her feel like she had to buy his pictures. When fans act up you take notice of them, the security guards certainly did. I signaled them to usher the guy out of the room and away from Janie. Eric came and several big guys in the crew, he fought them until they pushed him out the door. And stood guard in front of the door so he wouldn't try to come back in.

Tim found the name and address. "Find me a phone number." I told him. "We don't have much time to write him a letter."

Eric paced the floor, while I sat in the chair by Janie's bed. "Eric can you go down to the cafeteria and get me a cup of coffee?" Any thing to keep him from doing that annoying pacing.

"Uh what, Cam?" He hadn't even heard me.

"Can you get me a cup of coffee? I'll wait for the phone call and for the doctor, go and get yourself one too."

"Oh….. Yeah I guess I can….. I could sure use a drink, not coffee, though." He says. Running his hand through his hair. I would laugh, cause his hair is now a mess, but I'm not in the mood.

"Yeah so can I!" But I gotta have a clear head. "Maybe later, uh?" I say.

"Yeah…. I guess," he rakes his hand through his hair, again. He looks awful, this is really wearing him out. I hadn't realized he cared so much for her. My friends little brother. A grown man in love with a pretty girl. It was bound to happen. Who wouldn't fall in love with Janie.

He left with his hands in his pockets, a worried look across his face.

I watched him leave and get into the elevator. I pulled the chair closer to Janie's bed. I picked up her cold hand, and held it tight in mine, I hoped she could feel me. She was so pale looking, ghostly even. The dark circles under her eyes seemed darker. Her lips were dry and cracked. Those were the lips I so… enjoyed kissing. Soft and warm against mine. I sigh. I gotta stop thinking like this, right now.

I sent Eric away so I could talk privately to her. I wanted to tell her how I felt about her. I wanted to tell her I loved her, just like Eric did. I wanted her to wake up.

I didn't know where to start. I had to hurry before Eric got back. I look out the door to make sure the coast was clear. He wasn't back yet.

"Janie," I whispered her name, I liked the way it always rolled off my tongue. The tongue she would bite, "Janie….. Its me Cam. I'm here with you in the hospital, and so is Eric, I'm so sorry your sick. I didn't know you were so sick, I wouldn't have let you go on tonight. I'm sorry I ignored you, no scratch that, I'm sorry I forgot to call you. It's because Melissa made a surprise visit. Yeah a surprise. I didn't know she was coming. We've been together for a long time, I love her. But I also love you too. Oh man this is so wrong. But I cant help, I cant fight this feeling anymore." I take a long breath. I need to continue. To lay my heart out for her.

"I cant explain it, hell I don't even understand it myself. If I could have more than one wife I'd have both of you. No, that sounds stupid. Scratch that too. Your different than she is.

You challenge me, your so infatuated with me, I think its gone to my head. You put me to the test. I want to be a better, singer, writer, person than I am, you make me feel that way. Your fun to be around, things get exciting. I love when you tease me. The first time I saw you, I thought you were so beautiful, cute. You were trying to get away from me. When I've been so used to people chasing after me, it was refreshing to have it the other way around."

I take a look out the door again, maybe Eric got lost. "Then when you climbed up on stage that first time, and started dancing. It took me a while before I finally recognized you. Then it floored me that you were taking such great lengths to get my attention. I don't think anyone has ever done that before. You dance so sexy, if I didn't have to sing I think my mouth would have been hanging open the whole time. I couldn't get you out of my mind. And now I know that Eric has strong feelings for you. I feel like I have to compete for you. But I really don't have the right, I'm with Melissa. I feel lost, I don't know what to do. Maybe if I knew your real feelings for me, that might help. Please come back to me, Janie. Don't give up. I love you." I kiss her cheek.

CHAPTER 21

CAM

My phone rings, Tim's number comes up on the screen and I almost drop my phone. Tim has the name and phone number of the guy. Eric comes back with the coffee, just as I hang up the phone.

I dial the photographer's number. Someone picks it up on the second ring.

"Hello," she sounds elderly.

"Hello, is this George Smith's house?" I ask.

"Yes, this is his mother, who is this?" She asks.

"My name is Cam Konner, I was interested in some pictures that he took of my band. Is he there?"

She sounded tired, sad. "No, he died three days ago, I just came from his funeral." My blood went cold.

"I'm sorry, I didn't know," I said, "Can I ask you what from?"

"Some kind of a viral infection, the doctors really don't know what kind it was. He traveled a lot..... As a photographer." She says.

"Do you know who his doctor was, I'm sorry to ask you so many questions, but I have a friend who is very sick and we know she came in contact with your son. Any help you can give me, would be greatly appreciated."

"I'm sorry about your friend, and yes I can give you the phone number of the doctor who treated him. Do you have a piece of paper and pen?" She asked.

"Yes, go ahead," I scribble it down, tell her thank you. And hang up. "Eric go find the doctor, I'll call the number she gave me."

He nods and runs out of the room, my hands are shaking, I can barely punch in the numbers. I finally do, after three attempts. The phone rings, a man answers the phone.

"Is this doctor, Miller?" I ask.

"Yes, who is this?" He sounds like he was sleeping.

"My name is Cam Konner, you were treating a patient by the name of George Smith? He passed away about three days ago?" I swallow hard.

"Yes I did, why?"

"Because I have a sick friend who came in contact with him and now she is deathly ill, in the hospital, and I would like you to talk to her doctor, and tell him what you did and what you know about what he had." I sound hysterical, I try to remain calm, breath, I say to myself.

"Yes I can do that," he says.

"Okay wait, my friend went to find the doctor, he should be here in a minute," I get up and walk out in the hall way. To the nurses station. I ask the nurse where the doctor is, he's making his rounds. Did Eric find him yet?

The nurse pages the doctor, just as he's coming around the corner with Eric. I handed him my cell phone. I lean against the wall and sink down to the floor. Eric does the same. This is killing the both of us. I cant take stuff like this, this emotional stuff wipes me out. Neither one of us say anything. Were trying to listen to what the doctor is saying.

"Thanks," he says and comes back around the corner. He sees both of us on the floor, "Come on lets go to Janie's room," he says.

I get up, I feel like an old man. Eric isn't much better. How do men do it when their wives have babies?

The doctor closes the door, Eric is now occupying the chair by the bed. His eyes are red. Big men do cry. I haven't got the energy to cry right now, maybe later. The doctor looks grim.

"We have the test back," he says looking at the chart.

"It's some kind of virus like we thought, but we don't know what kind. It came back inconclusive." He looks at both of us over the rim of his glasses.

"Meaning what?" I ask.

"We don't know, I spoke to the other doctor, and he will send me the guys chart. Perhaps we can figure something out."

"Great….listen Doc we found the guy we think was the carrier, he was a photographer, he probably traveled all over the world, I have his mothers phone number talk to her too, maybe she can tell you where he's been. Maybe he picked something up from another country. Anything, do anything, for her." My voice quivers a bit and Eric looks over at me.

"Good, okay there might be hope yet, we wont give up, have faith." The doctor nods, I give him the mothers number. He leaves me and Eric pondering everything that he just said.

At least it gives us a tiny bit of hope, although it doesn't really feel like it. Right now its all we have.

Eric and I take turns staying up and watching Janie, until morning, in case there is any change.

The crew had packed up and left already for Canada. We'd fly there, once we know that Janie is out of danger. Sleeping in a chair is torture. The nurse brings in a cot to sleep on. We take turns. Janie never moves, never stirs in her sleep, the only thing that moves is the rise and fall of her chest as she takes a rasping breath. They put her in an oxygen tent. To help her breath. The doctor says she isn't in a coma, so why doesn't she wake up?

I want her to wake up, I want her to open her eyes, I want her to look at me. I want to see those pretty green eyes, sparkle the way they do when ever she looks at me. Damn it! I hate this.

I need a shave, I need a bath. I imagine they took all of our stuff with them, including clothes.

Early morning, my phone rings, had a horrible night sleeping. My eyes are glued together. It's Melissa. I take an exhausted sigh. Here we go.

"Where are you, Cam? I waited for you all night, everyone left for Canada." She practically screams.

"Hi, to you to," I say to her, " You don't say hi at least."

"Don't avoid my question, where are you?" She raises the tone in her voice. She's mad.

"At the hospital, with Eric." I close my eyes, and lean my head against the wall.

"Is Eric her boyfriend?" That's the one thing about Melissa, she gets right to the point.

"Yes."

"Oh, okay, well why are you still there, then?" She asks. She makes that little noise, she makes when she's mad.

"Some support, and take care of some bills, Eric is the little brother of one of my friends.

I'm leaving tonight, I'll be in Canada tomorrow. Are you gonna be there?" I ask her.

"Do you want me to be?" She lets out a little puff of air, I know she's exasperated with me.

Which no doubt she probably is.

"Yeah of course I do." Did I sound convincing enough? There's a long silence before she says anything.

"Okay, Cam I guess I'll see you there. Bye."

"Bye." We used to say I love you to each other before we hung up the phone. I guess were not exactly feeling it right now.

Eric is still sleeping in the chair. I check on Janie. The machines are still beeping, monitoring her vital signs. The little heart shape blinks on and off. Her heartbeat. I look at all the numbers, flashing on the machine. It remained at a steady beat.

I wonder if she's in any pain? She has several dark purple bruises from the fall, one on her arm, one on her forehead, on her hands, probably her legs too. A sprained ankle and a sprained wrist. She was probably out before she hit the floor, that's why nothing broke. Two bruised knees. That's gonna be bad for her.

I kiss her forehead and notice the heartbeat increase its beat. Hum..... I do it again. Her heartbeat rises again.

"Janie," I say to her, "Get better, please for me. I need you with me." I look over at Eric to see if he's still sleeping, he's looking at me, with a curious look on his face. I pretend I don't know that he heard what I said to her. He closes his eyes again, maybe he really wasn't awake.

I tell her "I love you, Janie," I watch the machine spike up again, she can hear me. "I'm going for some breakfast, I'll be back soon, Eric is still here with you." I kiss her again. I smile to myself, so that's what I do to her.

I make my way down to the cafeteria, where I smell hot coffee, eggs and bacon, my stomach rumbles. I'll bring breakfast up for Eric. I hope no one recognizes me. I'm pretty messy looking. Scary actually.

JANIE

I float above a bed in a place that looks like a hospital room. There's someone in the bed. There's two men in the room. I float down to get a better look, I'm shocked it looks like me. I get a closer look, it is me. I look deathly pale, with super dark circles under my eyes. I must be pretty sick. The two men look very sad. I look closely at the both of them, oh its Cam and its Eric. They look so sad. Both look like they've been crying. Its me their sad about. I want to tell them I'm right here, don't be sad, I feel fine. But I cant seem to get their attention.

A man in a white jacket comes in. He looks very serious. He's telling them something, only I cant hear what it is, it just sounds like wha wha wha. He must of told them something bad. Not good. Because Cam buries his face in his hands, and Eric walks outside the room and bangs his head against the wall. I followed him, and tell him to "Stop it!" I'm right here, I'm okay. But he doesn't here me, he slides down the wall on to the floor. And buries his head in the crook of his arm. This is so weird, I feel so weird.

Cam is asking the man " how much longer?" How much longer for what? I'm right here, I stand in front of him, I'm here. I'm okay, I'm fine. I jump up and down, and wave my arms. He still cant see me. Am I dead? I don't feel dead. I felt Cam kiss me on the cheek a couple of times.

I need to do something about this before it gets bad. I see this beautiful light..... And I know that on the other side there are people waiting for me. My Dad, my aunt, my grandparents, and my favorite dog, Jack. But I love Cam so much and I love Eric too. I don't want to leave them. If I leave them it will make them even sadder.

The pull towards the light is strong. But I fight it, and say no I'm not ready. I want to get married and have children, I want to grow old with the man that I love. Cant this wait for another fifty years or so?

I made my decision, and like a vacuum, I'm sucked back down into the body that's lying on the bed. I gasp for air and open my eyes. I suck in a big mouthful of air. I have to blink several times to focus.

Cam has his head on the bed. I touch his head with his soft curly hair. I'm very weak, but I just have enough strength to lovingly caress his head.

He puts his hand over my hand and looks up at me. Tears are in his eyes. He says my name.

"Janie," as soft as a loving whisper. "Your back, you came back." He says. "Eric wake up, Janie is awake." He nudges Eric's leg. And pushes what looks like a tent or something out of the way.

Eric jumps up and comes over to my bed. He looks as bad as Cam does. He has a big smile for me.

"Wow you guys look awful," I tell them both, and they both laugh, hysterically.

"It wasn't that funny," I say. My voice is dry and raspy.

"No were laughing cause you alright, you've been very sick." Cam says.

"I remember," I say. "I fell off the drum deck."

Eric left the room and comes back with the man in the white jacket. It's the doctor. "Hello, Janie, I'm Dr. Miller, How do you feel?" He asks me.

"I don't know, okay I guess. Hey my sore throat is gone." I try to move, but I'm very sore.

The doctor wants to examine me. "Doc please, can you give us a minute?" Cam asks him.

"Sure," I'll be outside. He takes the chart and starts writing frantically.

"Janie, how do you feel?" Cam's voice is so sweet and gentle, his hand is on my head.

"I guess I feel okay, better than I remember feeling. I left my body….. I saw the whole thing. I saw you and Eric in the room, and I saw myself in this bed. And you both were sad."

"We were sad, both of us." Eric says.

"I wanted to go with my Dad, and my aunt and my favorite dog, Jack. But I couldn't leave you guys. Cause you both needed me more."

"We do," Eric moves in, and kisses me too. His eyes are red. They both need a shave and a bath.

"Janie," Eric says to me, Cam walks outside the room. "We thought we lost you, you were so sick." He says.

Eric sits on the bed next to me. "We thought you were a gonner," he says.

"Nice Eric," Cam says from outside the door.

"That's okay, I guess I almost was." My throat is dry, "Can I have something to drink? Can I have some water?" Eric hands me a glass of water.

I drink the whole thing down, and want more. He laughs, "it's a good sign," he says, "that you want to drink something."

I try to move and make myself comfortable, I'm so stiff and sore, and notice the bruises on my hands, the sprained wrist. "How'd this happen?" I asked Eric.

"When you fell, off the drum deck, do you remember?"

"I said I remembered, why though?"

"You've been sick, I guess you passed out." He says.

"How many days has it been?' I ask.

"About three, I think we've been here. I don't know, kind of lost track of time."

"Oh, and what about the concerts?"

"Not until tomorrow night, Cam is leaving today."

"Then I gotta go to," I try to move my leg, but I cant, Ouch," I pick up the sheet to look at my leg. I have some kind of metal brace around my knee, the one that I used to slide on. "What's this? Get it off of me, Cam will fire me if I cant dance." I scream.

"Janie, Janie, its okay its suppose to come off before you leave, it was just to keep you knee from moving. It's not in your knee, just on it." Eric reassures me.

"Oh," I breath a sigh of relief, I got really scared they already operated on it.

"Did they want to operate on it?" I ask, touching it gingerly.

"Yes, but we told them what you said, so they just stabilized it. It was all messed up. Its still black and blue, a lovely color of black and blue and some other colors too." He says. You can still see the yellows, purples and greens, under my skin.

Cam has to go, and I'm very disappointed he cant stay anymore, but I know he cant.

He says good-bye to me, gives me a kiss on my forehead, and says he'll call me. Yeah I've heard that one before.

I still have Eric. "You need a bath," I wrinkle my nose at him.

"I do?" He smiles innocently.

"Yes you do and you could use a shave, hair cut and some clean clothes."

"Yes, Mom, what would you like me to do?"

"Go to Walmart and buy some clothes, I need some too. I wore my pink dress? Didn't I ?"

CAM

As much as I want to stay with Janie, I gotta go. The next concert is tomorrow night. I need a shower and a shave, some clean clothes. Besides I have to smooth things over with Melissa, I have to figure out where all this is going.

I need to sort out my feelings, for Janie, for Melissa. Is it just a game, has her attention gone to my head? Who I am, I'm not claiming to be anyone, I'm just a regular guy, who plays in a band. But people make you out to be something more than what you are. I could get any girl I want, I just have to point my finger and they come. Maybe I'm just kidding myself. I'm not that great.

I drink to much, I've been arrested, I used to sell drugs, and still like a little toot now and then. I have a bad temper. And I love woman's breasts, maybe a little bit to much.

I get to the airport, and buy a ticket to Vancouver. I have no luggage, nothing to claim. I have my hoodie over my head, and my sunglasses on, so no one recognizes me. Besides no one expects me to be here now, usually people know when were going to be some place.

I call Melissa, call Rob to tell them I'm on my way. Melissa is curt with me and cuts the phone call short. I'm in hot shit now.

The plane ride should take a couple of hours, so I settle into my seat and close my eyes, I try to sleep. But my legs are long and the seats have no leg room, so its uncomfortable for me. I have to sit sideways and stick my legs in the isle. Which the flight attendant keeps telling me to put my legs behind the seat.

I close my eyes, and my thoughts go back to the hospital with Janie. I should call her. I'm tired, tired of thinking. I'm so relieved that she's better. Will if Eric is the man for her, then he's a good choice. I wouldn't have picked anyone else. He'll take care of her and protect her, keep her safe and most of all love her with a fierceness of a father lion. They look good together too.

He's not a bad looking guy. When she gets better, she'll look like her beautiful self again.

I fall asleep, I must be really tired, because there's always crying or screaming children on a plane, and they always sit near me. But I fell asleep and dream.

Janie and me, married, some how I know that were married. There's lots of children. They look like me, they look like her. Were happy. Melissa is there too. She has children too, lots of them. They look like me. Holy shit.

CHAPTER 22

I wake up in a cold sweat, I don't want any children, Melissa knows that. What is that suppose to mean? Probably sleep deprived and those annoying kids behind me. Triggered that weird dream. The guy across the isle give me an annoyed look, "Sorry, bad dream." I say.

We land, and I run off the plane to a waiting taxi. Tell him the arena, I hope the tour bus is there.

Thank god, all of my clothes and things are here, it takes a while longer for the tour bus to drive here, but its here, its parked in the back of the arena. I shower and shave and feel like I'm human again. Janie's stuff is still here. I wonder if Melissa saw it.

No one is here, it's a strange feeling, almost like deja vu, Janie's things are by the door. Its so weird that she isn't here. I got used to her being here. Like I expect her to walk through the door any minute.

I pick up her bathrobe and smell it. I see her. Standing there in it, she always smiles at me.

There's a new picture of us together, it makes me smile. I don't remember who took it, but we look good together.

The shower I took was the longest one I think I've ever taken, probably no water left. Put on a t-shirt and jeans. Clean clothes are the best feeling in the world, I can think of one other feeling I like…. Rather love. Cant take care of it now…..

I head to the arena. Everyone is busy. The familiar sound, gives me goose bumps. I observe all the activity. Sometimes I have to pinch myself, I've finally made it. This is my life. I used to be one of the fans who stood in the audience at a Motley Crue concert. Now I'm the one on the stage, with an audience coming to my concert.

I walk down the stairs to the main floor. I walk over to the guys, "Hey Cam, you're here," brother Matt slapped me on the back. "Everything is just about finalized for the show tonight." "Good cause I could use a nap." I yawn.

"How's Janie?" Dale asks me. I knew he would be the one to ask, he likes her, unlike my brother and Rob.

"She's better, much better." I say.

"Good," he says, "I'm glad, I was really worried, man, the way she fell off the deck, I thought she broke her neck. It scared the crap out of me."

"Yeah, me too," That horrible feeling crept up my spine, when I stopped short where she laid on the floor. Just thinking about it now, sends shivers up my spine again.

"Okay, so what's up?" I ask.

"Nothing, but we were talking and we'd like to add those two songs we sang at the last concert. And the new one if "its finished."

"No its not finished, I haven't exactly had time to do anything. But we can sing the other songs and I think I'd like to do "Mistake," as a regular on the play list. Janie likes that song…."

I get some raised eyebrows, but no one objects.

Its hard to concentrate on anything the whole day. I tried to work on the new song, but couldn't get passed the first few lines. I find my mind wandering back to Janie.

I wanted to write a song. Something that would sound like it was for any woman, but its for her.

The concert is tonight, I got to get focus. My mind is a maze of cobwebbed thoughts. I hope I can remember the words to the songs.

I made the excuse I was a little jet lagged, and went back to the tour bus. I wanted to be alone. Alone with my favorite guitar, my notebook and pencil. I had a line stuck in my head. A riff. It just popped there, I thought I couldn't concentrate. I wrote the line down. I play a couple of cords. I decided it would be raunchy at first, because after all that's how she danced, and then it would mellow out, and become sweet and romantic. I wanted to put all the raw emotions I felt down on paper. I had so many emotions, I made a list. Guilt was one of them. Guilt my stupid conscience. Guilty for what I haven't done yet.... I crossed that off. This isn't a confessional song.

There was a pain in my ass. I was sitting on my cell phone, I forgot I put it there.

I call Janie. It rang several times before a raspy voice answers.

"Wow, listen to you, your voice still sounds bad," I say.

"Oh hi Cam, I do sound terrible don't I," she laughs, I love when she laughs, even if it is raspy.

"It doesn't hurt though, the doctor said it will go away in a day or two. Did you make it to Canada alright?"

"Uh yeah, it was a long flight, plenty of annoying children on board. Had a weird dream."

"What about?" She asks.

"Cant remember," I lie. It was vivid as if I was there. Its still haunting me.

"Oh, I like to know what you dream of," she teases.

Yeah she's feeling better. "How are you feeling, other than the raspy throat?"

"Much better, I have this stupid brace on my knee, I freaked out because I thought it went through my leg, but its just on the outside. It'll come off when I leave the hospital. I still feel very weak, and need Eric to help me out of bed. I walk a little bit. But other wise I'm good. Oh hang on Eric wants to talk to you."

"Hi, boss," Eric says.

"Hey man, you taken good care of Janie?" I ask him.

"Of course I am. You should see her, she finally has some color to her. Hey is it alright if I stay, until she's ready to leave? I don't want her to be alone." Eric asks me.

"Yeah Eric, I was hoping you would want to stay with her. That's fine, I don't want her to be alone either." I think to myself yeah alone with you.

"Okay thanks, here's Janie."

"Thanks, Cam, I appreciate it. It does get lonely in a hospital. No family to visit, so far from home. How are you feeling?" She asks me. She's been through so much, but yet she's still concerned about me. She's so sweet.

"I'm okay, just a little jet lagged, I think, I got a B 12 shot before I left the hospital and I've been washing my hands like crazy. I feel germaphobic."

"It's a good way to be, I'm like that too, generally. I didn't have any antibacterial wipes with me at the meet and greet, I think we should carry them from now on. I'll use a whole container if I have to." She says.

"Has the doctor found out anything?" I still want to know what the hell that guy had. "You know like what you had or where that guy came from."

"The doctor talked to the mother. He had just came back from Africa on a Safari thing or something for National Geographic. So he apparently was a photographer for all different kinds of things. So he brought something back with him."

"Yeah what a nice present," I say sarcastically, she laughs. "Most likely, he brought you something." I want to tell her I miss her. There's a long silence. "So listen when you feel better, and strong enough, come back to the tour, okay?" I tell her.

"Cam, you want me to come back?" She sounds excited. She coughs. "Sorry, this damn cough wont go away, the doctor said it might take a month or more."

"Yes, I want you back, fans look for you now. We all miss you, and I'm sure the cough has to work its way out of your system, however that works." I'm no doctor, I said it though we all miss her, except I wanted to say I miss her, ME! I miss you!

"I cant wait to come back, I miss….everyone…." She says. Did she want to say something else.

"Good, hey I gotta go get ready for the show, it wont be the same without you. I'll talk to you later, okay."

"Okay," another silence, "Bye Cam."

"Bye Janie," I hung up. Bye Janie, I love you. Will no time to sulk. I didn't realize how fast time has gone by.

Dinner should be arriving soon. I take my guitar with me, notebook and pencil, too. Somehow they make me feel normal, like everything is alright. I need that right now. I feel so out of sorts, I don't even know what's wrong. I guess its Janie, Melissa, me, gees everything.

I want to jot down every idea, thought, feeling, emotion, I have tonight. Everything is important.

This song has to be the best damn song I've ever written.

The concert goes okay. I have to fake being happy, I'm not really feeling it. I should have eliminated the song that Janie dances to. Because it ripped a hole right through my chest. I sang it with such anger, through gritted teeth. My jaw actually hurt afterwards. Rob and Matt, gave me the "what the hell was that?...... Look. Dale was feeling it too, he was beating the drum like he wanted to punch a whole in the sky.

I played like that the whole night, as a matter of fact. I'm not sure why, maybe I'm angry that someone so careless about others, made Janie sick. If your sick, stay at home.

No one deserves to be deathly ill. The night didn't have that excitement or that anticipation, of waiting for her to come out. To see what sexy dress she had on, or the sexy shoes, or the perfume that drives me wild. Without her is was.... Well boring. I tried to get woman to flash me their boobs, there was no takers. I always look forward to her dancing, every time she comes out I see something new. How she tilted her head, or how she smiled seductively at me, or she tried on those different perfumes, everything drives me insane. The way her hips swing from side to side, or the way she struts across the stage to wrap herself around my leg. Like I'm a dance pole.

She didn't care if I was covered in sweat or the way I smelled, or that my clothes were soaking wet from the hot lights. She touched me and ran her fingers across my back, sliding down my leg when the song is over. It was her, just me and her. Whew! I got it bad.

The concert over, I had my bottle of beer, my guitar and note book. I want to be alone and daydream. I have a meet and greet, then I'm free.

People however, had other ideas for me. One being, Melissa. She showed up half way through the concert. When I was done, went back stage, she through herself into my arms, and kissed me.

"Ewe...... your all wet and sweaty," she pushed away from me. Funny she never used to do that.

"Come on Cam, we're going out, everyone is, were going out to eat." Who in the world would be open at this time of night?

"One of the VIP guests, has a restaurant, he's got it open just for us." She says.

"Fine, why not."

"Why are you such a grump?" Melissa asks me.

"Jet lag, I guess. Why?"

"I don't know your acting funny," then as if an idea popped, which it did, in her head, she said. "It's that girl, isn't it? The one that was sick, the one that dances on stage. Isn't it?" She was tapping her tiny shoe on the floor waiting for my answer. Then when I was taking my time answering her, she asked, "Is she alright?"

"Oh yeah, she's better. But that's not what's wrong, I'm tired, that's all, jet lag." I manage a lame smile.

She give me that pout, that melts me, but its not going to, tonight. For some reason she's playing dumb, she's much smarter than that. She wants information, information I'm not going to give her. She's curious about Janie. I don't feel like discussing her right now.

We go to the man's restaurant. It's a nice Italian place, he serves us a ten course meal. Its only the band members and Melissa. It was fabulous, I love Italian. If I was hungry. But I wasn't. This to, was keeping me from my song writing. And this set me in a bad mood. Melissa wouldn't leave me alone, she kept hanging all over me. She touched me a lot, and that isn't her normal way. Talked about who knows what, cause I wasn't listening to her. And irritated the shit out of me.

I had this new song in my head and was scribbling it down on a napkin.

"Whatca writing, Cam?" She tried to see. I wouldn't let her, and crumpled it up. Stuffed it in my pocket.

"Nothing, a new song." I huffed at her.

"Okay……" It went on this way until we left the restaurant.

"Do you want to come to the hotel with me?" She asked.

"No not tonight, I'll see you tomorrow, okay?" I kissed her goodnight. She stood there with her mouth open, because any chance to have sex, I usually don't pass up.

I left in the van.

I crawl into bed, with my guitar and notebook, I have the napkin with the new song on it.

There it was, the best damn song I've ever written, in my entire life. It would make Janie cry. Its so beautiful. Hell it brings me to tears. Its called, "I'm living the moment."

Its raining out. I love to listen to the rain. It has such a soothing effect on me. I love a good thunder storm even better. I'm a people person, I have tons of friends. Famous, musicians, celebrities, non-famous people, friends from my childhood. So my behavior lately was making everyone crazy and confused. I just walk away from everyone when I'm done doing whatever.

I have a lot of things to think about. And I want to concentrate on writing some new songs, especially the one for Janie, tweek it a little bit better. I'll get over it soon.

The thunders rumbles over head. The lightening ignites the sky. My guitar is across my lap, my legs are hanging over the arm of the recliner, Janie would sleep in. Her perfume is on the fabric of the chair, it gives me inspiration, cause the song is about her.

Melissa would be pissed, I've never written a song about her. Although some of the songs I have written have things written in them about us together.

I wonder if its raining in Oklahoma? Janie is still recovering in the hospital.

I think the title of the new song is good, "I'm living the moment," because I am what ever happens between us, for that moment, I'm going to live it, right or wrong, I don't want to miss it. Wonder if she really is the one and not Melissa, then what? So I want to make sure I live every moment like its my last.

The guys come back, to the bus to sleep. Their pretty quiet.

"Hey," I say.

"Hey, Cam, are you feeling alright? Your not getting sick are you?" Rob asks me.

"No, I'm not sick, and yes I'm feeling alright. I've just been busy writing some new songs, I have a whole ton in my head, and while I have my mojoe going I want to work on them. You guys know." I say.

"Yeah, so your alright? You've been blowing everyone off lately. What's your problem? Besides writing songs, you always do that, naw its something else." Rob probes.

"No problem, Rob, I've just been writing that's all, why the inquisition?" He gives me a look of disbelief, he knows I'm lying.

"Believe what you want, Rob, I just want to get them finished, before they fly out of my head."

"Alright, then, goodnight," he says.

Dale taps me on the shoulder, I think he knows. Matt rubs my head, the big brother that he is. He's always got my back. Even if he doesn't agree with what I do.

"Night," he says.

"Night," I say.

A few years ago I was in a relationship, it ended badly. I don't want to make that same mistake again, I want to make sure I make the right choices. Its for the rest of my life. They can think what they want. Dale gives me that goofy smile. He always lightens things up.

Everyone hit's the hay, I go to bed too. Take my guitar and notebook, my brain always works overtime when I try to sleep, I sometimes come up with my best ideas. If I don't write it down I definitely will forget. Nite Janie.

JANIE

You can go home, Janie," Dr. Miller, tells me, he is the specialist they called in for my case.

"I can?" I am so happy and surprised, I had no idea it would be so soon. They finally take off the brace. My knee feels good. The way they've been fussing and pumping me full of drugs. I thought it would be another week or two.

Eric could use a break that's for sure. He looks tired, but he never complains. He even had me laughing at his silly jokes and stories.

He needs a haircut and shave, I'll tease him about it for a long time to come.

He came in after the doctor told me I could leave, he took off the brace, I sat there rubbing my knee. "I'm so glad Janie, cant wait to get back to work. And I'm glad your better, it was tough going there for a bit. When can you leave?" He asks.

"I guess as soon as I get dressed. Only I have no clothes to get dressed in. Except the dress, and its seen better days. Eric your gonna have to go to the store and buy us some clothes."

His face drained of all color, as he looked at me. "What?'

"Clothes for you and me, go to Wal-mart, I'm sure they have everything we need there."

"Like what?" He swallows hard. "I've never bought a woman any clothes before."

"Well its not hard, ask someone there, they'll help you."

"What do I buy?" He asks me. "A shirt, pants, underwear and a bra, socks and a pair of sneakers, for me, and for you a clean shirt, pants and some underwear too."

"I gotta buy you a bra....?" I laugh, his face, the look on his face, he's mortified.

"Underwear, I have to buy you underwear, too?"

I think he's gonna cry. "I'll tell you the size, you just pick it out, they'll be some woman there to help you, don't worry."

"That's what I'm afraid of, that everyone is gonna see me," he cries.

"Please, my dress is dirty, I cant wear it on the plane. Please......" I beg. And give him my best pouty face.

"Oh....... All right, but you owe me big time," he says. I write down the sizes for everything and what I want him to get.

"I already owe you big time," I smile and give him a hug and kiss, hand him the list and pat his butt. Send him on his way. In the mean time I'll take a shower and be ready for my new clean clothes.

I lost some weight, and some muscle mass. I'll have to get back to my workout routine. I still feel weak. The dark circles are just shadows now. I wonder how long its going to take Eric to find clothes, I should have told him to call me if he had a problem. I forgot.

The black and blues are fading as well. In fact the rest and the brace on my knee, kind of fixed it up. I asked the doctor if I could take the brace with me, you know just in case.

The two sprains, are much better and only sting if I twist the wrong way.

I look at the clock, he's been gone for a long time, poor Eric, he's probably sweating and cursing under his breath, trying to find clothes. He'd better come back with clothes for himself too, other wise I'm not sitting with him on the plane.

CHAPTER 23

"Your so funny," Eric says, he's got six big bags.

"What did you buy? The entire store?" He drops the bags on the floor and flops in the chair, closes his eyes and puts his head against the wall. "Never, ever make me do that again." He huffs. "Everyone was looking at me when I was trying to pick out your bra and panties. I was so embarrassed, I had no idea what to buy, so I bought you a whole bunch of stuff." He pushes the bags with his foot in my direction. He's to exhausted to move.

"I've been traumatized," he says, his head in his hand. "I'm exhausted, how do you woman do it?"

"Oh you poor thing," and I kneel down in front of him, take his hands away from his face, and kiss him, he's surprised. "Thank you, you are the best friend any girl could want. I know it was hard for you to do, but you did great. Thank you, you've always got my back." I look through the bags.

"You did buy the whole store, did you buy any clothes for yourself? And you better have."

"Yeah I did," he moans.

"Good go take a shower, I'll get dressed, and then we can leave. Cam said he has two tickets for us at the airport. I want to go, I want to leave,

I want to go back to the tour." I want to go back to Cam. Eric's been so good to me, that I didn't want to hurt his feelings. "And Eric thanks, for being here with me, I don't know what I would have done."

"It was no problem," he says, as he ducks into the bathroom.

While he takes his shower, I pick out something to wear. He picked me out lots of lacey under panties and bras. So this is what he likes. I search the bag for something less frilly, plain undies on the bottom of the bag. The kind my mother would call "Old ladies underwear." The plainer the better, cause that's how I feel, plain right now. No makeup, no sun. A plain white vegetable. T-shirt and jeans, socks and some cheap sneakers. I want my skechers.

I hand Eric his clothes, his hand is sticking out the bathroom door. I pack my dance clothes in one of the bags, its ruined, I'm so upset. It looks like they cut it off of me. And my favorite boots, one of the heels is broken. I must of done that when I fell.

Cam sent us some money and our passports, cause now you need them to enter Canada. I'm getting antsy. I want to leave now. "Hurry up, Eric," I say through the door.

"Almost done, I'm trying to shave, I've never had this much to shave before."

"Do you want some help?"

"If you think you can, sure, the door is open," he says.

I push the door, and then stop, "Are you dressed?"

"A little, not fully, I'm not naked, if that's what you mean."

I push the door all the way, the steam comes out, Eric has soap all over his face, his hair hanging in his eyes. "You need a haircut, too, if I had some scissors I could cut it for you."

"I'll get one when we get to Canada," he's standing in front of the sink, looking at me in the mirror. His face covered in soap.

I take the razor out of his hand, "Here sit down, and I'll see what I can do." He sits down in the chair. And holds up his face towards me.

"Have you ever done this before? He asks me. Eyeing the razor.

"No, not really, except my own legs, does that count?"

"I'm not sure, legs are different than my face." He's keeping his eye on the razor in my hand.

"The only way to find out, is if I do it, so hold still." I hold the razor against his skin at the base of his neck, and hold my breath, I don't want to cut him. I make the first stroke, and look for his reaction. I guess I didn't cut him. I do it again, and then again until I have under his chin finished.

"How is that? I ask him.

"Umph, good, you have a very gentle touch, it feels good, I feel really relaxed. I could go to sleep."

"Well don't fall asleep, cause I want to leave as soon as were done."

"Sure," He leans back and lets me finish with his chin and cheeks. "Do you want me to leave the mustache?"

"No, don't like facial hair, why you want me to look like Cam?" He says sarcastically.

"No, certainly not, your you, Cam does it for his image. He's got to have facial hair, it goes with the rock star thing."

"I guess." he says. I shave off the hair above his lip, he opens his eyes and watches me, cause I'm very close to his face. I bit my bottom lip, when ever I concentrate on something. I have to make several swiped with the razor before I get it all off. "There, all done, you look human again," I tease. I wipe off the excess soap with the towel. And he holds me close, searching my face and looking into my eyes, he's looking at me with such tender emotions, that I want to turn away, because he's starting to embarrass me.

He has his hands on my upper arms, we just look at each other for a long minute. Is there something here. Between us? I feel some kind of electricity, a small spark starting to ignite?

"Um, Eric.... We should get going, I'm finished...." I clear my voice.

"Uh, yeah we should go......." He says. Looking at my lips, and then back to my eyes.

I clean up the bathroom and throw everything out that we don't want to take with us. You cant take razors, and stuff anyway, on the plane. He's still in the bathroom and grabs my wrist, it takes me by surprise and he turns me around to face him. He's not kidding around, he looks serious, he pulls me into his arms, and kisses me. A big giant kiss on the mouth. It wasn't vicious, or rough. It was gentle, it was nice.

"There," he says, "I've been wantin to do that for a long time."

"Oh, well I'm finally glad you got around to it, what took you so long?" I smile up at him.

He still has me in his arms, he's doing that searching thing again. "What are you looking at?" I tease.

"Just your reaction, if your gonna kill me or not." He smiles.
"No, your good," I tap his shoulder.

We pack up the rest of the bags. I sign myself out and give everyone hugs, the nurses and the doctors who took care of me. "Hey how about some free tickets to one of the concerts," some one says.

I wave over my shoulder as we exit the hospital. "I'll see what I can do." I say. There's a taxi waiting for us to take us to the airport. We have tickets, that we can use for any flight, to anywhere in Canada. Will take what ever comes first, even if we have to drive the rest of the way to the arena.

I'm nervous, and excited at the same time, I want to see a tall, curly, dirty blond haired, sky blue eyed, nice ass, even better abs, gorgeous smile, amazing voice guy. And I cant get there fast enough. Its torture not seeing him for a couple of weeks now.

We board the next flight for Vancouver, luckily for us it's a popular destination. So it wasn't long before we had a flight. I call Cam and tell him were abroad the plane we should be there in a couple of hours. He's glad. He'll send a limo for us. He said he wrote several new songs, and cant wait for me to hear them. I am his biggest fan, after all. His voice gives me goose bumps. I try to remain emotionless as I talk to him, Eric is watching me. "Okay, bye Cam, sure, I'll call you when we land, bye." His voice always gave me goose bumps, not that Eric doesn't have a nice voice, he does. He probably can sing too, but I've never heard him. I hide my feelings pretty well sometimes, wonder if Eric has a clue as to the way I feel about Cam. I was always taught not to show people my true feelings, especially if it hurt someone else, I think it would hurt Eric.

Eric has the outside seat, cause he has long legs and the seat doesn't offer to much space. We watch a movie, he's eating some peanuts. I watch him out of the corner of my eye, he eats nice too, he doesn't shove it in his mouth, like most guys do. He can eat though, I've seen him eat half a cow, in one sitting.

The movie is over, it shouldn't be to much longer before we land, I can hardly sit, and get up to use the bathroom. Its so cramped in here, thank god I'm not a big person. I look at myself in the mirror, yuck, how could any man want me, the way I look. I look surprisingly old. I don't want to look anymore. I walk out really unhappy with myself.

"Everything okay? Eric asks me. "You were gone a long time, were almost there."

"Yeah fine," I sit down and look out the window.

"Janie, what's wrong?" He puts his hand on my arm, and tugs so I turn around to look at him.

"I'm sorry Eric, I should be really happy were getting back to the tour and everything, I should be really grateful, I didn't die, and I am, but look at me, I look horrible, I look so old." I cry.

"No you don't, you are beautiful, you've been very sick, you'll get back to your beautiful self again." He pats my arm, trying to reassure me, that what he says is true. Even though I don't feel it.

"I guess, thanks, I don't feel very beautiful, in fact I don't feel beautiful at all. I feel like an old woman." I pout.

"Well, your not, just give yourself some time, you'll see."

I look out the window again, I can see lights below us. I put up the facade that I've always put on when I want to hide my feelings, its true, all my life I've done it. Put on a brave face for everyone and then go home and cry when I'm alone. If I look like some old lady Cam wont want me dancing for him.

"I thought maybe you were nervous about flying?" Eric says. "Is that's what's really bothering you?"

"No, we've almost landed, I was fine about flying, I'll tell you what makes me nervous, right before I get on stage." Now that terrifies me.

"No you aren't, your always so calm, you never show that your nervous."

""Yes, I'm shitting butterflies," he tries to stifle a laugh.

"Shsssssssss, yes I'm always nervous about everything, but once I start the butterflies go away. I focus on what I have to do, besides with the bright lights you cant really see the audience. I focus on the music, anyway." And Cam, my mind adds.

The seatbelt sign goes on and we land at the airport. We find the limo, it shouldn't be long now. I call Cam and tell him we've landed. We're in the limo. I'm closer to you Cam, can you feel me? I'm so obsessed with him, its almost frightening, if he never liked my dancing or sign language, I would still be chasing him all over the country. Did he do this for every obsessed fan? No, so why me? Oh shut up I tell myself, stop analyzing everything all the time.

Eric is quiet as we drive to the arena, I stare out the window. My reflection staring back at me, Eric is asleep. I watch him. He looks so peaceful. And he really is cute, thoughtful, kind, and protective. So why couldn't I love him, Cam is really out of reach, he's with Melissa. And I'll have no one.

Enjoy every moment, enjoy every moment with the people around you, including Eric. I'm being unfair to him. I make a face at my reflection in the window.

Enjoy Cam and yes, Eric too. A big teddy bear. The best guy friend I've always wanted. He would do anything for me, I know he would, to protect me and keep me safe. I don't deserve him. I brush his hair out of his eyes. He opens his eyes. And smiles at me.

"How much longer?" I ask the driver.

"Another hour," he says.

I might as well take a nap too, I still don't have much stamina. I curl up against the door. And close my eyes. I should be happy, I survived a deadly illness, I'm living my fantasy, I have really nice new friends and I have two guys who care about me. I fall asleep. I'll be happy no matter what. No one can see the fantasy world I live in, the things I dream about, the things I think about, the things I dream about with Cam. No one knows what a lunatic I really am, when it comes to Cam. Its funny, do crazy people know that their crazy?

I dream of Cam, his smoldering blue eyes piercing me, burning into me. That's the way that I've caught him looking, at me. Uh….. I cant wait to jump into his arms.

The driver wakes us up, we are here. I always call them arenas. They may not be arenas. They might be pavilions, stadiums, gardens, theaters, colosseums, what ever they are, they are hugemongus.

The driver gives us our bags. Now I realize why people were looking at us. We look like bag people.

There's the brown tour bus. My heart pounds at the sight of it. Cam…..

"Where do you think they are?" Eric asks me.

"Probably asleep, look at the time," It was almost morning. Everyone would be sleeping.

We say goodnight. Eric will go to one of the trucks to sleep. The tour bus is locked. Great. I look under the mat, no key, I don't want to wake them. "Wait Eric, I'll come with you."

We wave back our limo driver, and went to a hotel. We slept until three in the afternoon, I hate that. But when your up all night, that's what you do.

When we get back to the arena, everyone is gone from the tour bus. I drop off the bags of clothes, I'm going to donate them, I never want to see them again, and remind me of what happened. My dress though I'll keep, and I probably can get the boot fixed. I change into my real clothes.

I take a shower, and put on my real clothes, my pink velour pants and jacket, with my tank top. My skechers, my butt feels like jello. I put some make-up on, concealer under my eyes, I even have a rosy color to my face, I look better. Some perfume, brush my teeth. Everything was where I left it in the tour bus, so I guess Melissa wasn't here, cause if I was her I would have thrown everything out.

I eat whatever is left in the fridge. A bowl of cereal. Fix my hair before I leave. Grab a bottle of water. Walk out the door, its still a nice day out. I'm so excited and nervous, who is going to be happy to see me back? Who isn't? I make a bet with myself, I know two people who aren't going to be happy to see me. I make a mental list. I wonder if SHE is here? I didn't see any evidence in the bus that she's here.

Eric is already working, he changed out of his clothes too. As I walk into the arena, I can hear people shouting, hammering, Instruments being tuned. I wait to hear that one voice in the mic, they practice before every concert. I wait for that voice that gives me goose bumps all over my body. I hear his laugh and it stops me. I walk into the darkness of the arena. Follow the sound, as it echo's down the corridors.

All of the arenas are new to me. I usually have no idea where to go. But I follow Cam's voice over the mic, then his laughter.

I hear other familiar voices too, there's always a ton of laughter. No matter how much work there is to do, everyone has a good time. Its one of those Kodak moments. The kind embedded in you memory, forever.

I walk up the ramp and some stairs into the arena. There's so many people here. I stand on the top of the stairs, taking it all in, its good to be back, it feels right. I stand on the landing a long time, watching everyone, I'm trying to pick out one particular person.

Someone stands next to me, "Can I help you?" He asks. "Only authorized personnel are suppose to be here."

I turn to see who is annoying me, its some fat security guard, who's a wanna be cop. I take a slow drink of water, from my water bottle, give him the once over and turn away from him, I'm not even gonna answer him.

He grunts to get my attention. "I said only authorized personal are suppose to be here, not fans."

I toss my hair, and give him a sly smile, "I'm part of the show," I say and walk away from him. But he follows.

"You are?" He questions me.

"Yes I am, now leave me alone." If he touches me I'll deck him. He sees Cam wave to me. "Hum", and I walk towards Cam, this time the guy doesn't follow me. Everyone has tags, you know the one I pretended I had, the first time I bumped into Cam, picking up the garbage.

I walk around the lower part of the arena, I want to start slow with my exercise routine. I still feel very weak. Cam disappears, from view, no one seems to see me, I must be invisible.

I'm getting upset. Did I think they were going to throw a party for me? I'm feeling a little emotional, no one cares if I'm here or not. I cant see Cam. And just as I'm ready to cry, the crowd separated and there he is. Standing there, with a big smile on his face, just for me.

My heart pounds in my chest, I forgot how gorgeous he is. I can see his sky blue eyes from where I'm standing. He has his guitar and notebook in his hands. He's got those jeans on that make his butt look sexy, and sensualizes the sexy way he walks. His hair is curly, the way I love it.

He's talking to Rob, as if he can feel my gaze on him, he turns to look at me again. I swear if I was the fainting type I would have.

My mouth goes dry, and I cant move from the spot I'm standing in. I hiccup twice. And remind myself to breath. He sees me and waves me over. I melt all over the floor, but get myself together enough to walk over to him. My legs are shaking, why am I having such a ridiculous reaction at seeing him? I've seen him a thousand times.

"Janie, you look so good," Cam says as he walks over to meet me. "How are you feeling?"

"I feel good, Cam, a little tired, but good. I was going to exercise." I feel so shy standing next to him. He gives me a big bear hug, and lifts me off the ground. "OH….. Its so good to see you, we've missed you so much." He puts me down. And looks at me. "Don't over do, and your not dancing until you are totally feel up to doing it, okay?" I shake my head up and down.

"I wont Cam, I'm gonna take it easy, I can sign I think, I'm sitting, so it wont use extra energy."

"Good, let me know, if your not up to it, then don't do it, okay?" He insisted." He smiles and pats me on the back.

I could have used a kiss on the cheek. He patted me like I was a puppy. Maybe because everyone was looking at us.

"Hey Janie, you sure look better from the last time I saw you." Dale says. "You're a sight for sore eyes," Dale picks me up and swings me around. He puts me down, "Wow, you look tiny, I think you've shrunk. You know when you fell off the deck, you scared the crap out of me. One minute you were there, and the next you were gone. Boom, flat on the floor. I almost had a heart attack. Cam was really upset too. We thought you were dead." He smiles his sheepishly cute grin at me.

"I know I scared everyone, I'm sorry, But I'm much better now, and I promise it wont ever happen again. And thanks, I wasn't sure if everyone wanted me back." Rob nods, as does Matt. "Of course we did, it wouldn't be the same without you," he gives me a kiss on the cheek and joins Cam, by the equipment. Some of the other crew guys, say Hi, and welcome back. I'm happy with that.

So two who are happy I'm back, and two maybes. Better than I thought at least.

CHAPTER 24

Cam comes back over to me, and whispers in my ear, "I've missed you, I'm glad your back,"

I cant look at him, he's made my head dizzy.

"Janie, look at me," he says. I turn my head to look into his blue eyes. "I mean it, I really have missed you."

He leaves me with my mouth hanging open, "Thanks," I say to him, "I'm glad you wanted me back," with that everyone turns to look at me.

I follow him to the center of the arena were he's finalizing the sound system. "Of course," he says, "I wrote some new songs. One of them I'm going to surprise you with tonight, so hang around okay."

"Sure," I say. I can not get my brain to function, I feel so dumb. Eric, of course sees me and comes over to say Hi, everyone around finally noticed me, and greeted me warmly.

"Don't over do it," Dale yells over his shoulder.

"I wont," I say. Dale is a big health and fitness buff. I think he's probably the one who got Cam to work out on his abs, cause Cam didn't always look hunky, like he does now. Not that he wasn't fit, he's always been thin, but now he's more buffed. And has a six-pack. He can eat anything and never gains weight. How lucky for him.

Dale has bigger muscles though, helps him play the drums, he's got tattoos, and some piercing. He's cool. And I know he has no animosity towards me.

"Take it slow," he says and waves.

I wave back and start to walk around the arena, up and down the stairs. It feels good, my butt feeling like jello and my abs feel like marsh mellow. I look at my arms, I think I've grown wings, cause there's some flabby skin hanging under my arms.

The two sourpusses were cordial enough. Some reception, but I'm not gonna let them bother me, I'm here to stay, I'm not going anywhere, unless Cam tells me to go. I wonder when I get to meet the wives? I'm sure Melissa has informed them of my presence.

I try a few of the dance moves, and put the song into my CD player. My knee feels good too.

I really want to dance tonight, I should just get back into the swing of things, like getting back on the horse, when you fall off.

I think I want to dance tonight, I feel up to it. Incredibly enough. I tell Eric, he's not to happy about it, my worst fear would be to get dizzy and faint or something like what happened the other time. I tell Cam, he isn't to happy either, I ask him if he can slow the song down a little. He says sure, but not to much.

I try on some of my old dresses, I pick the one I first wore and the boots. I'm nervous before the show. I pace back and forth backstage. I drink a lot of water, take vitamins, and eat a lot.

Eric is late, and I'm waiting for him down front and center of the stage. I keep looking for him. The show has already started. And my song is next. He comes running up behind me, "Sorry , I'm late, I couldn't find a clean shirt." He's trying to catch his breath. I roll my eyes at him, "Okay will you're here now, let's go." I always have a jacket on to cover the dress. Most are dressed in jeans and tees. So someone in a shiny dress would seem odd.

Cam spots me, I wave that I'm ready. Eric waves too, that's the signal. Cam hit's the first note and Eric lifts me up. Cam is playing slower. Singing every word with a definite purpose. Its to slow, and I motion to him to speed it up a little. I can keep up, I feel energized. I hadn't really thought about Dale's deck. When he starts banging the drums harder, I have second thoughts about climbing up there. But I'm not dizzy and I'm not sick.

I unzip my boots and pull them off. The crowd roars, they must think it's a striptease. I go up to Dale and do my little dance. I hang onto him a little more than I normally do. I don't think he minds, though. He always enjoys me holding onto him. I climb down. I pick up my boots and swing them over my shoulder as I walk over to Cam for the end of the song. He's got a smirk, just at the corner of his lips. I drop the boots on the floor and slide down Cam's right side, down his leg onto the floor. I'm out of breath more than usual, but that's okay, I finished the dance. Cam grabs my fingers, and entwines his with mine. I look up at him, and he smile down at me. He helps me up. "You did it," he says, "Nice job, hang around," he whispers, "I'm singing that new song, you'll want to hear it."

"What's your name?" He asks.

"Janie," I say. He smiles, was he expecting me to say Melissa?

"Let's here it for Janie." He says into the mic. I dive off the stage into Eric's waiting arms. We rush backstage.

"You were great," Eric says to me as we run backstage. "I think it was even better then, all the other times, I like the slow part."

"It was to slow," I say out of breath. I cough.

Eric gives me a concerned look, "the doctor said the cough would linger for a month or so, I'm okay, stop looking at me like that."

"Like what? I just don't want anything else to happen to you, that's all….." He trails off.

"I'm sorry Eric, I didn't mean to…… I know you care." He nods.

"I gotta go, I'll see you later." He squeezes my hand and runs back to work.

"Bye," I say.

I have to change my clothes, I'm gonna do the sign songs too. The tone of the concerts change, to a more slower pace, the stools are out and their sitting on them, Cam is talking to the audience. Telling them about "a crew member, that they almost lost. She's a big part of the show and a valued member, she would be sorely missed if anything happened to her." I realize he's talking about me. I swallow hard, and try to wipe the tears that are trying to escape my eyes.

He tells them it's a brand new song and it hasn't been recorded yet, there the first to hear it. He wrote it for someone special. The two guitars play together, one an octave or two above the other.

Rob is strumming his guitar to match Cam's. It's amazing, how they can mimic each other's every move.

I sign the two songs I usually do, I didn't forget them, and didn't miss a beat. Cam tells me to stay, and winks at me, it's the new song.

I stay on the stool I was sitting on, the one next to Cam, he starts to play along with Rob. He turns to face me, and starts to sing. The music is beautiful, romantic, his voice is hypnotic as he sings the new song. He's completely focused on me, and its making me feel uncomfortable, embarrassed even, I try not to fidget, in my seat. I focus on Cam's voice, and watch his fingers glide over the strings as this incredible song comes out of his mouth. My hands are folded over my lap, and I put one of my hands over my heart. The song is making my heart beat faster, is he singing about me, it could be any woman, or is it Melissa?

The last cord is played, and the strings vibrate the last notes. It echoes around the arena, for just one moment the audience is silent. Cam lays his guitar across his lap, smiles at me. I mouth to him, I loved it. My eyes are misty and I have to blink several times to clear them, then the audience roars their approval. His song has left me breathless.

"I hope you liked it? Cam says to the audience, looks at me, "Did you like it Janie?"

"I loved it, Cam." He says thanks to the audience. The stools are taken away, and the tone of the concert changes again to their more raunchier venue.

I once read a book, cant remember the name, cant remember who wrote it, but it was about angels. I remember it, because it came to my mind when Cam was singing this beautiful song. The author wrote, that he believes that angels write the songs that we humans write. They give us the songs, whether its through a dream, or a thought or whatever gives you the idea. They sit in a white room, several of them, with their white wings, and white robes, sitting at tables with quilled pens, writing these beautiful songs. That's where I believe Cam gets his beautiful words and music from.

Cam walks off the stage, for a quick break, usually he changes his shirt. He grabs my arm, "Did you really like it?" He asks me. He wipes the sweat off of his face.

"I said I loved it, it was the most beautiful song I've ever heard, even more than your other songs."

"Good," he says.

"Did you write it for Melissa?" I ask him.

"NO," he says a little annoyed, "I wrote it for someone else. Janie I wrote it for you." He takes a drink of water and runs back out on stage to finish the show.

"Oh," I say. I hoped he had written it for me. I had no idea that he actually did.

I head for the food and something to drink, I'm still so thirsty, and hungrier than I used to be. Dehydrated, and I didn't eat for a couple of days in the hospital. So I guess I'm making up for it.

The after party. Its really just the crew. The show went good. At least what I did went well. I didn't fall or faint, or make an ass of myself.

I shove a piece of cake in my mouth, when one of the crew guys ask me to go find Cam. He wants to know what to do with his guitars, or some stupid thing, that I have no interest in. "Why are you asking me, go do it yourself." I tell him. Trying to swallow the piece of cake, I just shoved in my mouth.

"Yeah sure, where is he?" He asks.

"Probably in the dressing room." So I head that way, instead, I am curious where he disappeared to. He usually eating most of the food. For a skinny guy he can eat.

I open the door to his dressing room, I hear the water running, I guess he's taking a shower.

The steam is coming out of the bathroom. "Cam?" I call. No answer, I walk in, "Cam," I call again. He cant hear me.

"Cam, are you in there? It's me Janie, one of the crew guys is looking for you. He wants to know what to do with your new guitar? I guess… sounds a little suspicious to me." I say.

"Cam, are you in there?" I tap on the curtain, to make it move. Still nothing. That's strange.

He's not answering me, what should I do? I pull the curtain just a bit so I can look in.

"CAM?" He's laying on the shower floor. I see his foot, he's lying on his side. I look in further, his head is up against the wall, the water falling over his face. His eyes are closed, he looks like he passed out.

"Cam?" I say louder, he doesn't move. I turn off the water. I get wet. I don't look at his private parts, of course not, I'm not that kind of girl. Yeah right…. But I put a towel over him, anyway. "Cam," I push him a little, then I shake him, I put my head on his chest to hear if he's breathing. He is, I breath a sigh of relief, okay then what the hell is wrong with him. I'm getting worried, I guess I should go get someone.

He doesn't do drugs, at least I don't think so. He drinks a little to much sometimes. But I don't think he had enough time tonight. He doesn't even smell like alcohol.

"Cam, oh my god, would you wake up, what's wrong with you? I gotta go get help." Maybe he slipped and hit his head.

I check his head for a bump or blood, but find nothing. I put some more towels over him to keep him warm. I try to pick him up, but I cant move him. I'm getting really upset now. I'm almost crying, that's what I do when I get upset and feel that things are out of my control. I bend down to wrap the towels around him better, "I'm going for help," I tell him just incase he can hear me.

He grabs me, scares the shit out of me. He gets me soaking wet, I'm drenched now. "I've got you," he kisses me.

"Oh you..... How could you do that to me, that was so mean. I really thought you were hurt, or sick, that was a really nasty trick to play on me. You really scared me...... Now I feel nauseous. Thanks a lot." I put my hand on my stomach, to steady the butterflies.

He's laughing, "It's not funny," I cry.

"Yes it is, you saw me naked."

"No I didn't, and its not like I haven't seen you naked before. And I didn't see anything anyway, I wasn't looking." I turn my back on him, with my arms folded across my chest. He can be infuriating sometimes.

"Yes you did, liar." He laughs again.

No one calls me a liar. I walk over to the shower, he's still lying on the floor laughing. "I'm glad your having so much fun at my expense," I say to him and turn on the cold water.

"HEY," he gets up.

"How was that?" I ask, " Was that good for you?"

He smiles, a very devilish smile, "Well, yes it was," and charges out of the shower after me. I'm not quick enough. Wet jeans feel yucky.

He's got his arms wrapped around me. The front of him is pressed against my back, his head is on my shoulder, he's got me in a big bear hug and I cant get free. Although I'm really not trying to.

"Did you like the song I wrote for you?" He whispers in my ear, his breath tickles my ear.

"I told you, yes, Cam, you told me you wrote it for me, thank you, it was so beautiful. Why do you keep asking me?" My head is leaning back on his shoulder. His arms wrapped tightly around me. I never want him to let me go.

"Because I want to make sure, you know it was for you and no one else, no other woman, not even Melissa." He breath is hot on my neck. Sending goose bumps all over me.

"It was the most beautiful song I have ever heard in the world, where do you come up with this stuff?" I ask him.

"I had inspiration, it just comes to me in a big giant wave of emotion." He nuzzles my neck. He's loosened his hug on me, but hasn't let me go.

"You gave me the words and the music, you were in my head when I wrote it, you were in my heart….." I shudder at his words. He is smooth isn't he?

"Turn around, Janie," he says.

"Cam you have no clothes on." I turn around in his arms to face him. He did manage to wrap one of the towel around his waist. But the rest of him is naked. He has very little hair on his chest, I hate hairy men. They remind me of monkeys. I unwillingly roam his body with my eyes. Didn't mean to do it, but I cant help myself. His six-pack is staring me in the eyes, and so is he. I put my hands on his chest, my wet clothes clinging to me, are pressed against him. I can feel every part of him.

"Cam," I say very low, "What are you doing? I mean your with Melissa right? This is so…… wrong and you know it."

"No, it's like the song said, "I'm living the moment, and the moment is with you." He pulls me tight against him. His arms around my back pulling me closer. I'm trying, but not really that hard to push him away. I have to make it look like I'm at least trying to fight him.

My hands are touching him, roaming his chest, every curve, every muscle I feel under my hand quivers under my touch. I love the reaction I make him have. The same he does to me.

He lets out a moan, "Cam?" He kisses my neck, then my lips, the kind of kiss where your lips are glued together. And your kissing each other at every angle, trying to feel them, taste them, become one with them. I have his bottom lip, between my teeth and run my tongue a long his lip.

He laughs. Its one of my favorite things to do, when I'm kissing a guy. The feeling makes me dizzy and breathless and crazy.

He moves back down to my neck and my shoulder. I keep having this sense of deja vu, every time we end up doing this.

"Your shaking," he says. "Wet clothes?" I shake my head no.

No not really, its you. I say to myself. You make me shake all over. All the time. When ever you look at me, when ever you say my name, when ever you touch me, when ever you are just here.

"Listen, I gotta go, their waiting for an answer about your guitar, their gonna start looking for me. And you know who will be leading the pack." Before he lets me go, he kisses my neck again. I step out of his arms. Turn for the door.

"Okay," he says. And gives me that smile, that makes me dizzy.

CAM

Janie didn't know I set the whole thing up. I guess I scared her. I want to be alone with her. I want her all to myself, just me and her. Not a big audience of thousands of fans, not the crew, or the band members. Not Eric.

JANIE

I walk back to the crew member who started this whole thing. I never did get an answer from Cam about his new guitar. I give the guy a real dirty look, "Cam says to do what you usually do with his guitars." I tell him and walk away, with the guy looking flustered by my attitude. Cam told him to do it. I know that.

Cam really had me scared. I should have thrown up all over him, that would have taught him not to play mean tricks on me like that. And that look on his face, when he gets that look, it scares me even more, cause I know what that look means. That animal attraction thing that goes on between us. Its not what I want all the time with him, cant it just be a normal physical thing. Not some over zealous animal lusting, ferocious wrestle with you, knock down drag out kind of thing. We never have a chance, just to be gentle, exploring each other. Maybe its just never meant to be.

CHAPTER 25

Why do people do such horrible things? Its something I've always asked myself. Why are some people, more evil than others? Why do people want to hurt others?

Ten years ago a very good friend of Cams was shot to death, by a so called fan, while on stage performing at a concert.

Just shot dead, while playing the guitar. People saw him with the gun, they saw him aim and shoot. Didn't anyone try to stop him? He was some kind of military man, a man who was trained by our government to shoot a gun and kill people. I don't know if anyone tried to stop him, I don't know if anyone tackled him after he fired.

In fact I really don't remember hearing about it. I guess I wasn't into that kind of music. The heavy metal, head banging stuff. I'm sure it was on the news.

So when I started going to concerts, I was a little shocked about how little security there was in the arenas. They really don't search you, they only checked my pocketbook, not my jacket, not my pockets. They didn't search my personal body. I could have hidden a gun anywhere on my person.

I would have followed Cam anywhere, in fact I was planning on it, I would have become a serious stalker.

Our next stop was Alberta, Canada. The guys can see their families. Is Cam going to visit Melissa? Or is she going to show up at the concert? I cant stop him, and I don't think I'd try to, he might resent me for trying to do that.

I guess I'll hang out with Eric. He wants to. "How about dinner tonight, a movie or something?" He asked me.

"Dinner sounds nice, how about bowling or ice skating?" I suggested.

"Oh yeah, ice skating, well I don't do ice skating, but I do bowl." He says.

"Good, bowling it is." I say. "I don't want to sit, I want to move, I need to move," I tell him.

After we get to Alberta, everyone goes their separate ways. Eric and I go to dinner. We have a nice casual dinner together. Find a bowling alley to play a couple of games. I'm not the greatest bowler, but I do strike out a couple of times, Eric wins of course, hey I let him.

We go back to the arena, its like were almost the only ones left. No one is in the tour bus. Everyone's gone. I have an empty feeling, because Cam isn't here, but then it quickly passes.

I don't live in Canada, like most of them do, even Eric lives in Canada. Why didn't he go home to? I ask him, he says he wanted to say here with me.

It is late, Eric tells me he wants to meet some friends at a bar, did I want to come? I say no. I hate bars, stale cigarette smoke, stale beer, and cheap perfume isn't my idea of a good time. So I tell him no and go and have a good time.

When he leaves, I look around the bus to find something to do. I'm bored. I've been cooped up in a hospital for weeks, I don't want to stay inside any more. There's nothing on TV.

It's pretty lonely with out the guys. Even Rob and Matt. I decide to take a run. Around the parking lot, its pretty big, probably a mile around. A couple of times, I run around it, I run until I'm out of breath and feel exhausted, that's how bored I am. It feels good to exercise, exhilarating in fact. But I'm still alone.

Eric is probably drinking to much. I have no interest in that. He was meeting some old friends. I hadn't even thought if it involve any woman.

So I'll make use of my down time, like I hadn't just had weeks of down time, I take a hot shower and pamper myself. I find a good old movie on TV, make myself a snack and stretch out on the couch. I still cant sit for to long, I feel antsy. I could drive the bus around the lot. Even Carl, the driver is gone.

So I try to sit and watch the movie. I switch seats, and swivel around in it. Looking at everything. The bus has six bunk beds, the guys have their stuff scattered around. Cam left his guitar and notebook, I'm surprised he forgot it, he never goes anywhere with out it.

I'm not usually a nosy person, when it comes to Cam I guess I am. I'm curious about all the other new songs Cam said he wrote.

I pick up the book and open it. It has doodling in it, I didn't think he was a doodler. The book is well used and worn, he could use a new book. Maybe I'll get him a nice leather one for his birthday.

I open it to the first page, the ones that are already on CDs are written here. The new ones are in the back of the book. Scribbling words are all over the pages, sideways, across, every space on each page is full. It tells me how his mind works. He's got a lot on his brain.

Lines written and crossed out. His thought process is complicated. He definitely writes the naughtiest songs he can think of. Without being censored. That's why I first loved his music. That's why people love his music. I turn the pages and read every single word he writes. I think how unfair it is that someone can come up with such beautiful songs. He's a story teller. Does he ever have a hard time coming up with a song? Or the right words? He picks a subject and runs with it.

Each song is dated. Some as far back as 2003. I turn the pages until I get to the new ones.

I read each song. Here's the song he sang last night. It says, "to Janie, thanks for the inspiration, for the beautiful person that you are, for making me want to be a better person. Who has the sexiest walk, the slamming body that every guy dreams of, the one that I want my body all over."

Holy shit Cam, I say. You wrote this so everyone can see this. The next page is a very dirty little song, its not finished, I wonder why?

Wow, can you be so deprived? No wonder he's been chasing me. He should be with Melissa now. I frown, that thought doesn't make me feel any better. I can just picture the two of them together, yuck. It gives me a lousy taste in my mouth.

I get depressed thinking about it. Cam and her, her and Cam. I feel sick. Their probably doing it right now. Ugh. Don't think about it. I read the next four songs. The one he wrote for me was the best. He's so talented, how does one acquire such talent? Are you born with it? Or do you develop it, or learn it, what? Cause I have none. Does it grow in you as you grow older. Does he know how special he is to his fans, to me?

On the last page is a letter. It doesn't say who its too, the words are beautiful as he pours his heart out. Its very touching, and I now feel I've invaded his privacy. But I want to know everything about Cam. How he thinks, what he thinks of. He cares so deeply about someone, probably Melissa. I close the book and put it back where I found it. Now I'm really depressed. I'm sick of Melissa, and I haven't officially met her, yet. As my real self, Janie. I met her as the fill in house keeper, Joan Collins.

I'm so glad I'm watching "The Notebook," the movie that makes me ball my eyes out. I feel like a good cry now, see that's what I get for being nosy.

I just ball my eyes out and make myself tired. My eyes are red and swollen. Reminder to self don't watch "The Notebook," anymore.

There's a knock on the door, which makes me jump, cause I wasn't expecting anyone. I did lock the door, didn't I? Who in the world?

"Who is it?" I ask through the door.

"It's me, Eric," he says, "Can I come in?"

"Yeah sure, hang on," I unlock the door and open it, the first thing I notice is how tousled his hair is. He's standing at the bottom of the stairs, and looks up at me. He's had to much to drink. He has a very silly grin on his face.

"What have you been up to?" I ask him, I'm trying to hide the smile that's slowly creeping onto my face. He looks so cute.

"Can I come in?" He slurs. I step aside, so he can get in the door, he's wobbly, way to much to drink.

"How did you get here?" I ask him.

"Friend drove me back, I couldn't drive," he says, "Look at me."

He rakes his fingers through his messed up hair and looks around the bus. "Sit down," I tell him.

"Hey I thought you could use some company, looks like I was right." He smiles that impish grin again.

He looks up at me, and notices my eyes, his face changes from happy to concerned. "You've been crying, why? What's wrong?" He has me by the shoulders, and I'm trying to hide my face from him, not unless I have a legitimate reason to cry I don't want anyone to know.

"Its nothing," I laugh, "Just watching a stupid movie, that makes me cry, that's all."

"Is that all?" He's not convinced.

"Yes that's all, I promise." He gathers me in his arms, and gives me a big bear hug, he smells like beer and cigarettes, but he still smells like Eric.

"Sometimes everyone needs a hug," he says as he squeezes me tighter.

I have my arms around his waist, he's taller than me and my head just fits into the crook of his shoulder. It's nice. Really nice, he's warm and strong. And he cares about me. I want him to hold me forever.

He kisses the top of my head. I want him to kiss more of me. Its funny, but I really want him to kiss me.

I turn my face up to look at his. I'm here alone, with no one, everyone in the crew has a someone, except me, I'm angry with Cam, he's probably doing it with Melissa right now. How he toys with me, and leads me to believe that he wants me. And here Eric is, wanting me, and only me. He doesn't toy with me, he doesn't play with my emotions.

He looks down at me, I still have my face tilted up to him, he's not sure what to do next. He puts his lips on mine, very gentle, very soft. Like he's not sure if I want him to kiss me. I don't pull away, and I suck him in.

I'm pulling him into me. He can feel that. If I pull any harder I'll be standing behind him.

I wrap one of my legs around his, I put my hands on his butt. That makes him kiss me even harder. He puts both of his hands on my butt to and holds me there.

I start to pull off his t-shirt, he drops my robe. If I knew I was having company, I would have worn something a little more sexier, instead I have on a plain white cotton nightgown.

I throw the shirt wherever. He's got a nice rock hard body. Muscles all over and a smooth hairless chest, damn. I rub my hands up and down his bare chest.

"Nice nightgown," he teases. He pulls it off over my head, he smiles when he looks at me. I will not be shy, I have a nice body too. Shapely, toned, and hot. He likes what he sees, and they are spectacular, pink, soft and they fit nicely in his hands. I hate big boobs, just like the word says, boobs.

I like my perky little ones. I undo his pants, they fall to the floor. He kicks off his shoes and the pants fly too. I hear change and keys drop out of his pants pockets. I take his hand. I turn off the lights and the TV. I walk him….. YES…..back to Cam's bedroom.

Cam's big bed, Cam's room, Cam's big bed that he sleeps in. One time with me. I close the door. There's some candles on the head board shelf of the bed I light them, it gives a nice romantic glow to the room. Cam never light them when I was here.

I push him on the bed, and he falls without a fight. I jump on top of him, we roll all over the bed, good get our scent all over the sheets, and I'm sending this out to you Cam, I hope you can feel this. I keep repeating it in my mind, sending this feeling of wanting, of desire, of passion, of incredible sex. I hope you feel this Cam. Like a litany, in my head, repeating it over and over again.

Its everything Cam tried to do, but never happened. Its passionate, its animalistic, wild, ecstasy. I think we even invented some knew things. It lasts for 2 ½ hours. The touching, the exploring, the sheer pleasure of Eric all over me. I know it was 2 ½ hours cause I looked at the clock. We touch every inch of each other, we click together like two lego's. Like we belong together.

"I love to hear the sound you make the minute your done," he whispers in my ear.

"Your quoting a line from one of Cam's songs," I whisper back.

"I know," he laughs. "It's Cam's bed, isn't it?"

"It is," I laugh. "He'll be able to smell us on the sheets, wont that piss him off?"

"Yeah he'll have a shit fit for sure." Eric laughs.

Eric stays the night, were wrapped in each others arms all night. It's a wonderful feeling to wake up in someone's arms in the morning. I'm sure Cam is lying in Melissa's arms too. I smile to myself. We fall asleep. I have no idea when anyone is coming back.

I wake up first, because I hear some noise out in the living room part of the bus, at first I'm not sure if I'm just imagining the sound, but then someone opens the bedroom door. I lay very still. Eric is still sound asleep. Sleeping off a night of drinking and sex.

The floor creaks, and someone walks over to the bed, I know who it is, I don't have to open my eyes to see who it is. I can smell him, his aftershave, its Cam. Surprise!………. I hear him say something under his breath. He grabs some clothes out of the dresser, he's very quiet. I hope I look really cute lying in Eric's arms. I hope Cam is jealous. Then the thought pops into my head, I hope he doesn't fire us.

He takes one long look at us again, then closes the door. I feel really smug, that he saw us together in his bed. But then a few minutes later, I'm regretting what I've done. We should have left earlier. Then I'm trying to rationalize this, one way or the other. I have a right to be loved, a right to love someone. Its not exclusively just for Cam.

Everyone has someone, in this group of people, everyone, whether it's a girlfriend, or a wife, or whatever, Eric and I have no one.

So if Cam thinks this is wrong, well I've got something to say about it.

Eric is adorable, he attracts the looks from girls every night. But he wants me.

So my smugness wears off. And now I'm scared to face Cam. I told Eric, that he stopped in. I've hurt him. I'll just pretend I didn't know he was there, that he saw us together in his bed. If he wants to confront me, than he can.

Its quiet outside, so I guess everyone went to the arena, its late morning. I get up and look out the window I see them headed for the arena. I wake Eric, "Hey good morning," he says. He holds open his arms and I jump back into bed in his arms. We lay there for a while.

"Its not morning, you know, it's late morning."

"Oh crap, I gotta get to work," he gets up to quick, "whoa," he says, "the room is swaying. Oh…. My head." He kisses me, I pull him back for another kiss.

"I'll see you later, okay, it was really nice." He smiles. "I need some aspirins."

"I have some," I give him two. "I feel like the cat that ate the canary, Eric."

"Yeah, me too, thanks for a fantastic night."

"Yeah it was," I say.

"Oh and Eric," he stops at the door, "Cam knows."

"Oh great," he says, he picked up his change and his keys, whatever else fell out of his pants pockets.

I get dressed. Its late, but there's plenty of time to get ready for tonight's show. I want to run, and run far. I run to the arena, everyone is working. The lights, sound check, instruments.

I stroll in. Everyone looks at me when I walk in, what? What do I have a big red letter across my chest. I try to act nonchalant, but I'm a mess inside.

Eric comes up to me. "Cam, just fired me," he says, out of breath. He must of ran over to me.

"What?"

"Yeah, he just told me, I think your next." He has his hands on his knees, bent over at the waist trying to catch his breath.

"Oh really, hang on, I'll go talk to him."

I find Cam, playing his guitar. I stop and watch him, I want to know if I can see if he's mad. I cant tell. I walk over to him and stand in front of him. He ignores me.

He looks at me, a really nasty hard stone face.

"Yeah, what is it?" He says curtly.

"Please don't fire Eric, please." I beg.

"Why not?" He raises his voice and everyone looks at us.

"Can we go talk somewhere privately, please?"

"Sure," he puts his guitar down. He has his hands in his jeans pockets, I bet he really wants to put them around my neck.

We find a quiet place to talk, outside the arena, in the parking lot.

"Why did you fire, Eric?" I ask him again.

"I saw the two of you in my bed, together, IN MY BED, how the hell do you think I feel?"

"I'm sorry but the bunk beds aren't big enough. I was lonely…… he was lonely, you know how it is, one thing leads to another."

"Yeah, but you were in MY BED," he yells. That echoes all over the place, I'm sure everyone heard that.

"I was lonely," I say again. "I have no family here, I have no boyfriend, or husband, I have no one, everyone had someone last night, even you, weren't you with Melissa? Having sex all night long. You're the only one who's allowed too? It wasn't planned, I was alone for most of the day and night. Eric went to a bar with friends. He came back drunk. I was by myself all day. No one to talk to, nothing to do." I yell back at him, " I missed you……." I say very low. I fold my arms across my chest and turn the other way. I don't want him to see the tears that are rolling down my face. I hate it when I cry, especially when I'm trying to be tough. And defensive.

He didn't say anything. I turn back to look at him, his blue eyes are staring off somewhere far away.

"Cam," I say softly to him. "Please give Eric his job back, I'll leave, if you want me to."

"NO...... don't leave. Tell Eric he can stay. I owe it to his brother. Next time get a room, and not mine, okay. And I missed you too. But I have to go to Melissa. We've been together for a long time, I just cant leave her, I cant just tell her no. I don't want to hurt her." He looks off again. Yeah I know, I've heard this before.

CHAPTER 26

"But you did sleep with her and spend the night with her in her bed, right? But it was okay for you, but not for me? What are you, my father?" I fold my arms across my chest and turn my back on him, again.

"No, I don't know.... Look can we discuss this later, we have a show to do." He says.

"Yeah sure, you're the boss." I say.

Well that went no where, other than getting Eric back his job and me not losing mine. I find Eric. "You have your job back."

"Thanks," he says, "Is Cam mad?"

"Yeah, pissed off that we were in his bed, I have to talk to him later," I get a quirky smile from Eric and he goes on his merry way. Nothing ever bothers that guy.

I'm going to have an angry dance tonight, I can feel it coming on. Cam changed the order of the songs, again, so my song is in the middle of the show.

I go down to the front of the stage, my usual place to stand, I'm there a little earlier than I need to be. Eric always following behind me.

We don't really say anything to each other about last night, the only acknowledgement is a shy smile passed between us.

Everything happened in slow motion, and all at once.

The crowd was packed in close to the stage. People crowd surfing, lifting people up and passing them over their heads. The security guards grab them when they come to the front. Right before they get to the stage. Its cool until someone decides they don't want to lift you along. Then they drop you to the floor.

Out of all the people I had to be standing next to, it has to be the one who pulls out the gun. My first reaction was, it didn't register that it was a gun, that it didn't belong at the concert. And why did he have it here, and how did he get it passed security?

The second was when he raised his arm and aimed it at Matt. At the same time, Eric and I saw him do this. We didn't say anything, but we both reacted at the same time.

I reach for the gun, I know it was a stupid thing to do. I try to pull the gun out of the guys hand. He was shaking and sweating profusely. Like he was a crazed, feverish psycho. Maybe high on drugs. Eric grabbed him around the neck, in a choke hold. The people who were standing closest to us, started screaming, "He's got a gun!"

Matt was the closest to the edge of the stage and saw us. He stopped playing the bass. Which got the attention of Cam and Rob, Dale was the only one playing, which was probably okay with him cause he likes to play drum solos. But he did stop.

People were still screaming, and trying to get away, the security guards were trying to get to us. They pushed each other, causing some people to fall and get trampled.

I'm still wrestling with the cold steel gun, its hurting my hands, and my strength is waning. He's got a strong grip on the gun, his finger is wrapped around the trigger.

"Let go," I keep saying, to him, I try to kick him in the shin, I was thinking of biting him, but suppose he has some kind of STD.

So I continued to kick him. "Do you want to be a murderer?" I yell at him.

The guy was maybe eighteen or so. He never said a word. Just struggle to get free from Eric's grip and get the gun out of my hand, so he could fire at one of the band members. I suspect Cam was probably next.

He was trying to squeeze the trigger, but I got my fingers in there too, so there was no room for him to fire it, my fingers hurt, I thought he was going to rip them off. I didn't care, no one was going to hurt Cam. NO ONE!

By the time some of the security guys finally got through, Eric has the guy on the floor, and I have my foot on his chest, still holding onto the gun. I can feel my fingers breaking. Even though the kid was thin and lanky, he was friggin strong. And it took five more burly guys to hold him down. Once they flipped him over and put on the plastic ties on his wrists and around his ankles. Eric let go of him and my fingers were ripped away from the gun. As I let go of it, I heard the click of metal on metal, and waited for the bullet to hit me, in the stomach. I closed my eyes. You know how sometimes you know its going to happen and you just accept the inevitable, there's no way around it, for that one moment I felt like that. That this was it, I was going to die.

But nothing came. No bullet, no pain, no blood, nothing. Was his gun empty? Or was it the one chamber that didn't have a bullet?

He was pulled off the floor roughly by the security guards, and pulled through the crowd. Cam, Rob, Matt and Dale were escorted off the stage by their body guards. When the guy was taken away, they came back out.

They saw the whole thing unfold, I looked up to make sure Cam was alright. He mouthed to me, "Are you alright?" I nod to him, yes. He looks relieved.

Cam addresses the audience over the mic. "Were taking a short break, for a few minutes, have a drink on us," he says.

We all meet back stage. The police are here and take the guy away. "The police want to talk to me and Eric, after the show." Cam says.

Cam pulls me aside, "Are you sure your alright?" He looks me up and down, I show him my fingers, "Get the paramedics," he yells. My fingers are blue, and swollen, and crooked.

He gently holds my hand and looks at my fingers. "Does it hurt?" He asks me. I shake my head, it hurts like hell. Why do I get hurt all the time?

The paramedics come and I show them my hand, I have to go to the hospital later to get it x-rayed, but the paramedic is sure that more than one is broken. He wraps it up, so I can continue in the show, Cam says, "I'm up next."

The show must go on, and too bad if you feel lousy, it sucks for you. Slowly the fans come back to the arena, everyone ran to get a beer. Did Cam realize what he had said? The drinks are on the band?

Eric hugs me, I can feel him shaking, and he looks into my eyes, his blue eyes are very serious, "Janie, I thought he shot you, I was so scared. Let me see your fingers," he holds my hand, I show him my blue fingers, "there my be more than one broken," I say.

"I'm sorry, hospital again?" He asks.

"Yeah," I smile, weakly, "Hospital."

Cam gets serious for a moment with the audience. He's really upset, I don't think I've ever seen him this upset, not even when he saw me and Eric in his bed. The guys all stand around him.

"My good friend was shot to death, ten years ago. By a fan who attended his concert, well maybe he wasn't a fan. What the hell is wrong with people?" He's shaking. The guys put their hands on his shoulders.

"I mean, if you don't like us, then don't come to our concerts. My friend, our friend, was a good guy. He never harmed anyone, and someone he didn't know shot him, killed him in cold blood. For what? For what reason, can someone tell me why?" His voice cracks.

The crowd is quiet, Cam is searching the face of the people who are closest to the stage. He's waiting for an answer from someone. "No one has an answer?" He screams into the mic.

He continues on, cause he's really upset, " Some lunatic had a gun tonight, it was aimed at my brother, Matt, then it was probably going to be aimed at the rest of us. Why? I didn't know the guy, he didn't know us. I try to treat people with respect and dignity, What did I do? What did we do? What did we do to make him hate us so much that he wanted to kill us? Does anyone have the answer?" Matt pulls Cam away from the mic.

"Its time to finish the show," he tells him, "Its okay, everything is alright."

"No we aren't finishing it," and with that they all walk off the stage. Eric has his arms wrapped around me. I think this is the first time I see Cam, for the person he really is, to understand what kind of a person he is, he's passionate about what he does, and when something happens like this it devastates him.

Thank god, he's got good people around him, they all do. Everyone will help them through a difficult time. I'll try too, I'm not very good with words sometimes. But I can let him know I'm here for him, and he knows that anyway.

Eric and I walk hand and hand backstage, to talk to the police. Matt is talking to the police. Cam went to his dressing room alone. The gun was pointed at Matt, and he's so calm about it. Rob too, even Dale. Dale is talking to a girl.

I wait around to see what happens. Some fans have left. A lot are still hanging around. The concert was only half over. Eric and I wait for the police to finish talking to Matt. I'll go to the hospital tomorrow, for my fingers.

Their saying were hero's, I don't feel like one. Neither does Eric. We just did what we thought was the right thing to do. When you don't have time to think or react. You just do it.

The rest of the show is officially canceled. The security guards usher the rest of the stragglers out of the arena.

Money will be refunded if they send in their tickets. I feel so bad for Cam, he's taking this really hard. I was so mad at Cam, for being mad at me for being in his bed with Eric, it all seems so petty now.

I walk to Cam's dressing room in a hurry so that I don't have a chance to change my mind.

I knock lightly on his door, I open the door, its dark inside, except for a small light at the desk.

Cam is sitting in a chair. He has a vodka bottle in his hand and a whiskey bottle on the desk.

"Cam?" I say, "What are you doing?" I say it automatically, not accusingly. I know he's upset.

"Cam, don't do this, to yourself, its not your fault." I walk over to him, I don't even know if he even heard me.

I put my arms around his head, which he buries his head in my chest. Which I'm sure he likes cause he's a boob man, but I don't think he's thinking of that right now.

"I know your upset, everyone is, do you want to talk about it? Do you want me to call Melissa?" I take the bottle out of his hand, which he lets go of, with out a fight and I push the whiskey bottle off the desk into the garbage pail.

"No," he says, "I can talk to you." He looks up at me, his eyes are filled with so much pain, I want to take it all away for him.

I kneel down in front of him, and take his face in my hands, so he looks at me. "Cam, please talk to me," I whisper to him. "I know it hurts, I know it scared you, but your safe, your okay, everyone is. I'm so sorry that this had to happen." I take his hands in mine. His blue eyes, misting as he pulls me closer.

"I know its brought back all kinds of horrible memories, but your really okay." I was going to be strong for him, he touches my face, his gentle touch completely unnerves me. I have to be strong to resist Cam's allure. Besides this isn't about how attracted I am to Cam, right now.

"I know I am, I know everyone else is safe, thanks to you. You're my guardian angel, Janie." He laughs a little as that sinks in.

"Oh…. I don't know if I'm your guardian angel, maybe I was tonight. I would do anything for you Cam, anything to keep you safe……cause I love you." I swallow, that slipped out, I wasn't suppose to say what I was thinking. But I did, sometimes I say whatever is on my mind, without thinking.

He seemed surprised, by my sudden burst of truth. "You do?" He looks into my eyes.

Now I have to back paddle, "Yeah, you know, you're a great guy, everyone loves you."

"Oh," he said he made a face and looked disappointed.

"I do love you, Cam, but its not right for me to, your with Melissa." I really hate saying that all the time. I wish he wasn't with her.

"Forget that," he says. "You saved my life, how can I ever repay that, how can I ever thank you for that?" I put my arms around his neck, and hug him, I hear him take a deep breath. He pulls me into him.

"You don't have to, it isn't necessary, just being here with you everyday is thanks, enough, I was an obsessed fan who chased after you, and did some incredible things to meet you, I should have been arrested, but you didn't. And now I'm living a dream I've had for a long time." I breath on his neck. And close my eyes. I breath him in.

He edges off the seat a little and plants his lips on mine. His kiss is blazing hot on my lips. His hands are red-hot on my skin. I don't want to extinguish how passionate he is. But I promised myself I would resist him.

The hell with Melissa. I kiss him back, just as passionately as he is kissing me. I kiss down his neck, and he moans. I take, rip off his shirt. I hope it wasn't a shirt that he liked. He unzips my dress, it falls off my shoulders and falls around my waist.

I'm still on my knees, I've got to get up, cause there starting to hurt. As if he understands, he picks me up in his arms, and carries me over to the couch and puts me down. The kissing and touching gets more intense, and urgent.

I want to devour him, I want to know every inch of his skin, every pore on his body, every nook and cranny, I want to explore every part of him. I want to know where every beauty mark is, where every dimple is, if he has any ticklish spots, I want to know what sends him over the edge.

My hands are in his curly hair, I pull it with each passionate kiss. He pulls my hair. I bite his bottom lip and suck on it. He does the same to me, what ever I do, he does back. We're both turned on by the same things. We're both making intense noises. Moaning and groaning, and sighing. If anyone was standing outside, they would think that something was wrong.

"You feel so good," he says in my ear.

"Sooooooo, do you, I want you Cam, now." I purr.

I finally have him, the way I want him. Cam Konner, and it's everything I hoped it would, could want it to be. He's passionate like the songs he writes and sings. He cares about making me happy, the more I moan the more he gives. The feeling is intoxicating, I don't have to drink to get this feeling.

He laughs when I make that little noise at the end.

"So what took you so long?" I ask him. His blue eyes are darker, as he studies me. "I love your green eyes, I love the way you always look at me. I could never explain what it meant, I think I know now."

"So you did notice, I didn't think you did," I tell him.

"I noticed the first time I looked into your eyes." He says, his voice low and sultry in my ear.

"Well you are nice to look at, you know, you have a very sexy walk, and a cute ass." I take his hands and look at them, " I love your strong hands. I love how intense you are about your music, I love everything about you, Cam, everything." I breath, there I've said it all, now he knows how I feel about him.

He's surprised about my feelings. "Really?"

"Yes, really, don't you believe me? Hasn't anyone ever said that to you?" I wanted to say, hasn't Melissa, ever said anything like this to you?

"No….not really."

"Hum, I don't understand why?" I sigh.

"Me either," he laughs. We kiss a little more. Its really late, I wonder for a second why no one has come looking for us. We get dressed. We touch each other.

I walk out first, our fingers entwined together, he follows behind me, our hands slowly come apart, we don't want to let each other go. But we cant let anyone see us.

I walk to the tour bus, he walks to the arena, to see if anyone is still there.

Everyone is sleeping, I tiptoe in and climb into my bunk bed. I hear Cam come in a few minutes later.

He peeks in, "Hey are you asleep?" He whispers.

"No, not yet." I whisper back.

"Come with me." I take his hand.

I get up and follow him to his room, he closes the door. And puts his arms around me, and kisses me passionately where he left off.

"Come to bed and sleep with me." I guess he's forgotten about me and Eric.

He's already in bed, stripped of his clothes. I jump in next to him. He's warm and it makes me feel so wonderful. I lay in his arms. The feeling is sheer bliss it envelopes me. I can hear his steady breathing, his heart beating. He's already asleep. I laugh to myself. I can look at him, really good, make a mental picture of him, sheer him in my brain. Trace my finger lightly along his nose, his jaw line, his lips, he smiles.

"What do you mean their gonna sue us, for not finishing the show last night?" Cams voice woke me up. He was talking on his phone to someone. "They want us to do another show tonight, to honor the tickets from last nights show. How about we sue the Arena for lack of security, they let a guy in with a GUN, tell them to go fuck off." He throws his phone on the table.

He's talking to the band, there's some other crew members in the tour bus. The ones that organize everything, the assistants, the coordinators. "They want us to do a show, tonight," Cam says. I lay in bed listening.

"We're packed already, Cam. Some of the trucks have left already." Someone says.

"The lawyer says, they might win, all that money, you know. I think we should do another show, then they don't have a leg to stand on. We can sue them for their bad security." Cam says.

"Maybe, but we better call the trucks back, if you want to do this." Rob says. Everyone agrees.

I hear a lot of unhappy people, I stay in the room. Until most of them leave. I guess we're doing another show tonight.

I peek out the door, he smiles at me when he sees me. I must look dreadful. "We have to have a meeting with the rest of the crew," he says, "I gotta go, I'll see you later," he gives me another sweet smile, the guys notice. They run out the door, before I say "I'll be there."

I get dressed quickly, and rush to the arena, some of the trucks have pulled back in, so I guess they weren't that far away.

We can do another show, were professionals. It would be tight, but we could do it. The crew agrees we could do it. Everyone helps to unload the trucks including me, Eric is happy to see me. I have a really big secret, one that I must hide from him. It would hurt him so badly, so I smile sweetly at him, even give him a peck on the cheek, he blushes.

The radio stations, get the word out about the concert. Twitter, face book, whatever even the local TV stations.

If you had a ticket from last night, you got in. And no one wanted to say it, but it was like a free concert.

You sign a contract, but under unforeseen circumstances, it's the arena's fault for having poor security. Someone didn't check the guy with the gun. Someone didn't do their job.

It would take a long time to go to court, so instead of arguing about it we just do the concert and take care of it later in court.

CHAPTER 27

The whole day is hectic, everyone is running around. Cam is in a very bad mood. So I avoid him all day. So does everyone else, that's something else I learn about him, he has a bad temper.

The concerts starts earlier than we usually do, because we have to leave as soon as we're packed to go to the next arena.

Every seat and every standing room spot is filled. This time security has metal detectors, a little to late, don't you think. Cam gets into an even fouler mood when he sees that.

They know its their fault, some day they'll put bullet proof glass around the stage. It may happen one day.

When Cam goes out into the audience, which he doesn't always do, he has his body guard, Hawk with him. Cause you never know, people are trying to grab you, and to touch you. You never know who might try to stick you with a knife, or shoot you with a gun. So this guy shoves people out of his way. What a crazed person is capable of doing. Tonight he ordered me to stay on stage, and I don't think he intended me to stay in the audience, anyway. He doesn't want me out there, anymore. He says the stairs are good enough to enter the stage or even come from the back stage, Eric agrees with him.

" Eric is my body guard." I say. Cam snickers at that. "Well he is," I say. Eric would do anything for me. And Cam knows that. Wow I cant believe how Cam's personality has changed. What didn't last night even happen? Its scary, and I'm confused. The night with him is already forgotten. Is this how its going to be?

The concert goes okay. Everyone is nervous. I come up the stairs the way Cam told me to. Eric is still with me at the bottom of the stairs. He's always got my back. They don't take a break and go right through the whole concert. Cam does little talking to the crowd. And no meet and greet. We pack up and we leave for Niagara Falls, I even drove to relieve Carl for a short break. The guys sleep.

We're always setting up until the start of the concert, their all perfectionists. Why should this night be any different? The crew works good under pressure. People start getting silly, though. Nerves, tired, who knows what. We had a water gun fight, where did they get them from? Whip cream was flying, silly string, and some goopy stuff in a can. We were like little kids. With no supervision at all.

I've been to Niagara Falls only one other time, when I was a little girl. With my family. I remember hanging over the fence to get a better look at the falls. I remember seeing a boat, disappear under the water, the people on the boat had yellow raincoats on. The sound of the water pounding, vibrating in my ears. All the tourist, I wanted to be a tourist today. I told Eric, he said. "Yeah, lets go," he's never been here. And he lives in Canada. It's like me, I've lived in New York all my life, and never visited the Statue of Liberty, or the Empire State Building, either.

I told Cam we were going to the falls. "Show starts at nine." He says. He seems awfully cold, and it bothers me for the rest of the day, what did I do to piss him off? I try to think of something, everything, I said or did. And come up with nothing. Maybe someone said something about me coming out of his bedroom. I don't know, but thinking about it, is giving me a headache. And I don't want to spoil my time with Eric. So I push Cam to the back of my mind for the rest of the day, until I see him tonight.

We have a lot of fun. We go on the boat ride. He looks like a big banana in his yellow raincoat. And I tell him that. " So do you," he says. We get wet anyway. There's a gift shop and a restaurant which we stay for dinner.

I really feel like I'm on vacation. When I first started the tour, I felt like I was on a vacation. Now it feels like a job, don't get me wrong I love it. And I'm having a lot of fun. It's just this, this is special, with Eric. Just him and me.

But when you wake up and most of the day is gone, and stay up all night, it's a little hard to get used to. And it kind of messes up your brain. We are programmed to sleep when its dark, and stay awake when its light.

All the cities look the same, especially at night. Niagara Falls is all lit up, its very romantic. Eric is feeling romantic. He stands very close to me. Our shoulders are touching as we lean over the fence. His fingers tickling my arm. I smile at him. I lay my head against his arm.

He leans over and kisses my cheek. I don't pull away from him, in fact I turn towards him for a kiss. He kisses me on the lips.

Like someone is talking to me, 'Your such a slut.' I hear in my head. 'You've been with two guys in two days.' I ignore that voice in my head.

I look at my watch, "We'd better get going, its late."

"Time to work, this was nice, we should do it more often." Eric says.

"It was, I hoped I got some good pictures." I fiddle with my camera. It got wet, I hope its okay.

We were laughing when we got back to the arena. But the mood quickly changed. My laughter stops dead in my throat, when I see her standing there. Her hands all over Cam. Melissa. Shit, it has to be. Those big brown doe eyes looking straight at me.

I turn to walk the other way. When Cam spots me and calls me over. Shit again. I don't want to meet her, I don't want to talk to her, I don't want anything to do with her.

I turn around, put on a fake smile and walk over to Cam. We were never formally introduced, not that I cared. I did see her once at one of the concerts. And met her briefly at his house as I pretended to be the house maid.

"Janie," Cam bubbles over, he's faking it too. "This is Melissa, Melissa this is Janie," he says to both of us, he looks at both of us, as if he's waiting for something to happen. Is there a light bulb above her head? Does she recognize me, from the house? Does she remember me as Joan Collins?

I nod and say, "Hello." She eyes me up and down. "How do you do," she gives me a smirky smile. Please, who the hell says, How do you do?

She's a little shorter than me, she has a shapely figure, cant say that I like her taste in clothes, kind of drabby. Medium boobs, go figure. I bet Cam drowns in them every chance he gets. She has blonde hair, dye job and its more of a silvery color. Not like my honey color. Its layered like the old shag style. How long has she had that style? Heavy on the eye makeup. Heavy on the lip stick.

Her eyes are brown, common color, big like a does. She has full pouty lips, that Cam probably chews and sucks on until they bleed. She's dressed in jeans, tight, like they were painted on, low cut shirt and a leather jacket. Expensive jewelry, I don't see an engagement ring. She's so smug, I want to smack her. And she's clinging to Cam like a leech.

"Nice to meet you, Melissa," I say to her. "I gotta go and change for the show. Cam….." I nod and walk as fast as I can away from her. I can feel the daggers piercing my back. I hear her giggle. I hoped Cam told her a joke and she wasn't laughing at me. What a bitch! Its written all over her face.

I walked to my dressing room and opened the door. It opened wider then I pushed it open. Before I have a chance to react, someone grabs my hair from behind and pulls me as hard as they can.

I try to grab their hand out of my hair. But cant, they have a good grip, the lights go on automatically when someone enters the room and in the mirror I could see who it is. Melissa…

She followed me, she looks like a crazy person, she sneers in my ear. "People saw you with Cam last night together in his dressing room." She yanks harder on my hair.

"Ow, you bitch let go of my hair. Cam is my boss, why wouldn't people see us together?"

"No…" She says. "The two of you were alone, for a long time. They saw you holding hands when you came out. And you look flustered, both of you." She screams. "He's my boyfriend, he's been for seven years. I'll kill you." She yanks again. She almost knocks me off my feet.

Somehow I managed to grab her wrist and dig my nails into it. She screams and lets go of my hair. We turn to face each other, like two alley cats.

"You slutty ho," she says in my face. "I'll make you sorry you ever met Cam. He's mine and a slut like you isn't going to separate us." She spits in my face.

She tries to grab me again, but I'm quicker, I make a fist and swing my arm. I land a perfect punch to the side of her head. Which sends her spinning. She lands on the floor, a little stunned, shaking her head. She tries to get up. I push her down with my foot. I lean into her hard, so she cant get up.

"Now listen bitch, I have a boyfriend, his name is Eric, I'm not interested in Cam. Sometimes Cam needs a friend to talk to, someone tried to shoot him last night, he was upset." I thought my explanation was good enough to calm her down. I took my foot off of her.

"Now leave," I said, " I have to get ready for the show." I turned to dismiss her, that was a mistake. She jumps on my back and starts pounding my head with her fist. I fling her off of me and the fight is on.

I didn't care if I mess up my knees, or my manicure, or if she even gives me a black eye. I was going to rip her apart. I was going to rip her pretty little petite face off. I want to hurt her as much as I could. I must have been screaming or something, because we attracted a crowd, standing in the doorway. Guys mostly. Guys love a good cat fight. Something about girls fighting that makes them horny.

I clawed her perfect skinned face. I ripped out her hair extensions, I had no clue her hair was fake. There was a pile on the floor. It made me laugh. Which got her madder. Her boobs were just about to spill over her shirt. I bet they were fake too. Maybe I should squeeze them to see if they'd pop. I grab both of them and squeeze as hard as I can.

She screams bloody murder. "Ow..." She screams. She tries unsuccessfully to grab any part of me. You see, I had a brother, growing up. We used to fight all the time. And I know how to fight. I used to beat up boys in school. With girls anything goes.

I dive on top of her to finish this. When I'm just about to hit her in her perfect little nose, someone lifts me off of her. My arms and legs are flailing around, I'm screaming "I'm gonna kill her."

It was Eric, he has his arms around my waist. Holding me tightly. Cam has Melissa around the waist too. He was having a little harder time holding her. We both wanted to go at each other.

"Calm down," Eric whispers in my ear.

"I don't want to calm down," I scream. "That bitch, jumped me, she followed me, grabbed my hair and started to attack me." I wipe the blood from my mouth. I was on the verge of tears.

"Keep that crazy bitch away from me." I yell.

She didn't say anything in her defense. But smiled a positively evil smile at me, while she wiped the blood from her nose.

"Cam, get her out of here," Eric says.

Cam nods and drags her out. I'm breathing really hard. The fight really winded me. I pick up the clump of hair and throw it at her, in the hallway. "Take your fake hair with you. You fake bitch." I hear her laugh, pyscho. God she's insane, doesn't Cam see that?

Everyone departed after Cam took her away. Eric closes the door.

I sat on the couch and cried. Not out of defeat. I certainly felt like I won. She was the one on the floor, not me. I was crying because no one beats me up. NO ONE! It was humiliating.

Eric stood there by the door for a couple of minutes. I guess he didn't know what to do. He went and got me a towel and some ice.

"Here," he said, he handed me the towel. "Let me look at you." I tilted my head up to him, his forehead furrowing, his lips pursed. He's usually so calm about things, I could tell this certainly had him rattled.

"Oh man, you look bad. Your gonna have a black eye that's for sure," he puts the ice on my eye.

"Owwwww……." I pull away, and touch my eye. "Damn that bitch."

"Sorry….. And your gonna have a big fat lip, too."

"Anything else?" I slurred, my tongue feels thick in my mouth, I think I bit my tongue when we were fighting.

"Any loose teeth?" He asks me.

"No, I don't think so," I feel around my mouth with my big fat tongue. " Nothing feels loose, but I do taste blood. Something is bleeding." I slurred.

"You probably bit something, good, at least that's one good thing, no loose teeth, I guess…. Plenty of scratches, you'd better take a shower, I'll try and find some medicine for your cuts. There must be a first aide kit around here somewhere." He starts to look around the dressing room, while I go into the bathroom.

"Will you stay, please, until I get out. In case she comes back."

"Sure, I doubt she will, Cam was pretty mad." I hear Eric rummaging around the room.

"Mad, mad about what? That his girlfriend didn't beat the shit out of me?"

"No, I don't think it was that, probably because you were fighting."

"I wasn't fighting I was defending myself, she's the one who jumped me, I didn't follow her and start hitting her in the head." I look at myself in the mirror. Oh my god, my face is swollen and red, she scratched my cheeks, my lip is split open, and my eye is swollen shut. The stupid bitch. How am I suppose to go out on stage tonight?

"I know you didn't start it, so does he, take a shower." He's still searching for the medical kit.

"Found it," he yells. I have the water steaming up the bathroom, I feel sore all over, especially my back and neck where she jumped on me. She may look small, but she weighed a ton. My sprained wrist hurts and so does my knees and ankle. I should sue her, take her to court. Get her jailed for attacking me, and in any normal situation, the police would have been called and she would have been arrested. But our little community takes care of situations on their own. Cam better chain her up.

Even though she messed up my face, I smile though. I messed hers up more, I made sure I did.

The shower eased my mood, somewhat. I cried some more, in the shower so Eric couldn't hear me. It upsets him, when he knows I'm upset. I only cry behind close doors, no one will ever see me cry.

I turn off the water, and dry off. "Are you done?" Eric asks through the door.

"Yeah, I am, be out in a minute." I dry off and put a dry towel around me.

"I found the medicine kit." He's standing against the door.

"Where'd she get you?" He asks.

I look in the steamy mirror again, "my face, neck, some on my arms. Mostly my face."

I open the bathroom door, Eric has a sympathetic look on his face. "Come on over here, sit down, I'll fix you up."

I sit down in the chair, "How am I suppose to go on stage tonight, looking like this?" I hiccup.

Eric gently puts the antibacterial cream on my cuts. Everything stopped bleeding, there just scratches, nothing to deep. I hope I gave her some deep cuts.

I twitch a little as he dabs the cream all over my face, "Makeup," he says.

"Yeah a ton of it, and I don't have a ton of makeup." I exhale a big sigh. There's always something to complicate your life. All the time. Nothing ever goes smoothly.

"I guess I'll have to try to cover everything the best I can. Can you help me get dressed?"

He turns a little red, and shifts his position, "oh come on, Eric, don't feel uncomfortable, its not like you haven't seen me naked before. I'm hurting all over. You can close your eyes if you want."

He gives me a lame smile. "Sure, let me just finish putting this stuff on your neck." I'm very surprised at how tender and gentle he is, for a guy as big as he is, with those big hands, and muscles all over, his touch is very nice. And I like the way it feels against my skin.

He helps me dress, he closes his eyes when I put my under wear on. Then he opens his eyes, and surveys the rest of my body. "Man, Janie, your gonna have black and blues everywhere." He says. He gently touches the places that are already bruising. "Here, here, and here."

He zips up my dress. I put on the sexiest one I own, he raises his eyebrows at me, but says nothing about it, I think he knows how my mind works. Red hot, firey, sequins, shiny, shakes and shimmers with every move, and emphasizes my shapely ass, its very low cut and actually makes it look like I have cleavage. Which I never have.

My red sexy 4 inch heels, that he has to buckle up for me. Lots of makeup, I put it on at least four times, each time letting it dry before another coat. Leave my hair, like the beachy look, wild and free, and its real. Its full and wavy, and a pretty honey blonde color. And its all mine.

I'll show that bitch, she has to be scared of me, in more ways than just beating her up. I'll steal your man, and tonight...... I'm gonna be all over Cam. More than I usually am. I'll put my hands on places I shouldn't be touching. It would be so funny if she came out on stage to try to beat me up. I'll tell Eric to watch out for her.

"Janie? Janie, where'd you go, I've been asking you if you need anymore help? You disappeared there for a minute." He says.

"Oh sorry, I was just thinking, wonder if she tries again, or while I'm on stage. Will you watch for her? And stop her if she does anything?"

"Or course I will, I've always got your back, remember?" He smiles and kisses my forehead.

"Ow...." I laugh, "I don't think there's a place that doesn't hurt."

"I know," he laughs a little too.

Cam hasn't said a word to me since the fight. He looked surprised though when he saw me back stage, dressed and ready to go. And then his face furrowed when he saw my black eye, all the cuts, my swollen lip, cuts on my neck and arms. He turns red, as if his blood was boiling. And walked away. Clinching his teeth together, shaking his head, with his hands in his pants pockets.

The makeup didn't hide very much. It dulled the redness a little. I smiled at him, before he turned his back on me. He's either really mad, or pissed off at one of us or both of us, I'm sure he'll talk to me later.

The bitch was no where to be found. At least I didn't see her for the rest of the night. Not that I was hoping to. I hoped he had her locked up in a closet somewhere. And I hope she was chained.

You know I could have told her about me and Cam last night. I could have told her how good he was, about all the beauty marks he has and where they are. Or how he likes to pull my hair or bit my lip, or how he likes the same things I like. But I didn't. I didn't want to hurt Eric. If he knew, about Cam and me. It would shatter him. I was beginning to really care deeply about him. So I let it go........ For now.

CHAPTER 28

Eric stays close to me the whole night. I lean into him a lot, for support. His strength gives me strength. God, what a great guy he is. He doesn't deserve this, I don't deserve him. I shouldn't use him, the way I do. I make a promise to myself, that I will treat Eric better, the way he deserves to be treated. I should stick with him, with him I have a future, with Cam, nothing but one night stands. But I know I'm still obsessed with Cam. I…can't…let…go…of…him……

"Janie, that's your cue, its time for you," Eric says in my ear, "You keep going far off somewhere," he says.

"Sorry, just thinking," I say, and climb the stairs to the stage, walking with a little more swagger in my step, giving my ass that extra swing. Eric is right behind me, up the stairs, and stands just out of sight from the audience. I see him scanning the stage and the audience for her incase she sneaks up on me.

When Cam strikes that first cord of the song, it transforms me into a totally different person. I play a roll. Like I'm an actress. I become the stripper, the teaser, the seducer, the woman most men dream about but never get.

I keep my face hidden from the audience, my hair hides most of the bruises. When I pass Rob and Matt they look surprised at my face.

My hair is wild, and my shoes give me this extra sexy step. And my dance is x-rated. I put my hands all over Cam, I told Eric I was going to do this and don't get upset. I said I had to get her back somehow. I'll probably do this for a long time, try to get back at her without physically beating her up.

I put my hands on places that make Cam jump. Between his legs. He gives me a look, like stop it and what the hell are you doing? I just smile at him. Your girlfriend just beat me up. So shut up.

I hope she was watching from somewhere. Whether from Cam's dressing room, I hope the TV monitor was on. It shows the entire stage. Where ever she was I hope she is miserable.

I did some moves, that mothers covered their children's eyes. My butt was hanging out, of course I have panties on. Cute ones too. And when it came time to give Cam the pink thong, I pulled off the extra, and yes, extra pair I have on, I planned this. His eyes almost bugged out of his head. And Cam is up for anything. I might have went over the line, though.

Dale was laughing hysterically, when he saw Cam's face. I was all over Dale too, my hands rubbing all over his sweaty chest, but Dale is fun to play with, and he plays along. "Phew," he says into the mic.

The other two, who cared. When I was done, I wrapped myself around Cam's right leg. I could feel his leg muscles tense, when I did it. He asked the usual question, who was I tonight?

"Let's here it for?" Melissa, I mouth to him, "Melissa," he hisses. He makes a face at me.

I wave, take a bow and then curtsy to the audience. Roars come from the crowd.

I walk off the stage to the stairs where Eric is waiting. "Janie, some day their gonna lock you up for that," he laughs and shakes his head.

"How'd you like a lap dance tonight?" I ask him.

"Yeah," he turns beet red, "I'd like that a lot, then I'll know how Cam feels when your dancing around him, can you do the leg thing for me, too?"

"Sure," I laugh, I cant believe he actually wants me to do it. "I'll do what ever you want," I purr in his ear. I feel so evil. I smile to myself.

I change my clothes for the sign language songs. Back stage I ask several of the crew guys, if they've seen the bitch. Everyone I ask, says no. Cam was still on stage, so I couldn't ask him where she is.

I look all around me, and peek around every corner. I look into doorways, and into rooms. I'm ready for her, if she tries it again, you may get me once, but that's all you'll get me. It never happens twice.

I grab my pepper spray, she'll get a face full of it. I have my finger on the trigger, every noise makes me jump. Eric meets me halfway down the corridor.

"Your looking, jumpy," he says.

"I am jumpy, where did Cam put her?" I ask him, eyeing every nook and cranny.

"I think he sent her home. She lives in Canada, too." He says.

"I hope he did, cause my nerves are shot. I'm bruised enough. From the time I fell off the deck, and now, I don't need anymore scars."

The rest of the concert goes well. It usually does. I've signed so many autographs, I've lost count. I used to count at every concert, just to see how many I signed. Now I don't anymore.

People know now I'm part of the act, I take pictures with them, tonight I bowed out. My eye is swollen shut. And its throbbing, I need some ice. My lip is swollen, and I look like a grouper fish.

Cam pulls me aside. "God, look at you," he examines my face. He touches my face, "I'm so sorry, Janie," he says, "I don't know who told her," he gently touches my lip. "At least I don't do that to you," he whispers.

I give him a sarcastic look, "What….. It was a joke." He chuckles.

"Yeah, ha, ha, what the hell is wrong with her? Cam. She followed me and attacked me."

He looks around before he asks me the next question, "Did you tell her about our night?"

"Of course not!" I say through gritted teeth. "What do you think I'm… an idiot?"

"Someone did, someone saw us, and told her?"

"Gee, I wonder who?" I say and my gaze goes to focus on Rob and Matt. They know, "Try Rob or your brother," I say.

"Why did she feel she needed to beat me up?" I ask running my finger over my swollen lips.

"I don't know, I wont commit, maybe," he says rubbing his chin.

"What you wont marry her?" I ask.

"Yeah, something like that." He rakes his fingers through his hair.

"I swear Cam, I'll kill her if she ever tries that again. So you better make sure she stays away from me."

"I will," he says, And touches my arm, as if to confirm his promise.

What else is there for him to say. But I'm serious about killing her. I will if I have to. I will defend myself.

"I think from now on I'd better stay at a hotel with you, Eric."

"Yeah, that's a good idea, I never liked the fact that you were staying with Cam in his tour bus. It just wasn't a good idea, and it didn't look good."

"There is six bunks, besides his room, and I helped with the driving." I say trying to justify why I stayed so long."

"Still I didn't like it," he smiles.

I gathered my suitcases and bags from the tour bus, look around, give a deflated sigh. I don't want to leave. It was fun to be in with the in crowd. To spend extra time with Cam. I feel really sad, but I know this is something I have to do. To smooth things over with the girlfriend, or at least to keep the peace. I really could care less about her.

I go to the hotel with Eric, we get adjoining rooms.

"Can I get a rain check on that lap dance?" I was so tired and swollen, I wasn't exactly feeling sexy.

"Sure, I understand, I'm tired too, its amazing how emotional stuff makes you exhausted. What a night!"

"I agree, good night, Eric," I give him half a smile, cause my lip is swollen, and split and any motion makes it hurt all the more.

"Good night, Janie, if you need anything, anything at all, just remember I'm just a scream away." He smiles. "Sweet dreams, Janie." He says so sweetly. It gives me goose bumps.

"I will, I'm hoping I'll just pass out on the bed as soon as I hit it." I open the door to my room. Give Eric a nod and close the door behind me.

If I have a nightmare about Melissa I'll jump out of the window. Eighteen stories up. I could stand on the ledge and fly like a bird until I went splat on the concrete below. She wasn't going to invade my sleep, I wasn't going to let her live in my head.

As I got undress, and changed into my night clothes, I was thinking what Cam was doing right now. I hated the fact that I didn't know. I wonder if he misses me? I miss him, I miss listening to him play his guitar, every night, and hear him sing quietly to himself as he composes a new song. I want to cry, but I'm to tired to. I left Cam a note, so he wouldn't worry where I went to. He'll notice all of my things are gone. I left our picture. No more booty calls in the middle of the night for him.

I shut my mind off, putting the white blank sheet of paper in my mind, concentrated on that and fell asleep.

Cam's music always plays in my head, it often keeps me up all night. My mind starts to wander, and scenario of him and me together, forms in my head.

Fantasies, fanatic, fan. Fantasies, something imagined, an illusion, yeah I was disillusioned wasn't I? About Cam and Me. The reality of it is, is that Melissa has him. My reality is Eric.

So I make up my mind, from now on, Eric would be in my fantasies, from now on. No more thinking about Cam. So with that thought I closed my eyes, and had a dreamless night.

I woke up around four in the morning, I thought I heard a noise, I got up to use the bathroom, and I opened up the door that connected our rooms together. Eric is sleeping soundly in bed. A big king size bed, that I could climb into. I closed the door and go back to bed. I could sleep for another couple of hours.

I lay in bed thinking, how bizarre things had gotten, how things had turned out. Like an addiction, drinking, smoking, drugs, an obsession, it was going to be hard to get Cam out of my system. To stop thinking about him all the time. He's under my skin, he's absorbed in my blood. His scent is fuse into my brain. And it doesn't help that I see him everyday. I always look for him, in a crowd, in the arena, when I see him, I'm happy. Now I have to train myself not to look for him. Focus my attention on Eric.

I have to quit CAM.

I made up my mind, starting today. I will avoid him, go out of my way to avoid him. I'll go out of state to avoid him. I went back to sleep and wake up, with Eric tapping on the door.

"Hey," he whispers, "Are you awake?"

"Yeah, come on in, what's up?" I rub my eyes, ouch, I forgot the swollen black eye.

"Whew," Eric says, he comes over to the bed and sits down beside me, turns my head into the light so he can see my face. "Whelp your eye is a nice color of black and blue, it looks like its swollen even more. And your fat lip its all dried up. Lets see your arms," I roll up my sleeves.

The cuts are swollen, red and raised up, there's some black and bluing. You are a mess." He lets out a big breath.

"Thanks," I survey my arms, I touch my lips, and my eye. "Och, damn this hurts."

"I guess you wont be kissing anyone all to soon," he laughs.

"I guess I wont," I move my lips around, stiff. "Including you," I smile back, teasingly. He makes a face, guess that hadn't accured to him.

Eric frowns. And I laugh again.

" Cam wants us to come to the arena early today. He wants to change the layout of the stage. So he wants to show you where you come in."

"Yeah, I'm sure he does," I say sarcastically.

"Are you mad or something?"

"No, just not feeling to good this morning, I mean look at me. I'm so sore." I whine.

I got dressed, in the frumpiest clothes I could find, except I really don't have frumpy clothes. So it was just a T and jeans. Didn't bother with any makeup, it was just no use. I did get some ice, and kept it on the eye and lip the whole day. We got a quick breakfast and headed over to the arena.

Except for the meeting and the change in the contour of the stage, that was the only time I talked to Cam all day. And for about a week, avoiding Cam was easy. The only time we saw each other was when I was on stage. He would look at me, raise an eyebrow, look like he wanted to say something to me and then would change his mind.

But avoiding him only worked for a while and then as if someone was playing a cruel joke, we bumped into each other more than we ever did.

We said "Oh sorry," more times then ever and touched for a brief second, more then before. It was if we just met each other and we were trying to figure each other out. He was very polite, and gave me his shy smile, but I wasn't falling for it. I put up a big high wall around me, and it was Cam proof.

Or at least that's what I told myself, his touch, however how light it was, left a tingly feeling on my skin. And he would leave an ache in my chest.

We look at each other a little longer than necessary, he always looked like he wanted to say something to me, but never did. And I wanted to say something to him, but both of us would clamp our mouths shut, and walk away.

I missed being around him, his laughter would vibrate around the arena and it was contagious. It would make me turn my head to see where he was. Not that I didn't love Eric's laugh, his laugh was very cute, and always makes me smile. He always has me in stitches.

But there is still a hole in my heart where Cam used to be.

Next concert Edmondton, Canada, a few miles from where, Eric's family lives. And where Cam grew up. We have about a week of free time. Eric wants to stay, but I told him to go home and visit his family. I'd be fine.

My bruises and cuts are faded to a nice pink, my lip is not swollen and the split is almost gone, I load up on lip balm. My eye is open, and there's just a hint of a black eye. The eye itself is still blood shot though, I hope that goes away.

Eric invited me to come with him for a visit. He said his Mom and Dad would love to meet me. I said no though, I'd pass on the invite. I'd promise I would go the next time.

"Are you sure?" He was disappointed. "I feel so bad, you'll be here all alone. Everyone is leaving."

"I have plenty to do, tons of shopping to catch up on," I say, "I'll be fine. And I'll call you every day, okay."

He reluctantly leaves me at the hotel. I have a list of things to do, including taking my tattered pink dress to a seamstress to see if she can repair it. Catch up on some movies. Maybe write some letters, eh scratch that, who writes letter anymore. Lots of shopping, clothes, shoes. Jewelry.

Everyone was gone. Band, crew, I'm here all alone. I was relaxing after taking a luxurious bath, I had a massage, offered by the hotel. Had my nails and toes done. A facial and waxing. Even had my hair layered a little to give it more volume and body. I was feeling fabulous.

I have a good book I want to dive into, an old favorite movie on the TV. A scrumptious snack. I stretch out on the couch. Take a nice cleansing relaxing breath.

I opened the book to read page one, when a pounding on the door, nearly made me jump out of my skin.

I hadn't ordered anything, and I wasn't expecting anyone. No one knew I was here, except Eric. So, maybe it was him, I got excited, he came back for me, I jumped off the couch and flung open the door.

I had a big stupid smile on my face for him. And I was going to throw myself into his arms.

I stopped myself. Standing in the doorway with my mouth hanging open, and my eyes probably as big. I had to stop myself from throwing myself into his arms. "Cam?"

He was standing in front of my door, his arms braced on either side of the door frame. Trying to hold himself up. His hair was hanging in his eyes, he smelled like cheap beer and cigarettes and cheaper perfume, he was at a bar. He looked up at me, with bloodshot eyes. And gave me a goofy smile.

"Cam…." I said again, in the most exasperated voice I could muster. "What are you doing here? What have you done?"

"Aren't you gonna invite me in," he slurs with a devious grin.

I look out in the hallway, to make sure no one sees him, he stumbles into my room, I close the door.

I stand there looking at him, he turned to face me, the grin faded from his face when he sees the look on my face.

"Janie, you look beautiful," he says and takes a few steps towards me. He reaches for me, but I push him away. I keep my hand there to stop him from coming any closer.

"Cam, your drunk."

"Yes I am," he laughs, and sits down in one of the chairs by the couch, stretches out his long legs.

"Why?" I ask him.

"Why?" He says, "Because I can."

"That's stupid," I tell him.

"Your going to get yourself into trouble again, and this time they'll throw you in jail for good, and take away your license for good too, you'll have to go to another state to get a license."

"Not if I stay here….. With you," he grins again, he gets up and with a speed that I certainly didn't expect from him, he's standing in front of me, trying to trap me in his arms.

"You smell so good," he says, I'm trying to wiggle out of his arms.

"You don't," I tell him and I push him away. "You smell like cheap beer and cheap woman, whew and throw up. You need a bath." I push him towards the bathroom. "Go."

"Oh come on Janie, I don't need a bath, and I'll only take one if you come," he moans. But he goes anyway.

"Take off your clothes and get in there."

"Only if you come," he tries to pull me in.

"I will, I have to call downstairs, go in I'll be there in a minute." I take an exasperated breath. I look at the TV playing my favorite movie, its already started. I look at the book, opened to page one. And take another exasperated breath.

CHAPTER 29

He goes in the shower, with the idea that I'm going to join him. I hear the water running and he's singing.

I phone down to the front desk and ask for some coffee, a mans robe, some sandwiches, some extra towels. Any kind of sandwiches, I tell them.

Cam is calling me, "Janie, I need help, can you come in here?" He yells.

I bet he needs help. "Okay, what do you want," I stand outside the door. For all I know he's probably drowning himself.

The bathroom is steamy. I had just cleaned everything that was mine up. Cam's dirty clothes are piled on the floor, I throw them into the shower with him. "Hey…..!" He says, "Whatcha do that for?"

He's sitting in the tub, the water is filling the tub up. His head is against the tiled wall. His eyes are closed. "Cam?" Are you alright?"

"Janie…." He's loud, and holds out his hand to me, I take it and he pulls me down.

"What are we going to do with you, Cam?"

"What ever you want," he says. And he kisses the top of my hand.

"Seriously Cam you have to stop this destructive drinking." I grab the shampoo bottle and pour it over his head.

"Nothing more sexier than a woman washing a mans hair," he says and I smack him.

"You're a sexist, and believe me I'm not enjoying this. You've got me soaking wet."

"Your not enjoying this?" He's blowing bubbles, off his hand.

"No I'm not, its ruining my hair."

"Your beautiful hair, I 'd love to drown in it every night." He says and I pour hot water over his head, it gets in his mouth and he spits it out and coughs. He looks at me through the soapy mess on his head.

"Your trying to drown me," he spits water.

I laugh. "Yeah something like that." He ruined my peaceful night, I'm thinking to myself.

There's a knock on the door. I get up to get it. "The front desk sent some food up," I say, "I have to get the door."

I get the door, a young man is standing there, "The front desk sent this up for you," he hands me the towels and robe. Gives me a tray with the food on it. "Thank you," I say and close the door.

Was I suppose to give him a tip? I always forget.

I put everything on the table, except for the towels and robe, take them into the bathroom with me.

"Who was that?" Cam asks.

"The front desk, there's food and coffee, I have extra towels, and a robe for you."

"I could stay naked!" He laughs. And laughs even harder when he sees the look on my face.

"That… isn't going to happen." I said.

I pull his hair, and rinse the rest of the soap out of it. "Lean forward and I'll wash your back."

He's got some bruises on his back.

"Cam, where did you get the bruises from?"

"Uh, what bruises?" He tries to look at his back, "Where are they?"

"Here and here," I touch the spots, where they are. "And there's some cuts too."

"Oh yeah, I remember, I was in a fight at the bar, someone told me my music sucked, so I punched him, then there was a big fight and they kicked me out."

"Oh, so because of who you are their suppose to give you a free pass?" I rinse off the soap.

"No, far from it, but I don't need people telling me how they hate my music, especially when I'm just drinking and being just a regular person, its not like I'm on stage doing my job. I'm drinking there just to relax and have a good time. Not to start trouble. But people seem to think that BECAUSE….. of who I am, they can bother me, and then they purposefully go out of their way to antagonize me. It's the same reason the judge threw the book at me, last year, I had no license for a year."

"You'd think you'd learn" I say under my breath, get the towel and the robe, give them to Cam.

"What'd ya say?"

"Nothing, come on and get out, there's food outside."

I leave him in the water, "Oh and leave your clothes in the water."

He comes out a few minutes later towel drying his hair. He has the robe on. "Do you mind closing your robe."

"Its not like you haven't seen it before," he grins. Why do guys find offending woman such a great pleasure.

"Just close it," I say.

And that's the problem, I have seen it all. And I liked what I saw. Liked the way it felt. Still want him, and I'm trying to forget, forget all of it, his touch, his voice, his smile, the way he smells, when he smells good, the way he kisses, the way he laughs at a stupid joke, his sky blue eyes. I want to tell him all of it. But here he is. Tempting me.

"Sure, so what's been going on? You've been avoiding me like crazy, is it because of Melissa?"

I pour him some coffee, hand him a sandwich, while I contemplate my answer.

"Sort of….." I say before I shove a sandwich in my mouth.

"Sort of what?" He asks.

"Well yeah its because of her, she scared the shit out of me. And your still with her. And someone is tattle tailing on us. I don't want to be the other woman. I want to be the only woman. Just like she does."

"Its kind of erotic, two woman. Two at once. Don't you think?" He says.

"Maybe for you. And every other man, but not me."

We finish eating. I sit on the couch and surf through the channels. My favorite movie is over. He comes over and sits next to me, because I realize he cant leave, he has no clothes. It would be so easy for me just to slid closer over to him. Take advantage of the situation. Curl up and cuddle with him. But its not right.

"Where am I suppose to sleep?" He asks.

"On the couch." I say.

I give him a pillow and a blanket, he really put a dent in my relaxing night. And I am pissed. Make up the couch for him. Tuck him in like I'm his mother, and he lets me do it to with a silly look of amusement on his face.

"Okay," I say, looking at my handy work, "Your good."

"I'd be better if you were here with me," he looks like a little boy right now. His blue eyes blinking up at me, I bet his mother had a hard time denying him anything.

"Good night, Cam…."

"Good night, Janie, oh hey could you tuck my feet in?" I give him an exasperated grunt. He's dragging this out. I tuck his feet under the blankets. He grabs me as I pass by him to go to my bed in the other room. Pulls me down to my knees, inches from his face.

"A goodnight kiss?" He puckers.

"NO," I push away. And try to stand up.

"YES," he pulls me closer.

"NO," I push away again, he's strong when he's drunk.

"YES," he plants his lips on mine. My resolve is disappearing quickly. I want to return his kiss. But I hold fast to my promise.

I pull away, this time getting to my feet and walking a few feet away. "Good night, Cam. See you in the morning."

"Janie……" He calls after me. "Please come back, I'm lonely." I close the door on the bedroom. I lock the door.

I am so tempted to go back, and fall into his arms. I think about Eric. Yeah, that's good, think about him. He trusts me so much, I cant let him down.

My obsession with Cam, has festered over the years, feels like my favorite damn disease. All those years before I knew him. How it built up to my obsession. Its hard to go cold turkey, to get him out of my system.

I forgot to call Eric, today. I grab my cell phone, and look at the time. It isn't to late. I press the button, and call his cell phone. It rings several times.

A sleepy Eric answers his phone. "Hello?"

"Hi," I say, god its so good to hear his voice.

"Hey, Janie! What time is it?"

"Oh I'm sorry, its not to late, but I wanted to hear your voice...... I miss you." I whine.

"Everything okay?" He asks.

"Yes, everything is fine, I just miss you. I've had plenty of things to do. So I'm not bored. But.....I'm just lonely." I sigh.

"I miss you too, you could still come for a visit, you know, Mom would love it if you came, so would I." He yawns.

"You sound tired, I'll let you go back to sleep."

"I am tired, but not to tired to talk to you, I've been helping Dad with the farm. There's always plenty of work to do."

"I'll let you know, if I change my mind.... About coming, okay?" I say.

"Okay," he yawns again. "I hope you change your mind. Goodnight, Janie"

"Goodnight, Eric." I hang up, I think I'll go and visit him, as soon as I get rid of Cam.

I crawl into bed. I've had a busy day today. And think about all the fun I had, until Cam showed up. I'm passed the point of falling asleep. Cam showed up so late. I lay there for a while. The time is slowly ticking by. I get up to check on Cam.

He's sleeping on his side. His hair is across his face. I study his face. He has nice skin, his mustache and goatee suite his face. Its darker than his hair, he has a beauty mark on his face, I never noticed before.

He has creases on his face, they come out when he sings, he has very expressive facial expressions when he sings. They'll be permanent, when he gets older. Only thing is they never look bad on a man, only on woman.

As if he knows I'm there. He opens his eyes. I stand very still, its dark enough, so maybe he cant see me. He stretches and looks around, then at me.

"Janie? What's wrong?" He props himself up on his elbow.

"Nothing, I was just checking on you. That's all."

"Oh, I'm okay. Changed your mind about joining me?" He smiles, and pats the couch.

"I swear Cam, you have a one track mind,"

"Always," he laughs.

I hesitate for just a second, and then close the door. I stand there and wait for him to fall back to sleep. I'd like to sit on the floor in front of him and watch him sleep. I'll wait. And go back.

I open the door after a few minutes. I hear him breathing evenly. I tiptoe out.

It didn't take long for him to fall back to sleep, that's the funny thing about being drunk, you sleep so easily.

See how obsessed I still am about him. I should stay in my room. Instead I'm tiptoeing over to the couch to sit and watch him sleep.

It's uncontrollable, I say to myself. Like chocolate if I don't have any, I'll go crazy. Besides, he'll never know, cause I'll leave before he wakes up.

I push the coffee table out of the way, grab the blanket off the chair, and wrap it around me, sit down on the rug next to Cam. He rolled over again, and is facing me. I can really study his face. Cause that's what I like to do, I study people. Some sign from outside the hotel, lights up the room just enough to see.

He's breathing softly. His lips are parted slightly. He looks like he's pouting. I want to trace his lips with my finger and then with my tongue.

CUT IT OUT, I say to myself, what the hell are you doing? Your such an idiot. Your such a contradiction, you betray yourself over and over again.

What do I have a bad and a good angel on my shoulder tonight? One is saying, its okay, no harm done. And the other is saying, leave, you're a obsessed sick psycho. I tell them both to shut up.

I'm enjoying myself, and Cam is nice to look at. I wonder if Melissa ever looks at him like this? I hate Melissa. Maybe she'll die or something. Then April's voice says to me, "Be careful what you wish for, it might come true. You might get what you want and get some things that you don't." April says.

I get comfortable on the floor. And rest my chin on the cushion of the couch next to Cam's chest. I watch his chest rise and fall as he breaths. His chest is showing, I bite my lip. I love a man's muscular chest, and six-pack abs. Cam is tall and lean. I wonder if Melissa puts her hands all over his chest? And I hope when she does, she lets him know how much she enjoys it.

Oh go to bed, I'm so friggin jealous of her it eats me alive. But soon my eyes grow heavy and I close them, I fall asleep listening to Cam's breathing.

Don't know what time it was, but his arm was draped over my shoulder. His fingers in my hair. He got up to use the bathroom and tripped over me. He came back and picked me up in his arms, I remember moaning or sighing, when I knew it was his arms I was in. He put me back in my bed. And put the blankets over me.

"Stay," I remember saying. He did. He climbed in next to me. Its a big king size bed, but he cuddled close to me and wrapped his arms around me, I never opened my eyes, cause I knew every movement he made. I was so in tuned with him, it scared me. You know how sometimes people finish other peoples sentences. That's the way it felt with Cam, like he was apart of me, and I was apart of him. There was nothing separating us.

How could something so wrong, feel so right? I wondered.

I think I said, "I love you, Cam." I'm not sure, or was I dreaming it? I heard a laugh, but he didn't reciprocate.

Dreams……..dreams have a funny way of dealing with your subconscious mind. I never thought I dreamed in color, until I had a dream about Melissa and Cam sucking the blood out of my neck. Blood dripping down their chins. They laughed at my limp body, lying on the floor in a crumpled pile of skin and bones. Eric crying in the corner. His neck bloodied.

Then it would go to an even stranger place. Always water, or fog. And I'm always lost. Especially in the fog. I call a boys name, I know he means something to me. I must find him. But I never do. I need to use the bathroom, its early morning. Cam is sleeping. If I want my free continental breakfast I better go now.

I look again at Cam, so I wasn't dreaming. Don't think we had sex, doesn't feel like it. I put on some clothes, and go down to the kitchen. They even have waffles today. I grab as much food as I can, a little bit of whatever they have. I make Cam a big stack of waffles, some fruit, and orange juice.

He's still sleeping, when I come back to the room. I bring the plate to bed with me. The smell wakes him up.

"Hi, would you like some breakfast?" I have the plate under his nose, cause the faster I can get him out of here, the faster I can pack and go visit Eric.

"Uh…….. Maybe later." He moans.

Great he has a hangover. So I eat, leave the waffles for him. He can heat them up later. I pack all of my bags up, except for the clothes I'll wear today. I'm still sleepy. I climb back next to Cam, he's so warm.

I fall asleep. I don't want to sleep to late. If I plan on going to Eric's today.

I'll stay a while longer, to make sure Cam is alright. Then leave. I'd stay the rest of the week we have off with Eric.

I sleep later than I wanted. Cam is still out. I write him a note, get dressed, and walk downstairs. I call Eric. "What's the address?" I ask him. I hail a cab. Eric is happy I'm coming, so am I. Cam made me exhausted. Not just the physical, not that we did anything, more the emotional aspect of it. Only because I'm obsessed with him, it effected me in the emotional way, like it always does.

I give the taxi driver the address, and sit back for the three hour ride to Hanna. My phone rings, I look at the number. The number is blocked. So I ignore it, it rings again, same thing, blocked. This time I answer it, "Hello," I say but all is I hear is back ground noise. So I hang up. It rings again.

"HELLO," I say. I'm pissed now.

I hear breathing, gees, I haven't had one of these kind of calls since I was in high school. I'm just about to hang up, when a woman's voice says, "Is Cam with you?" It takes me a second to realize who it is. Melissa.

"How'd you get my number?" I ask her.

"Never mind how I got it. Is Cam with you?" She asks again.

"NO," and that's the honest truth, he isn't with me at the moment, he's up in my hotel room, sleeping in my bed.

"Why?" I ask her.

"Because I cant find him." She lets out an exasperated sigh.

CHAPTER 30

"Oh, look don't call me again, okay. I have no interest in Cam, and I don't care where he is."

"Your lying," she accuses me.

'Look you bitch, leave me alone, or I'll get a restraining order against you." And I hang up on her, before she can respond. The driver looks at me in the mirror.

Who gave her my cell phone number? When I find out I'll cut their tongue out.

"Where do you want to go?" The driver asks me.

"Hanna," I tell him, "look at the address I gave you."

"Its gonna cost you extra, its far," he says.

"What ever," I frown at him.

"Hanna?" He says.

"Yes, Hanna, why?"

"Because no one ever goes there, it's a hole in the wall town." He says.

"Oh, well, my boyfriends family lives there, that's where I'm going."

"Okay," he says. As we head out of Edmondton.

"How long will it take to get there?" I ask him.

"A couple of hours," he says.

I call Eric, and tell him I'm on my way, and should be there in a couple of hours. We talk a little bit more, I want to tell him about Melissa calling me, but the driver is nosy. I'll tell him when I get there.

"Great I'll be waiting," he says. "How was your night?"

Why does he know something? He always seems to ask that question when ever I was with Cam. Crap did the bitch call him?

"I had a good night, I treated myself real good. Got my hair cut, a little."

"You didn't get your beautiful hair cut off, did you?"

"No, just a trim" he gives a "phew."

"You scared me, how will I run my fingers through your hair."

"Hey," I whisper, "I still owe you that lap dance."

He laughs, "Yeah well not with Mom and Dad here."

I laugh, "Brothers, sisters?"

"One brother, one sister, and one sister-in-law. Two dogs, three horses, and various farm animals." He says.

"Cant wait."

"Me either, you'll like it here, its so peaceful. And green. I got more work to do, call me when you reach the town, okay?"

"Okay."

"Cant wait," he says again, "Bye, Janie."

"Bye, Eric." We hang up, I look out the window as the scenery passes by.

I sit back in the seat, close my eyes. I can see Cam lying in the bed. Wonder what he'll do when he wakes up and doesn't find me there.

It was such a beautiful, sunny day. Canada is such a beautiful country. Lots of open spaces. Lots of big cities. Lots of trees and flowering fields. Farms dotted here and there.

Eric didn't tell me a single thing about where he lived. I looked out the window most of the trip. The cab driver kept a steady pace. I'm terrible as a passenger, I get nauseous. Car sick, have ever since I was a little kid. I have to be the driver.

The tour bus is different for some reason, maybe because of its size. I listen to my music, I cant listen to Cam right now, so I opt for my second favorite bands, DAUGHTRY. THREE DAYS GRACE, AND

BUCKCHERRY, HOOBASTANK, LIFEHOUSE, SAMMY HAGAR. I love them all.

If I listen to Cam, I may cry. Not that I'm not happy that I'm going to Eric, its just that…...I don't know, ITS CAM!

Cam's music used to soothe me, when ever I was down or depressed. Now I need Chris Daughtry, or Adam, or Josh or Douglas to soothe me because of Cam.

I should call the room and check on him. I change my mind, he's a grown man, and its not like he hasn't been drunk before. I left him a note and food. So he should be fine, his clothes should be dry, by the time he wakes up. I'm not his mother. If I was I would have smacked him for drinking.

But I change my mind, it wouldn't hurt to see if he was alright. I dial the hotels number and ask for the room number. It rings several times, but he doesn't pick it up. I hang up and wait a few minutes. After about five, I call again. This time a very sleepy Cam picks up the phone.

"Hello," he mumbles.

"Hi, Cam, its Janie."

"Janie? Why are you calling me on the phone, aren't you here?"

"No, I'm on my way to visit Eric in his hometown. I left you a note, and some breakfast, your clothes should be dry by the time you get up. I'll be back in a couple of days. Melissa is looking for you. She called my cell. Do you know how she got my number?"

"Yeah, she has my cell phone," he says. "I think I did something last night……but I cant remember what it is." He takes a deep breath.

"I cant help you there, Cam, you went to a bar, got drunk, got into a bar fight, got thrown out and came to the hotel, where you are now."

" I wish I could remember, I think it has something to do with Melissa." He says.

"She called me, but I didn't tell her you were with me all night and that you spent the night in my bed, with me and that's where you are now, so your safe."

"Oh good," he breaths.

"You should call her, she's worried about you."

"Yeah, okay I will. Where are you?" He asks again.

"In a cab on my way to Hanna, to visit Eric."

"Oh yeah, my hometown. Have a good time, if you can." He laughs. And he hangs up.

"What's that suppose to mean?" But I only hear air.

The drive went faster than I thought it would, the driver tells me the next town, is Hanna. I call Eric and tell him I'm almost to the town. When I get to the edge of the town, to call him again. He has to give me directions to the house, "What's the name of the road?" I ask.

"Its called Fox lake trail west, but you have to turn down an inconspicuous dirt road."

I open the window to feel the warm breeze on my face, I'm actually excited. And cant wait to jump into Eric's arms. I want to feel his big strong arms around me and I'm gonna kiss him too.

I don't even care if his family is watching us. Maybe its my guilt, about Cam I don't know. But I cant wait to see him.

The driver says we are there, and I call him again. He says the road we are on should take us down to the dirt road, go slow or will pass it. Look for a red mailbox. With the name on it.

I tell the driver, he nods. I sit up on the seat a little straighter, to get a good look at the sleepy little town, I swear if I close my eyes, I'll miss it. Maybe that's why Cam was laughing.

"I'll be outside waiting," Eric says.

I look in my compact mirror, put on some lip gloss, more perfume, fix my hair, check my teeth. Everything looks good. I tell the driver to slow down, it should be here any minute. I spot someone in a red shirt sitting on the fence by the side of the road. Its unmistakably Eric.

"STOP," I yell at the driver. I made him jump. "Sorry," I say.

"This is it," Eric is waving, he sits on a fence. On each side of the driveway is a split rail fence and a sign across the road that says, the name, Edwards.

Its very farmy, there's some horses, cows, a few chickens crossing the road. Houses scattered here and there. The people look poor.

There's fields of wild flowers, and vegetable gardens. I'd like to take a walk all over this little town, explore the unknown, where Eric grew up, where Cam grew up. What molded them into the person's they are today.

There's barns, some falling down, old cars and trucks dumped in the fields. We stop at the gate to pick Eric up.

"HI," I practically scream, I jump out of the taxi, before the driver has time to stop, and run to him, almost knocking him down, I jump into his arms, he swings me around and hugs me. "I've missed you," I say in his ear.

He looks at me, and smiles. "I've missed you too, come on their waiting up at the house for you."

"It's a ways up the road, we should ride there." He says. We climb into the taxi, and he takes us to the house.

Everyone is waiting on the porch, and it's a big porch. The house is a big two story farm house, maybe Victorian style. Its painted white. Its nice. A porch that goes all the way around the house. A big porch swing. A semi circle driveway that goes to the front of the house. There's a few cars and trucks parked in it. A big shade tree stands on either side of the house. Flower gardens on both sides of the stairs that lead up to the house. I can see a big green garden behind the house, a couple of barns, three horses in the corral. Two dogs come running up to the taxi.

There's a clothes line out back by the garden with some sheets blowing in the breeze.

Eric has a big grin on his face, he's watching my face. I love what I see. Totally country.

There's a ramp on one side of the stairs. I see someone in a wheel chair.

There's a pond by the horses. Wonder if you can swim in it? The cab stops in front of the house. And a crowd of people come to meet us. Except for the guy in the wheelchair, he's young, he looks like Eric.

Eric really didn't tell me to much about his family. So I guess I will learn all about them.

Eric gets out, and helps me out. The driver gets my luggage. His mom and dad are their to greet us first. Her name is Anne, and Eric looks like her.

Eric pays the driver, and he leaves. Eric puts his arm around me, "Mom, Dad, every body this is Janie," he says. Everyone comes forward to welcome me.

"Welcome, Janie," his mother says, "I'm Anne, this is his father Jeff, Sr., this is his sister, Anna lee, and her boyfriend, Mike. Up there is Jeff, Jr. and his wife Arlene."

I say Hi to everyone, shake hands, there's two dogs around my feet, begging for attention. Eric says, "and these two pesky guys are Duke, after John Wayne, and this one is Harlow, after Jean Harlow."

"Cute," I say as I bend down to pet them. There very friendly, and playful.

"You must be hungry, Janie? We made a big feast to welcome you." Eric's mom says to me.

"Thank you, Anne, I am hungry, it smells wonderful." I was introduced to Eric's brother, Jeff, Jr. and his wife, Arlene. Before we went into the house. The dogs followed close on my heels.

"Eric show Janie to her room, dinner will be in an hour." His mom says.

He carried my luggage up the stairs, to the guest bedroom, "Where's your room, Eric?" I teased.

He smiled, "Its over here, now bare in mind I left a couple of years ago, and Mom hasn't changed my room since I was a teenager." He pushes open the door.

I have to hide a laugh that wants to escape my lips. "Nothing has changed," he says. Its blue. He has a single bed. Posters of cars and girls. Pictures of friends, books, models, stereo, CDs. I pick one up, "You have the bands, CDs." I say.

"Of course, I'm a fan, too." He says. I walk around his room. "You have a nice family, Eric, a nice house, its really country here, I like it. I like your family."

"Thanks, they like you too, I can tell."

I pick up some more of his CDs. "You have the bands early CDs, too," there the least of my favorites, Cam definitely got better with age.

"Santana, too. There's a few songs on here I love to dance to, maybe we could sometime?"

"Sure, you know me, I can dance!" We both laugh, cause its true.

"Nice room, Eric." I'm still teasing him. "Where's the bathroom?"

"Over here," he opens the door.

We go back to the guest room, which is my room. Its pretty and cozy. Lace curtains on the windows, which are blowing gently in the breeze. A big bed in the middle of the room, a rug. Where the dogs have made themselves comfortable. A dresser, closet, mirror. The windows over look the back of the house. I look out. "I want to go out there," I point to the expanse of the fields.

"Definitely, I planned on taking you all over, there's a lot to see. We can go horse back riding, dirt biking. Hiking, what ever you want."

"That sounds great….!"

There's wood floors, the walls are yellow, one of my favorite colors, like my bedroom in my own house.

"Its lovely, Eric, everything about your house and family." And I meant it. There was this very calming feeling, like everything was perfect here. That must be where Eric gets his calm demeanor from. "Can we go outside before dinner?" I ask.

"Sure, lets go," he whistles for the dogs to follow, and they bound down the stairs in front of us. Push open the screen door and stand outside wagging their tails.

They make me laugh. I even think their smiling. "They seem like they have a lot of fun."

"Yeah, their quite silly the two of them, their the best though." He whistles for them to follow.

"Mom? Janie and I are going outside for a bit, call when dinners ready." He yells over his shoulder, he holds open the door for me.

"Okay," she yells back.

Its just starting to get a dusky pink in the sky, it was still light enough out to see. We walked towards the horse stable.

"You don't think your mother needs any help, do you?" I ask.

"No, she has plenty of help, besides today you're the guest." He squeezes my shoulders.

As we walk to the horse stable, I automatically put my hand in Eric's. He squeezes my hand. "I'm really glad you're here, Janie. I've really gotten used to you being around." He smiles that adorable smile at me. So I know he really means it.

"Me too, that's why I had to come and visit you, I missed you, it was making me miserable." Plus the fact that Cam was there, I wanted mostly to get away from him. But Eric didn't have to know that Cam was in my hotel room.

The air is cooler now, and smells like wild flowers and hay. The horses walk up to us when we get to the fence. "Its chilly," I shiver, Eric puts his arm around me. I put my arm around his waist.

"Better?" He asks. Squeezing me again.

"Much," I've got my head snuggled against his chest, for one quick second I realize I haven't thought about Cam to much, since I got here. I feel proud of myself.

"The ramp, Eric, for your brother, can I ask what happened to him?"

"Oh yeah sure, its no secret. He grew up with Cam. They went to school together. My brother worked as part of the crew. He was one of the guys that sets up the big girders, you know the big beams that hold the lights and the sound system. He was setting up one night, about two years ago. And the stuff came down on him. He's been paralyzed from the waist down, since then. So after he left, I join up with Cam, filling in for my brother. And that's how I came to work for the band. My brother still works for the band, he keeps up the websites for the them."

"Oh, I'm so sorry, I had no idea, he had such a terrible accident."

"When we got the call, we were all pretty upset, you know to see your brother lying in a hospital bed, paralyzed, pretty much like it was with you...... when you were in the hospital, sick, that was pretty awful."

"I know, when my Dad was in the hospital is was pretty awful too." I remember.

"Well Jeff wasn't to happy about me joining up with the band, so I don't do the big beam stuff. That was like a deal he made with the band. So I do everything else, though." He smiles.

The horses, nuzzle Eric's hand, he gives them some sugar cubes. There's three of them. Two I saw, the other came out of the barn. Walking so slowly, like he was taking his time.

"So do you ride?" He asks me.

I make a face. "What's the matter?" He asks.

"Horses scare me. I've ridden maybe twice, and was scared shit, that I was going to fall off. Give me a dirt bike and I'll ride the wheels off of it. A horse, ugh!"

"I can teach you, its easy," he pets the horses nose. "This is Geronimo, this one is Lilly, and this guy is Winchester. Geronimo is my horse. "And...." He says as we walk over to the barn and he slides the barn doors aside. We have dirt bikes."

The horses follow us just like the dogs do, and they seem to get along. "Yeah," I clap. "Your horses and dogs, get along, uh?"

"They grew up together, so yeah, besides the horses would kick the dogs butts."

I look inside the dark barn, "Oh wow, you have a 125 Kawasaki and a 250 Honda. I'll take the Kawasaki." I say.

"Your on." he says.

"What other secrets do you have?" I ask him. The horses keep bumping into my back.

"They want you to pet them, go ahead, they don't bite." So I turned around and the horse, Geronimo, sticks his nose right in my face, I get a breath full of horse breath up my nose. I sneeze. And Eric laughs. "Just pet his nose, he likes you." So I pet his nose and he shakes his head.

The other two are jealous and nuzzle their way in too. I have to pet all three of them.

"So what are the other secrets you have? I want to know everything." I smile.

"We have cows, milk cows, chickens, cats and llamas, and alpacas." He says.

"Llamas, alpacas?"

"Yeah, llamas, for the wool, we have some alpacas too, Mom is trying it out. It's a new venture for Mom and Dad. Its something my brother can be involved in. The whole family. We learning about them. Jeff does a lot of the research."

"Sounds very interesting." I say.

"They are, interesting animals, make good security guards, kind of smelly, very gentle, though, Mom wants to sell the wool."

"How many do you have?" I ask.

"About twenty, I think, and counting," he says.

"Look out there," he points out into the field in the back behind the barn. "You can just see them grazing in the field. There good watch dogs." I squint, but really cant see anything.

CHAPTER 31

Eric's Mom calls us for dinner. We walk back to the house, our arms wrapped around each other, I don't even think we realized we were walking like that, it just felt so natural, so right, so good.

We walk into the house, I need to wash my hands. "I like to meet the Llama's," I tell Eric through the bathroom door.

"Tomorrow, we can." He says through the door.

Everyone is in the kitchen, it's a big country kitchen, with all the modern appliances. In fact it's a very impressive kitchen, one a chef would be pretty proud to own.

Everyone gives us a big smile when we come in. The food is already piled on the table in the dining room.

"Everything smells so good, Mrs. Edwards." I say as my stomach grumbles.

"Sit down, Janie, and please call me Anne." Eric pulls out the chair for me, he's such a gentlemen. He sits down next to me. I can put my hand on his leg or play footsies with him under the table. That bad angel must be sitting on my shoulder tonight. I smile to myself, its always more exciting to be bad, when you have an audience, but I'll behave. I promise...

Eric's Mom sits down, and we say a pray before we eat. That's nice, I haven't prayed in a while. Its nice to thank God for your food and everything that he gives us.

We pass the food around. There's so much, I know I'm gonna eat to much. A baked ham goes around, my favorite, all kinds of veggies from the garden. Our plates are full. Everyone starts to eat…… along with, I knew it! The questions.

Their nice people, and I have nothing to hide. Their not pushy, just interested in who their son brought home. Of course they want to know who I am. I push the defensive wall, I always put up, down, when people start to ask me personal questions. And calm myself down, its just talk.

Its only normal that Mom and Dad want to know something about me. Who their son is sleeping with?

"So, Janie, Eric tells us you work for Cam too?" His Mom asks.

"Uh, yes, I do, I'm a dancer, and I do sign language for some of the songs." I say, between bites of food.

When I say dancer, Eric's brother, perks up an ear. Not that he doesn't have a bad looking wife. She's very pretty. Why do men always want what their wives aren't? Must be a fantasy thing.

I should understand that. I'm living the biggest fantasy of the world.

"Oh what kind of dancing?" She asks, Eric knocks my leg with his leg. I almost choke on a piece of ham.

"Um I guess, you could call it modern dance. It has to go with Cam's music."

"Oh I see," she says, she sounds sarcastic, or disappointed, Eric shifts in his seat.

"And the sign language? Arlene asks. "What songs do you do that to?"

"I do it to the slow, romantic ones." It gets every ones attention, "I was signing for a friend at one of the concerts and Cam saw me, he thought it was very interesting."

"How did you learn it?" Arlene asks.

"I went to school, I learned it for my friend. She taught me some simple hand signs, but I wanted to be able to carry on a conversation with her."

Eric doesn't like all the question, I can tell, I give his leg a squeeze to let him know, its okay with me, the questions aren't bothering me.

"Did Eric tell you, that he's my body guard?" I say.

"No he didn't say that," his mother says. And she makes this clicking noise with her tongue. Seemed like no one else noticed. Maybe she has dentures.

"He is, he's very protective of me. I feel very safe with him." I smile at him.

His sister wants to know what I wear when I dance, and to what song. She knows the songs. Their all fans. It's a dirty little naughty song. Everyone gets the idea.

Before they form any negative opinions about me, I tell her about the pretty pink dress, sometimes I wear silver or gold, I tell her I have a number of costumes to change into.

Eric's father is very quiet, so is his brother. That makes me feel uncomfortable. Its always the woman who ask the questions.

Dinner is over and I couldn't have eaten any faster, if I tried. I offer to help clean up the table, even wash. His mother accepts my offer. More questions. The men leave except for Eric. He gives me a sympathetic look. Maybe he feels he can protect me if he stays. But if he was my son I would ask the same questions. I'd probably ask even more personal ones.

Dessert would be a little later by the fire in the living room. They have a beautiful fireplace and a cozy living room.

Eric wants to show me around some more. Its gotten colder outside, even though its suppose to be summer. All the animals have come back to the barn for the night. As if they know, Eric says they do. The cows know when they need to be milked. Even though the animals have been eating all day out in the fields, they come back to the barn for more. I think that's funny.

"Tomorrow, I'm gonna teach you how to ride a horse," Eric says, I roll my eyes at him.

"I'm not thrilled, but I'll give it a try. On one condition," I say, "If you sit behind me on the horse."

Very romantic, I'm thinking, having his body pressed up against mine, the gentle swaying of the horse, could go somewhere. I like that thought and keep it in the back of my mind, so I wont forget for tomorrow.

"Okay, it's a deal," he grins, cause he's probably thinking the same thing, I bet.

"Oh say, Eric, and I don't mean to be rude or disrespectful, but did you notice a kind of clicking noise your mother made after I told her you are my body guard?"

"Ah yeah, she makes that noise when she's pissed. I don't think she was to happy with the body guard thing. That's why I stayed with you, while she still asked you some more questions. After my brother accident, she wasn't to happy about me signing up with the band. She'll get over it."

"I hope she will." I say. I don't need Eric's mother as a hater, I have Melissa to deal with.

CHAPTER 32

ERIC

I still cant believe I've got this girl. I mean look at her. She's like a Victoria Secrets model. She's the hottest thing to walk into my life since I discovered Playboy. I even took her away from Mr. Hottie, Mr. Cam Konner.

She's so pretty and so sweet. I think my family likes her. Although Mom and Arlene had some uncomfortable questions for her, but she answered everyone of them without batting an eyelash.

I'll wrap my arms around her when we go for the horse ride. Take her way out in the fields to be alone with her. That's one thing about us together, we never have much time to be alone. Maybe take her out to the swimming hole by the stream, go skinny dipping.

I want her to forget about Cam. I want her to think only about me.

I know she was obsessed about Cam, I'm not sure if she still is. If she is, she hides it very well. I see the way she looks at him, hell he even looks back at her. Its like some secret code or game they play with each other. Like they have a secret. Everyone sees it. I pretend I don't. Cause if I think to long on it, I might kill him.

I wonder what the jerk is doing now. He's suppose to be on his honeymoon or something. Well whatever. I don't think Janie knows.

Janie is here with me now. Even the dogs love her, and you know animals can sense what a person is like. And I trust my two dogs senses.

I hold her little hand in mine. Her voice is music in my head. I picture angels. She has a cute smile, and flashes it at me when ever she sees me. Her eyes light up when she laughs, and there pretty too, green like the wild grass that grows in the fields. She always laughs at my stupid jokes or stories.

I want to show her all my favorite places. This is the place I grew up in, all my fondest memories are here, everyone should have a place like this.

Its getting dark and colder out. I have to keep her healthy, so will go sit by the cozy fire. I want her to lay against me, her head against my chest, so I can feel her breathing. I want to devour her. I want her to love me, the way I love her. Damn, I sound like a love sick puppy dog, chasing her around.

"It got so cold. Eric? Earth to Eric, hey where did you go. For a minute there you zoned out on me."

"Oh sorry, just thinking about things, what were you saying?"

"I was saying that it got cold outside, does it always get so cold at night?"

"Yeah, it does, the days are warm though, it comes down from the mountains. You can sit out by a fire and stare at the stars, when its not to cold out. They might extend the tour, a couple of months. So we would go long into the next year." He says.

"When did you hear that?" I'm surprised. I hadn't heard this.

"Before I left, but I don't want to talk about work, lets talk about something else."

We got dessert, of course pie, which was delicious, and a hot cup of chocolate. The living room has a nice crackling fire going. And its cozy and romantic, sitting next to Eric on the couch. He patted the seat next to him, to sit down, I wasn't sure, how much of the lovey, dovey, touchy feeling thing Eric liked to show in front of his family. He seemed to have no problem with it, and neither did they. I think they were happy to see Eric with someone, and he looked happy, so that made them happy. And it made me happy, too.

He put his arm around me, and kissed my forehead. I lay my head on his chest and put my arm around him. The fire hypnotizing me. The warmth enveloping me, and Eric's calming touch, making me feel sleepy.

The day was long, dealing with Cam made me tired. I yawned a couple of times. The dogs were curled up on the floor at my feet.

"They've really missed you," I said, petting them on the head.

"I raised them from pups." Eric says.

I leaned in against Eric. He was warm from the fire, Eric is always warm, his whole being is warm. It comes from within him. It radiates off of him. From his smiling face, with just the way he stands there, ready to help. Whoever needs helping.

Anna lee and her boyfriend went out. His brother and wife went to bed. His Mom and Dad ate dessert and went to bed also.

Seems a little odd that everyone cleared out of here at the same time. Wonder if Eric arranged it.

My eyes are getting heavy. Eric's throws a blanket over me. And I cuddle closer to him. He's a big teddy bear. Warm and inviting.

"This is nice," I yawn.

"Yeah, I finally get you alone, I thought they'd never leave." He has his head leaning on my head and breaths into my hair.

"So what do you have planned for us tomorrow?" I yawn again.

"What ever you want, I said I'd teach you to ride a horse, I'll give you slowpoke Geronimo."

"How about a tour of the town, too." I ask.

He laughs, "Its not gonna be much of a tour, there isn't much to see, if you close your eyes, you'll miss it." Is that what the inside joke is? I laugh, I can just picture it, I did drive through it, but wasn't paying attention to the town. "I still want to see it anyway. It doesn't matter how small it is, its where you grew up, and I want to see every place you went too. Like where you got your first kiss, the school you went to. Where you learned to drive. Where you went on your dates. Everything, okay."

"Okay," he giggles.

"What was that giggle about?"

"I was just remembering the first kiss I got, I was so nervous that I nearly missed. She's married now and has a couple of kids too."

"Oh, well that's good." I yawn again.

"How about dirt biking too?" I ask.

"Are you trying to wear me out?" He tickles me.

"Cut that out, and no, just want to do everything before we have to leave." I giggle. I'm very ticklish.

I yawn again, the long day caught up to me. As I'm starting to drift off to sleep, I realize again, hey I haven't thought about Cam, the whole day. I guess I really can do it. Cold turkey, get off of the Cam addiction. The withdrawal wont be so bad, after all.

ERIC

I wonder if I should tell her? I don't want to spoil any of the time we have together. If I tell her, she's gonna flip. Maybe even have a heart attack. I wont tell her. Why ruin our week, away from him, by reminding her. I'll let her find out on her own. From someone else. I'll pretend I didn't know a thing. I wont tell her that Cam Konner…. got married.

I can see it now, she'll faint, or be hysterical or maybe throw herself off a bridge or jump off of the 18th story of a building.

I don't want her to be a prisoner of Cam Konner. And in my mind she is. I want to set her free. Free from under Cam's spell. As long as she's obsessed about him she'll always be. And that…… kills me. I want her to be obsessed about me.

I cant sing, I cant play the guitar, I cant write beautiful love songs, or romantic songs either. I cant write anything. But I can love her with all of my heart, body, give her my soul and mind. I'll keep her from falling. Protect her and keep her safe. I want to be in Janie's dreams, I want to be the one she dreams about. Not Cam Konner. I have to make her see that some how, some way. I'll try and prove, I'm the right one for her. I'm just not sure how to do it.

JANIE

"Eric?"

"Huh?"

"Where are you zoning out to? You keep doing that. Tell me what your thinking."

"Oh nothing, just how nice this is, that's all."

"Yeah it is nice, I'm tired, I think I'll go to bed, okay?"

"Sure, I'm tired too, farming is hard work." He pokes the logs, a couple of times, and closes the doors to the fireplace.

The fire is glowing embers, we walk upstairs together. The dogs follow. We stand in front of Eric's bedroom door.

"Goodnight," I whisper. And stand on my tiptoes to give him a kiss.

"Goodnight, Janie, I'm glad you're here," and he leans down to give me a kiss back. We take a long time kissing each other goodnight. And its really nice….!

I go to my room. He waits until I close the door. I need the bathroom. I try to be quiet as possible.

The dogs sleep with him. How lucky are they. I don't suppose I could do the same? But out of respect for his family I wont even go there.

I unpack, what I need. I have a system now about how to live out of a suitcase. Since I've been doing it for a while now. I've managed to learn how to fold and roll my clothes so they don't get wrinkled. And I can pack a lot into a tiny travel bag.

I bought a conservative nightgown with me and put that on. Brush my teeth. Pull the shades and curtains closed. Climb into bed. Its not a big, big bed, Eric and I could fit in it. He's a big guy, I wonder how he fits in his bed, it makes me laugh to think of his feet hanging over the edge of the bed.

Its so weird getting into bed early, were usually up doing a concert at this time. I drift off to sleep.

"Janie, time to get up," I hear Eric's happy voice in my head, I think I'm dreaming, he's tapping on the door lightly.

"Ohhhhhhh……what time is it?" I yawn, and try to open my tired eyes. I squint at the clock on the night table. It says 9:00 o'clock. UGH.

"Can I come in?" Eric whispers through the door.

"Sure… come in."

He's already dressed and has a big smile for me. "Why so early?" I have my face smushed into the pillow, I look at Eric with one eye.

"Early? Are you kidding, its late morning, I've been up since five this morning."

"UGH! What are you a morning person?"

"When I'm here I am, there's work to be done, the animals don't feed themselves. The horses are waiting for us. Mom made a big breakfast.

Come on down." He tickles my foot. Now that he knows I'm ticklish, there'll be no end to this.

"Stop that," I say into my pillow, I don't want him to know just how much it tickles. "Yeah, yeah, let me wake up, okay."

"Sure, I'll wait downstairs for you, see you in a few." He pulls the covers off of me, before he leaves.

I'm not a morning person, never have been. Maybe twelve. I smell breakfast cooking.

My stomach always betrays me. Thanks I say to it. Now I have to get up, cause I'm hungry.

I take a quick shower, and put on a pair of jeans and a t. My hiking boots. The dogs greet me at the door, as soon as I open it. Their just as happy as Eric is, must be the air here or the water.

They run down the stairs ahead of me. Eric meets me at the bottom of the stairs, and takes my hand and kisses it.

"You look awake," he says. "Come to the kitchen, Mom's got breakfast for you."

Before we walk into the kitchen, he pulls me into his arms and kisses me. Gives me that big goofy smile. I look into his blue eyes, how they twinkle when he smiles. He squeezes me and puts me down. "Good morning," he says.

"Good morning to you too." We walk into the kitchen.

Everyone is there at the table, greets me with a warm smile. I guess last nights conversation is already forgotten.

"Janie, how was your sleep?" Eric's mom wants to know.

"Very peaceful, wonderful actually." And it was, I haven't had that good night sleep in a long time. Not even one single dream about anyone, or anything.

"Oh good, now you'll be able to keep up with Eric." She smiles at me.

"I suppose so." I wink at Eric. I would wear him out, I can definitely keep up with him.

"He's our little energizer bunny," she says.

I stifle a laugh. He turns red, and rolls his eyes. Shakes his head at his mother.

"Mom……." He says.

"Really, how cute, I cant wait to see that." I tease.

I whisper to him, "And I'm not going to let you live that down either."

He rolls his eyes again, “Thanks Mom,”

“What else are you hiding, Eric?” I ask him.

“Nothing…..believe me… nothing, NO one,” he points a finger at everyone, “No one says anything else.” And everyone bursts out laughing, must be some inside joke.

“Now I have to know what secrets your hiding from me.” I say.

“None I assure you.” He holds up his hands.

“Uh hum,” everyone is still giggling.

We finish breakfast. Eric and I head out to the horses. “Remember what I said, you ride behind me until I get used to the horse, okay?”

“Yup, that’s what I was gonna do.”

He saddled Geronimo, cause he’s also the biggest horse. The others can follow behind.

He helps me up, which is not easy, I start laughing, which makes it even more difficult. But I cant help it, I feel stupid, and I probably look worse. We try several times to hoist me up onto the saddle. The horse is high. It makes me laugh again uncontrollably, cause its funny. I try to swing my leg over, but its just not going over the saddle. Eric is getting winded.

“Why is this so hard?” I say over my shoulder at him, he wont put his hands on my butt, which might help me get up there. “Eric, put your hands on my butt, and push me up.”

“Well okay, if you want me to,” he says.

“Every night you lift me up on stage, you’ve touched my butt before. What’s the problem?”

“I’m not sure, I just lift you, with out thinking what part of you I’m touching, the dress is loose, you have jeans on, it’s molded to your butt.” He says clearing his throat.

“Just push my butt up,” I tell him, because this is making me tired fast.

He gives me one hard push, and Eric almost pushes me over the other side of the horse. I’m breathing heavily, I’m finally on the horse. This is one reason, I don’t ride a horse. Plus they smell.

He climbs up behind me. We squeeze together, I sit in the saddle, he’s on the horses rump. My back is pressed to his chest. He wraps his arms around me and takes the reins.

“Okay, now that your on the horse. You’ll master getting on yourself, just takes some practice.”

"It's a good thing you have a patient horse," even though the horse kept turning his head and looking at me, once I was on though, he tried to bite my leg. Only grabbed my pants leg, with his teeth.

"He's a good boy," he pats the horse's head, which made me lean forward to far, I almost fall off.

"Whoa, I gotcha." Eric has his arm around my waist.

"Can we just ride now, before I get to exhausted to do anything more?" I say with an exasperated sigh.

He clucks at the horse, he starts walking a nice slow steady pace, the other two horses are following closely behind. And the dogs are running around their feet. Which makes me nervous that the dogs are going to trip the horses.

"Aren't the dogs going to trip the horse?" I look at them weaving around the horses legs.

"No, horses can see all four of their legs. That's way their so sure footed." He's way to confident about his horse. Wish I felt the same way.

The horse had a really nice gait, it gave me a little more confidence that maybe I could ride alone. Eric behind me. His body warm against my back. He smelled good this morning, like fresh air and sweet grass.

"Where are we riding to?" I turn my head a little to talk to him. I could plant a big kiss on his lips.

"A special place of mine. You'll see you'll love it." He clicks to the horse again.

"How much further," I ask, my butt is getting numb.

"Not much further, why what's wrong?"

"My butt is falling asleep and my legs are numb."

"Move around a little in the saddle, and try not to be so tense."

I wiggle around a little in the saddle, it doesn't really help. Its like a giant itch that you can get to.

Don't ask me how the cowboys did it. Maybe that's why they all walked so funny.

"You'll get used to it" he laughs.

"I don't plan on it, Eric, I'd rather ride the dirt bike, that I'm used to." He slows down the horse, I can hear water trickling, like the tinkling of bells.

CHAPTER 33

Up a little hill and down the other side, up ahead is a glistening stream, its sparkling in the sunlight, running over rocks, past tall grasses and tall willow trees that edge the border of a pond.

Its magical looking. Like a secret mystical place. My mouth must be hanging open, cause Eric says, "Its beautiful isn't it?" Gives me a knowing smile.

Eric got off Geronimo, and helped me down. "This is so beautiful," I couldn't believe how green it was, private.

"This is my little hideaway place. Everyone knows about it, but know one comes here, I'm the only one who comes here. I go skinny dipping here sometimes." He smiles shyly, and looks at me sideways to see my reaction to the skinny dipping. Little pink spots on his cheeks.

"Water looks cold to me. I bet I'd freeze and shrivel up like a little old lady." I tease.

He laughs, "I guess you could. Its cold year round, it comes from the mountains. Come on."

He grabs my hand and walks me down to the stream for a better look. There's rocks placed in rows that look like a walkway across the stream, and little trickling waterfalls.

"See where the pool is?" I nod, "I made that. I dug it out to make a pool. Its about waist high. And the rocks, I moved them around to make the waterfalls, and that walkway over there."

"Its tempting me, but not today," I tell him. "I'll take a rain check. I'm very impressed though."

"We have crawfish in here. You can eat them, their sort of like miniature lobster."

"Really?" I peered over the waters edge to see if I could see any of the crustaceans.

"Where do they live?" I ask.

"Under the rocks, usually in the shadows, their very quick, but fun to catch."

He grabbed my hand again and pulled me along the waters edge up to the top of the hill, where the horses were. "Look up that way," he pointed. "Do you see the forest there?"

"Yeah its beautiful," I shield my eyes from the sun for a better look. I haven't been out in the sun in months, I feel like a vampire. The sun feels really good. Maybe I'll come back with a tan.

"You think you can ride by yourself?" He asks me, I look at him, disappointed. With a little bit of a pout.

"Why, I like riding with you behind me. Its really nice." I smile. "I like having you hold me." I pout, some more, hoping it works.

"Oh no, I'm enjoying it to, just thought I'd ask, that's all." He says.

He helps me back onto Geronimo's back, I get on a little easier this time. He climbs on behind me. He clicks the horse. It's a clicking noise he does with his tongue. The horse knows the sound and what it means. We head towards the wooded border of the forest. The dogs are running up ahead, the two horses behind us.

The forest is very lush and green. Pines, maples, birch, hickory, and elm trees. Seems like a smorgasbord of trees. There's green moss and huge mushrooms growing out the side of the trees, you can even sit on them that's how big they are and strong.

"Magic mushrooms?" I ask.

"Naw, there as tough as wood, you could never eat those, you'd break a tooth." He laughs.

There's fallen trees, and paths made by big animals, like deer and moose. Small little animals scurry across our path, the dogs take off after them. Barking like excited little children, and it's a game to them. Thank god they don't catch anything.

"Any snakes?" I ask.

"A few, but they wont bother you."

"I hate snakes." I say.

"I'll remember that, anything else?"

"Spiders, I hate spiders." I shiver.

"Those, we have plenty of too, some are pretty big."

"Oh, great."

We travel a little further in to almost like a dead end. Which is a cliff or the side of a mountain and a cascading waterfall.

"This is the source of the stream, I think," Eric says.

"Its wow, who would have thought." The rest of the day we use up sightseeing the fields, surrounding the house and barns. I walk through them spinning like I did when I was a little girl. We go to an old train depot. Places have closed up all over the tiny town. How sad it is. When things were better for the people that lived here I wonder what it was like. A little bustling town, where everyone knew everyone.

We go back to the farm in time for dinner. Eric's mom comes out to meet us. She waves and gives us a big smile.

"Someone from the band called." She says. "They want you to call back." She tells Eric. "Its not an emergency." She says.

"Okay Mom, thanks, did they say who they were?"

"Dale, I think, oh and dinner is almost ready." She goes into the house.

"Can I help, Anne?" I shout after her.

"No, everything is taken care of." She closes the back door to the kitchen.

I help Eric wipe down the horses, and give them a quick brushing. Fresh hay and oats, clean water.

All the animals are in the barn for the night. Including the interesting llamas. I'm still very wary of them. Even though their like pets. But their big, smelly, taller than the horses. And they have weird teeth. I'm afraid they'll bite me. Their very friendly and come right over to me. We finish with the horses. The dogs run into the house for their dinner.

"It was really fun today Eric, thanks," I grab his hand, " But tomorrow dirt bikes."

"Okay tomorrow dirt bikes. And your welcome." He kisses me on the cheek. "Its fun with you here," he kisses my forehead. Uh.....Eric is not a pushy or aggressive guy, like Cam is. Who, if there were no laws, would be all over me. No matter if you said yes or no.

But there are times, like right now in the dusky light of twilight, that I wish he was like Cam.

Kiss my lips for Pete sake. I want you to. Take it slow must be his motto. Unless its just the place we are. You know Mom and Dads home. Has to behave.

I wont push him, so he wont be uncomfortable. I'll respect his family. The house is brightly lit. Its very homey.

Eric's sister, minus boyfriend, his brother and wife, Mom and Dad for dinner. The dogs are swallowing theirs down.

After I wash up, we sit down for dinner. "Oh don't forget, to call Dale," his mom says.

"Yeah wont forget, I wonder why Dale is calling, he never calls me." Eric says.

"I hope nothing is wrong." I think out loud. Something with Cam? I would die if anything ever happened to him. "He had a dream," he said. Cam once said and I absolutely hate this. Cam once said, "that he was going to die on stage on his 40th birthday and he'll have a heart attack. Everyone will think its part of the show."

When I heard him say that I got really upset. He better not. I have another idea about his death. And I don't want to say it, because if I say it, it might happen, it might come true. But it involves a certain orange Ferrari.

The one he drives, the one he got arrested for driving drunk in when he was pulled over for speeding. Do you get where I'm going with this?

Through out dinner, I hardly hear or join in the conversation, at dinner. I automatically answer the questions that someone asks me. I'm feeling a terrible foreboding in the back of my mind. And now...... I'm worrying about Cam.

Damn it. I had all but forgotten about him. At least for the day. This is Eric's time in my head.

We finish eating and I've made it a habit and wont take a no for an answer. To help clean up the kitchen. So I help Anne. Eric calls Dale. I try to listen to his conversation. My ears are straining to hear Eric talking to Dale, over Anne's chattering.

"Sure Dale, okay, yeah, I'll tell Janie." Eric hangs up the phone, and comes into the kitchen.

My heart and my stomach are in my throat. I try not to let it show on my face. I hold my breath, and prepare for the worse. Eric doesn't look any different.

"Hey Eric, what did Dale say?" I ask nonchalantly.

"Cam, has extended the tour, and he wants us to come back a day early."

I feel so light headed, that Eric has to steady me and puts me in a chair. "Everything's alright?" I manage to say.

"Oh yeah everything's fine. Its just that the concert is sold out and theirs people scalping tickets, and swamping ticket websites, and calling, so they've decided to give another show."

"Oh my, I know the band is so popular, everyone loves them. Especially Cam…." His mother adds. We both look over at her. She ain't kidding. Everyone loves Cam. How about millions of woman. And I'm one of them.

All finished in the kitchen.

"Come on Janie, were going to the movies tonight. All romantic comedies are playing." Eric says.

"I'd like to take a shower, do I have enough time?"

"A few minutes," he says.

I run up to the bathroom, the dogs running up with me, they even come into the bathroom with me, and lay on the rug, while I rush to take a shower.

"I'll be right down," I yell to Eric. I grab my purse, and cell phone. Hopefully somewhere in this town I'll get a signal.

I open it up to see if I have any messages. None at the moment. I'm so tempted to call Cam. Just to hear his voice. Even if I get his voice recording.

"Janie hurry up the movie starts soon," Eric yells up.

"Okay be right there," I put my phone in my bag. But take it out again to look at the pictures I have of Cam. I have several pictures of him, several of him bare-chested. Sexiest man alive….. Oh…. I sigh. It makes me thirsty just thinking about him. I'm still addicted to him. Crap.

I rush down the stairs. One day these dogs are going to trip me, and send me flying down the stairs. And I wont land on my feet either.

We walk to Eric's mustang. He fires it up. Sounds sweet. I'm a car girl. Anything with a motor. And its red. With a big white racing strip down the middle of the car. I buckle up. And he pulls out, the dogs are running after the car, but they stop before the gate at the end of the driveway.

"You feeling alright," He asks me.

"Yeah, I'm okay, just disappointed that we have to come back early, its almost unfair, if you ask me. Almost like he's doing it on purpose or something, I don't know……"

"You just had a funny look on your face after I talked to Dale, I was just wondering." I put my hand over his, he's got his hand on the shifter.

" Just my stomach did a little flip flop, that's all, I thought maybe something bad happened. And now one less day with you. I'm P.OD about that. But otherwise every things fine."

"Yeah me too, I was hoping for some more time with you too, but at least we have jobs."

"I guess…." I moan.

Its dark out and you can see red eyes staring back at you in the headlights. He's driving slow.

"Deer," he says. They always wonder by the road."

"Scary, those red eyes, Vampires?"

"Yeah Vampire deer," he laughs.

Its Friday night and it seems like the whole town is at the movies tonight. There's already a line formed in front of the doors. Eric's sister and boyfriend are on line already. We wave to them.

We park the car and walk to the end of the line. Everyone knows Eric. And their all curious about me. Especially the girls. There all pretty and cute. The guys are all right looking. Eric introduces me to some of them. Like I'm suppose to remember.

I look very plain tonight, like plain Jane. Jeans and a t-shirt. No jewelry, except my earrings that I always wear. My favorite old sneakers. My hair is long and hanging down. So why all the snide little looks from the girls? Eric introduces me to a friend named Ray. He's studying me intensely. "I know you," he says, his girlfriend gives him a nasty look, and a poke in the ribs. "I've seen you at L-K's, concerts, you're the girl that dances on stage and does the sign language thing.. Oh cool, I'm right, right?" He says. I look at Eric to see what I should say. He nods. "Yes I am," I sigh.

"I knew it," he says. "Can I have your autograph and a picture with you? Hey every body, this is the girl that dances on stage for Cam." He yells and waves for everyone to come over to me.

I look at Eric again, like rescue me, he smiles and just shrugs his shoulders. I get pieces of papers shoved into my hands and people are trying to stand next to me to take pictures with their cell phones.

The movie is about to start, but because most of us are still outside, they hold it up, until we all take a seat. We sit mid-section, crowded on all sides by everyone who knows who I am. Is this how Cam feels? Only it must be more intense then this. There all harmless people really. Just excited a sort of celebrity is here, and someone that knows Cam. Well Eric knows him too.

I prefer to sit in the last row, I hate having someone sit behind me. Always have, since I was a kid.

I can hear people talking about me, "Yeah that's her, yeah the one that dances. I've seen her. Yeah, yeah, yeah…….. She dances for Cam, yeah she's all over him, he seems to like it, from the look on his face. Yeah cool, man she's hot." Then I hear a slap, must be the girlfriend. Male voices, most of them. Then the negative voices of the females, "Oh she doesn't look so hot now, did you see her, she looks so plain." Oh gees. I 'd like to get up and tell them all to shut up, I'm right hear I can hear everything you say. Eric tells me to ignore them.

The lights darken, and the movie starts, good then I wont be able to hear all the comments about, this and that. I slid down in my seat to become invisible.

Eric bought popcorn, soda and some chocolate candy. Popcorn gets stuck in my teeth, soda gives me gas, but if the candy is chocolate, then that's okay. I'm happy.

He has his arm on the arm rest. I put my hand on top of his and entwine my fingers with his, I kiss the top of his hand.

He leans over and kisses me. Soft and gentle, I taste the popcorn, its salty and buttery. I want more, but not here. Maybe later. I pull him closer to me and kiss him again.

"Oh get a room." Someone says. Everyone laughs. Some throw popcorn at us. I can play too. What's left of Eric's popcorn, I throw the entire bucket over my head. It sails through the air, hits someone, "Hey!" someone yells. More laughter from the crowd.

We sit through the rest of the movie, playing finger sex. Its very arousing, I had no idea it was that erotic.

The movie has a couple of slow spots in it, not that I'm really paying that much attention to it anyway, my attention is more on Eric and his hand. My mind starts to wander back to Cam.

He's jinxed himself. About his death. And if I say what I think about his demise, then I've sentenced him to death too. I send out a little pray, please lord, protect and keep Cam safe. Every night I'm gonna pray this, before I go to sleep. I want Cam to live to be an old man, I want him to write more beautiful songs. His life, his talent, his beautiful smile, his sky blue eyes, all the fans that love him, all the millions of woman that want to be Melissa, who adore him, would die. If anything happened to him. I would die.

If he was gone, I'd throw myself off of that 20th floor of that building he sings about. I've said it before, but I mean it.

And my mind goes further, how does Melissa feel about this? When he said it, how did it make her feel. That the guy she is suppose to marry, is talking about his death at age 40. She'd be a widow before she was old. That isn't even funny. And on his 40th birthday, we all should make sure there is no concert, on that day.

I want to be Melissa. I've got to be that someone that your with. I want to put my hands all over his sexy body. I hope she does, every time she sees him, I know she did at the last concert, but I think it was just for show, for me to see. She didn't look like she felt comfortable doing it.

Everyone is laughing. At some scene in the movie, it brings me back to the present again. Eric next to me, holding my hand. Funny, I've missed most of the movie. Oh well. I've seen it before.

The movie is over, seemed like it went fast. We leave the theater, and there's a crowd waiting outside. They want us to go to the diner with them. Sure why not.

I get a chance to see some of the town in the dark. Most of the windows are blackened, empty stores, feels like a ghost town. Only the diner is opened now. Its probably their biggest night for business.

The waitress is tired. You can tell. She has no clue who I am. Glad for that. But Eric's big mouth friend tells her. She could care less. Good, I'll leave her a big tip.

She knows Eric though. And makes small talk with him, while she waits for everyone to decide what they want to eat.

I have a piece of homemade carrot cake and a glass of milk. Eric orders a sandwich plate. The guy can eat. The girls just have sodas. I dance and exercise so much I can eat pretty much what I want, in moderation.

I feel their eyes on me. Like a can their prying open, prying me open to examine me under a microscope. If I was their age, and I probably am, I'd either tell them off, or beat the crap out of them, but for Eric's sake, I keep my mouth shut.

I snuggle closer to Eric in the booth. He puts his arm around me, and looks at me like, what's up? Do I really need a reason why?

We leave the diner, its late, but not to late. Tomorrow is our last day, and I want to make the most of it. Dirt biking, and maybe some skinny dipping. I'll definitely get dusty and dirty, from riding.

The house has the porch light on. Hope no one is waiting for us. I plan on having some alone time with Eric.

The dogs bark, Eric hushes them. We try to be quiet. We should have stayed in his car, for some make out time. But we want to get to bed, wake up early to do all the things we planned on doing.

We walk upstairs, the dogs sit at Eric's door. We say goodnight. A very long kiss. He opens his door and I push him in his room. I want more make out time. Push him on the bed, and get on top of him. The dogs jump on the bed and think it's a game. There licking our faces, and nuzzling us with their noses. It makes us laugh. Shhhhhh…….

I push them away, I put Eric's arms above his hand and hold him there. And start kissing him. His face, down his neck. Unbutton his shirt with my teeth. Have it almost undone, so I can kiss his chest.

But nothing else. I love to tease. That's one of my favorite things to do, especially with a guy who cant really do anything about it for now. When I get off of him, he moans. He tries to grab for me, I straighten myself out, I would hate to get caught, by his Mother or Father. I'm sure they do know what we do. They did once or twice, too.

So I say goodnight, he's propped up on his elbow looking at me, with an wicked little smile on his cute face.

"Good night," he says.

I wave over my shoulder, look demurely at him, "Night," I whisper.

Up at nine this morning, the last day of our vacation together. I already packed. Eric has the dirt bikes out. Fueled and ready to go, he comes in to eat breakfast. After were done, he hands me a helmet. He tells me to start it up and ride it. I look at him like you have to be kidding, I'll ride you into the ground. I used to race these things. You don't have to tell me anything. But I don't like to brag. I usually let them be surprised, when they actually see how good I can ride. I put the helmet on. I wish I had my own gear, leg guards and gloves on too.

I start it up, a couple of good quick kicks gets it started. I'm already riding circles around Eric.

The dogs are running all around us. I forget how many muscles it takes to ride. Like everyone you have and ones you never knew you had, screams have mercy, it's a workout for sure. But I love it, and I don't care how much my muscles scream at me.

"Where are we going?" I yell to him.

"Where ever you want to go," I point to the fields. The dogs are trying to keep up. Tongues hanging out of their mouths, tails wagging, barking with excitement.

Somewhere in trying to keep my eyes on the dogs, and watching where Eric is going, I failed to see the giant hole some animal dug, in the field, covered over by the tall grass, until I hit it…. I hit it with my front tire and did a somersault over the handle bars. Not the first time, I've done that.

Whoa…. did that knock me for a loop, it knocked the air right out of me. I just laid there, in the grass, face down, my helmet smushing my face. I seem to do a lot of that.

"Let me catch my breath," I tell Eric, who dropped his bike where he was and ran over to me. The dogs sniffing and whining, they know something is wrong. Their sniffing my face and licking me, "I'm okay," I tell them. And push them away, with my free hand. I'm laying on top of the other one, and it hurts.

I sit up with Eric's help, "Janie are you alright?"

A little wobbly and dizzy. "Are you hurt anywhere?" Eric asks, and he's feeling my arms and legs, looking at my face and head. Looking at my eyes.

"No, just my pride," I say. "I wasn't showing off or anything, the dogs distracted me." Eric helps me up.

I get back on the bike, a little stiff, tighten my helmet back on. It's a good thing to wear all the time, its one of the most important gear to wear.

Have trouble starting it, flooded I guess. Takes several kicks to start it. This time I take it slower. "Lets try the road." I point to the driveway.

I have my eyes peeled for anymore obstacles. This time I know the dogs dart all around us.

Eric has a basket strapped to the back of the bike. A picnic lunch. We'll go to his special place by the stream. When we stop and I get to examine myself better, I see I have a lot of scrapes, some deep cuts, and those wonderful bruises. Dirt and grease all over me. Grass stuck to the dried blood. A nice dip in the pool would be what the doctor ordered.

We spread a blanket on the ground. Of course the dogs make themselves at home on it. Eric bought them something to chew on. Just some sandwiches and something to drink.

I look at my boo-boos, ouch……. They hurt. And my hand. A big cut across the top of it.

"Your all cut up" Eric looks me over. Takes my hand.

"It was a good thing I had my helmet on, I probably would have cracked my head open, and my knee guards, probably would have destroyed my knees." I say looking at the cuts on my arms. My hand dripping blood.

CHAPTER 34

My helmet is all scratched up, it could have been my face. We finish eating and Eric spreads out on the blanket. The dogs crawl closer to him. The sun is shining, brightly, not a cloud in the sky. I look up at the sky, the sky is blue...... sky blue like Cam's eyes. The air is sweet smelling. The stream has a tantalizing trickling sound. It calls to me.

"This is nice," I sigh, tossing my head back.

"Sure is," Eric says, "That stream sure sounds inviting," he smiles. Eyes closed.

"Yeah, maybe," I peek at him.

"I'll race you," I say and jump up, kicking off my boots, pulling off my t-shirt and unzipping my shorts, throw everything over my shoulder.

I scream when I hit the cold water. It numbs the burning scrapes and cuts. Eric is right behind me. Pulling off his shirt and boots. Shorts, jumps in next to me.

"Whew!" He screams, "Its cold," I laugh cause he looks blue. The dogs are running around the border of the pool. Big chickens, that they are. We splash each other, the dogs bark. The splashing gets vigorous, competitive, I'm pulling out all the stops, to win our splashing fight. We get closer to each other, as we splash without giving up. Splashing until we cant see each other.

We are laughing, “I think it’s a tie,” I spit water out of my mouth.

He grabs me and holds me in his arms. Were both breathing hard and still laughing. His kisses are unrestrained, he’s not holding anything back. He wants me and I want him.

We get out of the pool. And go to the blanket. Our teeth chattering. The water was freezing, but out passion is red hot. Everything I’ve pent up, everything I’ve kept buried for weeks, for Eric whether its because of Cam or not, comes spilling out of me. I aggressively attack him. We roll around on the blanket.

The dogs think it’s a game and bite our feet. Okay, the dogs aren’t going to let us have a mind blowing minute.

“Duke, Harlow,” Eric yells at them. Their having to much fun to care if he’s mad or not. Their tugging on the blanket like it’s a pull toy.

“Oh…….this ain’t gonna work,” he says. “Bad dogs.” We laugh because they are just so funny.

Our moment of desire is subdued. “Stupid dogs,” I say. Its late anyway. Dinner should be on the table, soon, and early to bed. We have to leave early.

Cam was sending a car to pick us up, so at least we wont have to drive. I patch myself up, the cuts and scrapes aren’t that bad, some black and blues, I always bruise easy anyway. The cold water helped.

We get dressed. Pack up the picnic basket, ride back to the barn and put the bikes away. I take a hot shower before dinner. I hope they don’t mind me in my PJ’s.

“What did you guys do today?” Eric’s mom asks.

“Dirt biking, picnic down by the stream.” I say as I chew a piece of chicken. “This is good, Anne.”

“Oh, thank you,” she says.

“Yeah, Janie can ride,” Eric smiles and pats my legs.

“I’m gonna miss you , Janie,” Anne says.

“I’m gonna miss you guys too, Anne, I’ve had such a wonderful time here. Your cooking has been so delicious, everything has been great.”

“Oh, thank you, Janie, You can come back anytime you want.” She smiles.

"Thanks, I'd like that." Eric squeezes my leg, again. It makes me jump, cause he's squeezing a bruise, I roll my eyes at him and mouth, "OUCH." to him.

"Sorry," he mouths back. He doesn't mention that I fell off the bike and landed on my head.

After dinner, we sit outside by the bonfire. There's so many stars out tonight. I have a jacket, jeans, shoes and socks on, over my PJs, wrapped up in a blanket, cuddled up next to Eric. Its so nice to sit out under the stars, when your in a big city you never see any stars.

A hot cup of chocolate in my hands. My head rested against Eric's chest. I look up into the dark night sky, at least it isn't blue. Trillions of stars. A shooting star.

"Make a wish," Eric says.

My first thought was Cam. What do I wish for? That he loves me, and forgets Melissa. That he wants me for the rest of my life, that he'll love me for the rest of my life. I wished I found the right person for me. I look at Eric and smile.

"Did you make a wish?" He asks me.

"Sort of," I said, I sip my chocolate.

"I hope it comes true," he says.

"I think it might have already," I say. And smile a very satisfied smile at him.

We're quiet for a while, the crackling fire, is the only noise, except for the bugs, the croaking frogs, the animals in the barn. The fire is making me sleepy.

"Come on Janie, we better go to bed, its late."

"Only if you come with me," I say between yawns.

"Someday I will," he says so sure of himself. He offers me his warm hand. He helps me up, and we walk into the house our arms around each other. I'm feeling very sore. My cuts are all bandaged up. Eric helps me out of my jeans, and jacket, I still have my PJS on underneath. He tucks me into bed.

"Night, Janie," he leans in and kisses me.

"Night Eric, stay please," I sigh and snuggle down into the blankets. "There's enough room here for you."

"No I better not, gotta respect the folks." He kisses me again.

"See you in the morning," I say.

"Sweet dreams." He says. He closes the door, and I fall asleep. The dogs are sleeping with him, Duke snores and Harlow makes noises. I fall a sleep, not thinking of anything in particular. Cam isn't even in my head tonight. I'll see him tomorrow anyway. I wonder how it will feel, to see him, after a week apart. Will that same dizzying feeling I get when ever I see him, hit me? I was hoping that maybe it wouldn't happen at all.

CHAPTER 35

The car, the one Cam sends to us, arrives at 8:00 in the morning. I'm not even up yet. My bags are already by the door, so Eric can load those into the car.

I got dressed as quickly as my achy body would let me. Eric rushes in to wake me up, but I'm ready to go, much to his relief.

The driver is standing outside the limo with the trunk still open, in case we have something else. He's smoking a nasty cigarette and Eric's Mom had given him a cup of coffee and a muffin.

Eric's mom packed us some breakfast, we say good-bye. I especially am sad to leave the dogs. No matter how lousy or down you feel, they always make you feel better. I said good-bye to the horses, last night.

I promise I'll come back again, we wave out the back window. Everyone is on the porch waving back. We settle in for a long drive.

I can tell Eric is a little upset, I put my hand in his. I would be too. If I had a life like theirs. He has a nice family and home, who would want to leave. But we also need jobs.

We eat the breakfast, about an hour later. I finally get to see the town in the daylight. Not much to see. The movie theater, and the diner we ate in. The burnt down arcade he used to play in. Even his high school, Hanna High.

I can see he has fond memories, I have none really of my town or high school only that I hated it and couldn't wait to leave.

As soon as I graduated I never looked back.

My parents moved too.

Three hours later the driver drops us off at the hotel, we leave our bags and go to the arena. Everyone is there, setting up the equipment. Before I go in, I take a deep breath. Breath, I remind myself. Breath.

Eric says, "Are you ready?" I nod yes. He grabs my hand and we walk in together.

It was awfully quiet, for so much activity, some banging and hammering, sound check, for the amount of people it takes to set things up. People were talking, it just wasn't the usual excitement, with laughter and teasing, jokes and things. Something was off. An eerie quiet, like something bad happened. It sent a chill down my back.

Some look up at us, and nod. Others didn't care. Eric shrugs. Like he feels it too, but doesn't know what's wrong either.

"Wow, what a welcome," I say under my breath.

"Yeah, what's going on?" He agrees.

He goes to find the guy who's in charge. "I'll see you later," he says and kisses me. "You want to go for dinner?"

"Sure," I tell him. "See ya."

Who do I seek out? Do I seek out Cam? I spot him.

But I hang back and hide in the shadows. I just watch him, for a long time. He looks up a couple of times. In my direction, but then looks down at whatever he is doing. He looks like he's waiting for someone. He keeps looking up and around. Makes a frown, then goes back to what he was doing. My mouth is salivating. I'm so nervous, like its my first date. My heart is pounding in my chest. I look at him and start from his head, to his face, to his chest, down his long legs and back up again. He pushes his hair out of his eyes. I notice all the rings on his hand, a shiny new one. But I cant tell. I don't know why I noticed it. I guess because I notice everything about him. I noticed it because he was playing with it. I'm curious now, I cant stay in the shadows any longer. He draws me to him. Even if he doesn't know it, he draws me like a magnet, a magnet to my soul. But I stop, I feel dizzy. My mouth goes dry, and my head starts to hurt. In the back of my mind I don't want to say what I was feeling, thinking, what I was trying to deny. What I knew to be true. I sit down on the stairs and leaned forward, my head in my hands. I feel sick to my stomach.

I feel paralyzed. If I didn't say it, it wouldn't be true. I got up from where I was sitting. I heard someone call my name. All I wanted to do was to run. Run until I couldn't breath anymore, run until I couldn't cry, run until I died.

I ran as fast as I could. And it was fast, I was in excellent shape. I ran out of the arena into the parking lot and looked in all directions. I looked for the exit. I had no idea where I was going to run to, maybe I could run home. I ran to the exit ramp. Someone is following me. Someone is calling my name, I don't hear them. I don't care who it is.

I run into the main road, look for a sign that says south and turn in that direction. My steps are strong, and my breathing is strong. I can go for miles. I turned to look behind me, the arena wasn't in my sight anymore. I wonder how many miles I've run already. It felt like the hardest workout I've ever done. But anger is propelling me to go on further. Anger and hurt, and disbelief. I'm trying to out run the hurt and the pain, the denial. I'm starting to get winded. I was thirsty, and its getting harder to catch my breath, if I don't slow down I'll have an asthma attack. And I don't have my inhaler.

But I'm gonna keep going and whoever it is, is catching up to me. Maybe its Eric. I tripped over a raised piece of concrete on the sidewalk, and fall. I just lay there. Panting........ Looking up at the sky. I closed my eyes and hoped to die.

"Janie?" He was swallowing big gulps of air. "Janie, what the hell are you doing?.....Janie answer me, are you alright? Answer me." Cam caught his breath and rolled me towards him, so he could look at my face in the light of the on coming cars.

I bet it looked like something really suspicious was going on, maybe an assault, passing motorists didn't seem to care. Even though it was dark. All they could see was a figure hunched over another figure on the ground. Some beeped horns, no one stopped.

"Janie, open your eyes, and look at me." I refused. He knew I was alive because I was still breathing fast, and the rise and fall of my chest. Tears squeezed out of my eyes.

He shakes me by my shoulders. "Janie why were you running away?" He stops shaking me, and I peek at him. He's looking at me, with a big frown on his face. "Janie?" He softly says.

I open my eyes. His eyes are dark as he stares at me. There hidden in the darkness of the night.

"Your ring," I choke out, "Its new."

He nods.

"Is it…….. A …. wedding ring?" I sniffle, and hiccup.

He looks at it, and twists it around his finger.

"I've known her for a long time, we've been going for like seven years now. She knows my mother and my grandmother. She used to do their hair." He laughs. You know every time he says that, about how long they've been together, "for seven years," I wonder if its been a wonderful seven years or a miserable seven years. Melissa says it too. Like both of them have an issue about the time. She, about waiting for him to commit. He, not wanting to.

Why is it ironic, that your mother and grandmother knew her before you did. They probably talked about you all the time. How is it she ended up at your concert, and you just happened to see her in a crowd of thousands of screaming woman, and you picked her out. I was there, you didn't pick me. She turns out to be about the same age as you. Comes from the same area as you, I don't get it. Why cant I have both of them, Cam and Eric. Why do I have to chose which one I want. There should be a law somewhere, were it says you can have more than one man. Why cant I have them both. And wonder if he never found Melissa that night at the concert and he's been alone for all these years. And then I come along. Would I have had a better chance of being his? What if everything had changed that day, he wanted to meet her back stage. And she hated him. What then?

CAM

"She lives in Canada, like me. That's where I met her. I gave her a big diamond ring. But didn't want to commit to her. I'm not sure if I was drunk or I got drunk. That's all I know." He rubs his hand with the new ring on it.

"So is that a yes or a no?" I say through clenched teeth. It's not even an answer. "I'm very confused."

"So am I," he says.

"I don't want any children, she does. So why would she want to marry me?"

“I don’t know,” I say. I don’t understand why he wont give me an honest answer, or he doesn’t want to give me one.

“Come on back with me,” he says. He pulls me up. My bruise knees I have from dirt biking, when I flew over the handle bars, are bleeding again. When I fell over the concrete sidewalk, they opened up again.

“Why did you run away from me?” He asks softly.

“Because, if I ran away, then it wouldn’t be true.” I whine. I know I hate it when I whine.

We walk slowly back to the arena. His body guard with the weird hairdo, Hawk is probably looking for him by now. After a long silence. I finally ask him. “Why don’t you want to have children?”

“Because I’d make a lousy father,” he says.

I’m surprised. “No you wouldn’t, you’d make a terrific dad.”

“I don’t think so, I don’t want to be like my father. I don’t want to make the same mistakes my father made. He left when I was young, it hurt, it hurt a lot. I hate him for that. I never knew my father until my teen years. I grew up without a father. My mom found Matt’s father, he’s a good guy, I adopted his name.”

“But you wont make the same mistakes, because of that, you would make sure you wouldn’t do, what he did.”

“I just don’t want any, that’s all.....” His voice drifts off, he’s looking off in the distance.

“You’ll be alone in your old age. You have to pass on your talents to someone, you just cant end it here. You have to pass on your blue eyes, and your voice, the way you sing, and the music you write, teach him to play the guitar, and to play hockey. And ice skate, teach him everything you know.” I plead.

“Oh it’s a him?” He raises his eyebrows at me.

“Well, you know, a boy or girl whatever it is. Your brother has kids, and Rob too. Your children are your greatest treasure, your greatest gift you can give someone.” I say.

“What are you a sales woman? You want kids?” He asks.

“Someday I guess, if the right guy comes along.....”

We cross the highway to the exit ramp, run across the road to the entrance to the arena.

“What about Eric?” He asks.

"I don't know, how do you know if the person is the right one?" Is it a feeling you get? Is it a look. I don't know. I like him a lot. Sometimes he seems like a big brother, rather than a lover."

"He's a good guy you know, he'd do anything for you." Cam says.

"I know. Cam…….?"

"Yeah?"

"You have to take back what you said about dying….you have to, you jinxed yourself. Please take it back. It isn't even funny. It's not funny at all…………...." I cry.

"I don't think I can, I already said it." He ponders the idea.

"And like I said, I don't see it ending that way anyway. Its that stupid car of yours.' I say. "Please get rid of it." I beg.

"Don't drive it anymore. Please." I beg, again.

"Do you really think anyone would miss me, if I was gone? Do you think it would make any difference if I wasn't around?"

"Oh my god, yes Cam, you have affected so many peoples lives….. including mine. Once your gone, there wont be anymore band. No more beautiful songs written or sung by you. I told you, I will jump off of the 20th floor of a building, if you die."

"Don't okay, I don't want you to die because of me."

"Then don't you die, you live to be a very old man, don't do a show on your 40th birthday. PROMISE ME." I want to grab him and shake him violently so it sinks into his head.

"I cant," he shakes his head. "I don't know what the band will be doing then, it's like five years from now. So I don't know, where will be."

When we get closer to the arena, his body guard is there, along with a crowd and Eric.

"Where have you two been? We've been looking all over for you," an exasperated body guard, Hawk says.

Eric looks at my bloodied knees, I follow his eyes, "I fell." I say.

"We took a walk," Cam says to Hawk. I walk up ahead, trying to get away from everyone, Cam is behind me, Eric is walking behind them. He's probably steaming mad at Cam.

I walked to my dressing room, close the door and plop myself down violently on the couch, I'm in shock, in the twilight zone. I know what he told me, but my mind cant get a grip on it, I don't want to get a grip on it, I don't want to believe it.

Cam went to his dressing room, I guess. Eric followed me. I think I slammed the door in his face. He cracks the door open and peeks in. "Janie? Can I come in?" He asks me.

"Sure," I stare off at the wall. My head feels so heavy, and it hurts. I feel so tired. I want to go to sleep. My knees hurt too. But I really don't care.

"Janie," he says softly, "What's going on?"

I slowly look up at him, I'm so numb. I see him there, and I cant remember who he is. Its like a bad dream and I cant wake up.

He asks me again, "Janie, what happened, with you and Cam?"

"Nothing, why?" I say defensively.

"I don't think its nothing, you look terrible and Cam didn't look to happy either, you know don't you?"

"Know what?" I ask dryly.

"About Cam and Melissa, getting married."

I stare up at him, "So...... its true?" I whisper, and turn my face away to hide the tears that are threatening to fall down my face.

"Yes, its true, didn't he tell you?"

"No, not in so many words, he said he couldn't remember."

"BULLSHIT," Eric says, " He couldn't remember what kind of shit answer is that?" He's pacing in front of me, running his fingers through his hair.

"He can't remember, its one of the most important days of your life and you cant remember, oh my god, what an ass. What a load of shit."

"Yeah, you said that already, he said he was drunk, that's why he cant remember."

"Don't kid yourself Janie, he remembers, listen...... I know I'm not suppose to know about this, cause you keep this to yourself, but everyone sort of knows, and I'm gonna say it anyway. You have to get over being so obsessed with Cam. It's gonna make you crazy, or worse yet its gonna kill you. I wont stand for that, I wont let you make yourself crazy over a guy who uses you." He stops in front of me, and gets on his knees. Takes my hands in his.

He looks into my eyes, he has such pretty blue eyes, different than Cams. But pretty none the less.

"I can see it happening, you do crazy things when it comes down to him, he makes you crazy and irrational......Can't..... Can't," he took a big breath, “Can’t you be obsessed about me? I love you, Janie. It makes me sick, to see you follow him around like a love sick puppy dog.”

I look at him through my hair, which had fallen in front of my face. A shield, he looks like a little boy, with pleading eyes. The ones that are staring back at me. I feel remorseful. I’ve hurt him. I touch his face and he closes his eyes. Pushes his face into my hand, and hold his hand over mine. I can’t find my voice, he said he loved me. What can I say to him to make this right?

“Eric, I’m so sorry, I’ve hurt you. I’m not making excuses. If I can explain how I feel, maybe you can understand, why I behave the way I do when it comes to Cam.” I clear my throat. “Its like an addiction, that’s the only way I can explain it. Its an addiction I cant control, I have no will to fight it. Its been a part of my life for quite a while. I’ve tried to quit cold turkey, as they say. I’ve tried to ignore him, and stay far away from him, I even came to visit you, just to get away from him. But the minute I see him, all those strong old feelings for him come flooding back.”

“Yeah, but he’s married now, and that should make it easier for you, he’s out of reach, Janie, he’s no longer on the market, and he really wasn’t before anyway because he was engaged to her. It’s wrong, in so many ways.” He breaths heavily, and lets it out.

“I know,” I whisper and I hang my head. I knew all along it was wrong, but I didn’t care.

“If you go any further with this, then it becomes adultery.” He says.

“I never thought about that, I know, I’ll give up, I will, I’ll be obsessed about you, Eric. I like you a lot, I could love you, just give me a chance.”

He smiles at me, but he also looks skeptical to, I don’t think he believes me. I don’t think I believe myself.

I look at the clock, “I have to get dressed for the show, can we talk later?” I ask him.

“Sure,” he says, “after the show.” He gives me a weak smile, opens the door and closes it behind him.

How am I suppose to do the show? How am I suppose to dance around him? Remain in the twilight zone. Just zone out, have no feelings about anything, just go out there and do my job. I do it every night, I touch him every night. Why should tonight be any different?

I don't even remember getting dressed, or leaving the dressing room, or even going back stage to wait for my cue.

I don't feel like doing this tonight, what's the sense, it was always to entice Cam, to seduce him, to lure him, to tempt him, to lead him into loving me. But it never quite worked. There was always Melissa, what kind of hold does she have on him? I was just a distraction, when she wasn't here and he was feeling lonely, I filled in the empty space.

I was just the something to play with, while she was away, and I let him.

He can go live with her in his big mansion. And drive his big black hummer, and his Ferrari, and his corvette, and his prowler, and live happily ever after. I'm not a jealous person, usually, but I feel like I've become one. I want to be Melissa.

Then I think about how many times I've seen him drunk. And how many times he's been arrested for DWI. How he's drinking more on stage now, how he's getting loud and obnoxious when he's performing, how he wants the audience to drink and get drunk with him. Do I really want a man who does that? And the answer is NO.

Eric drinks, in a very rare, few occasions and since I've met him, I've only seen him drunk once. I've seen Cam several times. He doesn't need a special occasion to get drunk. Is that a prize, really? I stand back stage trying to convince myself that this is it. I lean against the wall, with my arms folded over my chest. My head is against the wall. I don't even hear the music. I'm so caught up in my own thoughts, for anything else to register. He maybe sexy, and hot, and well endowed, cause he brags about it on stage, says that he could never wear spandex, like Steven Tyler, of Areosmith. He's tall, blue eyed and blond haired. And you know me I love those blue eyes. Has a beautiful voice, and a sexy walk. Is talented beyond belief, that it used to bring tears to my eyes. And its unfair that one single person can have that much talent, but he does. He writes poetry. Romantic love songs. Where they rip my heart right out of my chest when ever I hear him sing them. And now, I don't know if they'll have the same meaning anymore, they'll be bitter in my head, in my heart. What about the song he said he wrote for me?

He's around famous people all the time. Especially musicians all the time. Even discovers new groups and helps them out. He's a nice guy, most of the time. It was so out of reach. I was only kidding myself.

Someone has to tap me on the shoulder, to tell me its my cue. I nod, and walk out on stage. I go through the whole dance number. I think I did the usual stuff, I have know idea. I don't even remember the music. I don't remember seeing Cam's face or any of the other band members, or even Dale's face. Did I even go up on the drum deck?

I have to go change for the sign language songs. I look through my suitcase and pick out the costume I hate the most. Its all black, like for a funeral. In a sense that's the way I feel, a funeral for my heart.

I take off all the makeup, I feel like the plain Jane, I want to be. No jewelry, no perfume, to night. I put on my ugliest dress I had. My hair straight as a board. My hair is naturally straight, what I wouldn't give to have his curls. And every night, he tries to have straight hair. I bet she's the one who dyes it and cuts it. I bet she told him it looks good, you know what Melissa you have a lot of fans very mad, about Cam's hair. I hate it. He looked sexier with curly and wild, hair.

I wont smell like every flower in the desert tonight, either. He's lucky I took a shower after my long run.

I feel so hateful, right now. I hate myself. I hate myself for hurting Eric. I have to make this right.

I go through the sign language songs, I sit next to him, he seems oblivious to the way I'm acting towards him. Maybe I'll just vanish. And no one will know I was ever here.

I didn't show up for the meet and greet, no one even came to get me.

I know Cam was watching me while I danced around him. He kept his eye on me. I never looked at him, though. It was like I'm just doing my job, I have no feelings for you, what so ever.

I messed up really badly for the sign songs, my hands just looked like shadow puppets. I don't think any of the fans noticed.

Frankly if he fires me, I wouldn't care. I'm so numb. I cant believe how this is making me feel.

I have to consider Eric. Cam's face is furrowed the entire night. He doesn't banter with the audience, like he usually does. Good, were all miserable, ALL BECAUSE YOU GOT MARRIED!

Life is cruel, Love is even crueler.

I don't understand how some people can find a boyfriend or a girlfriend right after they break up with one and find another. And go on and on and on like that for most of their lives. They always have someone.

Then there's people like me, who never have anyone, who cant find anyone. Am I destined to be alone? I only find shit heads. Or drunks, or men that just want to use you for some reason or another. Or men who have no personalities at all. Who are so flat, you could stand them sideways and you wouldn't see them. Because there's nothing to them. Not in their heads, not in their hearts, no where. Its just so unfair, love is cruel, its laughs at you. Makes you feel like you have wings and then it pulls the wings out so you fall flat on your face. And it laughs even harder at you.

Then there's Eric. Eric is none of these men. I should be so thankful for him, that he wants me. I don't deserve him. I think I'm going to remain alone for the rest of my life. This way I wont hurt anyone and no one will hurt me.

Why would you want to marry someone, tell them you don't want children, tell them your going to die on your 40th birthday. And leave her a widow. How cruel is that?

My grandparents got married and were married for 57 years. They raised a family, went through the usual highs and lows of life, and survived. Then my grandfather dies and leaves my grandmother all alone. She's lost, depressed, doesn't want to do anything that she used to do. Just sits and stares, or stays in bed.

What's the sense in having someone, they die and leave you. I'd rather be alone. Yes I'm feeling sorry for myself right now, I'll get over it......maybe. I've been cheated and screwed in this life when it comes to love.

So I'm going to distance myself from Eric, so I wont hurt him anymore. He's been hinting at things like, living together, or even getting married. I'm tired of being hurt all my life, of loving things and then their taken away. My heart hurts so bad. I don't want to feel anything anymore.

We have about three more months of touring. Can I hold onto my sanity?

I had once said that Cam helped me keep my sanity, when my father died. Now who will help me keep my sanity over him?

I know Eric hasn't given up on me. He stays in the shadows keeping his eye on me. If I need his help, I know he'll be right there for me. He's right there giving me his strength. His support.

He doesn't say anything about Cam to me. But you can tell by his eyes that he feels my pain, he's in pain too. Because of me. My obsessed behavior, my obsession with Cam.

He may die from a heart attack on stage. I've seen him smoking lately and I just don't mean cigarettes either. So maybe it will be true. But it wont be…like I said. It will be a fast car, he's the driver, DWI and a tree.

About a week of moping around. Eric couldn't stand it anymore.

"Janie," he called after me ,when I was running up and down the arena stairs, I intensified my workouts, so I would be to tired to feel anything.

"Janie," he called again, and waved a towel and a bottle of water at me.

"Hey Eric, how thoughtful of you." I took the water bottle and drank half of it. And the towel to wipe my face and neck. I hadn't seen him all week, I mean like for a date or hanging out. We saw each other, but just working. I avoided him with great effort, when I felt this weight on me that was smothering me, I wanted to go to him, but didn't.

"How are you? What's up?" I tried to sound nonchalant, when really I wanted to through myself into his arms.

"Listen, I've been thinking…Maybe you should go see a doctor about your depression, maybe he could give you something, ya know?" I was taken by surprise, but I didn't stop him from continuing, I kept my face blank. I pretended that I had no idea what he was talking about. I pretended to tie my sneaker laces.

"I cant take it anymore, your avoiding me. Like I'm the bad guy, here. I'm not. You don't smile anymore, you don't laugh either. You need some help, even if its just someone to talk to." He looks at me intently.

"What do you say? Will you go for me please? I don't want to lose you…"

I look at him. He looks like he's on the verge of tears. I feel a pang in my chest. He's still hurting.

I throw my arms around him, and he squeezes me hard. "I will Eric, I will, I promise. I'll try and see someone this week. I didn't know it showed, I thought I was hiding it really well." I say in his ear.

"No, its all over your face." He whispers. Holds me tight against him, I can feel his strength, I can feel his love for me. I want to say it to him, I want to. But I cant. I'll hurt him again.

"Okay, good, I'll go with you if you want."

"No, I think I should go by myself."

"Alright, but if you need me to drive you."

"I'll ask," I smile.

I go to the weight room, the arenas always have them. And I use every piece of equipment there is. Treadmill, bicycle, elliptical and some of the weights. A punching bag. I remember one time, when a boyfriend broke up with me, I pretended the punching bag was him, and every time I kicked it or punched it I said his name.

Which I'm pounding the crap out of, with all my might. The sweat is trickling down my back.

"Anyone I know?" A laughing voice, says behind me.

Cam walks in. Why now, I ask myself. He had all day to come here. I don't answer him. Yeah it's you, I say to myself. Because I hate you. This is what I really want to do to your face, your body, your cold heart, your senseless head. With each piece of his body, I give a hard punch to the bag. Tears are starting to gather in my eyes. He wont notice anyway with the sweat that's on my face. And my back is turned to him.

He starts to lift some weights. Should have a spotter for that. I think, to bad. If it falls on him, I'll leave him there. I keep punching and add a few kicks, like right in the groin, whew that would hurt. It gives me a grin on my face, just thinking about it.

My shoulders, arms and legs, my back, hands are starting to feel the burn. The madder I get, the harder I hit the bag. I picture his face on the bag, its not that hard to do, his face is embedded in my brain.

I can see him in the mirrors. He's trying to lift something that's to heavy for him. He's glancing over at me every minute or so. I keep punching. Even though it hurts, it feels good. I can feel all that pent up anger towards him, being released.

I'm just about through with my workout. And maybe I'll move on to something else, when the rest of the band walks in. They stop just inside the doorway. When they see me beating the crap out of the bag. And look at Cam and then at me.

Cam is lying on his back, trying to lift the weights over his head.

I'm laughing inside, he's so weak. Those skinny chicken arms.

I finish one last punch, for Rob and Matt. Take off the gloves. Blink away the tears. Wipe my face with my towel. Take a big long drink and pour some of it over my face. I'm ignoring all of them. Their probably thinking, why doesn't Cam fire her? She's brought hostility to our band. She interfered in our lives. She's no longer a team player. He wont though. He wants me around. I make his ego feel good. Cause I'm young and gorgeous, he knows I'm obsessed with him. It boosts his ego to the ultimate high.

I pour more water over my head and it soaks my shirt. Right away their eyes go right there, wet t-shirt. What's the song? "Cant touch this." Nope no more Cam, no more booty calls either. Not that I've given him any since I've been with Eric. Since the shooting incident.

A couple of sit-ups, oh around 300, I do sets of 25. And I'm done. I do them in different leg positions to get the most out of it.

I'm done. I pick up my things and leave. But I linger just a while outside the door in the hallway. "Did she say anything to you, Cam?" Dale asked Cam.

"No… not a word. I asked her who she was beating to death on the punching bag. She didn't have to say who it was, she just looked at me and I knew it was me." He grunts.

"Man, you have got to get rid of her, fire her, will you? She's making everyone uncomfortable." Matt says.

"I don't want to…., she'll get used to the idea. Besides she goes, then Eric will leave. And I promised his brother I'd take care of him. So I cant. Let me deal with this, okay."

"Yeah, okay, its your call." Rob says.

I laughed to myself and felt really smug. Good, good, good. He feels the sting. I'm glad. I will never get used to the idea, EVER!

CHAPTER 36

I made an appointment with a regular GP for now. Get a physical, all of that stuff, that goes along with it. And talk to him about my depression and obsessive behavior. How one minute I feel fine and the next my emotions are a roller coaster.

Maybe he can point me in the right direction. I have Eric drop me off. He goes and eats lunch. The doctor took me as a special patient when I explained to him who I work for etc…. and that I didn't have much time to get a physical done for my job. Because were always on the move.

He asked a lot of questions, takes blood, urine test, all the usual tests.

Of course tests results take a while to come back, so he wont know right away if something is off. He says I'm in excellent shape, of course I am. Blood pressure is good. He asks me my age. Asks if I'm married, boyfriend, sexual partners? I'm a little puzzled why he's asking me such personal questions. And what do they have to do with my physical.

He has a stick and puts some urine on it. "What are you doing that for?" I ask him, concerned he isn't being straight forward with me.

"Why are you doing that?" I ask, again.

"Just thought of something," he says. We go on with some other tests. Reflexes, eyesight, hearing, EKG.

He looks at the stick, after a few minutes. "Hum," he says.

"What?"

"Your pregnant," he says.

You should see the look on my face. He shows me the stick, pink lines. Its positive.

"That's why your feeling the way you feel. Hormones run amok."

"No, your wrong, come on doc, its got to be wrong."

"Nope these tests are 99.9% right, there never wrong, if you want to take it again, its gonna come up the same, you'll see. You are pregnant." The doctor says.

"Great," by who? I think. And do I tell Eric?

"So you'll have to go to a GYN/OB, I can give you a good doctor to go to." He says.

"Sure," I say, I'm in shock, dazed and confused. I try to think back. I hadn't even noticed that, that time of the month never came. This very heavy feeling over taking me. What do I do now?

"I don't live here, Doc, I live in NY, I'm traveling with the band." I tell him.

"Well go to the doctor for now and get the usual done, ultra sound, some advice, vitamins. And then go from there, I'm sure she'll be able to tell you what to do next." The doctor says.

"Okay, I will, thanks Doc." I shake his hand and head out the door. Get the number for the next doctor. How do I say, "Who the father is, to him?"

I don't want to say, I've been a slut and slept with two different guys in two days.

"The doctor is a woman?" I ask.

"Yes, there are several, but she's the best, and she'll be able to help you." He writes down the number on a card and hands it to me.

I pay and call the GYN doctor. Explain the same way. I'm on tour, and need to see her now.

There busy, but can squeeze me in. Eric drives me there. He raises his eyebrows, when he sees the sign for GYN/OB.

"Don't ask," I say, " the doctor said it was a good idea, okay?"

"Okay," he says.

He drops me off. It's a wait. But I finally get called. The doctor gives me an exam, ultra sound. She's very nice. I feel I may be able to tell her my predicament.

She confirms, what the other doctor had said. Then I just come out and tell her about the two guys I was with, and ask her who's it could be. She says you have to narrow it down to the exact time of ovulation, although it could be up to 72 hours later. Oh great, the time line is to close to figure it out.

She says as long as I'm feeling good, I can still dance. Take it easy. I tell her, I've never really felt nauseous, that I can remember. So many things have been going on, that something like a missed period I hadn't even noticed.

November would be the estimated due date. Cam is born in November too. What a birthday present that would be.

This cant be happening, oh my god. I don't want to have kids, yet. I don't want to get married yet, either. And then I said I wanted to be alone.

Eric is waiting for me outside in the car. I take a big breath and walk to the car, get in. Its a borrowed car.

"Well?" He asks. "How did it go?" He's fishing. I can tell, I know he's concerned about me.

"Oh well, they say I'm in great shape. Wont have any of the tests back, until next week. Will be out of here by then, I'll have to call."

"Every things, okay though?" His blue eyes stare at me, why does he know something?

"Yeah, uh, fine." His stare is making me uncomfortable. "Your staring at me. Why?"

"I'm not sure," he says, " I just want to make sure your okay, that's all." He starts the car. I stare out the window.

We drive back to the arena. I want to be alone for a while and think. I could have an abortion. But I don't like that idea at all. So I guess I go through with it.

Maybe I can keep it a secret. Yeah, sure… lots of girls keep it a secret.

I'll tell Eric soon. As soon as I except it myself. As soon as I can get up the nerve.

I think about it for a couple of days. I'm feeling tired, but not to tired. I do the shows. I workout, but not the intense way I used to. I decide after a week of thinking about it, now was the right time to tell him.

I ask him if we can go out or something. Maybe a cheerful restaurant.

"What is it Janie, you've looked serious all evening. Are you alright? What's going on?"

"I'm fine, Eric, just have a lot on my mind, and I have something to tell you. All week I've been trying to find a way to tell you." He's doing that staring thing again.

Before we go into the restaurant, we sit outside on the concrete walls they have around the place. "You'd better sit down," I tell him.

"Okay, now your starting to scare me." He says.

He sits down next to me. He takes my hand and looks at me intently.

"Well I don't know how to tell you this, so I'll just come right out and say it." I hold my breath. And blurt it out.

"I'm pregnant." I sneak a peek at him, his face is kind of blank, but he takes in a deep breath.

"Eric?" He's mulling it over in his head.

"Are you okay?" I put my hand over his.

"Yeah, that's like WOW, incredible, are you sure?" He's excited?

"I'm sure and your okay with this?" I'm really surprised.

"Yeah, I always wanted kids. So then you'll have to marry me." He smiles. And hugs me in a big bear hug.

"Well, lets take it slow, okay. It hasn't really sunk in yet. And please don't tell Cam. I don't want anyone to know yet, okay." He shakes his head.

"Why not? I want to tell everyone," he smiles and kisses my hand. Hugs me again and swings me around.

"Eric, Eric stop, put me down, I'm serious, if you tell anyone, then they make me leave the tour. And I don't want to leave, yet. We only have a few more months to go and its over."

"Oh sorry," he pats my stomach. "Can I tell my parents?"

"Yes, only them. No one else. Okay?"

"Okay. "I cant believe it, I'm gonna be a father," he says.

"Your okay with this?"

"Yes, yes, yes, I said yes." He hugs me again. His arms feel so good around me, so comforting, like maybe everything will be alright. I needed his arms around me. After avoiding him for a week, I wanted his touch.

While eating in the restaurant, Eric and I talk. "Will your parents be disappointed? You know we aren't married. Shouldn't we be married first, then the baby?"

"No, I've been talking to them about asking you, they know." He smiles that bright smile.

"Oh..." I'm surprised again. He's full of surprises, tonight. I didn't think he was serious about me. "So just for a while lets keep it our secret."

"Just for a while, not much longer. God, Janie you've made me so happy." He kisses me all night and has his arms around me.

I wonder if he'd be happy knowing, that I don't know who's it is. That this might involve Cam also. And if Cam found out, what would he think? I don't want to think about what might happen. I just want to be happy for a while, like Eric is. He's just radiating happy, from every pore of his body. He better wipe that smile off his face though. He looks like he's going to explode.

Things have settled down, between all of us. We just avoid each other, except when we have to work, it's become very professional. We all do our jobs. We still have fun in the arenas before the show, and even after the show. Melissa visits, we avoid each other also. Boy would she be pissed if she knew the parts that he was kissing. I smile at that thought, I nod as I pass her, she nods back.

I don't feel all that bad for someone who is pregnant, I don't know am I suppose to feel that bad? I'm not really sick or nauseous, like they say I should be. So I'm very happy about that, so it'll make my dancing easier. My clothes still fit. I'm not that far along.

Eric tells his parents. They were ecstatic about the whole thing. Couldn't wait to be grandparents. Eric wasn't sure if his brother Jeff could have children, because of his accident.

I'm glad everyone else is happy about this. Why wasn't I? Honestly, I'm scared. If Cam found out would he think it was his? Or would he wonder if it was his? Would he try to take it away from me. Him and the bitch. They don't want kids. So why would he? After all they, he certainly have the means to raise a child, he's got tons of money.

And wonder if Eric found out about Cam and me? I know he has his suspicions. After all he did warn me about Cam. It would hurt him beyond belief.

Every time Eric sees me, he gives me a big grin. His face has been smiling ever since I told him. He's been singing and whistling. Funny what you think of, my Dad used to whistle, when he was happy. And then when he started feeling ill, the whistling stopped.

He mouths to me, "I love you." And I mouth back to him, "Stop it," and I look around to see who is watching. No one that I can see. Although I catch Cam, once in a while staring at me. I make a face at him and then he realizes he been staring. Sometimes I stick my tongue out at him. Then he smiles and it's a dirty little smile. An evil smile. Like yeah I remember you, and I remember what you liked to do. What you did with that tongue. What you loved to do with that tongue….

We have a week in between the next concert. The end of the tour is mostly in Canada. Because that's home base. Everyone except me lives here.

Eric and I are going back to Hanna, for a visit with his family. I'm excited. The weather has been very nice, everything is starting to turn green again. Eric wants to help his father get the fields ready to plant. Sounds like fun.

I forgot to mention Jeff, Jr. Eric's big brother. Manages Cams official website. That's his job, besides whatever he can do on the farm. I know that his wife wanted children, she mentioned it once. I never ask personal things, especially when it may be a sensitive subject with them.

I don't know how they are going to feel about me and Eric. And baby.

We left on Sunday, and got there in the afternoon. I slept the whole way, it seems like these days I cant get enough sleep. And that's all I feel like doing.

I laid my head on Eric's lap. I was getting car sick, the best thing for me to do is sleep. Eric rubs my head and plays with my fingers. Puts his hand on my stomach, often, like he's checking to see if there really is a baby in there. I can just feel a little bump. So can he, he's amazed.

And he's so bubbly happy, that it amazes me. And upsets me at the same time. Why cant I feel the same way he feels? But I don't. I feel like I have this huge weight on my shoulders. I hope it passes, soon.

The limo is rooming, so I can stretch out. Eric's long legs appreciates it too.

The limo pulls up in front of the house. Everyone comes running out. The dogs too. The dogs are barking for attention.

"You ready?" Eric asks me.

"Yes," I smile. I stretch and feel refreshed.

"Hi, you guys," his mom says as we get out of the limo. She's the first one to come running up to the car. She gives me a big hug. "Janie, were so happy to see you again, let me look at you," she says as she backs up a bit to take in a full view of me.

She looks at my stomach, and puts her hand there. "Oh I think it a boy," she says. I smile. His Dad hugs me, his sister, and Jeff's wife. I go up to the porch, to say Hi to Jeff. "Hi, Jeff," I say.

"Hey little sister," he says. I bend down to give him a hug, he whispers in my ear. "He loves you a lot, you know." I shake my head, I know.

"I know." I say, as I look at Eric.

"Yeah Dad I'll help you plant the fields," Eric is saying to his Dad.

"How are you feeling Janie?" His mom Anne asks me.

"Oh good actually." I tell her, I'm still watching Eric, so strong, so confident, so hot.

"Oh good, I'm glad. It can be hard in the beginning." She says.

We get our bags into the house. The limo leaves. We still have separated rooms. Which is okay with me. We still aren't married. And out of respect for his parents.

At dinner though, his mother confided in me, she whispered while we dried the dishes. "I was pregnant with Jeff, Jr. before we were married." She nods as if remembering those days. "We had no money, and my parents were furious with us. I had to quit school and get a job. Jeff already had a good job, and he worked on this farm with his father. So we moved in with his parents, here and have been here ever since." She smiles at me, I smile back.

"I didn't know that Anne, does Eric know?" I ask.

"Yes, they all know, its like one of the family stories we tell. It's not that I'm bragging or anything, but everything worked out for us." She sighs.

"So are you saying that this is alright with you guys? I mean I was worried you would think bad of me. And I care a lot about Eric and what you guys think of this whole thing."

"Janie, we are very happy for you and Eric, we cant wait to be grandparents." We finish the dishes. And carry the dessert into the dining room. Where everyone is gathered.

Anne made a special dinner and a special dessert, just for tonight, to celebrate.

She told me to come into the living room, where it was decorated like a baby shower. Ribbons, and garland, pink and blue. "OH…you guys." I said, "You didn't have to do this."

"Yes we did," everyone chimed in. "Its our first grandchild."

There's presents for me and the baby. I tear up. Eric smiles. "You knew about this?" I nudge him with my elbow in the ribs.

He looks up at the ceiling. "I plead the 5th." He says.

"Oh you guys must of spent a small fortune. Its all so beautiful."

"Its from Eric, too," his sister says.

Anne crocheted blankets and sweaters, booties and hats. Sister and sister-in-law, made a baby quilt. Dad made a cradle. Jeff set up a bank account and trust fund for the baby. And Eric says I can pick out an entire nursery set. He has catalogs. When everything is unwrapped. We eat dessert.

I take another look at all the lovely gifts. Homemade things are the best. I cant crochet, I can knit a little. I do quilt, or I used to. Don't exactly have the time any more.

The animals need to be taken care of, so Eric and I offer to go and feed them. Oh yes, I forgot the dogs, who haven't left me alone since I stepped out of the limo. I've spent most of the night petting them. I fed them, I always give them an extra treat in their bowls.

Eric has gotten awfully quiet. Eric is actually acting weird. He seems a little nervous. Why in the world, would he be nervous, were finally here. I've opened all the gifts, and his parents are fine with the whole thing.

"Are you alright?" I ask him. I gently touch his arm, and he takes my hand as we walk back to the house.

"Yeah I'm fine, just happy to be back home.' He opens the back door for me. Everyone has disappeared. I look around.

Eric walks into the living room, he's making a lot of noise. "Eric, maybe everyone is in bed."

He motions for me to come and sit down on the couch. The dogs lay on the rug at my feet. He makes a sudden move and startles the dogs, he gets down on his knees. "What are you doing?" I ask him.

He pulls out a little black velvet box and opens it.

"Janie, will you marry me?" He looks very serious, and very scared. And very nervous. I'm floored, and blown away. I never expected this. I really don't want to get married. I don't. This will change everything. I don't want to hurt him or disappoint him. I check my feelings for him. He's waiting for an answer. I look into those beautiful blue eyes. I do love him, I know I do.

So I accept. I say "YES."

The ring is beautiful and he puts it on my finger. It fits. "How did you know my size?"

"I measured your finger while you were sleeping," he whispers.

"Hey, you guys, Janie said Yes," he yells.

Everyone comes running in, hugs and kisses. I yi, yi. They were all waiting in the kitchen, they all knew about it.

I'm lying in bed in the guest room. Staring at the ceiling in the dark.

How did this happen? How did my life get so out of hand? Where did it take such a dramatic turn? I know when, the first time I ever heard Cam's voice, that's when.

I don't want to get married, I don't want a baby now. But I didn't know how to say no to him, I didn't want to hurt him again. Everyone is so thrilled. I took the ring off. It feels funny. I turn on the light to look at it. Its so pretty. I put it on again.

So that's why Eric was acting funny most of the night. He had a secret. And we have a bigger secret, him and me.

No dirt bike riding for me, I think I can ride the horse if he rides with me. Eric says his horses are the most gentlest around. Especially slow poke Geronimo. Who is so happy to see Eric. He keeps nuzzling Eric neck with his nose.

Eric's horse should have been named, Lazy daisy, or something else. Geronimo was a fierce warrior. He's the slowest horse I've ever seen.

We go for a ride every morning. Eric is always sitting behind me. He puts his hand on my stomach. “I can feel, him.” he says in my ear. I smile. The whole idea is really starting to sink in.

He takes me to different spots everyday. We even rode to town on the horse. That was fun. The dogs followed behind. There’s hardly any traffic. People in town are out early. Everyone waves. Congratulates us on our engagement. Nice people, I could see why Cam would write a song about this town. News travel fast here. I guess were big news.

CHAPTER 37

Eric helps his father plant two big fields of wheat. I helped his sister and sister-in-law plant a vegetable garden for his Mom. Everything but the kitchen sink went into the ground. Even a herb garden.

I still walk a lot, jog not to much. No heavy lifting.

In the evening Eric and I go for a twilight walk. The dogs jump all over the place finding new smells and new things to explore. Some times all is you see is their tails sticking up. They disappear in the tall grass.

I've gotten friendly with the llamas and alpaca's. Anne showed me how she gets the hair from them to make it into yarn. It's quite a process.

Since I've been here, I've been getting anonymous phone calls on my cell phone. We don't get service here, so its on my voice mail. Most of the time I don't have my cell phone on me. Its usually a private number. Most of the time its off. If I go someplace by myself, I bring it with me and have it on. We can use it like a walkie talkie kind of thing.

By Friday, I had 25 missed calls. No phone number left. Said private every time. I call my family members, in case something happened to anyone. No one called. I call April, she says no. But since I have her on the phone I tell her the news. She cant believe it, and when I have more time I'll give her all the details.

So as long as everyone I cared about was okay, I didn't care who was trying to call me.

It just seemed strange that's all. You always wonder who it is.

The week went so fast. We had to leave Sunday morning. Eric's family would hold all of the baby gifts for me. We piled everything in the guest room. The cradle is beautiful, wood with little heart cutouts. His dad did a beautiful job.

We talked about where we were going to live. I told him I wouldn't mind living here, in Hanna. Eric was pleased about that. So was his family.

His Mom and Dad gave us some land to build a house out behind their house, out in one of the fields, that never gets planted. There's to many rocks or something. I didn't want to give the okay, though. But I said, "it sounded wonderful."

Both of us made good money on the tour. I sent a lot of mine home to take care of my Mom.

But Eric saved all of his up. He wanted a mansion built, "like Cam's?" I said. "NO, are you crazy? No way do I want a mansion like Cam's, who is going to clean all of it?"

He laughed. " Okay, okay, something smaller."

He thought I wanted something that big, I said, "Just because Cam has a hugemogus house, doesn't mean I want one. I want to be able to find you in the house," I told him, he laughed again.

Cam's house is way to big. What do you do with all that space, especially if its only the two of you. And a cat.

Saturday night we went on one last date to the movies. Scary night week. I love scary movies. My favorite is vampire movies, the one that was playing tonight was Stephen Kings "IT."

After the movie we went to the diner.

Someone asked me if I was pregnant. I asked them, "why would they ask that?" I looked at Eric , "why do I look like it?"

They said, "I looked different, but didn't know what it was." Great, so if someone looks at me, their going to figure it out. Especially woman.

I ask Eric's mom what it was that looks different about me. She said, " No honey, you just glow that's all."

Great, I glow!

I was trying to sleep, Saturday night after we came home. It was late and I was tired. I must of left my cell phone on. I checked to see if I had any calls, five more today. Same thing no number.

I was just about to doze off, when it rings, and bounces all over the night stand. It startles me, and I jerk awake. I haven't heard it all week.

It was late, like around 2:00. I answer it. It could be important, it could be something about my mom.

"Hello," I whisper.

Silence, but I can hear back ground noise. So I know its an open line. I hear music, and voices, laughter, but its all like far away.

"Hello, who is this? Look it late and I'm really tired and I need my rest. I'm hanging up if you don't say anything."

"No.... please don't." A scratchy raw voice says.

"Cam? Is that you?" Silence.

"Cam, are you okay? I know its you."

"No....I'm not okay, I'm in my Ferrari and I see a big tree up a head..... I'm gonna wrap my car around it, just for you.....Janie."

It takes me a second to realize it doesn't sound like he's kidding. "Cam, cut it out, this isn't funny, what's wrong?"

Silence, I hear the engine start up, it roars through the phone.

"What's wrong, why do you want to do this?" I ask him.

"I had a fight with Melissa, and I've screwed everything up, like I always do. With you, with me, with her." He sounds so depressed.

"Me? Why me? I ask him.

"I don't know, when we don't talk to each other, when we avoid each other. I guess."

"Oh..." I take a breath. "Yeah, but its not the solution, its not the end of the world, everyone has fights. You don't have to punish yourself. Just because you had a fight."

"I don't know... why she didn't run as far away from me as she could." He says.

"Because she loves you," I said.

"Like you do?"

"NO...... I think my love is more like an obsession, infatuation, it was something I wanted so badly, I couldn't have you, so it made me crazy, kind of thing."

"Does it still?" His question hangs in the air.

"Sometimes.... I'm trying to control it, you know now that your married. Why?" I ask him.

"Just wondering," he gives a quick nervous laugh.

"Did you turn off your car?"

"Yeah, for now."

"Listen everyone fights, that's how we express ourselves when were unhappy about something. I prefer the silent treatment." I say.

"Yeah, I know," he laughs again. I'm sure he remembers my silence.

"As I was saying, every relationship you have, you have to work at it, to make it work. You just cant coast along, its give and take from both of you. You cant just take and take, and the other keeps giving and giving, it has to go both ways. It's a shared even thing. Both of you have to give."

I'm getting a headache, now I'm Cam's psychiatric doctor or maybe his priest. I don't want to know about him and Melissa.

"Did you get out of the car?" I ask him.

"Yeah," he slams the door. I hear the car alarm.

"Where are you?"

"At a bar," he's walking, cause I can hear the gravel crunching under his feet.

"Go into the bar, give the keys to the bar tender and call a cab." I tell him.

"Do I have to?" He asks.

"Yes...you have to. Cam no one wants to lose you."

"Does that include you? He takes a deep breath.

"Yes of course it does."

"Say it, Janie."

"Say what, Cam?"

"That you'd jump off of the 20th floor of a building if I died."

"Yeah I did say that didn't I? I guess I would Cam. The tallest building I could find." I say.

What can I really say to him. Things have changed Cam, I would never throw myself off the side of a building for you anymore. I wouldn't throw myself off of the 20th floor or the 11th floor or the 5th floor or the 1st floor for you, not any more. I have a baby to think about and a new man, who loves me. But I don't say that, he's fragile right now, I have to save him, from harming himself. Or worse yet, killing himself in that stupid orange Ferrari.

There I did it again, I fed his ego. That's why he called, because he knows I will say what he wants to hear. His big giant ego. I said I wasn't going to do that again. But I did. I fell right into it. Well, I did it so he wouldn't drive that car. He did get out. He gave his keys to the bar tender.

I decided I already lost Cam when he got married, every woman in the world who wanted him, lost him. I'm not sure if it made it any better.

Sunday morning after Cam called I had a difficult time falling back to sleep. We were suppose to leave this morning. I kept mulling over everything that has happened in the past few months. When I first discovered Cam and LK, my life was pretty boring, then one thing led to another, and another. How fast everything changed. I don't think I would change any of it. The only thing I might have changed was the way I was aggressive towards Cam. I would have demanded his love. And excepted nothing else.

Eric came in to wake me up, I was still lying there thinking. He stood in the doorway gloating. He's had that silly look on his face forever. Ever since I told him I was pregnant and ever since I told him I would marry him. "Come in my love," I said to him. He waltzed in with a flamboyant step. And stood by my bed looking at me.

"You still have that silly grin on your face," I told him.

He laughed, "And its going to stay there forever." He sat down on the edge of the bed and put his hand on my stomach.

"How are you feeling this morning?" He lays his ear on my stomach.

"I feel wonderful, can you hear anything?" I touched his head.

"I hear your stomach grumbling, if that's what you mean. Am I suppose to hear the baby yet?"

"I think its to early, soon though."

He takes my hand, and looks for the ring. "Where's the ring?"

"I took it off, I'll put it back on, don't worry, it was to big to sleep in."

He raises his eyebrows, "What are you saying that you don't like my taste in jewelry?" He grins.

"Oh don't be silly, of course I like your taste in jewelry, and you can get me jewelry any time you want. I'm just not used to wearing it that's all."

"Okay, if that's all. I will buy you what ever you want." He nuzzles my ear.

"Good, can I have that in writing?" I smile a mischievous smile.

"No, not today," he laughs.

"Come on we gotta get going. The limo will be here in an hour."

"Oh I was so comfortable, I don't want to go. How about joining me for a few minutes?" I pat the bed.

He looks at the bed and me, then at the clock on the night stand. "Okay, just for a few minutes."

I pull the covers aside, and he crawls in next to me. Were so warm together. He puts his arms around me and I lay on his chest.

"Is this how its going to be all the time?" I sigh.

"It can be, I think it will be. Its nice I agree, even nicer when were married. Then it will be right and no one can say otherwise."

"Your so old fashion, Eric, will sort of. We do have a baby before the marriage."

"Yep, we kind of got the buggy before the horse."

"Hum." I sigh a contented sigh.

"Watch the clock, I'm already packed. I smell breakfast, I guess your Mom cooked us a big one again?"

"Yeah Mom believes in a big breakfast to get you going. When we were kids, especially in the winter time, she would make us a big bowl of hot oat meal cereal with fruit. And lots of sugar. I would be so stuffed, I couldn't walk to school with out waddling down the road."

"That's funny," I say. "I remember my mother, would slather on the baby oil all over my face, so I wouldn't get wind burn. I'm not sure if it even worked. It smelled good though."

"We'd better get up now, or will be late." Eric says.

I get dressed, while Eric carries my bags downstairs. The kitchen smells good, I sneak a couple of pieces of bacon to the dogs.

"You look tired, Janie," Anne says to me. "Didn't you sleep well?"

"I was sleeping well, until my phone rang and woke me up. It's been those annoying calls." I chew on some toast. So I don't have to give the details. I cant tell them it was Cam calling me at 2 in the morning. Eric would be pissed I even talked to him. And he would be even more pissed off at him because I couldn't fall asleep again. So sometimes its just better not to say anything.

"Oh, you still don't know who it might be?" She asks.

"No, it could be one of those computer things, you know where its on a loop and it just keeps going around and around making calls."

"Maybe," she says. She gives me a suspicious look. Maybe she knows its Cam. It's none of her business anyway.

I stuff my mouth with more food, so I don't have to talk. Eric has his food eaten already, and he's taking the bags out on the porch.

I help Anne clean up the kitchen, just as the limo pulls up in front of the house.

"Well, this is it," Eric says. He put the bags in the limo. "Will call you when we get to Calgary."

We all hugged and kissed each other good-bye. We wave out the back window at them. I was glad I was leaving with Eric, that I wasn't the one staying behind.

We talk a little during the ride. I lay on Eric's lap again, and fall asleep. I have his ring on. I'll get used to wearing it. It's beautiful, old fashion in style, square cut, with tiny diamonds around the pink diamond, the band has diamonds on each side of the stone. It sparkles in the sunlight.

He holds my hand as I sleep. Its so amazing, when your starting a new relationship, everything is touchy feely, and you want to be with that person all the time.

I will always wear his ring, when I'm with him. I want to shove it in Cam's face. I think my ring is prettier than Melissa's, anyway.

I told Eric I wouldn't wear it when I was working though, I didn't want to loose it. He has no problem with that.

The driver drops us off at the hotel, across from the arena. Tomorrow back to work. I'd like to share a room with Eric. I pout, so he gives in. Hey its not like the damage hasn't been done already, I'm pregnant, remember?

I'm not sure if anyone else is here in the hotel yet, or if their in another hotel, but we haven't seen any one yet. Eric went down to the pool, for a couple of laps.

There's a knock on the door. Eric forgot his key? I didn't order room service either.

I open the door. It's Cam.....

I get that same funny feeling, I always do when I first see him, that little pang in my stomach. Its become a habit, I suppose. I'll have to practice, not letting that happen. Or it could be the baby.

I swallow the butterflies, and take a drink of water.

He's dressed in his black leather jacket that always makes his eyes look bluer. Jeans and a t-shirt. His hair is curly, and wild. My heart pounds.

"Hey," he says, with a grin. "I'm still here." He holds out his arms in a sweeping motion.

"Hi," I say trying to sound composed. Even though I'm not.

"I was just checking on you, to make sure you were here." He looks in my room, I guess he's looking for Eric.

"Yes we are here, just got here, a while ago. And yes you are still here, I'm glad."

He looks in the room, again, expecting Eric to come charging at him, maybe.

"Eric?"

"Down stairs in the pool." and as soon as that left my mouth, I knew I shouldn't have said it. That was his foot in the door, so to speak.

"Can I come in?" He asks.

It's a bad idea, a very bad idea. But I stand a side to let him in.

"Sure, come in." I leave the door open, though.

"Nice room," he looks around. "One bed?"

"Yeah….one bed. Were sharing, you know to save money on another room." I know its bugging him.

I put my hand on the back of the desk chair, the one with my engagement ring on it.

He looks at it. He turns a little red. And his forehead furrows. I follow his eyes to my hand.

"From Eric," I say.

He takes my hand and looks at it. "Wow, its huge and beautiful. Is it…..?'

"An engagement ring, yes." He's still holding my hand. His thumb is on the ring and he moves it back and forth, which is annoying, me.

"What's wrong?" I ask him.

"I don't know, I guess I'm just surprised, that's all, I didn't think you guys were that serious." He looks at the ring again.

I flip his hand over and look at his hand. At his ring. He wears one on his thumb, one on his middle finger, "And this?" I say. "It's the same feeling I had when I saw this." I thumb his ring.

"Same nauseating feeling?" He asks.

"Yeah, same nauseating feeling." I say.

"We cant undo what has been done, Cam. So lets leave it at that, okay?"

"I know we cant undo it," he says.

"So lets make the best out of it. Be the best husband you can be."

Eric walks in the room and stops short, when he sees Cam in the room. I drop my hand out of his. Cam takes a step back away from me.

"Oh, Cam, hey how are you?" Eric says, his face beams.

"Okay, Eric, hey congratulations on yours and Janie's engagement."

He shakes Eric's hand. Eric puts his arm around me. And smiles.

"Thanks," he says.

"Have you picked a date yet?" Cam asks, looking at me when he asks.

"No not yet, after the tour is over. We haven't really talked about it."

"Oh I see, will I gotta go, and check on everyone else, I'm glad for you guys. Be at the arena around three tomorrow, we have to go over the schedule." He nods to Eric. Eric goes to the bathroom, "see yea, Cam."

I walk with him to the door. Go into the hallway with him, I close the rooms door. It's stupid I know, but I cant let him go. I just want to be near him a while longer.

"Well I guess I'll see you tomorrow," he says.

"Yeah tomorrow," I say. " Good night," he starts to walk away to the elevator. Then says, "Oh hell." Walks back to me, pulls me in his arms, and kisses me like he never kissed me before. Then pulls away. Looks at my face, then walks away with his hands in his pockets.

Well now. What was that all about. He certainly left me something to think about. "Didn't I blow your mind, this time, didn't I?" That song suddenly pops into my head.

CHAPTER 38

I'm never gonna get over him, I shake my head as if he'll fall out of my head. I go back in the room. Eric came out of the bathroom wiping his hair with the towel.

"So he knows?" He asks.

"Yup, he knows, but only about the engagement, not the baby," I say.

"Okay, good, how'd he take it?"

"Oh not to bad, better than I thought he would, well he has nothing to say about it. He was surprised, he didn't think we were that serious." I say looking at my ring.

"I bet!" Eric laughs.

More like stunned, like the deer caught in the head lights of the car.

I still feel his lips on mine, I run my tongue over them, he was drinking again. Like my drink is Snapple Ice tea, his is beer, now its coke and vodka.

We watch some TV and eat some dinner, order from room service. Its nice being here with Eric. I'm not alone for once. I realize this and I really like it. He's easy to be with. He's never obnoxious, or rude, always thoughtful and caring. I'm amazed. How can one person be so kind?

I'm with someone who cares, and who loves me and wants to marry me.

I smile up at him. Cause I'm always lying in his arms. In bed watching TV, his arms are always around me. Its warm and cozy, I let out a big sign. This feels so right, god it has to be.

"What was that for?" He asks.

"Oh I'm just happy," I said.

"Good, I'm glad. Are you tired? Do you want to go to sleep?"

"I guess we should, after all we only have to be there at three."

"Which side of the bed, do you like to sleep on?" He asks.

"In the middle with you?"

We snuggle down together, I close my eyes. We talk about the house, the baby and our future together, until I cant talk anymore. I drift off listening to Eric talk. Not that he's boring, he just has a soothing voice. He always relaxes me.

"I love you," I know I said it. Before I went to sleep.

"I love you too, Janie." I hear him say as I drift deeper into sleep.

Monday morning, Monday afternoon. I got up a couple of times to use the bathroom, and checked on the time, went back to bed. The alarm was set for 2:00 in the afternoon, it gave us plenty of time to get ready before we had to go to the arena.

Eat, get dressed and go. Before we left I had an inkling about something. I decided to try on some of my dance dresses. A little tight, around the tummy area. "How did it look?" I asked Eric over and over again, as I tried on each dress.

"It definitely shows," he says. Funny it wasn't like that two weeks ago. I tried everyone on, all the same, tight. You have to remember, all my dresses are skin tight, barely room to breath. Although they have room to stretch somewhat, they could have been painted on.

I better go and buy something bigger.

We went to the arena, arm and arm. Smiles on our faces, we talk quietly to each other. We have so many hopes and dreams, Eric and I. And it amazes me how much we think a like. Its almost scary, in fact.

Cam changed the songs again, way he does this, I have no idea. It gets me confused. Honestly I hate it when he does that. They added some old songs and some new ones. One of them is my favorite, favorite, that Cam sings, he sings it so beautifully, even though he didn't write it. It's still one of my favorite's. They play is acoustically, just Rob and him with their guitars. I cant wait to hear it again.

After the meeting. I take a taxi downtown to the shopping district. I find a dress store. I find a really cute dress one size bigger. Yuck. I hate this. I'm a size 10, could be an 8, but a 10 is comfortable. And I want to stay a size 10. The woman notices my facial expression as I look in the mirror at the dress I have on.

"What's the matter, don't you like the dress?" The woman asks me.

"Oh, no I do, I just don't like the size, that's all." I tilt my head to get a back view of myself in the mirror.

"Well then you should lose some weight." She says.

"I will in about 6 months," I say.

She still doesn't get it.

"I'm pregnant," you dits, I want to say.

"Oh, I see." She says, making a face.

I pay and leave the little shop, with my dress. God what a dimwit. The day goes pretty fast. I tell Cam I have to tone down the dance a little cause my knee is really, really.....hurting. So I warn him not to be surprised, if I change anything.

He's fine with it. My knee isn't hurting at all. It's a good excuse, and thankfully I have one.

Back at the hotel, for a few hours before the show, I try on the dress for Eric. "So what do you think?"

"Hides it," he says. And comes over to me to put his arms around me, his hands always rests on my tummy.

"Good, soon it wont be easy to hide, and I'm gonna have to tell him." I say.

"When the time comes." He says.

We have three shows this week and two on the weekend. All here. I wish we would stay longer in the other arenas too. Like the first time I went to the Jones beach Theater. I would have gone to all of the shows they had. They were there for only one night. Then off to another state. It wears you out. Not to many places in Canada to play in, that we haven't played in before.

Everything I own is getting tighter. I wear one of Eric's t-shirts over my velour pants, lucky for me they stretch too.

I'll try running up and down the stairs, slowly, but it gives me cramps, running, so I walk.

I want to stay in shape, through out the pregnancy.

I get dressed for tonight's concert. Cam has invited some friends to perform with them. I get to met all of these performers, I'm still a dazed fan, like anyone. I get autographs too. Jerry Cantrel of Alice in Chains, Tommy Lee of Motley Crew, Jacoby Shaddix of Papa Roach, ZZ Top, Josh and Keith, of Buckcherry, Adam and Brad, of Three Days Grace, Douglas and Marku of Hoobastank and more. To much drinking, to much cigarette smoke and other things. Wild after parties.

Some of the guys are down right scary, some are outrageous flirts.

I pretend to limp and sit with a bag of ice. Cam is concerned about my knee. I tell him I'll be fine. Eric is so busy, I hardly get to see him until I need him as my body guard for the dance. And then the next time I'll see him is at the hotel. For a second it seems like he's a stranger.

But his big smile, tells me he certainly knows me.

For every band, they have to set up their own equipment. No one uses someone else's stuff. It costs to much. Take it down, pack it away, set it up again, some nights there is three different bands playing. Even before Cam takes the stage.

I'm happy just to sit and wait for my cue. I'm still having cramps and it's the only thing I've been thinking about all day. I called the doctor, she said to take it easy, try and lay down as much as possible.

Cam's been avoiding me after that passionate kiss. Big deal. Its not like we haven't before. When he looks my way, I smile. I'm certainly not mad or anything. I don't want this…. I hate it when we feel like we have to avoid each other. Then we feel funny around each other, its hard to keep that up, I'm tired of it. I want him in my life, no matter what. I want him to know everything is okay between us.

I want him as a friend, forever, if I cant have him any other way, I still want him as a friend.

Which ever way it is, a brother, a friend, it doesn't matter, he someone who amazes me every day.

My cramps have stopped, and I'm relieved. Maybe it was something I eat. But stuff like this scares me, especially when this is the first time I've been pregnant. I just don't know what to expect.

As much as I said, I didn't want a baby, now I do want it, no matter who's it is.

My cue. Cam says some words to the audience, then hit's the first cord. We've decided that I come out from backstage, now. Chased by a couple of security guards. But then Cam waves them off. He gives me a ruthless smile, and wants to see what I can do. I'm moving slow to the 4th beat, but its more seductive, like in slow motion, the moves are all precise.

Not wild and all over the place, you can tell it was rehearsed. Not like my general dancing. This is more like the India shimmy. Each move is rehearsed and has a meaning.

Certainly draws attention. I make my way over to Dale, climb the drum deck. The deck as been fortified ever since I fell off and its certainly bigger. Because now I'm even more afraid of falling off of it.

I wrap my arms around his sweaty neck, he whispers in my ear, "really nice dance." It's not really a whisper, more like a shout so I can hear him.

I make my way back to Cam and slide down his leg to the floor. Its getting harder to do that.

"Nice job," he says, and he grabs my hand to help me up.

"Thank you," I smile my prettiest smile at him. His sky blue eyes, light up.

"Lets hear it for….?"

"Janie," I say, "Janie Newton."

Eric comes out to get me, like a security guard. People start booing.

"It's alright, nothing will happen to her," Cam reassures the audience. "She was good, wasn't she?" The audience roars.

If they've seen the show before, then they know, if they haven't then its made to look real.

I change for the sign language. Cam has a stool next to him, for me.

This time I don't mess up. I ask him if I can sign for the new old song, the one with the acoustical guitars. I tell him I practiced with the DVD.

He says sure. I've noticed over the months that Cam really doesn't say no to me. Not that I really ask for anything that he cant deliver.

I wear jeans, which I have to leave the button open. A t-shirt and a loose leather jacket.

I don't want to buy a new wardrobe of maternity clothes yet. You can spend a small fortune.

The song I've been waiting for is the last of the three slow songs. I've never signed a curse word before, its, "bullshit."

I had to figure it out. When Cam and Rob begin to play, and Cam begins to sing, I close my eyes and fall into his voice. I love his raunchy voice, so much that it makes me cry. Yes, everything makes me cry now. I've been an emotional rollercoaster, as they say. When he's done, he wipes my tears away with his finger. It makes me bite my lip.

"That's so beautiful Cam, if your voice was the last thing I ever heard before I died, I'd be happy."

He smiles, I'm sure he cant figure me out.

Show one down. The doctor calls my cell phone the next day to ask how I'm feeling. I tell her the cramps are gone. And I'm resting. She's says good. But if I feel really bad, get to the hospital immediately.

One day to rest. I lay by the pool, catch up on some sun bathing. No bathing suit. Shorts and a tee. Get a manicure and a pedicure. Massage that the hotel offered. Feels nice to be pampered once in a while. Eric gives me back rubs.

Everyone is off doing whatever. Eric is sleeping in the lounge chair, next to me. He sure has a fine body. As my eyes roam up and down his sleeping form. Whew! I roam his body with my eyes again, Damn, I am lucky.

Cam's too. Sexy, hot body, nothing is more appreciated then a hot bode.

I'm reading a book, writing a letter to April and my Mom. I wish I had continued my guitar lessons, when I was a teenager. I could be plucking away. I'm not gifted like Cam or any of the other band members. I have to have sheet music in front of me, unless I memorize the music, but even that is to hard, I sucked at it anyway. I got a B in guitar class. I took Clarinet for 5 years. I can read music. Cant make a career out of it. Even played the tuba for a week, one of the hardest instruments to play. Played an organ, like a church organ, for some reason my mother got one, traded in her piano for it, what a mistake. She hated the thing. I played it for about two weeks and gave up.

Eric is still sleeping and I leave him a note. I kiss him on the cheek. He mumbles something.

He's so cute.

I go upstairs to take a shower and change. Maybe I'll just wander around, maybe to the stores or something.

Cam sees me in the hallway by my room.

"Oh, hey Janie, I was just coming to talk to you."

"What about?" I ask him, as I get to my door.

"About us, do we have a truce?" He asks me.

"I think we do, Cam I cant stay mad at you, forever, and not that I'm ever really mad at you, anyway. I want you to be a part of my life, no matter what way you can give it to me. I would miss you." I say so sweetly to him, and give him one of my prettiest smiles.

"So what you said, at the concert, "you would die happy if my voice was the last thing you heard when you died?"

"Yes its true, I still....love you. But I've accepted that you are married, and I'll be happy for you and Melissa."

"What about me kissing you the other day?" He asks.

"Oh I'm not mad about that, it was okay, but you shouldn't do it any more, a kiss on the cheek is fine." I say and he frowns.

"Okay, I guess on the cheek it is, so will be nice to each other from now on?"

"Yup, for the rest of our lives. Oh say I've been thinking, about something. And you can say no, if its to awkward for you, or you can think about it for a while, before you give me an answer." He raises his eyebrows, curious. "But when I get married, do you think you could walk me down the aisle being my dad is dead?"

"Really?' You want me to do that?" He's surprised.

"Yes, you'd be filling in for my father. You don't have to give me an answer now, think about it."

"No, No, I would love to, Eric's a great guy. I would be honored to."

"Oh thank you, Cam, it means a lot to me. We haven't set a date or anything, after the tour I guess."

"I'll be there," he grabs me and hugs me. "Whoa your getting a little tummy there?" He pats it.

"Oh I have a hernia, from dancing and exercising to much, so it protrudes out a little." I lie. Good one I think. Sounds good.

"Oh I'm sorry, I didn't know, man you are getting hurt all over doing this dancing gig. Does it hurt?"

"No, not really, only if I lift something heavy, I might feel a little discomfort. I have to stay away from the weights."

"Well you have it operated on?"

"Maybe if it gets to uncomfortable, I could do it when I have the knee done. I have to see what the doctor says, he didn't say I needed one though."

"Yeah get it fixed if you need too."

"I will." I smile up at him.

"Say what are you doing now?" He asks me.

"I was taking a shower, getting dressed and I was going down town to walk around and shop. Why?"

"Want some company? I have nothing to do." He smiles, those cute dimples by his mouth appear.

I really wanted to go look for baby clothes. But..... "I guess, sure. It might be boring."

"Doesn't matter, cant be boring with you. I'll meet you downstairs, in say ½ hour."

"Okay, that should be enough time." The Cam of old would have wanted to wait in my room, while I showered. And then he would say something about the towel, or that he would join me in the shower, or he'd try to rip the towel off of me, or SEX. Cause that's all he thinks about.

Cause SEX is always the answer, never a question, like he says.

I'm done in a half hour, meet Cam downstairs, I look for Eric, but he's nowhere in sight.

"Ready?"

"Yup."

He's got a limo waiting. Tells the driver downtown. Its amazing how everyone jumps for him. Wouldn't it be impossible to get a limo in that short of time?

"Hungry?" He asks me.

"Always." Or at least most of the time, lately I've been a little nauseous on and off.

"Good, I know a really good little eatery, we can go to." He says.

"Sounds good," Except I'm not feeling that good. I didn't tell Eric I was gonna be with Cam.

The driver pulls into a little side street. And stops. It looks more like an alley way, where creepy things happen. We get out. The driver pulls out, and Cam tells him he'll call him when were ready to leave.

"Its down this way," he points, "I found it last year, when I was roaming around. I got lost. Stumbled onto this place. Come on its just around the corner." He grabs my hand, and pulls me along. His touch, like always, makes me feel like I'm over heating.

We round the corner to a fenced garden with a quaint little house in the corner, with red shutters, tables, chairs, and umbrellas outside on a cobble stone patio. A few people are sitting at the tables eating. Its like stepping back in time, another country, another era. Vines of wisteria are hanging down, from the huge elm tree. They aren't in bloom yet. White picket fence, potted plants, window boxes with pansies in them. Stone patio, and walls. Pizza oven, with pies cooking in the oven.

"Italian." Cam says.

"I love Italian," I say.

"I know you do. I like it too, that lasagna you made. Cant stop thinking about it."

"I'll make it again, don't worry." I say.

The waiter shows us to a table, a flicker of recognition crosses his face, I guess he knows who Cam is. Doesn't everyone?

He gives me a menu. "Order what you want." Cam says.

"Lobster looks good," I say, "But I think I'll have the stuffed flounder."

"Lobster sounds good, but I think I'll have what your having."

The waiter comes back and takes our order, we get drinks, and a salad. I look around the quaint little place anywhere, except Cam. I feel uncomfortable here with him, without Eric knowing. Guilty maybe. I left him a note….

"So…" Cam says, drawing my attention back to him. "Where are you guys gonna live when your married?"

"Hanna, by Eric's parents, they have some land for us. Will have something built."

"Nice… you like Hanna?"

"I do, I love the farm land, the open space. Eric's family is really nice."

"He's a good guy. You guys look good together."

"Well you and Melissa look good together too. So…"

"Yeah….. She's put up with a lot of my crap, she deserves a medal." A long silence. The waiter brings our salad, and some bread. Ice tea for me, and beer for Cam, he's on his second bottle already.

"You don't drink, do you?" He takes another big gulp.

"No, never have, don't like the taste or the smell. I like to be in control of myself."

"You mean like me?"

"No, everyone is different, lets not get into this okay."

"Right…."

The place has nice music playing, some Italian stuff.

"Care to dance?" He asks me.

"No one else is dancing." I look around, he offers me his hand.

"We should practice for the reception, I have to dance with you for the father and daughter dance." He laughs, a slight grin on his face.

"Yeah you would have to have been about 10 years old to be my father," I tease.

"Yeah wouldn't that be something."

He puts his arms around me, I'm hoping he cant feel the baby bump. Its gonna get bigger and bigger.

"Now see it isn't that hard," he smiles.

No innuendo there.

"No, its not hard," I smile. He laughs, now he gets it.

"You have such a dirty mind, Cam." He gives me an innocent look.

"Who me?" We both laugh. "That's where all the good songs come from." He says, tapping his finger to the side of his head.

It's so easy being in his arms. He's not to bad on his feet. When he's doing his concerts he never dances, or even sways to the music. Something I noticed about him. Were as some band guys go crazy on stage. Joss Todd of Buckcherry for instance.

The song ends and our food arrives. We have a really nice, easy going conversation, about everything, and nothing. Its really a comfortable night. I know Eric wont be mad.

We walk down town, its really only around the corner, I could remember this place. I buy a couple of things to wear. It's a good thing Cam really isn't interested. I glance at baby things, now that, he notices. "I have a friend who's pregnant," I say in my defense, I'm the pregnant friend. I buy a few baby things, he grins at me. "What…..?" I say. He just shakes his head.

Shoe's……my vice.

Cam is looking at Croc's.

"Cam," I say, "Don't even think about Croc's, they are the faggyist things I've ever seen. Especially on a man." He smiles.

And puts them down. I've seen him in Croc's. He looked so uncool.

Show two. More guests show up. Its crazy. I make sure I get every autograph and picture with them. Who knows someday they might be worth something.

Even though, like I said before, that some of the guests are down right scary, they really are nice people. Cam wouldn't surround himself with anyone who wasn't worth his time.

The only thing I don't like is that they all like to drink, and heavily, which is a bad influence for Cam. I'm not his mother, and he sees my disapproving eyes watching him. I have to walk away. I still see that big tree in front of him. And that tree is not going to budge when he hits it.

Show two is down. Sometimes its like holding your breath. We still have a few more months to go, I like the fact that were staying here for a week. I have enough packages to start my own store. I always show Eric the baby clothes, I bought. He looks at everything, and smiles, and says how cute everything is, is that normal for a man?

I've been feeling very tired. The doctor gave me some vitamins, and a shot of B 12. The cramps are still coming and going. I should tell Eric, I don't think that this is normal. But I don't want to worry him, he's looking at me way to much as it is. His job is crazy right now, and he's not partying like he used to. He's really taking this whole daddy thing seriously. I'm proud of him.

Sometimes there isn't one sober mind in the whole place.

CHAPTER 39

Melissa comes and goes. She eyes me. I think she suspects something. Woman know these things. I just smile and wave to her.

Show number three down. Two more on the weekend and then were done with Calgary. Where are we going next? This week went fast. I invited my doctor to come to the concert. Special backstage pass. She said she'll look me over.

Saturday nights show was wild. I'm not sure why. But the audience was moshing, like crazy, people were getting hurt.

The mosh pit was brutal. People pushing and knocking others down. Punches, and kicking. People surfing over the tops of the crowd. Security knocking them down. Is it the goal to reach the stage to get to the band?

I had no problem, like I need it. Only because it was a different style of stage. I always wonder how the band can keep a straight face, or how they can remember the words to the songs, when they see all of this happening out in the audience.

It kinds of upsets me, actually, I don't like to see people get hurt. The doctor arrives and gives me an exam in my dressing room. I don't want anyone to know why she's here. She says, "I look okay, but cant tell without some of her machines to monitor me." Another words come in for an office visit. Like I have time for that.

She loves the show, and tells me to come in tomorrow for a sonogram, and blood tests. What ever else she can think of. And before she leaves, I tell her not to say a word to anyone about me or anything else. She says patient privacy is always her practice. I can just picture Melissa grabbing her and asking her a ton of questions.

One more show and then we close. Every concert is sold out. I remember those sold out concerts when I used to try to get tickets. And then I'd cry because I didn't get the ticket that I wanted. Or I waited to long and couldn't get a ticket at all.

I wanted to meet Cam way back when I wasn't even obsessed with him.

Sunday night. Everyone is so hyped-up. I wonder if any are doing drugs. Cam used to sell drugs when he was a teenager. I figured, he's the real bad guy.

This day though, something feels really strange, I don't mean the day, I mean me. I feel lousy. The cramps have come back and there stronger. I lay down most of the day. But it doesn't help. I have to tell Eric and he's worried.

"Maybe you shouldn't go on tonight," he says to me. He puts a cold wet towel on my forehead.

"I'll be alright, they usually go away."

But as the night time comes, the cramps get stronger. I call the doctor. "Get to the hospital," she says.

"I will, after the show," I tell her. She's not to happy about that.

It could be all the craziness. Although I've stayed away from it all day. And had a quiet day in my hotel room.

I get ready. Eric takes me to the arena. I'm very quiet. A wave of cramps convulses my body. And it takes every bit of strength to keep from doubling over. There coming more frequently and stronger. I just want the night to end. The first three acts go on. I ask Cam if I could go first tonight.

I tell him, "I'm not feeling good," he doesn't question me. And says yes. He says, I'm looking very pale. He puts his hand on my forehead, "A little clammy too."

The show always starts with piros. They are introduced and come out playing the first song. I want to pass out. I have chills. Cam looks back stage at me, he nods, I sort of nod back at him. He hit's the first note and I stroll out. I block the pain out of my head. The pain in my abdomen is pushed out of my mind. The 3 minutes and 36 seconds of the song are the longest few minutes of my life, like it was the first time I jumped on stage. The song is probably longer on stage, then on the CD. The band always adds some more instrumental notes. I tell Cam to make it short.

I slid down Cam's leg. Thankful that its finally over. I have beads of sweat on my face. As bad as Cam does.

"Janie, give me you hand, Janie give me your hand," Cam holds out his hand for me to grab, he pulls me up, he gives me a worried look, "Are you alright?" I wobble and I'm shaky. Rob went to get Eric. Eric comes and helps me off stage.

The pain has gotten almost unbearable, and I roll my eyes. "I gotta go."

He lets go of my hand, and he says, "Lets hear it for Janie Newton." He says. I can feel his eyes following me, as I hurry off stage.

I tell Eric to hurry up and get me to a bathroom. Something is wrong. Were practically running to the changing room, the pain is unlike anything I've ever experienced before. It felt like something is twisting my insides all around. I get into the bathroom and pop. Like a balloon, that's been under to much pressure, it popped. And everything comes out.

"Janie, what's wrong?" Eric can hear me moaning.

"I think I just had a miscarriage, call Dr. Harris, I need to go to the hospital."

"Oh…no….," he says, "Can I come in?"

"NO….There's a mess," but he comes in anyway.

"Janie…." And he holds me in his arms, while I'm sitting on the toilet. The pain and pressure is gone, but the discomfort is still there. I need to get to the hospital.

Eric called her, she'll meet us there. Eric tells Cam I wont be finishing the show. He'll talk to him later and explain.

I feel like I can walk out of here okay. I change my clothes. And wear several pads. The hospital isn't far.

Call a cab and tell the driver to floor it. I'm so cold. Eric has me in his arms and I'm wrapped up in blankets.

We get to the hospital in through the emergency doors. The doctor is there waiting for me. Takes me in to the examining room.

"You did have a miscarriage, I'm sorry, we have to do a, D and C. You have to stay the night. They put me out. I tell the doctor I'm so cold. Then I go to sleep.

I woke up in the recovery room, and I'm nauseous. From the anesthesia, and its not unusual.

I only gag a little. Cause there's nothing in my stomach, I feel empty inside. I go back to sleep.

Woke up in my room, with Eric he's here by my bed. I feel so empty inside. Not just no food, in my stomach, but in my abdomen. Empty. I was vacuumed out. Which is exactly what they do.

I reach over for Eric. He's been crying. He grabs my hand and buries his head against me.

And starts crying again. I rub his head. There's no words to say. So I say nothing. But hold him in my arms, I feel worse for him, then I do for me.

Dr. Harris, comes in to check on me. She asks me," how I'm feeling?" I say, "Empty." She wants to know my mental state? "Disappointed, very disappointed," I look over at Eric. She follows my eyes. "Come talk with me Eric," she says to him. He gets up and goes to the hallway.

Maybe later it will come, right now, I'm just numb. I feel as empty in my head and heart as I feel in my stomach. I was more upset about who the father was. Then this.

I ask her why it happened? It wasn't because of the dancing. She said sometimes the mother's blood, is different then the babies. They have to have the same blood type. She said that was most likely the case. And that the fact that I wasn't nauseous to much, was not a good sign either. Being nauseous is good. And that I was very sick, a few weeks before. There could have been something wrong with the fetus. I hadn't thought of that. I was pretty sick. Then I ask her, "with all the tests they did on me, why didn't the test show, that I was pregnant?" She looks at me, from over the rim of her glasses, perched on her nose, "they weren't looking for it." "Oh I guess, it might make sense. But they took a ton of blood from me. It had to have shown up." I say. Dr. Harris has no answer to that. So I leave it at that. Maybe they did know, but didn't want to tell Eric, or for that matter Cam. Until I knew. Let me decide.

She knew Eric was taking this really badly. He really wanted to be a father. When Dr. Harris spoke to him. And she said I can have more. When Eric came back into the room, he seemed a little better. But not much. He had to call his parents. They were upset too. And that started Eric crying all over again. He asked me why I wasn't crying? How could I explain it to him?

Shock, was what the doctor said. It would take a few days for it to sink in. I also didn't want to say, will it may not have been yours, it might have been Cam's. She also tells me I was further along then she first thought. More than a couple of months. And then I count back, that would have been exactly the time I was with Cam at his house.

I asked Dr. Harris about a DNA test, but it was to late now. So I will never know for sure who's it was. So in a very sad way this solves….. everything…..sort of.

Its really late at night now. Eric's cell phone rings. It's Cam and he wants to know where we are?

Eric walks out of the room. I hear him explaining everything to Cam.

"Where in the hospital….why…..because Janie had a miscarriage…. yeah I know you didn't know. We didn't tell anyone. Yeah she's okay. She'll be here over night, maybe tomorrow. No she's sleeping. No I'm not alright. I was really happy about it. Sure okay, bye."

He comes back in.

"That was Cam," he says. "He sends his love."

"Hum," I say. I wonder if it crossed his mind?

"He says he'll come in a while."

"He doesn't have to, tell him not to come." I tell him. I cant face him right now.

He tries Cam's cell phone number, but he's not answering.

"I guess he wants too." He shrugs his shoulders.

"Your staying the night, aren't you?" I sound desperate.

"Yes, or course I am." He sits down on the chair next to me. "So…I have a question to ask you…." He says. Uh oh, here comes the question I was dreading, the one I hoped he would never ask, or think of, who's was it?

But he doesn't ask that one, instead he asks me. "Its been bugging me for a couple of hours now. Its kind of stupid, kind of my insecurities, but I have to ask it." He shifts in the chair.

"Okay, what is it?" I swallow, thinking that this is the question. "Well?"

"Well, since this has happened. You know no baby." He looks at me to see my reaction. "Do you still want to marry me?"

"Of course I do. Whatever gave you that idea?"

"I don't know, maybe we were just getting married because you were pregnant."

"No, I was getting married, because I love you. And I want to spend the rest of my life with you." I touched his cheek. He holds my hand there.

"Why do you have doubts? About us?" I ask him.

"Cam?" he says.

"What about him? No, Cam and I are just friends that's it, we have come to an understanding, him and me, okay so you have nothing to have doubts about, ever!"

"Okay, I'll never bring it up again." He says.

"Good."

Eric goes to get us something to eat, for some reason the hospital forgot to send up some food for me. Its okay anyway, hospital food is horrible. While he's gone, Cam shows up. He has impeccable timing, its as if he knows when ever Eric isn't around. He peeks in my room, a big bouquet of flowers in his hands.

"Hey." He says, he looks around, for what? Eric maybe? Sees the coast is clear.

"Hey." I'm happy to see him.

"Can I come in?" He asks.

"Yeah sure." He looks like he feels awkward. He's tiptoeing in. He makes me smile, like maybe he'll wake someone up. In the short time I've known Cam, I've never really seen him look this awkward. But here he was standing in the doorway, not sure what to do.

"Come sit by me," I pat the bed and hold out my hand to him.

He comes and sits on the edge of the bed and takes my hand.

"Oh here, these are for you." He gives me the flowers.

"Thank you," I say and sniff them. I wonder where he found flowers this late at night, but like I said Cam can get any one to do anything for him.

"I'm sorry," he says, "I didn't know, I wouldn't have let you dance, tonight." He shakes his head and squeezes my hand.

"The doctor said it was okay for me to dance. And I wouldn't have if I didn't feel up to it. But I did up until yesterday. So don't feel it was your fault. Because it wasn't. Okay?" And I squeeze his hand back.

"Okay….. How is Eric taking this?"

"He's very upset, he told his family, they were thrilled, then he had to call them and tell them the bad news, it was just to much for him. He was so happy, he wants to be a father."

"Can I ask you a really stupid question?" He asks. He lowers his voice and clears his throat.

I knew it he's gonna ask me that question. The one I hoped he wouldn't even think about.

"Yes."

"Will…..," He looks at the doorway. "We did it, you know," I shake my head, yes, I remember that day, at his house, twice as a matter of fact. "Was it possible it could have been mine?" He whispers.

I swallow hard, should I answer him honestly or should I lie?

In a voice I cant quite get out of my throat, I tell him, what I think might be the truth, I talk so low he has to move in closer to hear me. I clear my throat, "it could have been, I'm not sure, it was you or Eric." I hang my head, to embarrassed to look him in the eyes. "It would have made a difference, if I had known for sure, but will never know. Both of you would have had to take a DNA test. Right now Eric believes it was his, please don't ever say otherwise. Okay? It would destroy him."

"I wont ever say a word about it. I give you my promise, but why didn't you tell me?" He lifts my chin up so he can look into my eyes.

"Well thank you for keeping my secret. I didn't tell you because you said you didn't want to be a father. And then you married Melissa, I wasn't sure how she would take it. And I didn't want to cause any more trouble between the two of you." It all comes out in one breath.

"Maybe when your up to it someday we can have a talk about it, I'm curious, if it was mine, if things would be different too." He says.

"Maybe, would you be happy if it was yours? I ask him.

"I did say I didn't want children, didn't I? I've been thinking about it since I found out what happened to you, I kind of liked the idea." He says.

"Well you and Melissa can."

"Yeah, maybe." He lets out a long breath.

He kisses me good-bye, leaves before Eric comes back. I just laid there staring at the ceiling. A nurse came in to check on me and put the flowers in a vase.

"Hey, I just saw Cam leaving the building," Eric says as he comes back into the room with a bag of food.

"Yeah he was here for a few minutes. Said he was sorry, and he wouldn't have let me dance if he knew, he feels its his fault. I told him it wasn't."

"Oh…. Of course it wasn't his fault, sometimes he feels he has to take on the weight of the world." Eric says.

"I guess."

The next day I can leave the hospital. I hate hospitals. I seem to be in them a lot lately.

I go back to the hotel to sleep. And then to the arena. Everyone by now has heard. Everyone looks up at me from what their doing. Some wave, some smile and say Hi, glad your back. No one knows what to say. Since most of them are guys.

I get a nice welcoming smile from Cam, even Rob and Matt. Dale gives me a big hug. "Hey you," he says, "I'm really sorry," he whispers in my ear, " I feel really bad," he says.

"Thanks Dale, that means a lot." I tell him.

The guys leave me and Cam alone. He smiles at me, "How are you feeling?"

"I feel good," I say. And I actually do, I feel incredibly skinny, all the pressure on my abdomen is gone.

"You look better," he says. He takes my hands, "next time you don't feel well, tell me, please tell me everything, whether good or bad, I would rather have you well, then not have you at all." He squeezes my hands, the warmth of his hands running up my arms. Since he's been married, he's been less touchy feeling with me. But he really cares about me, I can see it in his eyes.

"I will Cam, I promise."

"And you aren't dancing tonight, or for a month at least, okay. If you want to sign you can. Cause your sitting. Did the doctor give you a clean bill of health, yet?"

"She said to take it easy for a couple of weeks."

"Good and that's what you'll do." He says, lets go of my hands.

I should talk to Eric to see what he thinks, should I sign tonight or not, I think I know his answer. He's been getting pissed off at Cam for his insensibility towards my well being.

He's off to rehearse, Rob is tuning his guitar, Dale is at the drums, beating lightly, Matt is too.

Cam picks up his guitar to play.

Everything feels right, this is my life. This is the life I chose to follow for myself. And for once I feel content.

Eric sees me and waves. I wave back. He's trying to be strong for me, but I can still see it in his eyes, the sadness and the disappointment. At least the talk with the doctor, made him feel a little better. She told him we could have more.

CHAPTER 40

Eric is helping out with a camera. Like the first time I ever saw him. Every concert is filmed. Cam likes to put them out on DVD's. Then he takes his own camera and films the audience. He's got plenty of woman's boobs on film, that's for sure. I sometimes think that's why he does it. They do watch it later on, the whole crew. I smacked Eric once when he went to watch it. "Why are you watching that, when you have me, you can see my boobs anytime you want." He turned bright red and shrugged his shoulders.

"Its fun to watch with the guys......it's a guy thing." He says.

Oh brother.

Weekend shows...more energy, more crazy people, drinking, smoking pot. Cam says no dancing for me until the next set of concerts in Michigan. Which is like a month and a half away. Even if the doctor says its okay for me to dance before that. I want to protest, but he wont hear any of it. He holds up his hand to me, "Not a word," he says. And I huff off. I think Eric had something to do with that.

I'm so bored. A little drained of energy, sleep a lot. I crave oranges, orange juice. I have eaten so many oranges that my lips, my tongue and the inside of my mouth and throat are burned from the acid in the orange. But I cant stop it. It's so weird.

Eric wants to start to build our house. Now that I said I would still marry him. We've already decided on the type of house it will be, and we have the floor plans. He bought several architecture books, and we ordered the plans. After we get married and the tour is over we can move right in. I still cant say yes. So I don't say anything.

While I sat backstage and listened to the concert, I look through the books. I don't want a mansion, like Cam's, with black granite, and marble. I just want a simple two story house with a big porch, a big kitchen, a big bathroom, a big den, big dining room, and a big living room. And most importantly a big master bedroom. Can we fit that into a modest farm house?

Eric has the camera and is being guided along the floor in front of the stage. So he doesn't trip on any of the wires that are strung across the floor, all over the place. That's the first time I met Eric, when he focused the camera on the tattoo on my leg. It gives me an idea.

I have about 6,000 dollars worth if camera equipment and its just been laying in the camera bag. From digital to my favorite 35 mm film camera. I have no pictures of the band performing, except the couple of times I went as a fan, and sat in the orchestra section, or up by the stage, and got nothing but, butt shots. My pictures were good, took 168 pictures at one concert. But I didn't have access to the entire stage, like I do now. So I can go every where, and get better shots of the guys on stage.

I have mostly butt shots of Cam. Would be nice to have front shots of him, too. Its my hobby. And I'm good. I have a portfolio that would rival any professional photographer. I have a few photos published in a book. My cameras are in the tour bus, for safe keeping.

Before the concert starts I run back to the bus and get my bag of cameras. I might as well take it all, take out my favorite camera, and stuff several rolls of film in my pockets. My standard lens, wide angle and zoom lens. Get some close ups of Cam.

I'll follow Eric around and take pictures. I want to get unusual angles, different positions, different lighting, everything unusual. I want close ups of Cam's facial expressions. I love to watch him play, because his face shows exactly the way he's feeling when he plays. And he has a vast and expressive facial expressions.

I love what he does with his left eyebrow when he sings. How his forehead furrows, he has a lot of expressions, that amuse me. My favorite of his expressions is when he grits his teeth when he's playing a riff on the guitar.

I used to take pictures of race cars and professional go-karts, and dirt bikes, so I know how to set up a shot, how to wait for the perfect picture. When I wasn't racing myself.

My idea excited me. Maybe it would help get me over this boredom, that has me on the verge of hysteria.

I love photography. I love it even more when you get the pictures back and you see things in them that you didn't even know was there.

I get a whole bunch of the band too, the crew and of course Eric, cause he's just so hot. I follow Eric out into the crowd, of course their behind a fence and security stands in front of it. So there's no chance that anyone could grab me.

Eric has a puzzled look on his face, I hold up my camera, and he nods, he understands what I want to do. Cam sees me and has a questioning look on his face too, I hold up the camera for him too. He nods.

I think we should do a calendar. Some of the pictures should be of Cam half naked, and of course Dale, with his rockin body. I wonder if Cam would pose nude? I'll have to ask him.

I'd like to do a book about the band too. With lots of pictures. I have to see what he says, I take flattering photos. I hate the pictures that the tabloids put in their magazines. Most of the time they are not flattering to the celebrity. The tabloids always get you at your worst. Cam is gorgeous anyway, so I'm sure I wont get any bad pictures of him.

I have a new roll of film in the camera and five more in my pocket. As soon as they come out I'm shooting. My sign songs aren't until the end.

Cam changes guitars several times. He's got a beautiful new blue guitar. It has an awesome sound. So I get that. He walks the stage from one side to the other. I get close ups of his face, and his butt. His fingers fly over the strings, I love to watch him do that.

For a kid who taught himself how to play at age 13, it absolutely amazes me. He's so talented.

I've never been to talented about to many things, maybe getting into trouble. Cause trouble seems to find me.

Cam looks at me a little to much I think, maybe cause he knows I have a camera, I get his blue eyes, and they are so blue tonight. Intense and passionate. He loves what he's doing.

When its time to sign, I hand Eric my camera and tell him to take some pictures of me with the band.

After the concert, we all go out for dinner. Eric gives me back my camera. I used all of the six rolls of film.

Eric sits next to me at the table and whispers something in my ear, that makes me catch my breath. And almost choke on my food.

"When I was taking pictures of you signing…." He takes a bite of food. "I noticed you look at Cam an awful lot…with goggily eyes."

I nearly choke on the food that's in my mouth. I put down the fork a little loudly on the table. Some turn to see why.

I turn to look at Eric. "What's that suppose to mean?" I whisper through clinched teeth.

"Your still in love with him," he whispers back.

"I am not…I am over him, we have come to an understanding, I told you that, I am in love with you, Eric, why do you doubt me? You still doubt me?" I sip my drink so he doesn't see my lip quiver. "Its not true, Eric, I love you, I'm in love with you. How many times do I have to tell you that?"

"As many times as I need to hear it, and pictures don't lie, Janie." He shoves some more food in his mouth. I hear his breaths coming out in short little huffs.

"Are you mad at me?" I whisper to him again.

"No, just a little upset, that's all." He wipes his mouth with a napkin and pushes away from the table. Gets up to leave.

"You can stay if you want, I want to be alone for a while." He says, he doesn't look at me as he leaves.

Well… isn't this just fine. What is he so pissed off about, he must really be jealous of Cam, except I'm not marrying Cam, I'm marry him. I don't know what I'm suppose to do to make him understand this.

Cam has witnessed our little war of words. And has been watching us from the other end of the table. Do my eyes always wander back to him? Do I always seek him out? Maybe I do with out even knowing I do. I am allowed to look at him and anyone else I want to. I have no more appetite. I push my plate away, and push away from the table. I get up, how long should I let Eric be alone? How long should I let him sulk? Maybe he's thinking about not marrying me. Maybe when I go back to the room, he's going to tell me.

Cam always pays the check. He sees me leave and I'm in a hurry, I don't want Eric to have time to think about canceling our wedding.

Cam grabs my arm and stops me. "Everything okay?"

"Just a little tiff," I say. "About the pictures, I'll tell you later, I have to go find Eric." I give him a lame smile. He lets go of my arm. I still notice his touch, like I always do, his touch burns me with the familiar warmth and desire. I push the feeling away, I have to find Eric.

"I look forward to it," he yells after me. "I'll see you later."

I wave over my shoulder at him and hurry my step to a run. I need to fix this with Eric, for once and for all. With out him I have no one.

He's standing by the van, his back against it, his leg on the bumper.

"Eric?" I catch my breath, "please talk to me."

"What's there to say, Janie, he's got such a hold on you, I don't think I stand a chance." He shakes his head, runs his fingers through his hair, he wont look at me. He closes his eyes.

"But you have broken it, cant you see that? I'm marrying you, not him, I love you….." I put my hand on his arm and slide it down to his hand. He doesn't pull away, but he doesn't hold my hand either. Like I have a damn disease.

"Your marrying me, because Cam is already married." Oh that was cruel. That hurt. Maybe its true.

"That's really mean, Eric….. So what are you saying? You don't want to marry me anymore?"

"I don't know what I'm saying, I want to get drunk."

He combs his fingers through his hair again, walks a few steps away from me.

"Like getting drunk is going to solve this?" I say.

"Yeah, maybe it will," he walks away, leaves me standing by the van.

We had an audience, the crew had walked out of the restaurant . My back is towards them. Another reason why they can hate me.

Cam comes to my aid. "Just leave him be for now, he's upset with me too. I'll keep my eye on him." I shake my head, no thanks, yeah Cam is going to watch Eric drink. I don't think so.

I ask one of the other crew guys, who I know doesn't drink nothing stronger than a coke, to keep an eye on Eric. I tell him to watch Cam too. I'm going back to the hotel. I'm tired. I clean my camera equipment, and pack it away. Put the rolls of film in a bag. I'll take it to the one hour photo store. I really hope Eric is wrong. But I know its probably true.

It was four in the morning when Eric finally walked through the hotel rooms door. I remember briefly looking at my cell phone clock. He stumbled in the dark a few times, before he finally found the bed, hit his leg on a chair and cursed, sat down on the opposite side of the bed. He felt around the bed until he found my leg.

I lay in bed listening to him, I pretended I'm asleep, even though I've been awake waiting for him. Worried the worse, especially if he was with Cam. I could picture the two of them getting into Cam's car, both drunk, and there's that tree. I shiver at the thought. I never said what my dream about Cam was, if he was alone when he dies. I just never saw anyone else with him.

I breath a sigh of relief, he's safe. What about Cam? I guess he is too. Eric fumbles with the door knob to the bathroom.

He's talking about Cam, about me. Mumbling words I cant make out. He is drunk, that's for sure. He uses the bathroom, takes a shower, walks over to the bed and stands there. Dawn is lighting up the room, just enough that I can see him.

He scratching his head. I cant stand it any longer. I move in bed. And sit up.

"Eric?" I say.

"Yeah, Janie its me, who were you hoping for Cam?" He laughs a cruel laugh. One I've never heard come from him, before.

Now I'm mad, enough of this. Enough of this accusatory comments. I jump up on the bed, so I'm taller than him.

"Now you stop this," I say right in his face, and poke him hard with my finger in the chest.

"Stop this shit right now, stop accusing me of something that isn't true."

He backs away a step, and I move closer to him on the edge of the bed.

"Stop it or I'll beat you up," I say, as I put my hands up in fists in his face.

He starts laughing. "Oh your gonna beat me up?" He laughs again. "If I have to tie you up and tape your mouth shut, you are going to listen to me." I tell him.

I jump into his arms, which takes him by surprise, he wasn't ready for that, and he falls backwards, falls flat on his back with me on top of him.

He smells like soap and shampoo and beer. I knocked the wind out of him. But he holds onto me.

"You are the one for me, the one I want to be with, the one I love, you are my soul mate." I have his face in my hands, so he as to look at me. I can just see his eyes, grow soft, in the dim light.

"You still love me after the way I acted?" He chokes out.

"Yes, you fool," I kiss him even though I hate the smell and taste of beer.

"Did drinking solve your problems?" I ask him.

"A few," he says.

"Like what?" I ask.

"Well Cam and I, had a heart to heart talk about you. That Cam is really happy for us. He's glad we found each other."

"Oh....Cam said all of that?" I say, I'm not sure if I really believe that.

"Yeah, he did."

"Well see, you have nothing to fear." I get up, and pull him up.

"Come to bed will you. One more show tonight and then we leave. Will be tired. And your gonna have a nasty hangover."

We get into bed. I lay in his arms, like I always do.

"Oh not as bad as Cam," he laughs. "They had to carry him out."

"Oh gees, he didn't drive, did he?" I ask, trying not to sound to concerned about Cam.

"No." He sighs, he's already drifting off to sleep.

We fell asleep and didn't wake up until three in the afternoon, which is typically our usual time.

I'm hungry. Eric is sick in the bathroom. I order some food. Does tomato juice really work? Coffee? Some aspirins? It's a good thing the bands equipment is already set up.

Eric has been doing the camera, so that doesn't take to much brain power.

I get dressed and call a cab to go to the CVS drug store for the one hour photo developing. That was one thing I never learned, was how to developed my own photos. Except if there on a memory card, I have a printer. But its at home.

I wait around. I tell the guy its urgent and I'll slip him a fifty if he can hurry. I tell him, I'm with L-B's band. He doesn't believe me. I show him the pictures before I leave. I want to look at the pictures before anyone else sees them. I sit outside on the sidewalk, in the sun. They are really good. I look through them quickly, until I get to the pictures of me. I look haggard. For one thing. He took a whole roll of me. Me and Cam.

I don't see it. I don't see that I'm looking at him with love sick puppy dog eyes. I have to look at him to sign. What is Eric talking about?

I go through them again. There's one picture, you could almost say, its when I first come out on stage. And sit next to Cam, what I'm not suppose to smile at him or be friendly to him? He is my boss. Is it that look that Eric is talking about?

He's getting paranoid. He must feel that Cam is a threat somehow, even now.

I put the pictures back in the envelope and wave down a cab, "Take me to the arena."

Our last night, then a new city. Good I'm ready for a change, to many bad memories here. Back to the USA, Michigan, just over the border. I hide the photos in my jacket. I'll have to show Cam, the pictures, and tell him my ideas about the book and calendar. Ask him if he sees "that look," that Eric claims I give Cam, the love sick puppy dog look.

CHAPTER 41

CAM

In my drunken stupor with Eric, I wanted to open up to him about Janie. But I thought otherwise about doing that. Eric was pissed off at me as it was. I didn't need to add fuel to the fire. We drank tequila shots, and beer. Eric was drunk way before I even had a buzz. It was funny though, how easy he was to talk to, especially about Janie. I don't know if Janie ever told him how we met or what happened after, maybe I should keep that a secret. It would be another excuse for him to punch the daylights out of me.

We laughed about stupid things, how Janie would make a pouty face when she was unhappy about something. How sexy she looks in those jogging suits she wears. Should I mention the sex?

I thought twice before I almost spilled the beans, I'm sure Eric already knows. It makes my mouth water remembering the nights we spent together. Eric left the bar before I did. I think I had to be carried out.

After he left, I let my mind wander, and it wandered right back to Janie. I've never had a fan quite like Janie before. Melissa was a fan, I think, she was in the audience at one of my concerts. I said I was going to find my future wife at that concert, and when I walked through the crowd I spotted her. My mouth dropped open. I told my body guard, Hawk, to find her and bring her back stage. He did, and the rest is history. I'm not sure if Melissa really liked me at first. I'm not even sure if she even knew who I was.

Melissa knows my grandmother and my mother, I have a feeling they talked to her about me. I never asked her. She didn't stalk me, it was more like the other way around.

I remember the first official time, I call it official, because that's when I can really remember her. I remembered her green eyes, and how nervous she was, when she met me. And then I bumped into her backstage. She some how snuck backstage and pretended to be a worker for the theater. I thought she was very cute, and very pretty. Extremely shy. Which intrigued me all the more. She went through all this trouble just to meet me. I know I had met her at several meet and greets, but everything goes so fast, and there's so many people, that you really don't remember who you meet. Although her blonde hair and green eyes, and the intense stare when she looked at me, the way she couldn't tear her gaze from me, sort of stuck in my mind.

The second official, or at least the time I can remember, was when she climbed up on stage and blew me away with that seductive, sensuous dance, to one of my naughty songs.

She ran off so fast, I couldn't even talk to her and find out her name, at least. She looked like a scared rabbit. She flew into some guys arms, and disappeared. I thought it might have been her boyfriend or something.

The third official time, I think, was when she did the sign language thing to one of my songs. She had a friend with her who was deaf. I thought it was a nice gesture. It was so beautiful to watch her hands sign the words I sang. I called her up on stage and asked her to do the song again, she did. I wasn't sure, but I thought it was the girl I met before. When I saw her green eyes, the way she looked at me, I knew it was her.

I asked her to come backstage, to talk to her, but for some reason, everything went wrong and she ran out with her friend, and I didn't see her again.

Now I remember what it was, I asked her if she was stalking me, she was worried I was going to have her arrested. I made her cry, which really upset me. So I concocted a contest for her to go to Canada.

She entered it and or course she was the only one who won. I wanted her to come and stay at my house. I arranged everything for her, car, hotel, and I made it easy for her to find me. Of course my driver had me will informed. When she was close enough to Abboutsville, I hopped in my car and drove down to the gas station. I waited for her there. It didn't take her long to get there. She drives fast. I made sure she spotted me, I made it so obvious. The glasses, the hoodie, and the jeans. I let her follow me, and made sure I kept her in my rear view mirror. She had a flat, how that happened I don't know, but she ended up in front of my gates.

I invited her up to the mansion. She was awed by the whole place. She was very sweet and shy, and very polite.

I knew she was nervous. All kinds of thoughts raced through my head. What would it be like with her? Would she let me? Does she want me that way? My mouth salivated every time I thought of her that way.

I was lonely, not dead. I said I would call a tow truck, but I didn't. I wasn't sure if she knew that I knew who she was. She looked prettier, than I remember, older a little, more sure of herself, she was a teenager I think when she first came backstage. Now she's what maybe twenty one or so. I didn't want to scare her, by telling her I knew who she was. So I kept my mouth shut for the time being.

She looked all over my house but only went where I went. She wasn't nosy. Her eyes were darting all over the place except at me. Like she was avoiding looking directly at me.

She sure had gotten prettier, it kept running through my head. I smiled a lot at her. Her eyes were still as green as I remembered them to be. She kept sneaking peeks at me, looking with that intense stare, and when I caught her looking, she'd quickly turn away, and turn a lovely shade of pink.

She moved with gracefulness and a sureness in her step. Like a dancer. She must of continued with her dancing.

I wanted to ask her about the last time I saw her, why she ran out. She was keeping her distance from me, I think she was unsure about me, so I didn't ask.

She offered to cook dinner for me. It was nice to have homemade food, and nice to have someone in the kitchen. It hardly gets used. I had no idea why I bought such a big house. Its to damn big for one person. All I need is a recording studio and a hammock.

She's a good cook too, I remembered some of the food she made. I hadn't eaten food like that in a long time. She even made dessert.

I had been working on some new songs for an up coming CD. And some collaborating songs with other artists. A song for a new movie.

She obviously likes my music, she had a box with all of the bands CD's in them. She liked the things I liked too, dirt bikes were up on top of the list. Most woman like girly things, she likes guy things, even movies, ice hockey, NASCAR, hot, fast cars, my music. She looked at all the cars I own, looked under the hoods at the engines. Was pretty interested in the horsepower. It was easy to get along with her.

I know for sure she's good for my ego. I found out later that she loves my voice, she loves my songs and she's infatuated with me, her eyes sparkle when she said my name. Hell, her eyes still sparkle when she says my name.

She didn't want to sleep upstairs with me, well not in my bed, not in one of the guest rooms, either. Maybe she didn't trust me, or maybe she didn't trust herself, I saw her watch me every chance she got, when she thought I wasn't looking she would steal a look. I watched her make dinner.. I sat at the kitchen table, and pretended to play the guitar and finish writing my song. But no way could I concentrate with her there, she kept looking over her shoulder at me. Smiling every time she turned around.

Even though I was writing songs for a new album I was still bored, she thought she was inconveniencing me, hell she was a nice distraction.

I had hurt my hand trying to change her tire, she wanted to take care of my wounded hand. I found what I had in the house as far as first aide and dumped it on the counter. She took my hand in her small one, very gently cleaned it off and bandaged it. There was definitely electricity between us, I know she felt it too. She was concerned about my hand, because she knew I played the guitar. She hurt her toe too. She got so mad at the tire, that she kicked it with her foot, I tried not to laugh. I thought she broke her toe, she did break it. I took her to the doctor, the next day.

She has a really hot figure, the next day, I remember, she was wearing short, shorts and a tank top with no bra on. Oh my god, I almost died. I'm a boob man, and for her to be wearing a white tank top with no bra, made me want to run out screaming. In fact, I had to get up and leave, she was driving me insane. Go outside, and get some fresh air. Helped a little. But not to much. I wondered if she wore it on purpose, or not. Did she know what it was doing to me?

We ate dinner in my cozy den, with a nice crackling fire. She even made dessert, again for me, another delicious treat.

We talked about lots of things, she kept going about a round about way of asking me questions, about the band and about me. She wanted to know if I had a wife or girlfriend. She was disappointed when I said I had a girlfriend.

I heard her calling me frantically at first, I didn't sleep at all that night knowing that she was downstairs. I finally dozed off in the early morning. Then I heard her calling me, she couldn't find the bathroom. From the top of the stairs, I had a nice view of her breasts, and they were spectacular.

She made me breakfast in bed, and she was so nervous when she came into the room, that I thought she was going to drop the tray on the floor. But she didn't. I was in bed, under a sheet, my chest was bare and she kept looking at it. Hey, I'm buffed, ever since Dale joined the band, I've been working out with him. So I have a six pack. So I'm proud to show it off. I asked her to join me, but she could barely say yes, she had to run downstairs for some napkins. She made me laugh.

I hadn't had breakfast in bed since my mom made it for me when I was sick. It was nice.

And it was the sexiest thing, breakfast in bed. She had her PJ's on. I had to concentrate on eating, rather than Janie in her PJ's. The buttons were still open. I was trying to be polite and not stare at her cleavage.

She asked me what I had planned for the day, nothing would have been my answer, except for her green eyes waiting for an answer, so I thought of the first thing that came into my head, and that was the dirt bikes. She was excited to say the least. I hadn't ridden in a while. And to have someone who was so enthusiastic about dirt biking, well that just made my day.

To my surprise she was good, I could tell she did this often. Can you imagine someone who liked to do exactly what you liked to do. Melissa is scared of the things.

We rode a long time, all day, and then went on the go-karts. Her broken toe didn't stop her. She's competitive, just like me, and we had a race in the go-karts. I let her win by a small margin. Even though I said I won. On an impulse I kissed her. And not once but several times, she didn't push me away, or anything. In fact she kissed me back, and with such a desirable force I thought she was trying to suck the life out of me.

I ran into the garage with the go-kart, leaving her standing there, my heart was thudding so hard, I think I could see it through my shirt. I thought it was going to pound out of my chest.

She's standing there, her mouth open, her face flushed and she smiles at me shyly. Holy shit. She better run.

She wanted to use the Jacuzzi, just a segue to see her body in a bathing suit. Cause I'll join her. She probably thinks I'm hitting on her, am I ? Maybe I was. Of course I was.

I gave her several bathing suits for her to wear, the ones my girlfriend leaves when she's here.

I put water in the tub, add some bubbles too. Get it heated up. I haven't used it since Melissa was here, I blocked that out of my head. How long ago was that?

I put on my trunks, which was something I really didn't want to do, I usually don't. Melissa doesn't either. But out of respect for Janie I did. I'll be a gentlemen. I sank into the hot tub and waited for her.

I had my eyes closed until she came in. She had a towel wrapped around her. She was so self conscious of herself, I hid my smile.

She climbed in and then dropped the towel. I did manage a glance at her body, and man she was hot. I kept my eyes closed until she relaxed. She cleared her throat several times. Whether she was nervous or trying to get my attention. So I opened my eyes. She had that scared look again. I smiled back at her.

She asked me if I was wearing a suit, I wanted to tease her, so I said, no. She was almost ready to jump out of the tub.

We sat with our legs touching each other. I told her she looked very pretty. She blushed. Which just added to her beauty. She said I was pretty cute too.

No one has called me cute since I was in Elementary school.

She asked about the tow truck, and she told me she didn't have to much time left on her vacation. I could give her a job as a dancer with the tour.

If she still does it. I wont ask her yet, she still thinks I don't remember her.

She asked me about dinner. Man I could get used to this. Dinner, Jacuzzi, and Janie. She keeps asking me about Melissa. I don't want to talk about her. I swim over to her and put my arms on either side of her. I'm inches away from her face, I can feel her breath on my face. She keeps looking at my lips, she licks hers. She looks at my face. Into my eyes, like she's memorizing me. Since she came to my house I haven't had a decent thought about her.

I lean in to kiss her and she sneezed in my face. I thought it was funny, and I look at her face and I think its even more hysterical cause she looks horrified. I burst out laughing. I thought she was gonna cry. So I wipe my face off with my hand and lean in again to try for another kiss. I give her a big wet sloppy kiss. She tries to push me away, but I grab her. She wraps her legs around my waist and pulls me to her. God almighty. I took off her top and through it over my shoulder.

I pulled her into the steam shower, with the glass doors. I want to make love to her like the song says," one last time in the shower." Cause maybe it will be the last time I see her.

I make slow, delicious love to her. Were in there for a long time.

She made another incredible dinner afterwards, and sat very close to me. I give her a hug and kiss for the dinner, she fits so perfectly against me. We'd fit together in bed like that too.

She made yet another dessert, at this rate I'd have to work out twice as much to burn off all these calories. I made a fire in the den, while she was in the kitchen. She's humming one of my songs. I was trying to finish the song I was working on, you know dead line. But with her in the next room, in those tiny shorts and t-shirt, and she was barefoot, well it was next to impossible. She gave me a beer and dessert. I love her food. She likes my music. We were good together no matter what it was we did.

Is it possible to have two woman, who could be so right for you? Couldn't I have both of them?

I played her some of the new songs, she listened to them, watching the fire, her eyes glistening in the firelight. She looked sad, about something. I asked her what was the matter, and she turned her head to look at me, a tears escaped her eyes, and she laughed nervously, she said they were so beautiful, that my songs always made her cry. That compliment floored me. No one had ever said that to me.

Sometimes, and there are days when I wonder if I really make a difference to anyone. I think she just answered my question.

I play for her a while longer until she looks sleepy. I invite her to my room, this time she came.

I sit at the bar drinking my beer, I feel a buzz now. Janie wouldn't be to happy, to see me this way and wouldn't be to happy to know I got her boyfriend drunk too. Melissa would be pissed too. I have put her through so much these past few years.

We went out to dinner, and a movie, more dirt bike riding, another time in the shower. We had a mud fight, that was pretty funny. She can get pretty rough, when she wants to. I didn't mind, she's tough. And not afraid to have some rough fun. I like that, especially in a girl. Melissa isn't anything like that, she's a girly girl.

The next morning the tow truck did come, I didn't tell her, I wanted her to stay longer. But I knew she had to go home. She was packed and ready to go. She tried to smile, I could tell she didn't want to leave.

It was hard to let her go, I asked her if she wanted a job dancing for the band on the tour, she said, "yes." That I was ecstatic about. I would make the arrangements for her to meet us in Raleigh, North Carolina.

Her jeep was in the garage, I pulled it up to the house for her, put her bags in the jeep. I watched her drive off, I stood in the road a long time after she left. I've never had such a hollow feeling in my stomach before, as I did when she left. I went back to my huge house feeling so empty, so lonely. And that was it. I wonder how much of that story did Janie tell Eric. He never seemed to act like he knew anything.

When I went into the bathroom to take a cold shower, I noticed a spot of color on the floor. A ruffled pink thong. I smell it, it has her perfume on it. Her pretty face flashes before my eyes. The cute dimples, when she smiles. Those intense green eyes, that looked at me like I was a god.

How she hung on every word I said. I wondered if she was in love with me. I wondered if she cried all the way back to Vancouver. I'm so full of myself.

I put the panties in a box, a secret box of momentous. Its funny I haven't looked in that box in a while. A copy of her ID. I forgotten about. The pink thong someone threw up on stage. Some Mardi Gras beads. Some pictures. The day I met Melissa at one of the concerts. Its makes my heart sick. I'll call her tomorrow. I'll call Janie too.

CHAPTER 42

ERIC

I have such a headache this morning. Cam and I met at the bar. I'm not sure if Janie asked him to keep an eye on me. Yeah right, Cam keep an eye on me. I was pissed when I saw him walk in. I didn't want any one to bother me tonight. I was mad and I wanted to stay mad. I love Janie with all my heart, but I'm also jealous. Jealous that Cam still has this hold on her. And she cant see it, she denies it. When he asked to sit down at the bar, I said, "it's a free world." I guess I could have gotten up and walked to another table or went outside, he probably would have follow, so I just stayed there.

At first we didn't say anything to each other. I sat and watched the TV. He ordered me another beer. So I drank it. Then he ordered some shots. I drank those too. By that time I was pretty drunk. Then we started to talk. We ended up talking about Janie. I wanted to know just how much he knew about her. And he knew much more than I did. No wonder I'm jealous. He probably had sex with her before I did. In fact I know he did. I'm not sure what I'm pissed off at him for. He did know her before I did.

Maybe the fact that he knows things I don't, I want to know everything about her. Her past, her present and her future. I want to be her future. I know she'll never leave Cam, Cam will always be in her life some way or the other. So that I cant fight.

But why do I have such a desire to punch him? I WANT TO BEAT THE CRAP OUT OF HIM. We talk about the cute little things Janie does. How funny she is when she doesn't even know it. And how sexy she is, when he said that, we both fell silent, like we were both remembering just how sexy she is. That was when I wanted to punch him. If he was thinking disgusting things he would like to do with her, or what he already did with her. Whew, I needed to leave before I killed him.

He may be my boss. But it didn't mean I couldn't deck him, for Janie. So I left before anything happened. I was already to drunk to remember my own name. Someone drove me back to the hotel, I don't even remember how I got back up to our room. But there was Janie asleep in the bed. I thought maybe she wouldn't be there, to my relief she was. She woke up, and attacked me. That made everything right. Ha, ha, Cam, I've got Janie in my arms and what do you have. I don't even know if Melissa was there with you. That thought cheered me up considerably. I think Janie for gave me for getting drunk, at least she didn't yell at me or anything.

I think she understands.

JANIE

A week before Cam's fortieth birthday. No concerts were scheduled. After Cam's birthday past and he was still alive, suffering no heart attack on stage. Like he predicted. No concerts were scheduled after either just to be on the safe side.

Everyone was walking on pins and needles, as they say. We all looked at him like we were waiting for him to explode.

He acted like nothing was going on, I even think he forgot about his prediction.

We had a huge party for him at his mansion. It was Deja vu for me when I pulled up to the driveway, up the hill to the mansion. All lit with lights the way it was the first time I was there. I never told Eric I was here before.

It's hard for me to breath. What happened between us over the years is still there. The anticipation of seeing him always made me nervous and excited.

The day of my wedding, I was beyond nervous. I threw up, I don't know how many times. I was shaking. And couldn't stop. It wasn't because I wasn't sure about this, it was because I was so sure about me and Eric. I wanted to be his wife more than anything in the world. I wanted to have his children. Lots of them.

I had the prettiest dress. It was simple, but yet elegant. It was long to the floor, didn't have a train, but it flowed like it did. It had lacey folds all round the bottom from about the knee down. It had thin straps on the shoulders, with little lacy capped sleeves that hung down on my arms. It had a vee neck that was low. It was very beautiful.

Eric wore a dark blue tux as did all the ushers, my girls wore a pale pink gown. April was my bridesmaid. She wore a darker pink gown. We had the wedding at Cam's mansion, and the reception. Cam walked me down the isle, which made Melissa ecstatic, because now I would finally leave Cam alone.

When I finally finished dressing, the music playing softly outside, all the ushers and bridesmaids standing at the alter. Cam waiting for me down at the bottom of the stairs. I heard him suck in his breath when he saw me. He stared up at me, and I down at him. For one brief and I mean brief moment, it could have been our wedding. He was wearing a dark blue suit like Eric. He held out his hand to me, and I walked down the stairs towards him. If I cry now it'll ruin my makeup.

"Oh, my little Janie," he said, "Look at how beautiful you are. How you have grown up." he kissed my hand. Put my arm around his, "Are you ready?" He asked me, I shook my head, yes.

Its true I did grow up when I first met Cam I was still a teenager. Now I'm 25 and getting married.

"Eric is a lucky guy," Cam says. I have no idea why Cam feels he has to talk as we walk towards the door to my future.

"I feel like I'm giving away my only daughter," I look at him and roll my eyes. Now Cam is being sentimental.

"Yes, but your gaining a son," I smile at him.

We stood at the French doors that led out to the patio by the pool, the carpet that was laid down that led to the alter, through the glass I could see Eric standing by the pastor of his church. He wasn't standing still, he seemed to be rocking on his heels, back and forth.

"Are you ready?" Cam asked me again.

"Yes," I said with a certainty, that I felt was the right decision of my life.

We stepped through the doors, into the sunlight on to the carpet. All the guests stood and the music played the traditional wedding march song. All the guests were crew members and their mates. Some relatives, I or course did not have to many left. Aprils parents, and her new boyfriend. Eric's family and relatives. Mostly it was small and intimate affair.

I wish I had a veil, which was one of the things, I didn't want. But right now I wanted something over my face. I wasn't sure if I should smile or if I should cry. I was so nervous. Cam must of sensed it, "I can feel you shaking, look at Eric," he said.

So I focused my eyes, on him and saw his smiling face. And I smiled back at him. It seemed like a long walk to the alter, but then it seemed like I was there without even knowing how I got there.

Cam kissed me on the cheek, told me he loved me, and handed me over to Eric. Then went and sat down next to Melissa. That smug look on her face, irritated me. But I forgot about it, as soon as Eric squeezed my hand. I turned my attention back to him.

The pastor said the vows which we repeated, we had thought about writing our own, but neither one of us were very good with eloquent words. So we just stuck to the traditional vows.

After we said them and were pronounced husband and wife, Eric grabbed me and kissed me so hard that he sucked my breath out of me. He grinned at the cheering crowd, like the cheshire cat. And then someone played a really obnoxious song for us to walk back down the aisle.

Since the reception was right there the party started, Cam and the band played for us. Of course I had to dance with Cam, that was really nice. He looked at me with such love, that this time I was convinced that he loved me all along.

The reception lasted well into the night. Sleepy children lay on the chairs, even I was getting tired. Our flight wasn't until the next day. Cam was sending us to Greece for our honey moon.

He asked me where I wanted to go and I said Greece. So as a gift he made all the arrangements. And handed me the tickets. Told me to have fun.

When we came back from our honeymoon. We went right to our new house, it was finished. Eric picked me up and carried me inside. And the rest is history as they say. He still continued to work for Cam and the band.

I have two sons, one is now five and his name is Eric, Jr. and the second is Cameron, named after his godfather Cam.

I hadn't seen Cam in a while, I stood outside the car, holding onto the door handle. The boys jumped out of the car and ran up to the door.

The week before his day, Cam's birthday, the band took all of Cam's car keys away from him, emptied all the gas out of the dirt bikes, the go-karts, and even the lawn mower. The week after the same thing. He was pretty P.O.D. He was getting bored.

But here we were celebrating forty years of Cam's life. And he was okay.

The boys were waiting for us at the door. Knocking until someone came to the door. Eric asked me "Are you coming, Janie?" My hand seemed to be stuck to the door handle.

I'm shaking a little, I don't know why. Its not cold out. Maybe it's the same reaction I've always had, the anticipation of seeing Cam.

I've kept my weight down after having the boys, and still have a pretty good figure. I work out at the farm, and I still continue to run.

Chasing after two little mischievous boys also keeps me fit.

Eric is still looking at me funny. The door opens and Cam is standing there. He hugs Eric, and the boys scream, "Uncle Cam!" He picks them both up and kisses them.

I swallow hard, he puts them down and they run into the house, Eric turns to look at me again, then enters the house after the boys.

He knows I still have some feelings for Cam. But he also knows how I feel about him. So it didn't bother him to leave me alone with Cam.

Cam stands on the steps. His hands in his pockets. A slight smile on his face. My breath catches in my throat, as his smile widens. His blue eyes sparkle, just like I remember. God, he's one of the lucky ones who gets better looking with age, like George Clooney.

His hair is still blond and curly. He looks taller. He has his favorite ripped jeans on. Its November, but its not really cold out. He has a sweater on. I'm shaking more now than I was before. Its hard to swallow. I could use a drink. He takes one step at a time and lingers on each one. The effect is making me crazy and dizzy. It's only Cam, I say to myself. And these words that I hear in my head, its like fire running through my veins, every time I look at you.

And then he's standing in front of me. "Janie," he whispers. "I'm so glad you came." He lifts my chin up so I look into his eyes.

He searches my face. I can feel tears welling up in my eyes. They escape my eyes and trickle down my cheeks. He wipes them with his fingers and kisses my lips. I lean into him and he puts his arms around me.

"I've missed you," he says in my ear.

I take a deep breath to calm myself. And my entire body shudders as I let the air out. He still effects me in such a profound way.

"Cam," I finally manage to say. "Happy birthday."

"It is a happy birthday, now that you're here." We still play the game so well.

I have my arms wrapped around his waist. So many times I've had my arms around him. Every part of him is so familiar to me. We cant let go of each other. I want to stay this way forever. My eyes are closed, my head on his shoulder.

I feel a tug on my jacket, my son, "Mommy, come on they have a big cake, come and see it."

We smile at him, and let each other go. "Sh, honey, I don't think Uncle Cam is suppose to know about it." Cam lets go of my hand, and my son takes it. He pulls me to the stairs, and into the house. I look back at Cam, he has a weird smile on his face.

"Come on Uncle Cam," Eric Jr. calls. I smile back at him.

Everyone is here. The band and their families. The crew and their families. Some guys are eternal bachelors. Some have girlfriends.

The kids are in the heated pool. There's people everywhere. I'm greeted warmly by the band. It took them years to see I wasn't there to divide them. The wives were the ones who took me under their wings.

Its funny how one day you have no children, and the next you have many.

Cam and Melissa don't have any. It was Cam's choice, whether Melissa agreed or not, I don't know. Their both good with children.

It's a catered affair. Sort of dressy. I have on a little black dress, with heels. Pearl necklace that Eric gave me on our wedding day. My hair is up, a few tendrils have escaped, I feel sexy.

Eric comes over to me and puts his arm around me. Kisses my neck, "You're the prettiest thing here tonight," he says. Cam like always watches as he sips his beer. I can feel his eyes on me. Old habits never die.

"Thanks honey, your pretty hot yourself, you're the most handsomest guy here too, isn't it amazing how we found each other," I say teasingly, so only he can hear.

Eric is still hot to me, but Cam who I smile at, holds a magical part of me. Almost like a spell. That he's had on me, for all these years.

What do you buy a man who can buy himself anything he wants? How about a Greek isle? It was my idea. On our honeymoon, we liked Greece so much, we saw the islands all around Greece, some had for sale signs on them. It gave me an idea.

Well, we all chipped in and we rented the Greek isle for Cam. We all get to go and visit. We couldn't buy it, although we have the option to. Who has millions?

The party lasted well into the night and the next day. The kids had a slumber party. And everyone found a guest room to sleep in, or on the huge couches Cam has.

Cam was talking about starting a tour again for the new CD. He asked me if I wanted to dance? And he said it with a very devilish grin on his face. I'm sure he had my image in his head, like the first time I danced on stage.

I said I would think about it. The same crew would come back, everyone was itching to go. It would mean Eric would be gone for a year or more. That would be tough on the boys and me. If I went we'd have to take the boys with us. Have home schooling. It might work, and then again it might be hard on them. They wouldn't have a normal childhood.

It was something we needed to discuss.

Before we were married Eric had our house built. Big old farm house, but it was far from old. All the latest gadgets, and appliances, it was beautiful and perfect. We'd have to leave it too. Eric's brother could move into it, with his wife.

It was another thing we needed to talk about. Everyone wanted to do this, and the night ended with everyone excited.

There's something about being on the road. Sometimes you loose touch with reality, every day runs into the next, sometimes you don't even know what state or city your in. But isn't life like that sometimes, anyway?

Everyone had just about left and gone home. It was early morning, I felt like taking a walk in the woods behind Cam's house. It's the most beautiful forest of green, I've ever seen. I feel like reminiscing, a little. The trail that Cam and I rode the dirt bikes on, is over grown with tall weeds about four feet tall. The trail I wanted to bury Melissa in, the one where Cam would ride over her, body. I keep walking up the hill, its chilly out this morning. After all its November. It should be snowing or something. Everyone was still sleeping. The boys on the rug in their sleeping bags, and Eric in one of the beds in the guest room. I like being by myself. It gives me time to think about things. Mostly what Cam had offered me..

The air is crisp and clean, I breathed in deeply. I could hear the pounding of the waterfall off in the distance, I had walked further than I thought I did.

It starts to snow. I try to catch some of the flakes on my tongue and laugh. I used to do that when I was a kid. Its been warm this year, global warming?

Not sure how long I've been gone, don't wear a watch. I hear leaves and sticks crunching. I stopped to listen, could be an animal, if so what kind? Sounds like something big, something that could eat me? Maybe I shouldn't stand here and find out. I head back down the hill, following the over grown trail. Avoiding all the debris that has fallen in the path.

I see something bright red. I'm sure a bear doesn't wear a bright red jacket. I duck behind a tree to hide. It could be a hunter, it shouldn't be, this is private property. I'm getting scared. I never thought about dangers out here. In the middle of nowhere.

The red color comes closer and I take a look around the tree to see what or who it is. To my relief its Cam.

"Oh Cam," I say I hold my hand over my heart, and feel it pounding. "I thought you were a really big animal or a hunter. You scared the crap out of me."

"Sorry Janie, didn't mean to, I saw you leave. Didn't want you out here alone." There's a few awkward moments of silence. Its funny after all these years we still find it hard to talk to each other.

Before I finally say, "Thanks."

We walk together down the trail, "How was your birthday?" I ask him.

"It was great, I cant believe you guys rented me an island. It'll be a nice place to recuperate in."

"Recuperate? From what?" I asked surprised, by this.

He walks with his hands in his pockets. "Melissa has breast cancer."

"What?" I practically scream. But don't because its so quiet out here. It would echo all over the place.

He sighs, "The doctors think they've found it in time. She has to go for chemo, so the island will be a nice place for her to go."

"Oh Cam, I'm so sorry. I had no idea. Is there anything I can do?"

"Just be around if I need to talk." He smiles at me and then its gone.

"I will, you know I'm always here for you." I put my arm through his, he takes his hand out of his pocket and grabs my hand. Its warm and strong just like I remember it.

"She went for her usual physical and the doctor said she found something. Melissa had more tests, they came back positive. They did a biopsy, came back positive too. So she starts chemo next week. Were both scared."

"Of course you are, its only natural. But Cam, they have so many new treatments for cancer. I'm sure she'll be fine. I've known so many woman who have had chemo and now their okay. Melissa will be fine you'll see, she's a fighter." He squeezed my hand.

"I hope so," he says. We walk back to the house.

"Thanks, Janie," Cam says. "She isn't really telling anyone about it, yet. So please don't say anything until she's ready to, okay."

"Sure Cam, I wont say a word, but know my heart is with both of you, and I'm thinking of you both."

"I will," he says. He kisses me before he goes inside.

"Cam?" He stops.

"Tell me how it goes okay, let me know if you need me, for anything, alright?"

He nods. And goes inside the house. I can hear everyone in the kitchen getting breakfast. I linger outside a bit longer. I walk around to the go-kart track. It seems so long ago. When everything was new and exciting, at least for me. Filled with anticipation. Cam's always been here for me, when I was sick in the hospital, when I got married to Eric and he walked me down the aisle. Steadying my nerves.

When my kids were born. He was there too. Giving Eric support. Cause Eric was a nervous wreck.

Now I can be there for Cam and Melissa. My heart is heavy as we say good-bye. The tour will be postponed until Melissa's chemo is over.

I don't know what happened. From the time we left Cam's birthday party, to the time when Melissa started chemo. By that time everyone knows about her cancer.

What causes a person to drown their sorrows in alcohol? I told him to call me, know matter what. No matter where, when or what time of day it was. I will always pick up the phone.

Talk to me about anything, I'll talk to you. Even if its just to say hi. But he never did. I called him everyday, but he was never home, or wouldn't answer his cell phone. Was he celebrating, the news about Melissa was good, and everything went well. Or was he grieving? But what ever the reason, if there even has to be one. He was drunk. Melissa was in the hospital.

He was drinking at one of the local bars. No one stopped him, on one took his keys away from him. No one cared. Sometimes he'd have a fight in the bar. For what ever reason. Maybe some one insulted him or his music. Sometimes people wish for awful things to happen to you, just because of who you are. Because their jealous of you. So no one stopped him from getting into his car and driving home.

CHAPTER 43

His alcohol level was two times over the legal limit. We got the call on a Monday night.

Cam was in the hospital. Hurt pretty badly. Rob called. If anyone of us was with him, we would have taken his keys away. But he was alone.

Eric talked to Rob. I knew the minute Eric hung up the phone. The cold chill that ran through my body. The weird feeling that passed through me, a few hours before. I knew something had happened. But I didn't know what. I thought Cam would stay with Melissa. He left while she was sleeping.

Eric said I should go. He'd stay with the boys. Maybe he'd come later, have his parents watch the boys. I said okay, if he was sure. He said yes. I packed a few things, and drove to Vancouver hospital.

No one told Melissa and they wouldn't until she was feeling better. But she was asking about him, where was he? I told her he went home to get some clean clothes, and to have a good night sleep. Sleeping in a chair was torture.

So I drove to the hospital, wondering what I would find. I was so upset. And half the time I cried driving down the road. I still loved Cam.

He made it through his 40th birthday, we all made sure of that, now two weeks later, he's in the hospital.

I told him, he'd wrap his car around a tree. Only he was suppose to die. That thought caught in my chest, oh god, wonder if he was worse then Eric told me. He could still die. Like my friend Scott, he had survived a motorcycle accident, but died three days later in the hospital from head trauma.

I pull into the hospital parking lot, I've been to this hospital so many times then I care to remember. Yes the birth of my children was a wonderful thing, but this. This was the worst.

I hate hospitals, my father died in one, so did all of my aunts and uncles. The chill came back. I got out of the car, and phone Eric that I had arrived safely.

I head to the doors. Each step is harder and harder. I ask the desk for Melissa's room, and Cam's room. Cam is in ICU. Only relatives can go in. I'm his sister, I tell the nurse. She looks at me funny, "You don't look like him," she says.

"Different parents." I tell her.

She just shakes her head, I don't care if she doesn't believe me. Nothing is going to stop me from seeing, Cam.

I go to Melissa's room first. I've composed myself enough, that she shouldn't know that anything is wrong. She's happy to see me. She says she's had a lot of visitors today. People she hasn't seen since the party.

She asked me where Cam was, again. He hasn't been here all day. So no one told her yet.

She showed me the port they put in her shoulder for the chemo. It's a little sore. And she's had her first treatment. She can probably go home tomorrow. If everything is okay.

I smile grimly at her. She's talking on and on. I want to leave and go to Cam. I hardly hear anything she says.

I don't want to be rude. So I stay for a while longer. She's up beat and optimistic about her therapy. I smile and nod a lot. I ask her if she would like anything to eat? Or if she needs anything? I lie and tell her I haven't eaten, all day. She says she's fine. I tell her I'll be back either later, if I can or tomorrow. I'll bring her some magazines, or something. Someone will have to drive her home. It'll probably be me.

I run to the elevator, press the button for Cam's floor. Its so quiet up here. Except for the beeping of the machines. I go slowly to his room, afraid of what I'm gonna see. I look in. I lean against the doorframe for support. I wish Eric was here. Because when I looked in at Cam, it makes my knees buckle, my stomach nauseous, my eyes blurry.

Cam is wrapped up like a mummy. Bandages wrapped on his head, his arms, his legs. Machines monitoring his heart, painkiller, his breathing.

This must have been how I looked when I was sick. Except without all the mummy stuff.

I should move closer to him. I swallow and walk over to his bed. My breath catches in my throat. It doesn't even look like him, except for his curly blond hair sticking out from under the bandage.

"Oh Cam," I cry. I take his hand, very gently, his beautiful hand, its cut up, but that's all. The one thing that isn't wrapped up.

"Cam, its me, Janie." I lean in closer to his face. "Why didn't you call me? If you were that upset about Melissa. I would have come for you, so you wouldn't be alone. You can ask me for anything. You know that." I just cant believe this has happened.

The doctor walks in, I'm surprised because its Dr. Armond."

"Hi, doc," I say. "Its me Janie Newton, will now its, Janie Edwards."

"Yes, Janie, how are you?" I hug him.

"So you are Cam's sister?" He smiles.

"Yes, I am, how is he?" I smile back.

"He's in a coma right now, head trauma, broken bones, cuts, scrapes. He wrapped his car around a tree, big hit to his head." He says.

Its come true, I have to sit down. What I said, came true…..

"Will he wake up?" I ask.

"He may, his head took most of the impact. Its good right now that he's in a coma. It will keep his brain still and will help heal it. Only time will tell." He writes in the chart.

"What about all this stuff that's wrapped up?" I point to all the bandages.

"Well he was upside down for a bit in the car until it hit the tree, he got scraped up pretty good. He'll need some plastic surgery. Skin scraping." He says.

Ugh…I thought.

"Can he hear me, if I talk to him?" I ask.

"They say they can, they say it helps in the recovery. You can." He says.

"I will. Will someone tell his wife, Melissa?" I ask.

"I guess soon, I guess you could." He says.

Oh great. We've come to an understanding, her and me. She knows how I feel about Cam. We both love him. So she's accepted that. But she's the one he chose to marry, not me. She'll have to know cause she keeps asking and calling his cell phone. It was ringing when I came into his room. I found it in the closet in his pants pocket. I turned it off. She's called him about fifty times.

"Can I stay with him tonight?"

"Yes, I will tell the nurse, it's okay for you to stay." The doctor says.

"Thank you, doctor."

I made myself comfortable in the chair by his bed. Tears rolled down my cheeks, I just couldn't hold them any longer. If I cried all night, I'll have a head ache.

The nurse comes in about every 15 minutes. She gives me a blanket and pillow.

"I'm a big fan," she says as she's checking his machine and tubes.

I smile, a lame smile at her. "He's really cute looking," she says. How can she even tell, his face is covered in cuts and scrapes, along with the bandages. And she's got to be kidding, why are you even saying this crap to me. Just shut the fuck up.

"Yeah he is," I say. "And you should see his eyes, they are the most gorgeous blue you ever saw." I tell her.

I remember everything about him. I've stared into the blue eyes, for hours. And dreamed about swimming in them. I'd get lost in them and be happy for the rest of my life.

She leaves. And her words sends me on a journey about the first time I met him. The first meet and greet, where I was so nervous, my mind went totally blank, where I forgot my own name. How I was so nervous about getting caught, and how I devised this stupid idea to get to him. How obsessed I became with him. How I loved everything about him, how I loved every part of him. I loved his touch, the way he says my name. I'm still so madly in love with him.

"God Cam, if anything happens to you," I say to him, I hold his hand again. All night, I wont let go. I whisper in his ear. "I'm here Cam, your Janie. I still love you. You know that. Come back to me, to us, to Melissa and me. Melissa needs you. I need you. We all need you. Melissa is asking for you. She's asking where you are? And they don't want to tell her yet. The doctor told me to tell her, and I don't want to.

I'm not looking forward to it. Why do I get the lucky job? You better get better cause we all need you. All of us. I need you. I'll always need you. I needed my Dad and he left me. I still need him. But he's gone. Don't you dare, leave me. I love you so much. You broke my heart when you married Melissa, but I forgave you. I always forgive you. And I forgive you for drinking and wrapping your car around a tree." I swallow hard, I feel like throwing up.

Tomorrow I'm going to look for his car. I'll ask the police where it is. Its probably in some impound lot.

I don't get much sleep in the hospital. I'll get a hotel room today. I go upstairs to see Melissa. I have to tell her. She can stay with Cam when I'm gone.

"Melissa, I have something to tell you." It's the first thing I say to her when I come into her room, might as well get it over with.

She looks up from the magazine, she's reading.

"There's no way to gently put this, so I'll just say it." She looks at me. With a questioning look.

"Cam had a bad car accident, that's why he hasn't been answering his cell phone. He's upstairs in ICU. I stayed with him all night, he's in a coma." I swallow and wait for her reaction.

She blinks several times, and looks up at me. Her eyes are wide and full of tears. Her hand on her throat.

"Would you like to see him?" I ask her.

"Oh my god, Janie, yes. Why didn't anyone tell me?"

"I guess they were afraid for you. You know you have so much on your plate right now, the doctor thought I should tell you."

"Wow, what a bunch of chickens," she says. Half laughing.

"Yeah they are, men you know," we laugh a little.

"Take me now," she says, "How bad is he?"

"He's in a coma, he has head trauma, he's wrapped up like a mummy, he's got scrapes and cuts all over, he's got some broken bones. The doctor said he will need some plastic surgery, he also said he will heal." And I pray that he will. I will it.

"Oh my god," she says. I found a wheelchair for her. I put my hand on her shoulder.

"He'll be okay," I say. I'm not sure if I believe that. I pray that he will be. I send up another pray for him.

I push her to the elevator. I see Dr. Armond. I wave. "Dr. Armond," I call. He turns to see who called him. "Dr. Armond this is Cam's wife." I introduce them.

"Melissa this is Dr, Armond." She holds out her hand.

"She had chemo yesterday." I tell him. He nods.

"How is Cam today?" She asks.

"No change today, he's resting, his vitals are strong. The swelling in his brain has gone down a bit." He says.

"But he's still in a coma?" I ask him.

"Yes, but its not necessarily bad. He will be healing, his brain has been injured. Give it time, he will wake up when he is ready." He smiles at Melissa, then at me.

I push her to Cam's room.

"Thank you, Dr." She says.

"Can I be alone with him, Janie?" She asks me.

"Sure, I'll go down to the gift shop. Do you want anything?" I ask her.

"No, I'm good," she's looking at Cam. She gasped when she saw him. I know the feeling, it's a shock, to see him this way. A vibrant man, so full of life and energy, lying in a bed all wrapped up like this. I cant even describe the feeling I had when I first saw him. It was awful.

"Okay, I'll be back soon." I told her.

"Thanks," she says over her shoulder.

I walk out and stand by the door. I hear her moving around, she can walk, she doesn't need the wheelchair.

"Cam?" She says. "I love you, why did you do this? I'll be fine, you'll see. I love you so much. Please don't leave me." Then she starts crying and I leave.

I don't want to hear anymore. I leave the hospital and go to the police station. They have his car in the impound lot. They have to check out the car. But say his drinking was the cause of his accident.

The officer takes me to the lot and to the car. Its his corvette. It doesn't even look like it. Its compacted into a small flat piece of metal. Its amazing he's even alive at all.

I look all around it. I take pictures. I just cant believe what the car looks like, its beyond totaled, it's a piece of junk. Scrape metal.

There's blood inside the car. Cam's blood. All the glass is gone. I reach inside the car.

There's a picture of me and him. His CDs. A beer bottle, incriminating evidence. I remove it. A picture of Melissa.

I cant believe it. Its in every news paper. They say if he pulls through he may be charged.

The picture of the car around the tree. A police report. A small article about his life and his criminal record. How they took his license away from him for a year, once before. I wish he was driving his hummer, maybe he wouldn't have been hurt so badly.

I leave the police station and head back to the hotel. I'm really tired. The beeping machine kept me awake all night.

I'll take a nap and go back to the hospital. I call Eric and send him the pictures of Cam's car.

"Damn Janie, what a mess." He says.

"It is, Cam looks as bad as the car, he's in a coma, there's blood all over inside the car." I tell him.

"I hate to say it, Janie, but it was bound to happen." Eric says.

"I know, I think so too, he never quit drinking. I'm gonna take a nap, I'll call you when I wake up. Okay? I love you."

"I love you too," he says. "Sleep well, the boys say hi, they miss you."

"I miss them too, bye." I let out a big deep sigh, as I hang up the phone. It was so good to hear Eric's voice. I miss him so much. I feel so drained, so tired. I don't know what I'm feeling.

I dive into the bed and fall asleep. I don't want to think about anything.

I wake up hours later. Feeling tired still. I call Melissa and ask how Cam is? She says the same and wants to know if I'm coming back. I say, yes, after a shower. She seems relieved to have some support.

Isn't it funny, we beat the shit out of each other over Cam, now where here together for him.

Melissa is waiting in Cam's room, when I arrive a few hours later. She had another chemo treatment. Soon her beautiful blonde hair will fall out. I guess she knows that. She's been sitting by Cam's bed. She's been crying.

"Hey," she says when she sees me.

"Hey, how is he?" I look at him. My heart nearly stops. I just cant believe what's happened.

"Resting peacefully, I guess. I mean what else can the doctor tell me. He doesn't know, its just a matter of waiting." She sighs. "I'm so tired, Janie." She cries.

She puts her head in her hands and starts to cry again. I don't move right away, my reaction to her hasn't always been that sympathetic or caring when it concerned her. But I move over to her and put my arm around her.

"Oh, Melissa, I know." I hug her, and hold her tight in my arms.

"I'll stay with Cam, if you'd like to go to your room and sleep."

"Maybe I should for a while. You don't mind?" She yawns and sniffles. I hand her a tissue. She blows her nose.

"No, I don't mind. I'll bring you some dinner later. Okay?

"Okay." She gives Cam a kiss and leaves the room. Gives me another hug.

I thought she'd never leave, now I can talk to him. I have so much to say to him, so much to tell him. I want to tell him everything from the beginning. Everything I never told him before.

"Hi Cam," I peek out of the door to make sure she isn't lingering outside. Like I did. I kiss him on the cheek. His face is healing, they removed some of the bandages. He has facial hair growing all over, not just on the spots that he keeps the facial hair. Its fuzzy, and I'm not used to the way it looks. I wonder if I can shave him? Or if we can get someone to do it. Melissa is gone. I walk back over to his bed and put the rail down, and sit on the bed next to him, I take his hand. Its getting soft. He has calluses on his hand and fingers from the guitar. I rub them. I feel his hand, in mine and put it up to my face, then trail it down my neck, to my chest, to my cleavage, where his fingers would linger there. I close my eyes. How I loved it when he would touch my face with his fingers, how he would watch my reaction. How my reaction would make him smile.

"Everyone would notice if you went away, Cam." It's the first thing I want to say to him. "There would be such a void if you left us. If you left me….." I'm gonna cry again. But I don't care maybe he'll hear me. Its all the emotions I have for him, spilling out. I want him to really know, that my addictive personality continues to hold me to him, that I'm addicted to him.

"I hate this, I hate this, I hate this, I hate all of this," the stupid beep of the machines, in his room, him lying in the bed in a coma. All these bandages. I look again to make sure no one is listening.

I lean in closer to Cam.

"Cam, I always thought it was your baby, I counted the days. The doctor said I was further along then I thought I was, and it ended up to be about the time I spent at your house. I wanted it to be yours. I was so sad when I lost it. I let Eric believe it was his, because it would have hurt him so much. I wanted your baby, I've never told anyone this. I wanted to tell you along time ago…." I wish he could hear me.

"It's funny you know, you always make me dizzy," I laugh a little. "It was amazing I could function sometimes, you still leave me breathless. You make me crazy. Being near you every day. And then the days when I wouldn't see you, my chest would hurt so bad from the aching I felt, from not seeing you. I couldn't eat or sleep. Eric never tried to figure it out, at least I don't think he did. Even though I think he knows how I feel." I sigh.

"They say bad things always come in threes…..I wonder what else is going to happen?" I think I've given him enough things to ponder. If his brain is even pondering.

I sit back in the chair. I hold his hand and play with his fingers. Twist the wedding band. I wonder if I could twist it off. It comes off easily. I read the date inside and it says, "to Cam love from your sweetest cookie." Yuck. She isn't the only one with a sweet cookie. He enjoyed mine plenty of times.

I try the ring on. It fits me. He has thin fingers. My finger got bigger from having two kids. I think. I slip it back on his finger. And whisper, " with this ring, I thee wed. Cam Konner. I feel silly, thank god no one is listening to this babble.

My first marriage, I threw the ring in the ocean. I hoped it drowned the asshole.

Melissa's treatment continued. I had to go home. Cam's parents came. And there was always someone here visiting with Cam. I would come back on the weekends, with Eric and the boys. Other band members, and family would come. Most they wouldn't let in. Flowers and cards and gifts kept pouring in from fans. It could fill up the entire room from floor to ceiling. But none of it was allowed in the room. It had to be sterile.

"See Cam, this is how much you are loved, by your 1.5 million plus fans. We all cant be wrong in loving you. It isn't time for you to go yet.

I wish I had your talent, right now, cause I'd write you a song. To tell you how much I love you."

I told Melissa, good-bye. Cam's mother, father and step-father came to visit. They stayed with Melissa, too. They would take her home. She'd never be alone.

I wanted and needed my family. This emotional crap wears me out. I needed Eric to hold me tight in his strong arms and my two boys to cuddle with.

I told Eric I was on my way home. He said it was suppose to snow. I said I was coming home even if there was ten feet of snow. Nothing was going to stop me. He laughed and sighed at the same time. He knew me, if I was determined that was it. No one or nothing was going to stop me.

Beside I reminded him "I'm a damn good driver."

Home never sounded so sweet. Who ever coined the phase, home sweet home, should have gotten an award. The reunion was even better than that. My heart was heavy though, as Eric held me in his arms before we fell asleep. He didn't have to say a word. He always knows.

CHAPTER 44

The next week I played catch up with all the work needed to be done. We were canning vegetables. Stocking the farm for the winter, why we do this I have know idea when we could go to the supermarket and buy canned food. I guess its just the idea of it, and the stuff is fresh. It was the last of the summer harvest. The plants that liked the cold weather. Winter was bearing down on us. Eric was repairing the barns for the animals. We took the horses and the dogs for a long run. It relieved some of the heaviness in my heart for a while. I called everyday to see how Cam was. Still no change. The weekend came to quick. Eric said I wasn't obligated to go back, there is a whole bunch of other people to keep watch. I said "I know, Melissa wanted me to come back."

But if there's to much snow and the weather starts to get bad, I wont come to often. I'll have to tell Melissa that. Why she's found comfort in me, I don't understand. Yes, we came to an understanding with each other after our cat fight. But we always kept our distance. Now she seems to cling to me all the more. I guess we have something in common. Our ferocious love for Cam.

I checked into the same hotel and asked for the same room. I like familiar things. It was Saturday. The day I do wash and change sheets on beds. Vacuum and dust. Wash the floors. How I wished I could be doing that right now.

I sat across from Cam. I brought a book and magazines with me. I have nothing else I want to spill to Cam. Melissa was taking a break.

I was engrossed in my vampire book. Yes, I read those. I can block out everything around me and immerse myself in the pages. When a movement caught my eyes. I think Cam just moved. Maybe I was imagining it. So I waited and stared at him to see if he moved again. His leg twitched, like the sheet made a rustling sound. I should run and get someone. The doctor or a nurse?

If I got up and left the room, I might miss him waking up. I got up to stand by his bed. I leaned closer to his face. They took all of the bandages off his face. Just a lot of cuts from the glass, he needed his face scraped to get the rest of the glass out and even part of the road. Some gravel, pebbles and tiny rocks. His face was bright pink. But looked so much better. His eyelids were moving fiercely back and forth.

I held my breath. I took his hand. "Cam can you hear me? Its Janie, Cam. Open your eyes. I love you, Cam. Come back to us Cam."

The machine spiked up. One of the nurses came in.

"What's going on?" She asks me.

"I think he's waking up." I said not looking at her. "Go get the doctor."

I should call Melissa, so her face should be the first one he sees. But I don't, cause I want him to see me first. All these years. That's all I wanted was for Cam to see me.

I squeezed his hand. "Come on, come on," I say like a coach. "You can do it."

Dr. Armond comes in with the nurse following behind. I step away. He lifts Cam's eyelids to see. He sees the fluttering of his lids. The movement of his leg.

"Well doc, what's happening?" I ask. He's looking at the monitor, at the tape that comes out of the machine.

"It could just be a reflex, like a muscle reflex," he says. I'm not buying it.

"A reflex?" No, he's trying to come back, I know he is." I snap at him.

"It's a spasm." He says. "Its very common, he's been immobile for so long, that his body is tired of doing nothing."

"No, your wrong, Doc." I insist.

He's not going to argue with me and I'm not going to accept some stupid explanation. Spasms, reflexes.

"I'll go talk to another doctor, one who specializes in this," he says and leaves the room, looking at his chart.

I go back to Cam's bedside. Slide my hand into his.

"Come on, Cam, fight it, I know you can. You're a warrior, a fighter, you never let anyone else win. Don't let this win." I cry.

The fluttering continues for a few more minutes, then stops.

Disappointment making me weak, I fall into the chair, by his bed. My head in my hands. My eyes closed. A warm, strong, hand on my shoulder.

I look up. Its Eric. I jump into his arms. "Oh Eric, I'm so happy you're here." I sigh so hard it makes me shudder, against him. I start crying.

"Hey, hey what's this all about?" He says, he's rubbing my head and he's holding me tight in his arms.

"Cam," I say, wiping the tears away. "I thought he was waking up. His legs were moving and his eyelids were fluttering. The doctor says it was just some king of involuntary reflex thing. And I don't except it. Then it stopped. Now he's not doing anything. I had hoped with all my power, with all my strength and energy that I'm sending him, that he'd wake up. I'm so upset, so drained. So.........I'm so exhausted." I say against his chest.

"I know, that's why I came, we can do this together. I'll sit with him, you can go and refresh yourself. If you want."

"Okay, I need a break, Melissa is somewhere. She was suppose to go home."

"Go ahead, go," he kissed me and shoved me out the door.

I needed some fresh air, so I went outside and walked over to the McDonald's to get something to eat.

I sat down to eat, I hadn't realized how draining this all was, again. My cell phone rings. Its Eric.

"Cam's awake," he says. That figures.

I ask him, "Who did he see first?"

"Me," he says. He laughs.

"Is Melissa there?" I ask.

"No." Eric says.

"Did they tell her yet?"

"No." He says.

"I'll be right there." I run out, towards the hospital, my uneaten food in a bag. I have to get there before Melissa does. He has to see me first. I don't know why its so important to me, but it is....

I race passed people, the elevator is to slow. I take the stairs. By the time I get to his floor. I'm out of breath. Wheezing by the door. I'm so out of shape, I used to run up and down stairs with no problem. I open the fire door to the hallway. To Cam's room.

Eric is standing by the door, waiting for me, he sees me and smiles.

"What happened?" I ask him, bending over and trying to catch my breath.

"The doctor's checking him out, go in, he's been asking for you." When Eric tells me that my heart pounds with joy. Cam asked for me, he wants to see me first.

But he really wasn't, asking for me, I think Eric said it just to ease my pain. Cam didn't even know me.

Cam's eyes are open, a sleepy open. But there open. Seeing his blue eyes, makes me catch my breath. He sees me and smiles. That beautiful smile, he always gives me.

Dr. Armond turns to look at me. "Janie," he says, "Come here."

I walk over as if I'm stepping on broken glass. I stand next to the doctor. "I think you may have been right." He admits. And smiles at me over the rim of his eye glasses.

"Can you remember who this pretty woman is?" Dr. Armond asks Cam.

Cam smiles his gorgeous smile at me, his blue eyes shining at me.

"No," he says. My heart falls to my feet. And I feel like I could drop to the floor. Melissa comes in. Dr. Armond says the same thing to Cam. "Do you know who this pretty woman is?"

Of course Cam smiles at her, looks at me, then back at her. I hold my breath, cause if he says he knows her, I'll die.

"No," he says. I put my arm around her to steady her. We both lean on each other. "He didn't remember me either," I say to her.

"Are one of these woman my wife?" He asks. He holds up his hand and shows the ring on his finger.

"I am married, right?" He asks.

"I feel like throwing up," Melissa says.

"So do I, " I tell her.

"No I really do, from the chemo, I haven't eaten since last night." She says.

"Oh," I say, "Here I have some Mickey D's." I hand her the bag.

The doctor asks Cam some more questions, who is he, what's his name? What year is it, when is his birthday?" Just some simple questions, everyone should remember.

Cam's face wrinkles, as he's trying to remember.

"No I don't think I remember...... anything, what am I suppose to remember?" He asks.

"Well," I step up to his bed. I pull Melissa with me, "This lady is your wife, her name is Melissa, I'm a friend, my name is Janie, this tall good looking guy is my husband, Eric. He works for you."

Cam looks at each one of us. Shakes his head. He doesn't recognize any of us.

"And you, you are a famous front man of a very popular rock band. You live in Canada. You write songs and you sing them. You play the guitar." He's listening to it all, with a frown on his face.

"I do all of that? So you aren't my wife?" He looks at me. I shake my head, no. "And I sing and play the guitar?" He's not convinced, and he frowns again.

"Cant remember, your joking right, I cant sing." He shakes his head.

"Someone should bring him his guitar." I say.

The doctor tells us to come outside. We follow. Melissa is pretty upset.

"Bits and pieces of his memory will come back, slowly, everything sooner or later. It will take time, something my trigger, certain memories." Dr. Armond says. "Bring him things that might trigger his memory, like you said, his guitar, pictures, what ever you think might help."

We shake our heads. Eric is already on the phone, calling the band and the crew. Rob will bring his guitar, his mother is bringing pictures.

"What happened to me? Why and where am I?" Cam asks. He looks at all of us for the answer.

"You had a car accident and your in the hospital. You don't remember the car accident?" I ask him.

"No," he looks at his arms. They're all cut up too.

"I'm hungry." He says. We all laugh, a little.

"That's a good sign," the doctor says.

"What would you like?" I ask him.

"I don't know, what do I like?"

"Big juicy hamburger," Melissa says.

"Okay, sounds good, what do I like with it?"

"French fries." Melissa says.

"I'll run and get him something," Eric says, "You girls stay here." There is no way in hell I'm leaving.

The doctors and nurses study him, probing, asking Cam so many questions. Melissa is relieved and overwhelmed, she has to sit down. It's a lot to take in. What do we do if he never can remember? Where does it leave the band? Where does it leave the crew and all the workers?

Cam is watching both of us with amusement. I wonder what he's thinking? Two beautiful woman in his room. I smile at him, cause that's all I can do, he smiles back at me.

Eric came back with Cam's food. And food for all of us. Cam wolfs it down. As I watch him. This feels so strange, I wonder if any one else had this weird feeling. What happens when you wake up from a coma? Do you resume a somewhat normal life? Wonder if you cant remember your normal life? I hope and pray he remembers his life. Cause his life is amazing, the long ago childhood, his turbulent teen years and his adult career. I want him to remember, it all. To remember me, Melissa, his family and friends.

Rob and Matt come. They bring his guitar. And hand it to him. He takes it and looks it over. Its well worn, its old, but well loved.

"Who are you?" He asks Matt.

"Your brother," he says.

"Put your fingers on the strings," Matt says. "You'll remember."

But Cam frowns and tries to play it. Were all holding our breaths.

"Just try, Cam, close your eyes and don't think about it, just let your fingers remember." Rob says. "I know you can."

Cam looks at him.

"Who are you?" He asks, Rob.

"I am your back up singer, backup guitar, friend and band member." Rob says. "My name is Rob."

"Nice to meet you Rob." Cam says.

He takes a deep breath and closes his eyes. Puts his fingers on the strings, puts his finger on the cords. He remembers the cords, that has to mean something. You never forget these kinds of things, like riding a bike, or driving a car. Or how to talk. How to read. God he has to remember.

He starts to play, a little rough, something I don't know what it is. But its something. We all clap.

"So I play this, uh?" He says.

"Yes," we all say.

"We need to show him some concert DVDs , pictures, anything to trigger his memory." I'm desperate for him to remember. I want Cam back…..

The doctor wants him to rest. "Gees give the guy some time to recover." He pushes most of us out. Except Melissa.

Eric and I go back to the hotel. We spend a romantic evening together. The kids are at home with Eric's parents. I tell him" it might be nice to have another baby."

"I thought you said no more," he smiles, "After having two C-sections."

"I know," I rake my fingers our his chest. "You forget though. And the pain doesn't last long, it goes away, another baby would be nice or two."

He laughs and picks me up in his arms, carries me over to the bed, "your wish is my command." He kisses my ear, and a lot more.

Cam is up walking around his room, when we arrive. We've decided to go home. The farm needs us. But Melissa's eyes plead with me to stay. "Please cant you stay longer?" She begs me.

I try to be gentle with her as possible, and explain that the farm and the boys need us. Will come back in a few weeks. I'm not sure how much and how progressive they are going to be with her treatments. But she has to stay here or in the area, anyway.

Cam has a cat-scan, MRI, and they find his brain is still swollen, it might effect his eyesight. Maybe that was why he was staring at Melissa, and me, he couldn't focus on us.

He has many visitors, celebrities, crew members, family and friends. But mostly is just us.

We've showed him pictures, and DVD's, played his music on CD's. Showed him his note book. He's interested, but not convinced. He doesn't believe he's a famous guy in a band.

Carlos Santana even stopped by, oh my god. I ran down to the car, to get his CD's to sign. I know, I should be thinking of Cam's recovery, but I may never, ever met Carlos Santana again.

We're leaving on the weekend. Cam is having trouble with his balance when he walks. "Another side effect," the doctor says. "Head trauma, is tricky. You never know the full extent of the injury and its going to take lots of time and plenty of rest."

Which will be hard to do, because Cam is already itching to leave. Even though he's not sure where to go.

Melissa and Cam have been talking, a lot. Like when you met the person for the first time, and you want to learn everything about them. I hope they can give each other support. She needs him now more than ever.

Maybe this bump on the head, will help him forget that he likes to drink. That would be about the only thing good that comes out of this whole thing.

Sometimes when I'm watching them together, I feel as if I've let him go. I've given him totally to Melissa. I'm not obsessed with him any more. I've walked away from him plenty of times now, happy and sad at the same time. That I think I have let him go. Happy for both of them. Sad that it was never me. Right from the start it was always her, but I could never see it. Or I denied what I knew what was true. She always had him. When he first picked her out in a crowd of millions, he found her. And wonder if she didn't like him? Would everything be different now?

He looked right at her, did she look at him? He said that's my future wife. She just happened to be at the right place at the right time. She wasn't married, no boyfriend? Sometimes I want to puke. God had it planned all along? Does god even care? Does Cam even believe in god? He may now.

Melissa called excited. Her cancer was in remission. "How wonderful," I told her. "I'm so happy for you."

She's done with chemo and getting the port taken out.

I ask her how Cam is? Silence, for a second, then she says. "He's remembering things, little things." She's upset, cause he cant remember her, or that they were married. "But he's willing to try to remember," she giggles at that. Yeah, I can imagine how Cam wants to try to remember.

"He never stops thinking about sex. Ever!" She giggles, "That's one thing he hasn't forgotten." She giggles again. And lets out a long sigh.

She says even his cat doesn't like him. Me personally……I hate cats. And I'm allergic to them more than dogs.

Duke and Harlow are slowing down. But still the best dogs ever. Watched over the boys like mother hens, when they were babies. And still keeps them out of trouble, on the farm.

The doctor says Cam's swelling in his brain is gone. He says he wants to resume whatever it was he was doing. "A tour," he says, "How do I pull that off."

He's still having trouble with his fingers playing the guitar, its like his brain and his fingers wont work together. He gets frustrated. And throws the guitar and wont pick it up for days. This behavior is troubling to all of us. He's never been one to give up on something. And he isn't drinking. Melissa said he broke one of the guitars into pieces, he was so pissed off at it or himself.

I asked her if it was his favorite old one? She said "No." I was relieved to hear that.

If he broke that one I'd truly cry. Because that's the guitar he made all those beautiful songs with.

CHAPTER 45

Then one afternoon, I get a call. Its Cam. "Hi, Janie?" He says. I'm really happy and surprised that he's calling me. This is the first time since his accident.

"Cam?" I say, because there is a long silence. "You remember me?" I ask him. And I wait, for his answer, I hold my breath and hope the answer is yes.

"I do," he laughs. "Every single thing about you. That dance you do on stage. The fantastic sex we had. Your beautiful body, Everything…...!"

"Are you alone?" I ask him. I'm standing outside in the garden with a rake in my hand and dirt on my face. The dogs are sleeping near me, in the sun. The boys are at school. Eric is in the barn repairing the roof. That always needs to be repaired.

"Yeah I'm alone." He says. "Why?"

"Just wondering, you don't want anyone hearing this, especially Melissa. Where are you?"

"By the pool," he says, "Melissa went to her mother's."

"And what about Melissa? Do you remember her yet?"

"Yep, I remember her too, everything, I don't know I was standing in the kitchen, looking out the window at the mountain. And the dirt bike trail. I was cooking myself some lunch. The smell triggered it, like when you were cooking for me, when you got a flat. You remember that right?" He asks.

"Of course I do." I say, this is fantastic. "But you do remember, that is so great, Cam, I'm so happy. So are we going on tour?"

"That's what everyone keeps asking me, why do I have to decide? I want to. Melissa is better, I'm better. The album is done. And were releasing it this month. Yeah I would say yes it's a go. Do you want to dance? Hum……?"

"Yes," I say, "I'll start working on it right away. Getting back into shape, that is."

"What about Eric? Does he want to come back to work?

"I believe he does." I say excited.

"Great everyone is in. I'll schedule a meeting and will work out all the details. I'm glad Janie… It wouldn't be the same if you didn't come. I always want you around….I always want you in my life……" He trails off.

I swallow hard, my body getting hot. "Thanks, Cam." Why does he do that to me all the time? Yeah I love to hear him say that, but just as I let him go, he reels me in again.

"Okay, I'll call you with the date and time. Gotta go. Bye, Janie."

"Bye, Cam." I hang up the phone. And take a big happy cleansing breath, Cam is alright, everything is going to be alright.

I'm so excited I can hardly breath, my mind starts to race, all the things I need to do, a mental list. Where do I start, finish the work on the farm, what do I do with the boys? Start to get into shape again, costumes, and accessories, revamp my dance routine, see if I still remember sign language. And what about Eric, does he have a list too. I know he wants to work. He's been talking about it for a while. Can his ailing father handle the farm? Will have to hire some help.

Then I think about what Cam said to me. There he said it again. We still wants me in his life. I want to be in his too. Its as if and as long as we can see each other, everything will be alright.

We have to talk, Eric and I. "What about the baby we were talking about?" He asks me. As if that would stop me. "It didn't happen, has it? Maybe there isn't any more babies left in me."

"What about the boys? He asks. It sounds to me like he's trying to get me to stay home. I give him a sideways look.

"What exactly are you trying to say, Eric? That you don't want me to go? The boys can either come with us, or they can stay with your parents. They can come an visit us, when ever were close by, I'm sure we can work something out."

He shakes his head, "I don't know, they miss us, and if they go, they'll miss school, it could be a whole big upset for them." I give him a nasty look. "Seems like your thinking up all kinds of excuses for me not to go."

He shrugs his shoulders. Which makes me mad. Cause its not really an answer. "Don't you dare try to stop me, Eric Edwards or you'll be sorry. Don't you destroy my dream." I went off stomping my feet and crying to our room. I slammed the door shut.

I heard him say behind me, "okay, okay, I'm sorry, I just thought that maybe you might like to stay home, that's all." He knew he lost. Never could take a crying woman.

"It wouldn't be for another month anyway," I told him through the door.

But it turned out to be longer. Melissa's cancer came back and Cam wasn't getting his stamina back to quick either. He was finding it hard to move around with all the bruises and aches and pains he was experiencing. His balance was still wobbly, some headaches.

That was okay with us. At least with Eric. Sometimes he makes me mad, he has those old fashion beliefs that a woman should stay home with the kids. His mother did. Yes, but his mothers job was running the farm, it just happened to be at her home. Those are the times I ignore him.

It did give us time to finish the remaining projects we were doing on the farm. Eric was almost done with the barn roof. Always a fun job.

We had more alpaca's and llamas. A new horse. And Eric, Jr. was starting school, full time.

I started walking and then running, about 5 miles every day, if I could.

I choreographed a new dance routine for Cam's song. One that didn't require my knees slamming on the floor, and taking the abuse. Cam said he was writing again, he wrote some more new songs. But he was having a hard time mixing up the words and rhymes, and things that made sense.

He got frustrated a lot. And would call me, upset. His world caving in on him and he didn't know how to stop it.

I told him everyone feels that way at one point or another. I sometimes feel that way every day. When I look at all the work I have to do for the day. Sometimes you just have to walk away from it. Come back to it tomorrow. It always looks different in the morning.

The doctor said he was making progress in his recovery. Some memories and abilities my never come back. Every one helped him. The band members helped him write some of the songs. They helped with the lyrics. Helped with the music. The crew if he needed to go somewhere. And everyone gave him moral support.

Some days he was so depressed, there was nothing you could say or do for him, that would help. Other days he was passive.

Today was not one of those days. “I’m taking the hummer out,” he says to me on the phone. “I’m gonna drive it off the bridge.”

“Cam no your not, stop talking like this. What is the matter?” I let out a loud breath of air, I was right in the middle of cleaning out the fireplace, ashes flying everywhere. The black soot covering my hands.

“I don’t know, everything, me, Melissa, you….” He says.

“Me? Why me?” I let out a long breath.

“I don’t know, maybe it should have been you.”

“No, Cam it was never me, we all know that. Remember you saw her in a crowd, of thousands of people, you picked her out. If I was in that crowd, you would have never picked me out, you would have never seen me. You never did. That’s why I had to do the things I did to get your attention. Melissa didn’t… do you remember? How many times do we have to go over this?”

“I don’t know, thousands of times until it sinks in. I remember some of it.” He says.

“So stop talking like that, everything will work out. You’ll see we haven’t abandoned you yet.”

“I guess…just feeling sorry for myself, I guess.” He says.

“Its okay, we all feel sorry for ourselves once in a while, its okay to feel sorry for yourself. You’ve had a lot to deal with, a lot has happened, its only natural that your gonna have these kinds of feelings, everyone does sooner or later.” I close my eyes, and sit down, being Cam’s psychiatrist is tiring.

“Did you ever feel sorry for yourself?” He asks.

“Plenty of times, especially when I was a teenager. I was this awkward, to tall, gangly girl. Clumsy, prone to accidents….come to think of it I still am prone to accidents.” I laugh.

“Like what?” He asks.

"Well all the times, I've fallen. When I found out you married Melissa, I felt like I wanted to die. I wanted to die, I thought about ways to do it. And then I'd make you pay for not picking me. By placing a shit load of guilt on you. For making me kill myself." I say.

"Really I didn't know that."

"Yeah, there's a lot you don't know. I could write a book. And you didn't know, because I have good people around me, and I let them help me. Just like you have good people around you, let them help you, I have Eric. You have all of us. So your not the only one with these feelings, everyone has them." I close my eyes. I feel a headache coming on.

"I guess your right, Janie." He says. "You've always been good for me, Janie. I'm glad I still have you."

"Thanks Cam, I'll always be here," feeding your ego, I say to myself.

"I think I've thought of the next line in the song I'm writing, I better write it down before I forget. I'll call you later. I want you to hear it." He says.

"Cant wait." I have heard this so many times. This whole thing. I've heard so many of Cam's new songs. I'm glad he trusts me. I could steal them, and write my own songs. I always feel honored and special that he always wants me to hear the songs. But this feel sorry for me is wearing thin.

"Bye." He says.

"Bye." I say back to him. And put the phone on the table.

I sit down exhausted from Cams conversation. Lately they've been making me feel that way, I don't know how to deal with this kind of thing. Cam has been unloading all of this on me. Mind you I did tell him to. But its getting to me.

Later on in the day I went for a long run. Duke and Harlow run beside me. I start out pushing myself hard, because I'm mad, upset, not really sure what I'm feeling. But Cam's ups and downs, are getting me up and down. I don't tell Eric though, because it would be all he needed to hear to get in the truck and head towards Cam's house, and punch the daylights out of him. So I keep it quiet.

I run to the stream and Eric's homemade waterfall. The dogs wade in the water, lapping up a ton of water. Their trying to catch the fish that swim around their feet. Its very funny to watch. They bite at the water, burying their noses in the water, almost covering their heads. Jumping up and down, as if the fish are biting them. That would teach them. Splashing water all over the place. They always make me laugh with their antics. I sit by the side of the stream. My fingers make circles in the water.

My phone rings, which is unusual because I usually don't get a signal. I should have left it at home. But its Eric, to my relief.

"Hi," I answer.

"Hey, where are you?" He asks me.

"I'm by the stream, with the dogs, you should see these silly guys. Their trying to catch the fish." I laugh.

"Yeah they are silly, I hope they never catch a fish, I don't know what they'd do with it. When are you coming home?" Eric asks.

"Soon, I guess. I have some things to workout."

"What? Oh wait....let me guess....Cam?" He says.

"Yeah something like that, Cam is just being Cam. I'll be home soon." I tell him.

I hear him take a deep breath, I know he's trying not to get mad. "Do you want me to tell him to stop calling you?"

"No, I think that would hurt him, he's suffering enough, right now. He'll start feeling better soon, it's a process he's going through, I guess."

"Yeah I guess, well his process is making you crazy. He dumps everything on you, so you can carry it around."

"I know, but I'm stronger then him."

"You are, but still it isn't fair to you or your family, hey I'll met you on the trail." He says.

"Okay. Come on guys, you silly doggies, lets go home." I call the dogs. They gallop from the stream, dripping wet, and like always stand next to me, and shake themselves off. I get wet, I'm already running towards home. The dogs pass me and bound on down the trail. Their barking. It's probably Eric.

Eric is riding Geronimo. He waves, I wave back. The dogs are running all around the horse. Its amazing they've never been stepped on. It's a good thing the horse and the dogs have grown up with each other, because any other horse would have dumped Eric on his ass.

He reins in next to me. "Want a ride?" He smiles and offers me his hand.

I've become the master of getting up on the horse. I sit in front of Eric, I snuggle up against him.

He presses up against me, he's nice and warm against my back. Puts his arms around me, clicks the horse to walk.

I put my head back against his shoulder. His chin rests in the hollow of my shoulder. How many times we've done this. I turn my head to kiss him. He always makes me all fluttery inside.

"So did you workout all your stuff about Cam?" Eric asks in my ear. His hot breath tickles my ear.

"Well I didn't come to any conclusions, if that's what your asking me, but I did workout how irritated it made me. I don't feel so irritated anymore."

"Well that's good, I guess... don't want you irritated." He pauses a few minutes. "What did Cam say?"

"He said Melissa's cancer is back. He's having trouble writing, he's feeling really down. Wants to drive his hummer off a bridge. If he can find one," I laugh slightly.

"He's depressed, maybe he needs some medicine or counseling." Eric says.

"Drugs for him? No.....that would be bad, as his drinking is."

"I guess your right." He says, and lets out a big sigh in my ear.

"That tickles, every time you do that."

"Does it? I'll have to do it more," he nibbles my ear. I giggle.

We ride back to the house, slow and steady. The boys are outside with their grandparents. Everyone waves.

What a picture perfect day. The boys come running over. Their bright eyes looking up at us. "Hey you guys," I lift them up. Poor Geronimo, he never complains, we walk to the barn.

We have to explain to them will be leaving soon for the tour. It'll be hard for them, we've never been gone for a long time without them.

Cam wants to have the concert in Vancouver. To raise money for breast cancer research. We all think it's a wonderful idea. Melissa will be the guest of honor. The spokes person for this tour. But we're not sure if Cam is up to it. He says he'll be fine.

He finds an available date that the arena is free, the arena has been asking them to come and do a concert. The word goes over the radio and e-mails, newspaper. The concert is sold out is two days.

We all arrive one week early. Set up. Dress rehearsals. The band hasn't played together in a while. My new dance is approved by Cam. I intensify my workout, one thing I love about the arena's, is the stairs, it's a great workout for my butt. My stamina isn't to good though.

The amount of energy and excitement in the arena is contagious. It feels like it used to before all the bad things happened.

Cam sits on a stool a lot on stage. He's winded a lot. Some of us are worried he my not make it through the show. Will make sure, he takes it easy, eats good, gets enough sleep, give him a ton of vitamins.

Everything is set to go. Every day we practice. Its got to be the best damn show we've ever done. Cam wants to do the new songs, from the new album, that hasn't even been released yet. Is that a good idea? The band opts for a few off the new album.

My boys come the day of the concert, along with Eric's family. Being boys of course, they are fascinated, by the huge lights and cameras. How big the arena is. They run up and down the stairs with me. I have to say, I'm feeling good. My ass is looking good. You want a little jiggly in your trunk, no ass gets you no where.

The night of the concert, we have a big party with the crew and some fans before the concert. We have to celebrate, all of us back together. Cam's recovery, Melissa's new charity. The breast cancer research. Her new treatment.

Lots of great food, I notice Cam has a bottle of beer in his hand. I walk over to him, and give him a big kiss on his lips, which takes him totally by surprise, I take the beer bottle out of his hand. And walk away with it. He just stands there and looks at me. I look over my shoulder at him, to see his reaction. I smile at him, his face is blank at first, then he starts to grin at me. I throw the bottle away. I know he can get another one. But I sent him a message, he doesn't need to drink to have a good time, and he doesn't need to drink before the concert. He needs all his wits about him for the show.

Before we go on, he says, "he's nervous." Always before a show starts. Sometimes he says he forgets the words, and how to play the music, but then once he starts to play it all comes back. Will he forget tonight?

I suppose everyone goes through that, I even forget the steps I have to dance, until the music starts to play and I start to dance, it all seems to come flooding back.

If he needs the stool to sit, it'll be available. His body guard with the weird hair do, Hawk, his real name is Tom, is close by.

The three opening acts go on first. Each taking about 45 minutes to play.

I'm dressed in a brand new slinky dress, new 5 inch heels, forgot how hard they are to walk in. My hair is straight with just a hint of a wavy curl. Makeup a bare minimum. Sometimes the more I put on the more it brings the fine lines out, and we don't want that.

My kids are a little confused, their not even sure if its me or not. But after I say, "Its me, mommy," they run over to me. I kneel down to get a hug from them. They touch my face, and my eyes, and my hair.

"You look pretty mommy," Cameron says. "Uncle Cam keeps looking at you, he thinks your pretty too."

"Thank you, honey," I kiss both of them, stand up and straightened my dress back into place, and yes, Cam is looking at me. He gazes at me, the way he always does, in a way, that halts my breath.

"Stay here with Uncle Jeff," I tell them.

When its time to start the show, Cam takes a big deep breath, grabs my hand, before he goes out and lets go. I seem to give him, some kind of reassurance. Hey I do, what ever I can. Maybe he thinks I'm his lucky charm, I don't think I'm a lucky charm, far from it, I got ill from a fan, fell off the drum deck, messed up both of my knees, no lucky charm here. Wasn't there for him when he was drinking, got into his car and wrecked his corvette, not to mention, himself. Yeah, no lucky charm here.

CHAPTER 46

Cam welcomes everyone and thanks them for coming to this special event. He introduces Melissa to the audience. And incase anyone didn't know this is an event to raise money for breast cancer. All proceeds will go to the foundation.

They start to play the opening song. My song is the next one. I wait for that famous note, I have dreams about sometimes. I'm not in the audience anymore, waiting for my cue, we ended that a long time ago, when that guy tried to kill all the band members. I wait backstage now. Sometimes I pace, or tap my foot to the beat, I'm always nervous too, just before I go on.

And then Cam hit's the note that's embedded in my brain, and that's my cue. Its so good to be back, to having fun, dancing is fun. Dancing around the band members is fun. My new dance is a big hit, I even hear people yelling my name. I've slowed the dance down, even though the music is still the same beat, but it works, the dance becomes the seductive, sexual dance I always intended it to be. I tease them all, even Matt and Rob. Cam responses to me while I dance around him. Something he's never really done before. My dance over, and he says, "Lets hear it for Janie," he kisses me and says, "thanks" to me with misty blue eyes.

This is hard for him I realize. Everything that's happened. Its all up to him tonight. The whole show rides on his shoulders. I squeeze his hand before I leave the stage. He's got to remember that he doesn't need to go through this alone. We are all here for him. And he doesn't need alcohol to get through, either.

The first couple of songs are fast paced, get up out of your seat, and jump up and down fast. Ass slapping lyrics. And requires a lot of hard hand movements on his guitar. He's having a little bit of a hard time keeping up, Rob takes the lead. Rob is just as good, as Cam. Even his voice is similar to Cam's.

Cam is covered in sweat already. His clothes are soaked. The sweat is pouring down his face, into his eyes. When he finishes his song, I sent Eric, Jr. out with a towel and a bottle of water for Cam.

"Hey buddy, thanks," he says, "This is my nephew, Eric Jr.," he tells everyone. Eric, Jr. runs back to me.

"You did good, honey," I tell him. He's so proud of himself. He's got a big grin across his little face.

Cam drinks the entire bottle of water and wipes the sweat off of his face. I'm very nervous for him. I'm watching him like a mother hen. Everyone in the crew is too. We even have a doctor back stage. On stand by. Its Dr. Armond of course. Melissa knows him very well. She sees him every other week.

Cam signals for a stool. He sits down. Explains to the audience, he's still not 100%, but felt that this was to important not to do, no matter how he was feeling. The audience applauds.

He's going to play one of my favorite songs, "Mistake." I requested it years ago. And he sang it for me. I think I was the only one in the audience who knew the words to the song.

The concert is halfway over. After "Mistake," he needs a break.

He comes backstage. Dr. Armond, makes him sit down, gives him a drink, takes his blood pressure and listens to his heart. We are all hovering, like vultures, Cam gives us, all an evil eye.

Checks his eyes, pulse, reflexes, like a mini physical. Tells him to drink all of the water, Eric gives him a clean shirt. To many doctors hovering over Cam, he's getting annoyed, at all of us.

"I'm okay you guys," he sighs, "Just a little winded, that's all, I'm fine, and don't look at me in that tone of voice." He shakes his head at all of us. And says, "get back to work." He barks.

Dale, Rob and Matt are still out there playing. Dale always has a drum solo. Which always rips the place apart.

Rob tells him to show everyone his guns. Meaning flex those big muscles of yours. Everyone goes wild, specially the girls, always makes me laugh. He's tattooed and pumped. New piercings too. Like me. I've got more holes in my head, more holes for more gold jewelry. I sometimes think were in competition with each other, over who can get the most holes and tattoos. I think Dale wins though, cause my tattoos are small, and he has piercings in places, that I don't want to have pierced. Or that I don't even want to think about.

Before Cam goes out he says he feels a little dizzy. I wipe him down with a cool rag. Hoping that will help. Melissa is upset, and doesn't know what to do. The doctor may not let him finish the show.

But Cam says he must continue. The doctor says sit for the rest of the concert. But you know Cam….he's the showmen. He wants to give the audience the best show he can. He takes the stool and starts to play. Then stops and says, "I bet you thought we were gonna play this sitting down." Gets his electric guitar, and starts playing, that crazy way he does. With all the energy and enthusiasm that bubbles out of him.

About halfway through the song, he falters. He wobbles. Matt is by his side, Rob on the other.

My heart skips a beat. Jeff says, "he's going down."

His bodyguard comes out and grabs him. Takes him backstage. He's passed out.

The whole arena is hushed. I feel I need to do something. I come out and take the mic.

"Hi everyone," I say. "My name is Janie, Cam is a little winded right now. As soon as he catches his breath he'll be back out. We really appreciate your coming for such a good cause. We'd like to do something different. Rob and Matt pick out five people out of the audience and have them come up on stage." I tell them. They look at me like, what are you friggin nuts?

I mouth to them," just do it." And they shrug their shoulders, okay. Security is looking at me too. So they point to five people each. The ten people come up on the stage. Their excited, the fans that were picked. Mostly woman.

I say, "Lets all sing a song together. Anyone have a favorite?" Someone says," the one their most famous for."

"Rob?" I say. "You take over," Rob can do it, he's very capable, he does on stage anyway. He starts to play and everyone crowds around the mics, I back off the stage a little. I'm not the greatest singer, I wave my hand for Jeff and Eric and the kids to come out on stage. Melissa and anyone else who wants to.

Rob plays, my kids take my hand. Rob starts off singing, Dale's backup. Matt doesn't sing.

Dale can sing too. And then the audience joins in. It's the most beautiful thing you ever heard, like a big choir, a big church choir. Like a choir of angels singing. And were all singing for Cam.

The fans on stage are awesome. We have cameras filming the whole thing, everything. This should make an incredible, DVD.

"Let's sing another song," one of the fans on stage says. "Which one?" Rob asks.

"How about the one about being a rock star." The fan says.

Rob starts the song off too and everyone is singing. Even my kids, who know the words, after all they've grown up listening to it. Even when I was pregnant, I'm sure they heard the music.

You know how you stand back and take everything in, and your amazed at what your seeing. That's the way I felt, like this was some magical dream, the perfect fairy tale story. It was so incredibly miraculous, like a miracle was happening right before your eyes.

We sang more songs, and invited ten more people to come up for a turn to sing with the band.

The concert was already over an hour passed the usual end. But who cared. This night was something no one wanted to end.

Before we finished the last song, we heard a familiar voice, singing. Cam comes out holding a mic. The audience goes berserk. I go to him and put my arm through his and Eric is on the other side of him. He's shaky.

He stops at the end of the stage. I'm not sure if he's sweating or if its tears. He smiling. Melissa comes over and I let her hold Cam's arm.

"Thank you everyone, for this incredible night." He says. "You guys are the best fans in the world." He looks at all of us. "And the greatest crew and family. You made this the damndist best concert I've ever been to, the best we've ever done. All thanks to you." And he points to the crowd. Everyone cheers.

We close the concert with one of Cam's favorite songs. And it's over. The energy in the arena was high, and everyone stood around, no one wanted to leave. But security pushed the crowd out the doors, to close and lock them up for the night.

The after party continued back stage, long into the early morning. My kids were asleep in one of the dressing rooms. Melissa was sleeping. Eric is with the boys.

I changed my clothes, I'm tired too. It's a good tired. And I doubt I could sleep anyway.

Cam finds me as I'm packing up my dress and shoes. "Hey, Janie."

"Hey Cam." He's looking better than he did earlier.

"Come and talk to me," he whispers, he notices Eric and the boys sleeping.

"Sure," and I close the door quietly.

"I'm kind of tired, Cam cant it wait?"

"No, I've got to say this now. Come on."

So we walk out into the parking lot of the arena. The sun is just starting to turn the sky a soft pink.

He grabs me and hugs me. "You saved my neck tonight, where did you come up with that idea? Never mind, you have no idea how incredible that idea was. That was the best show, I've ever done, the best I've ever seen." He's shaking his head, remembering the night.

He sits down and takes a long deep sigh. "Cam, what's wrong?" I put my arm around him, he buries his head in my chest. Then looks up at me.

"When I passed out, I felt it coming the whole night. I fought it the whole night, until I couldn't fight it anymore, then it kind of took over. Then when I woke up….and I heard everyone singing. I thought I died and went to heaven. I thought the angels were welcoming me into heaven. I've never been so overwhelmed with love and respect for our fans. Our crew and especially for you. You truly are my guardian angel." He looks at me, again and searches my face.

"Thanks, Cam, but I really don't think I'm your guardian angel…..I wasn't there for you when you were drinking and you got into your car, I wasn't there to protect you and to keep you safe. I'm in no way your guardian angel, I failed you if I was your angel. You would never have gotten into that car, and you never would have driven into that tree….. If I was your guardina angel. My wings would have been taken away from me." I frown when I think of it, if only I had been there, that night at the bar. I would have taken the keys away from him and driven him home. But I wasn't there, I wasn't even thinking about him. Sometimes it weighs on me, that somehow I let him down.

I have a dumb look on my face, I know it. He's embarrassing me. I don't know what to say, he once said," I was his guardian angel." I never believed it though. So I say the only thing I can think of, "Thanks."

"No Janie, Thank you, even that word isn't even enough to tell you how I feel about you. My heart is going to explode… that's how it feels. It was a piece of history, we made a piece of history. The kind that I want people to remember for ever. And all of us were a part of it. We've even made a bigger amount of money for the cancer research, people are still donating. The last I heard we were close to a million in donations. All because of you."

"I just did what I thought was necessary, Cam it felt like the right thing to do."

"It was perfect," he holds my hands. I can still feel a little tremble in them.

We walk back to the arena. He gets Melissa and goes to the tour bus. I lay on one of the couches with my family. I fall asleep.

Vancouver newspaper, radio internet, all had the concert as head line news. Big success, raised more money than any charity event combined.

They liked the impromptu singing and fan participation. Said no concert has ever been quite like it before.

Dr. Armond wants Cam to come for more tests and another CAT SCAN, MRI. Even though he doesn't want to go, we all made him. The CAT SCAN showed some swelling, but nothing serious. The MRI the same thing.

Rest was what the doctor ordered. But to get Cam to rest, is almost impossible, he's always doing something. He liked how well the concert went, that he wants to do one in Edmondton, and all the large cities in Canada. Then if every ones health is better, maybe the US and beyond.

Melissa had a double mastectomy. It was the only way to get the cancer out. It devastated all of us. It was that or she would have died.

She got breast implants and she hates them, because they feel so cold and funny. They took out her chest muscles, so the implants aren't laying on anything but her skin. They feel cold and heavy, but she wants to look as normal as she can. She told me she has no nipples. They could take them off of a cadaver. Or maybe make them out of some other part of your body, but she said as long as it didn't bother Cam, then she wouldn't worry about it to much. I didn't know that Cam had thought that much about what her boobs would look like.

Cam never says anything about Melissa's cancer, I mean, we never have had a full out conversation about it.

But you know he supports her. His eyes hold all of her pain, you can see it, sometimes. Especially when he looks at her, when he thinks no one is watching him. I have to turn away, its to painful to watch.

Cam gets the okay from the doctor that he's healthy enough to get back to touring and concerts.

He announces the new tour is on and Edmondton is the first stop for the concert schedule. Will stay close to home for now.

The new CD is released, it goes Platinum in a few weeks. The tour is named after the album. The band will sing all of the new songs. And where does that leave me?

I ask Cam, "What about me? What do I do? What do I dance to?" And he tells me any song I want. But there aren't any slutty songs about a woman who prostitutes herself, none with a fast tempo, none that are teasing or tempting to a man.

He sees my disappointment, then says, he'll play my song. Great, now its called my song. I say, "Fine."

I have to learn new songs to sign. I sit with the CD player, the earphones in my ears. Try to figure out the signs. I should call April. I feel pressed for time. We only have a few weeks. The tickets go on sale and are sold out in two days, again. Its an all time record in sales.

There's also a special lottery for 10 people to come on stage and sing with the band. Will see if it has the same feel as the spontaneous thing we did the last concert. I call my sign teacher for some help.

We go home for the weekend. Eric's father isn't feeling well. The doctor says its his heart. He may need heart surgery. So we go home to help out on the farm. They don't need us until the week before the concert. We'll get things caught up on the farm. Eric will have to go back one week before me though.

His brother Jeff has created a new website for the new CD and concert. The last concert is available on DVD. They make 10,000 copies. They sold out in a week and have to go for a second print and copy.

Cam calls me everyday. Just to hear my voice. Eric shakes his head, and walks away, when I'm on the phone. If he tells Cam not to call, then Eric may not have a job. So I push him away and try to soothe him later. He has to understand that I'm the only person who can calm Cam down when ever he feels like his world is falling apart. He just needs an understanding soul to listen. I guess I get the job.

He shouldn't feel like that at all, like his world is falling apart, because its far from it. The band is given awards from the record company, for their new CD, that went platinum. Another award for Cam to hang up in his studio.

He says he's having some new ideas for songs. He's putting the lyrics and music together like he used to. Most of his memory is back, except for the car accidents. He cant remember any of it. My friend had a bike accident, he didn't remember how that happened either. Maybe it's the way the brain protects itself. Maybe its just better if you don't remember, something so horrible.

But then again maybe if he remembered the accident, he wouldn't drink anymore.

After he was stable, I showed him the pictures I took of his smashed up car. It was more like a flattened pancake. He couldn't believe he survived that. The rescue team had to cut the car practically in half, to get him out. Inches away from his face was a sign post that was lodged in the windshield. He must of hit it first, dragged it along with the car until he hit the tree. If he had turned his head to the side, an inch, if even that. God I hate to think what might have happened. Where that post would have ended up. But it didn't. So I push that thought from my head.

Eric's father has a heart attack, while working on the farm. Eric rushes him to the clinic in town, where they stabilize him and transport him to Vancouver hospital.

Before surgery he has another heart attack and passes away. We are all at the hospital, when it happens.

As soon as the doctor walked through the doors, we all knew. From the way his face looked. It was hard to hear. Hard to believe. One minute your there and the next your not. Eric's family is strong. But his Dad was the nucleolus of the family.

His mother keep saying, "Now what am I going to do?" And wringing her hands. Saying is over and over again. Eric went off some where to be alone. Jeff and his wife clung to each other, and took Anne home. Eric's sister Anna lee sat by herself crying, they took her home too.

I sat with Eric, Jr. and Cameron. They were upset and confused. Didn't understand why every one was so sad. Where was Grandpa? Is he going to get better? Where did Daddy go? Why was he crying? Why is Grandma crying?"

How do you explain it to a five year old and a three year old. I hugged them both. It felt exactly like this when my Dad died. You know it was a possibility . You try to prepare yourself for it. You bring in the pastor of your church to pray with you. You try to be strong, but it takes more energy then you have. It wears you down. Every time I left the hospital, I cried the entire way home, and that's were Cam's music helped me out. And then you had to come back to the hospital, the next day, pretending to be strong when inside you were falling apart.

CHAPTER 47

I made all the arrangements for the funeral. I figured I knew what to do, since I did it for my Dad. Eric's father served in the Vietnam war, so he was a vet. He would be buried at a War Vets cemetery.

We hired two men to work on the farm. And life went on. We went on as best as we could. Every once in a while, Eric's mom would stop what she was doing and close her eyes. Take a deep breath.

I asked her if she was alright, the first time I saw her doing that. She said, "I feel him here, every once in a while I can feel him standing next to me." Then she'd go on about her daily routine smiling for the rest of the day.

Jeff said he looked out the window towards the barn and thought he saw Dad in his red checkered coat by the horses.

Anna lee said she was lost in the car and was scared. It was dark out, she said her father told her the way to go.

Eric even said he thought he saw him out in the field. I've never seen him. I never saw my Father. My father was gone for good, from this earth. Why would he want to stay. His job on earth was done.

The next week was the start of the new concert schedule. Eric has already left the week before me. I interviewed and hired two new guys to help out on the farm. Two local men who were out of work, who lost their jobs, they were eager to start working. I made them a list of things that needed to be done every day. I wasn't sure if Anne could handle the responsibility of ordering men around. She still seemed out of it, like she zoned out ever since Eric's dad passed away.

I packed up my new dresses, shoes, makeup, and accessories, street clothes. I'm sure I forgot something. I always have that feeling when I pack.

I promised the boys they could come and visit on the weekend. Cam could send a car for them. They'd love a limo ride.

Cam is going to milk this concert for every thing it's worth. How many years can you play the same songs off of an album that is already two years old. Although the new CD was a big hit, most people preferred the old songs. Tickets were made affordable for fans, who otherwise couldn't afford a ticket. Made available concert tickets to win on the local radio stations. This was an all out assault on cancer. For two weeks we were staying in one city and would have a concert every other night. When tickets stopped selling, then it's time to move on.

Melissa was still recovering from surgery. We were all recovering from to many tragedies.

The night of the first concert for the new CD, we were all nervous and excited. I was so nervous about signing the new songs. I wasn't sure if I was doing them right, and like the nightmare I once had about signing, the wrong signs and everyone laughing at me, I hoped it never came true.

I called my old teacher several times. She sent me some signs over the internet.

My new dress was super sexy, if it wasn't for the rows of beading that wrapped around it, it would have looked like I had nothing on. It had that nude colored fabric underneath, from far away it probably looked like I was wearing nothing.

I through in some new Latin steps. Cause I love Latin dance. As long as the beats the same it will work. The dress has red beads. I know Cam likes red, red is suppose to be the sexiest color to wear. People notice you more in red.

I always have Eric approve the dress first though, he's my biggest fan. Tells me I'm hot even when I don't feel like I am. I have a little bit more boobs since the kids, but not a whole lot more… I have a tiny bit of cleavage. Something I never had before, I even tried a push up bra, did not work at all. And you know Cam's a boob man.

I stop and wonder sometimes. Am I still trying to please Cam? Am I still trying to get his attention?

Some days I say, yeah, other days I say no… when I dance around him and the sweat is glistening on my chest, I know I see his eyes go right there, he cant hide it. And he doesn't try to either. He gives me that devilish grin of his. His blue eyes turning darker blue when he smiles at me.

We'd have so much fun on stage, the teasing, sensuous, seductive game we play with each other, that some times Rob would have to twang his guitar a wrong note to get our attention. Every time it would be a different way of teasing each other. Come on we're allowed to have fun.

I hate the microphone stand in front of him. Or course he needs it there to hold the mic, while he sings and plays the guitar. But I always wanted to get in front of him, when I danced. So spontaneously I grabbed the stand, put my feet on both sides of the base and danced with it. Rocking it back and forth. I never once tipped it over. Cam of course looked at me, this was unusual. But it worked. I never did it again though, felt like I was stealing the show from Cam.

Eric wondered about it. It still makes him uncomfortable. I tell him, "I'm just acting. Nothing to be alarmed about, it doesn't mean anything."

He's still jealous after all these years.

The concerts are the best. And there always getting better. I think all the fans have met all of the band members by now. Which makes them feel like their Cam's best friend.

This is Cam's ultimate plan. He wanted every fan to feel like they personally know him, know us. Every concert Cam has a guest singer come and play with them. Usually the lead singer from another band. Like tonight its, Jerry Cantrell from Alice in Chains.

Melissa is the spokes person for breast cancer, at the concerts. She makes an appearance at every concert. We still have the sing along. Most people ask for the old songs.

Sales of the new CD went through the roof, donations still keep pouring in. There's a reason their named "the band of the decade." Another award from Canada, Juno Awards, for one of Cam's songs, he wrote.

Some things gotta go wrong cause I'm feeling so damn good. Would be one way of putting what happened next.

Everyone was riding on a high. We felt like nothing could go wrong.

The band was on every late night show. Interviews by magazines, the cover stories of many. I started to keep a scrap book, collected every little piece I found about them. I have five books stuffed with articles and pictures.

I still pressed Cam for the calendar. He finally agreed. I took the pictures, which were tastefully done, I took him to the beach and took the pictures. White sand, drift wood, blue sky, and Cam. One of the band, all the members. And one totally of him. One picture, which is my favorite, he's only got on a ripped pair of jeans. Low on his waist. And nothing more. You can imagine what's below. You'd know to much. He wanted to, too….I said we were doing a classy calendar, not playgirl.

Melissa found a lump under her arm. Her cancer came back. They removed the lump, but it had spread to her lymph nodes. Spread to her liver. Chemo was doing nothing. They pumped her full of medicine, she was so sick. And couldn't take it any more. There was nothing they could do for her.

We postponed the next few concerts. Told fans not to return them they would still get their concert.

Shortly after Melissa found the lump, and she started her new treatments, she died.

Cam was with her, she didn't want to die in the hospital, so he took her home. It was unbelievable grief. Her funeral was as big as Princess Diana's was. Well maybe a little bit smaller. Even though it was meant to be private, people found out anyway. They wanted to pay their respects. Cam was angry at first, because he felt they were invading something that was suppose to be sacred.

I told him his fans were mourning her too. After all she became a big part of the concerts.

We made sure that Cam was never alone, at all afterwards. Someone was always with him. To keep him out of trouble, to keep his head above the water.

How long do you mourn someone? Fans wanted to know when the concerts would start again. Especially ticket holders.

We all had a meeting, together without Cam. Its true everyone grieves differently. But for months now he's been moping around. It was time for him to join the living, to continue living.

So we dragged him out of his cave and tell him its time to get on with life. It was a slow process, but he came around and was playing his guitar and writing songs, again.

Every concert was dedicated to her. So she was never forgotten.

Cam still carries around this sadness though. Sometimes I see it in his eyes, when he thinks no one is looking. How sad his blue eyes look. He stares out into space. He fell in love with her the minute he saw her. Her big brown eyes, her pretty face, her petite size, the way she fit perfectly against him. The way they loved each other.

Then he would feel me looking at him and he would look over at me, and then look away. Time heals, is that really true? How do you mend a broken heart? How can I mend his broken heart?

He never did go to the Greek Isle, we rented for him. Maybe it was time we all went for a little vacation.

I mentioned it to Eric, every one had forgotten about it, he said it sounded great, Rob, Dale and Matt agreed it would be perfect. Getting Cam to agree was another thing.

The sun, the warm fragrant air, the beautiful blue green water, the white sandy beaches, and the food. It was a magical place. The white houses dotting the hillsides. The little fishing villages, that were tucked in to the side of the mountains. It was so charming, so peaceful, so beautiful.

So romantic, and Eric and I took advantage of that. We'd sneak off and find some secluded place to have a romantic swim or dinner.

The band brought their families with them. I asked Cam if he could teach my boys how to play the guitar. For a few minutes every day Cam would show them a few cords and notes. They even had their own little guitars, it was so cute. And this was also the first time they were on an airplane.

It always and still does fascinates me to watch Cams fingers fly over the strings. He is an awesome guitar player. Even my kids love to watch him. And every day the lesson gets a tiny bit longer, as they begin to understand more and become more interested in playing. Just like Eric started to teach them how to ride the dirt bikes, and how to fix them. They have no fear, no bad habits, its like a clean slate to teach them, the right way to do something. To ride a horse, to do anything….

We stay a month on the Greek isle. Everyone is relaxed and tanned. Cam looks so hot with his curly blonde beach hair and a tan. His rocking hard body, that sexy walk. I stand on the deck of the villa, and watch him strolling on the beach with my boys. He knows I'm watching, and looks up at me, his hand shading his eyes, he gives me a wave. I wave back, and sigh.

Eric is just as hot, "Come here, Janie," he says to me, and pats the lounge chair to sit next to him. I lather on sun screen all over his chest, which gets us kissing and touching, "Oh get a room," someone says.

I dared wear a bikini, which Eric appreciated. I think it might have given Cam deja vu. Hot tub, me, him, his house.

But he would look the other way. It got me upset. Did I lose Cam? I mean I never really had him anyway, he never was really mine, he was always Melissa. But I felt like I had a small part, how ever small it was of him. It made me sad. Eric asked me why I was sad. I couldn't tell him. I just said I was sad because we had to leave and go home. Which was partly true.

This was a fairy tale vacation. Everything about it, the food, I never had to cook. The cleaning, someone did that for you. Even your laundry. All we did was have fun, relaxed and bought what ever we wanted.

So for a time it was hard to talk to Cam. About anything. Did he resent me in anyway? Like maybe it should have been me instead of Melissa. We were polite to each other, but that was it. I wanted to ask him, but his eyes said otherwise. Like just leave it alone. I don't want to discuss anything right now. I don't want to analyze it either. So I'd walk away. I could feel his eyes on me, but he wouldn't come after me, like he used to. Come and try to make things right between us. I knew it would take time. So I left him alone for now.

On the plane ride home, Eric started to feel sick, was it something he ate or the water? His stomach hurt, even said his arm was hurting. He plays rough and he eats everything in sight. Even the octopus legs that were in the soup. Ugh!

He slept on and off in the plane. His long legs stretched out in the isle. The air attendant would try to get me to move them, but I'd give her a dirty look. Just leave him alone, look. The guy was tired and didn't feel well.

We weren't going home, home. We were going to Edmondton. Close enough to home for the boys. So his mom came and got them.

They had to practice their guitars every day and Cam is going to send them some DVDs of guitar lessons. He was going to do them for them. I always said "thanks," to him. It never seemed like it was enough, funny he once said that to me.

Eric didn't feel good for the entire week after we got back from the Greek isle. I was very worried about him. He wasn't eating to much. His color turned gray and his skin was clammy. He worked, but would come back to the hotel exhausted, eat very little, take a shower and go to bed. I wake up a lot during the night to check on him. I'd put my hand on his forehead to feel if he was hot. Just always that cold clammy feeling.

After a week, he still wasn't any better. I insisted he go to the doctor. I went with him to make sure he went. He hates doctors, he says, they make him nervous.

Turned out he was having a mild heart attack. All the signs were there, he just ignored them.

"But he's only thirty five," I said to the doctor. "How can that be, I mean look at him, he's always so healthy as a horse."

Turns out he has a hereditary heart condition, I learned from his mother. He never mentioned it to me. Was it fixable? Was it preventable? And what about my children? I was getting hysterical. All of these questions.

More test, pills, maybe even heart surgery, to fix the problem. My stomach was filled with butterflies or maybe more like a hornets nest.

They always say things, bad things, come in threes. A silly superstition I hope.

What would I do without him? He was my best friend, my lover, my husband, my boys father. They were to young to be without a father. I didn't want to think about it. So I pushed it to the back of my mind.

This was to much to bare. "Schedule the heart surgery," I told him. "As soon as possible."

"Janie, honey," he said, he took me in his arms. "I'm feeling much better, now, the pills are working, the medicine is helping." Its true, he wasn't looking so grayish and his skin wasn't clammy. He even got back most of his appetite.

"Don't worry," he said.

It still didn't have me convinced.

I called the doctor the next day.

He said with more tests and the right meds Eric may not need surgery. "But if its hereditary, and his father died from it, how can some pills fix it?" I wanted to know. I don't even remember what the doctor said. My mind was racing.

So many things Eric and I haven't done yet. So many things we wanted to do. Like another baby. The farm to run. Watching the boys grow up. And growing old together. I wasn't ready to give any of that up. I wanted every thing and more. No…...this wasn't happening, this wasn't the plan. Second opinions, always get a second opinion. Or even a third, until you get the answer you want.

So I called another heart specialist. He must of talked to the other doctor. Because he said the same thing. He did the same tests.

So I had to except it? No way, no how. Was I excepting this. I didn't want to, I didn't have to. Eric seemed fine about it. Every time he sneezed I had a panic attack. "Stop looking at me like that," he'd say to me while we were eating lunch.

"Looking at you like what?" I say, practically jumping out of my skin.

"Like I have two heads or I'm going to explode or something." He'd say.

"I'm just concerned Eric, about you, I'm scared. I don't want to lose you. How can you be so…...so nonchalant about this whole thing?" Tears escaping from my eyes.

"Because…I've had it my whole life, I've lived with it every day. Every hour, every minute, every second, of my life. I decided I wasn't going to let it ruin my life, or let it run my life. I was going to live it the way I wanted to. Whether it was playing football or dirt bikes, or horse back riding or farm work. I wasn't going to let it control me." He takes my hand in his and squeezes it.

"Oh," was all I could say. From now on I would say a little pray for him just in case. And for me to give me strength to accept it, like Eric has. But it didn't mean I liked it. Hell, except it no way, he was going to have this fixed.

I wanted the boys to spend as much time with their father as they could.

On our days off we planned outings. At night he would read to them or sat and listened to them play their guitars. We watched DVDs or went to the movies. They really make some good kids movies now.

I take a lot of pictures and video pictures of Eric and the boys. We watch them together, laughing along with them and then I'd stop, and want to throw up. That feeling of him not being here, would overwhelm me. I'd have to hide my face from him because the tears would come rolling down my cheeks. I didn't want him to see me crying. So I'd wipe the tears away, and try to block it all from my mind. When I couldn't, I did a lot of heart research, called a lot of doctors.

Live every moment, like today was your last day. Eric did that everyday. He always did. From the first time I made him blush to now, buried in beach sand up to his neck. Always laughing, always smiling, always having a good time.

The boys come to the concerts, Cam always let them come out on stage with their little guitars to play. Everyone thinks they're so cute.

"Lets here it for my nephews, Eric Jr. and may name sake, Cameron." Cam would tell the audience. They would have huge grins on their little faces, when they walked backstage.

Sometimes I stood out in the audience, so I could film them. I documented everything these days. I didn't want to forget one thing. Like the "Notebook" where she writes their life story down, in a notebook. So she'll remember later. I cried so much when I saw that movie. I cant watch it any more. So I'm making my own notebook. So I'll remember, so the boys will remember. So Eric will remember.

This is my footprint on this earth. So everyone will know we were here. Cam will be remembered for his music, for the band. Like Elvis Pressley or Michael Jackson, their footprints are forever planted on this earth.

The night after the fifth show in Edmondton. It was rainy and very dark outside. Nothing to do but stay inside. Watch a movie, eat popcorn, play some games.

Eric went to bed early. Said he was tired. The boys and I stayed up a little longer to finish watching a movie.

I put them to bed. Climbed into bed next to Eric. I kissed him goodnight. And wrapped my arms around him. He held my hands to his chest. I could feel his heart beating strongly. Around five in the morning, I rolled over. And went back to sleep. I remember because I looked at the clock.

We slept late. The boys always wake up early. They want breakfast. So I order some. And ask Eric what he wants. He never answers me. The boys eat. I crawl back into bed. I noticed how cold Eric is and how still he is. That coldness going right through me, right to my bones.

I touched him and I knew. He's never going to wake up again. "Oh Eric," I remember sobbing, and I held him in my arms for the longest time. What should I do? Who do I call?

Cam, I have to call Cam. I'm shaking so violently, I can hardly see the buttons, much less press them. But I do. He answers. I'm crying now, I barely can get the words out of my mouth.

"Janie," he says. "I'll be right there." He doesn't even knock. He comes right in the room. Looks at the boys. Looks at me. And walks into our room, where Eric is lying in the bed. Calls the police. I'm a total wreck. I throw up in the bathroom. I'm shaking so hard, I cant even turn off the light switch. My knees collapse. I sit on the floor, and wait for the police. Cam takes the boys down to the pool. Before the police come.

He holds me in his arms before he leaves, and puts me in a chair. "I'll be right back," he says. "I'll leave the boys with one of the crew. Don't worry okay. As soon as the boys are taken care of. You'll get through this, I'm here now." I shake my head, and he kisses my forehead.

The police and ambulance come. They ask me a lot of questions. What do they think? I killed my husband or something. I tell them he had a heart condition, and show them his medicine.

Cam called Eric's mother. She stands in the doorway, as they take Eric outside. She has a blank look on her face. Just like when her husband died. How much more of this can she take? How much more can we take? I scream in my head, "ENOUGH, I'VE HAD ENOUGH."

We hug each other. She tries to be strong for the boys. I know she will be. Then she'll cry when she's alone, like I will.

Cam makes all the arrangements. I'm so lost, I have nothing in my head. No thoughts, no feelings, just a blank, dark, empty space in my head. My eyes blink a lot. But there's nothing there.

Cam tells me to go take a hot shower. But I cant. I don't know what to do. So he helps me. He says he wont look. I don't care. He shoves me in under the water. And talks to me the whole time. I don't even remember what he talked about. Then he helps me out. He finds me clothes. What do we do next? Do I go somewhere?

I want Eric back. Cam wants me to eat something, at least some soup. I eat something, I think. That whole entire day is a blur. A big whole in my heart. Punched right through. I wish my heart would stop too. Cam stays with me the whole day and night.

He's not canceling the show, but says I don't have to come. But I want to, because it's the only one thing that feels normal. But I'm not performing. Its funny, but I never knew that I looked for Eric so much when we were working. And I realize, I'll never see him again.

CHAPTER 48

Sometimes, I thought I saw the top of his head or the back of his shoulders. I missed him so much. Cam mentions yet another lose in our camp. He plays one of Eric's favorite songs, and puts his picture on the screen, its our wedding picture. And I pass out.

Someone carried me to the dressing room, and laid me on the couch. Cam's face is the first one I see, when I wake up. And for a minute, I think its all a dream.

I reach out for him, my hand on his cheek. He takes my hand and presses it harder to his cheek.

"What happened?" I ask.

"You passed out," he says. "I'm sorry, Janie, I didn't mean to upset you so. I thought you would like the tribute I did for Eric."

"I did, I was just surprised to see our wedding picture up on the big screen. I guess I wasn't expecting it. That's all. Don't feel bad okay." I hiccup.

"Okay, sure, I'll change the picture if you want." He scratches his head and shifts his feet. I know when he's uncomfortable. But every thing is to soon, we haven't even buried him yet.

"No really its okay, it's a great picture. Thank you for doing it. For remembering Eric." There was a strained silence between us. Why has it been so hard for us to talk to each other?

Eric's funeral was three days later. And a lot of fans show up. Family, friends, some other rockers of Cam's. We just did this a few months ago.

The same black dress. I'm throwing it away after today. I hold Eric Jr's hand, Cam holds Cameron in his arms. I'm so numb, I cant even feel his hand in mine. I've cried a million tears, I have no more left to cry.

There's so many flowers, so many mourners, but I see none of them. They all come up to you, and say how sorry they are. How great Eric was. Blah, blah, blah. I just shake my head, and say thank you.

People I have no idea who they are come up to me, I say nothing to them. Cam thanks them for me. Eric Jr. wont let go of my hand. Cameron hangs on to Cam. Eric's family stays together. His Mom will take the boys back home. Jeff will try to be a bigger part in their lives. I'm grateful. Its over. All of it. I say. No more bad things will happen to any of us.

We drive in the limo to a restaurant to eat. Cam is sitting next to me. He wont leave my side. He hasn't left my side. After we leave, everyone is in the limo, everyone lost in their own thoughts. Even my normally noisy boys are quiet.

Cam booked the entire restaurant for us. No fans, no photographers. I have no appetite, and pick at my food.

Cam whispers to me in my ear. "I want you to come with me to the Greek isle," he says. "We need a vacation, the boys too."

I turn my head slightly to look at him, I shrug my shoulders. I have no opinion one way or the other.

"Fine." I say.

I throw that awful black dress out. In fact I take a pair of scissors to it, and shred it to pieces. I'll never buy black again. We pack for the Greek isle.

The sun, the warmth, the friendliness of the people, the blue water, the pristine beach, cant fill the emptiness I feel inside.

Cam watches me from the house, I can feel his gaze, as I walk on the beach. He knows exactly what I'm going through.

The boys play in the water. "I miss Daddy," Eric Jr. says.

"I know honey, I miss him too." I tell him.

I have a new bikini bathing suit on. Just for Eric, if he's looking down. That makes me smile.

"What's funny, mommy?" Eric Jr. asks me.

"Oh nothing honey, just you guys."

I remember the first compliment Eric gave me about my sexy outfit, I was wearing. How he turned beet red. How I realized that I liked him.

I feel lighter somehow. Memories of Eric fill my head. The moment when we knew we loved each other. How I always felt safe in his arms. When I told him I was pregnant again. I keep my memories of Eric close to my heart.

The two weeks Cam said we'd stay on the Greek isle were over. Time to go home. Time to start our lives again.

Start a new chapter in my life. The last chapter closed. A new one begins. We have to live. I have to live for my boys.

We have a full week of concerts. I'm going to immerse myself in my work. If I'm exhausted, I have little time to think about anything else.

I exercise every day for hours. Cook for the band. And perform at night. I'm so tired. Just like I want to be. I fall asleep, the minute my head hit's the pillow. I never dream of Eric. I don't feel him anywhere. Just an empty stillness when I'm alone. I reach over for him at night, to find he isn't there. The boys still come on the weekends for a visit. To them this is a lot of fun. I try to make it as much fun as possible.

Eric Jr. has started school full time. Cameron pre-school. And music lessons. Three times a week. For one week they go over the same lesson. The men we hired make sure that they ride the horses and dirt bikes.

They have regular chores to do on the farm. I want them to learn everything they can. So that when they grow up they can stand on their own two feet.

We still raise money for breast cancer and for heart research too. A simple operation would have fixed Eric's ailing heart. Sometimes I feel angry at his parents for not looking into it further, to find a cure for him, or to have that operation. I wont be like that with my boys. I've already had them checked out. So far a clean bill of health. Every few years will have the same tests done. Ignorance is stupidity.

I pass Cam's dressing room before the next concert. He was playing his guitar and singing a new song he just finished writing. I listen outside his door. I love his voice, I still do, I'll never get tired of it.

"You can come in," he says.

I push open the door with my foot and stand in the doorway with my arms folded across my chest.

"How'd you know I was out here?" I ask him.

"I don't know, I can feel you." He says.

"And why is that, you seem to be ignoring me again." I lean on the door frame.

"Janie, every pore of my body is aware of you. No matter how far away you are, its like you pull me towards you." He gives me a half grin.

"Really…you don't act that way. I feel like I have the plague or something, the way you go out of your way to stay away from me." I'm still leaning on the door frame. He puts down his guitar and gets up, walks over to me. He stands very close, looks down at me. Takes a deep breath.

"I was giving you some room to heal, it hasn't even been a month yet. But I'm very much aware of you. I don't want to just jump you… yet." He smiles.

His breath is warm on my face. His hands are warm on my arms. Tingles run up and down my arm to my fingertips. He drops his hand to take mine. My heart is pounding. My breath is short. I clear my throat. "So what are we going to do about this?" He asks. I blush. The heat rising up my neck to my cheeks.

I cant answer him, because I don't know what were going to do about him and me. It didn't work the first time. If there ever was a first time with him and me. Or was it just my imagination? Why would it work this time. Instead I put my head against his chest. He puts his hand on my head. And we hold each other for a long time.

Two lonely people, brought together by uncontrollable circumstances. We can share each others pain and grief, and loneliness. Its not spoken, but felt. My heart pounding against his, his against mine.

"Hi Mommy," I hear little voices and feet running towards us. Cam and I quickly separate. Awkward moment. They wouldn't understand if they saw us together like that. The way Mommy and Daddy used to hold each other…

"Hey, you guys," I say to my kids. They jump into my arms. Anne bought them to visit. "Thanks Anne." I say to her. Looking past my sons head at her.

She leaves, she never hangs around. I think she knows how I feel about their decision they made for Eric, when he was younger, about his ailing heart.

So she cant face me. Maybe that pain will fade too. She knew when I took the boys for the tests. She said it was a good thing to do. She knew that a stupid test would have saved Eric's life later.

My kids wiggle out of my arms. And jump at Cam. "Hi uncle Cam," they both say in unison.

"Hey you guys, how are you? You are getting so big." He gives them both a hug.

"Why were you hugging Mommy?" Eric Jr. asks him. He's been very protective of me, since Eric died.

He smiles at him and looks at me. Kids, they always say what's on their minds. "Because your Mommy was lonely and she needed a hug. You need a hug once in a while too, right?"

Eric nods his head. "All the time," he says. We laugh.

"How's your guitar lessons going?" Cam asks them. Rubbing his head.

"Great," Eric Jr. answers.

"Well, when you guys get really good enough, I'll let you come on stage and play with the band, okay?"

Eric's face lights up, "Can I mom?"

"Sure," I say. "When Uncle Cam thinks your ready."

I have to get dressed for the concert. The boys go with Cam. They feel right at home in the arenas were in. Everyone watches over them. Eric Jr. watches his little brother.

Since Eric died. Eric Jr. has sort of become the man of the house, even though he's only six. He looks so much like his father, even has some of his gestures. That always makes me laugh. And made me sad at the same time, sad that Eric would never see his sons grow up.

I look through my wardrobe trunk. Now it's a trunk, instead of a suitcase, because I have so much crap to lug around. I want to wear something new or something I haven't worn in a long time. I want a bright color tonight. Maybe red or fuchsia. I push past the ones I don't want and find something shoved in the back. I pull it out. Its that pink chiffon dress. The one I gave to Anne to take home. How in the world did it get back in my trunk? It's the dress I wore on my first date with Eric. The one I fell off of the drum deck in. Its ruined but I kept it anyway. And I gave it to Anne to put in the house. Is this some kind of cruel joke? Why would someone put it back in my trunk?

I look at it. Remember how special Eric made the date. How we danced together. I smell the dress and there's just a hint of his cologne. I start to cry. Balling my eyes out. I have to stop this. I've been crying so much. It makes my eyes look old and wrinkly. And it makes me sick, when I cry to much. I put the dress in a bag. I'll send it back home again, with Anne. I wonder if she put it in the trunk, so I wont forget Eric.

I get myself together. I find the red sequined halter top dress with the beaded fringe on the bottom. My black paten leather pumps. A silky white scarf. Makeup. I need to ice my eyes. When I have the time I have to go through the trunk again and clean out all the things that make me cry.

Just send it all home. I don't want to forget Eric, I'll never forget him, there's never a moment that goes by, that I don't think of him. But I also cant keep having these crying fits. I cry before I go to sleep every night any way.

I check myself in the mirror, before I go out. Cam is going to know I was crying, he always does. I think he knows me better than I know myself, sometimes.

The scarf is new, I figured I could use it as a prop. Do something with it. So as I'm dancing, and making my way over to Cam, I wrap the scarf around his neck, and slowly pull it off of him. Or I'd wrap it around his waist. Or wrap it around his leg. Whatever way it was, it was very sensual and sexy, something I never did before.

Cam likes it. I could try it on Dale too.

Rob and Matt, I might drag it across the back of their shoulder, or maybe hang them with it. Maybe. No we've come to an understanding. Everything is good.

"Janie," Cam calls after me. "Wait up." The show is over. "Tomorrow," he says. "Its our day off, lets do something together, with the kids."

" Really? Okay, that sounds like fun, like what?" I ask him.

"Yeah really, we could go to the zoo, amusement park, picnic, bike ride, boating. You name it." He says.

"How about we let the boys decide." I say.

"Okay, say around noon."

"Great. I'll see you tomorrow. Then." I smile shyly at him, why do I always do that?

"Hey, Janie." He calls, I stop.

"Yeah?" I turn around to look at him.

"I liked the scarf thing." He grins that gorgeous smile at me.

"I knew you would," I yell back. As I walk away, I can feel him looking at my ass. "I know your looking at my ass." I yell to him, I hear him chuckle. He doesn't deny it. And it makes me smile.

I find the boys and we go to the hotel. I tell them about Cams idea. They want to go to an amusement park, of course, I hate rides. They make me nauseous. Cam will have to go on all the rides with them. I can go on the kiddie rides.

My dad once told me when he was around 12 years old, he went to Coney Island. With his aunt. They went on the wooden roller coaster. He said he almost fell out when it was moving. Some how his aunt managed to grab him and hold onto him. In those days they didn't have the harnesses they do now. My boys wouldn't be able to go on the really big rides anyway.

Cam comes to get us at noon. The kids are excited, its been a long time since they've done anything, outside of the arenas. It's a nice day. I have the usual jeans and t-shirt on. So does Cam, except his are always ripped and torn all over. Which makes it all that more sexier when he wears them. I can see skin. And the back pockets with the flaps and the buttons, emphasis his butt.

We each have one of the boys hands on either side of us. And some how, I'm not sure how, we ended up holding each others hand as we walked to the next ride. It seemed like the most natural thing to do. It was nice, it was as if we had always done this.

I noticed of late that Cam touches me a lot more. Whether its just his hand on my arm or my back, or he stands with his shoulder touching mine, I've noticed he's gotten closer. Its okay with me, I actually like it. I'm so aware of his touch. No matter if he just brushes past me. It tingles all over, makes me catch my breath. And then I have to remember to breathe. I'm to old to be shy about such things, but I am. Aren't I?

Sometimes I feel the way I did when I first met him. All stupid and clumsy . Now it's the same sometimes. When I let true feelings for him surface, I could trip over a cow. I feel shy and awkward, tongue tied, and stupid around him.

We spent the entire day at the amusement park until the park is ready to close. The boys tired. We carried them back to the hummer. Cam isn't allowed to drive anything else except that. Everyone said so.

He says, "he loves how everyone bosses him around." Sarcastically.

I tell him, "its only cause we love you." He raises his eyebrow. No I wont explain that. Everyone meaning the crew, the band, his family, all of us.

Maybe he wants to hear me say it to him. Maybe he's waiting for those words, I once said to him. Three little words, that mean so much. I love you. I remember this song, L is for the way you look at me, O is for the only one for me, V is very, very extraordinary, E is for the ecstasy? No that's not it. I cant remember what the E stands for. We used to sing it when we were kids. Now its gonna bug me, that I cant remember what the E stands for. E for Eric, who used to love me…..

We take the sleeping boys back to the hotel. I put them to bed. Cam helps me. Its still early at least for the adults. I ask Cam if he'd like to stay for some dessert and a movie. His eyes light up with the thought of staying longer in my room for the night.

Of course he says sure. I make popcorn and order some drinks. Cake and coffee. I have my Snapple ice tea. Cam has a beer. One is okay, not a six pack or a twelve pack. He really has taken control of it. I'm so proud of him.

We sit on the floor in front of the big screen TV. I feel like a little kid at a sleep over party. I pick something funny. Robin Williams RV. Anything Robin Williams.

Cam has his arm around the back of me, resting on the couch. It ends up around me. Its about the most lamest move every guy makes. Its suppose to be a subtle move. Where I'm not suppose to notice when he does it. I don't mind. I smile to myself. I lay my head on his shoulder.

I could go to sleep, but I want to watch the movie and laugh with Cam.

"We should do that someday," he says. "Rent an RV and go cross country."

"But we do Cam, every day." I laugh.

"No, just us, you, me and the boys."

"That would be interesting, I'd love to go to Yellowstone Park. Or Sturgis during bike week, or Daytona's bike week, or the Grand Canyon.

Anywhere I haven't been. We could during the fall or winter, when the tour is over."

"I'll go on the computer and see what there is." He says.

Even though we've started a new tour for the new CD. We still take time off in between to unwind. You have to. Otherwise you lose track of reality. Reality is the key to a happy life. I think.

The movie is almost over. Its time to call it a night. Only Cam doesn't think so. "We have a concert tomorrow." I remind him. "Don't want to be tired for it. Then it sucks for you, if your tired."

"Oh, okay, I know when your kicking me out," he pouts.

"Really Cam, how old are you and your pouting." I put my finger on his bottom lip. And he bites it. I leave it there and bit my lip. And suddenly I'm in his arms and were kissing each other. I don't care. I need someone to kiss me. I want him too. I want him.

CHAPTER 49

We come up for air. He pulls away and looks at me. His hands on my arms. "Goodnight, Janie, I had fun. I'll see you tomorrow or later today." He smiles.

"Bye Cam, I had fun too, and I know the boys did too, thank you for this." I touch my lips. "I liked that. If you ever want to do it again." I hint.

"Yeah I do," he says. He grabs me again. Kisses me hard. And leaves me gasping.

"I gotta go," he says. "Maybe sometime when were alone," he looks at the door where the boys are sleeping.

"Yeah," I breath. I close the door behind him.

He makes me feel alive. Something I haven't felt since Eric died. I like the way he used to make me feel. I've got butter flies again. I feel like I'm bouncing all over the place, like I have little wings on my feet. I feel giddy.

Is it okay Eric? I ask. I miss you so much. I'm so lonely. And so is Cam. Could you please let me know if its alright with you? Please....

If Eric is looking down on me, I never got an answer. I guess I have to figure this out on my own. Do we belong together? I once thought we did. I was convinced we did. That he chose the wrong woman, but he chose Melissa over me, and I chose Eric.

Now were both alone, single and still attracted to each other. We can have each other. Without anyone saying anything about it. But yet I'm reluctant to jump at this. I wanted him so badly that it made me crazy. So what's wrong with me, now?

The boys go home for the week and I give Anne that bag with my pink chiffon dress, she looks guilty. But I don't ask her. I tell her to take it home and leave it in my room. I'll take care of it, later, much later….cause I cant even look at that pink dress. It still hurts to much. How long does it hurt anyway? How long is it suppose to hurt? I have a lot of thinking to do. So I put on my sneakers and shorts, ipod and run every place around the arena. Up the fire stairs, down, up the tiers and down. Through the corridors, in the parking lot, around its perimeter, a couple of times. Until I'm wheezing and feeling the burn. Have drank my entire bottle of water. Eric used to bring me a fresh water bottle, I frown. And my heart aches.

"Working out some demons?" Someone says behind me. Its Cam's body guard, Hawk, the guy with the weird hair do. I don't like him to much. His eyes always rove over me.

"Aren't you suppose to be protecting Cam?" I say, not bothering to look at him. I pretend to tie my lace.

"I'm on a break," he says. He comes closer. Go away I want to say to him. Your bothering me. I take a big step away from him.

"Do you want something?" I ask him. And look at him out of the corner of my eye.

"Cam sent me out to make sure your okay." He folds his tattooed arms across his chest.

"I'm okay, you can tell Cam, thanks, I just want to be alone, if you don't mind."

"No problem, I'll tell Cam," he gives me a nod and heads back towards the arena. But I know he didn't go inside, but stands just in the shadows watching me. Okay, I guess he was told to keep an eye on me. But its creepy.

Besides I'm not as important as Cam is, I don't need a body guard. I catch my breath after sitting for a few minutes. I still want to run. I start out walking again. I stretch, it feels good to pull out all those kinked up muscles. I look up at the sky, it looks like a storms coming. And sure enough, as I just finish saying it, a big drop of water hits me in the face.

Its starts to rain a few drops. The wind has picked up. I haven't listened to a weather report, since being on the farm. Farm work and life depends a lot on the weather. So I had no idea, we were due for a storm.

I start to run again around the parking lot, I'll be damned if I'm gonna let a little wind and rain stop me from working out. Besides it feels good. It starts to rain a lot harder. And I'm getting wet. But it still feels good. Cause I was drenched in sweat anyway.

It starts to thunder and lightening. I've been out in it before. If god wants to strike me, then go ahead. It's a down pour. And it blinds me. If it wasn't for the bright lights of the arena, I wouldn't be able to see where to go. Heavens tears. I stand with my face up towards the heavens, the water pounding my face, soaking me. I stretch out my arms towards the heavens.

"Eric, I miss you," I scream. "Why did you leave me?" A roll of thunder passes over me. My hair is matted to my head and face. I'm chilled now. I head towards the arena.

Cam is by the door, his hand shielding his eyes, as he squints and looks out into the rain. He sees me coming.

"Are you crazy?" He yells to me. Cause another loud clap of thunder, just boomed over our heads.

"Your soaked," he says. "And your lips are blue, your cold." I shake myself off so he gets wet.

"No way," he says and starts to run into the arena. "Your funny," he says, over his shoulder.

"Don't want to get wet?" I yell after him.

"No, not today," he smiles back at me. I go to grab him from behind, but he starts to run faster.

"You aren't afraid of a little water, are you?" I yell at his back.

He wants me to chase him? Why do men want you to chase them?

But I go the other way. So I'll meet him head on. As I round one of the massive cement pillars, the thunder claps over head and vibrates the building. The lights flash a couple of times. And then they go out all together.

I stop short, for a minute and wait for the emergency lights to go on. It takes them a second to click on.

There a lot dimmer, then the regular bright lights. So I have to keep my hands out in front of me.

I peel off my wet jacket. I hate wet clothes. And my wet clothes are annoying me. I have to try and find my dressing room. So I can change. The game of chasing Cam is long forgotten. The way I went is way to creepy and empty of people. I think I took a wrong turn some where. Maybe I should turn around and go back the way I came. But the arena is a big circle, so how hard can it be to find my way.

I see the fire exit and the stairs, which should lead me to the dressing rooms. I climb the stairs and another clap of thunder shakes the building. This is scary. I can see how black the clouds are outside through the wall of windows, the wind whipping around the building, you can hear it hissing through all of the doors. The rain pelting the windows.

I hope we don't have to cancel the show. I find my way to the dressing room doors. There isn't anyone around and this has me scared too. Wonder if they abandoned me here.

I find my dressing room its even darker inside, then in the corridor. I feel my way around the room. Bump into my trunk and suitcase. Find my dry clothes. I peel off the rest of the wet clothes and take a shower, there's just enough hot water to get warmed up.

I try to focus my eyes on the room. I stub my toe, the one I once broke. I hit my knee on the corner of the table. I trip over the suitcase. OUCH! I put on my velour pants and jacket. Cause I can feel the material, so I know what they are, I just hope they match.

I crawl around on the floor for my sneakers. It's a good thing, I have more than one pair. I hope the rain didn't ruin my shape-ups.

I dry myself off quickly and dress just as fast. Feel my way to the door. I have to squint to adjust my eyes to the dim emergency lights. Still no one is here, I open the other dressing room doors, all empty.

"Hello," I yell, and it echoes down the hallway. "Hello," I call again. Right about now, Eric would be looking for me. Anytime I needed to be found. Eric was always the one to find me. Lead me to safety. Put his strong arms around me, keep me safe and warm.

I slip to the floor, my back against the wall in the hallway. I sob, in the darkness, the loneliness, no one to rescue me, it overwhelms me. I sob, my legs drawn up to my chest, my arms wrapped around my legs and I just sit there and sob. Uncontrollably . Gasping for air in between my crying.

Its been a long time coming. I couldn't cry for a month. I had little fits of crying, but nothing like this, this flood of emotion, that released my tears, the built up tears, from the sadness in my heart. I don't know how long I was there. I just wanted to curl up into ball and disappear…..

…..forever.

I didn't hear anyone come up the stairs or even knew that anyone was standing in front of me. It was so noisy inside the arena. From the windy, storm outside. Until they touched my arm.

"Janie," my name a whisper in the air. He left his hand on my arm, so I looked up at him.

"Cam?" I wipe my eyes with my sleeve.

"Where have you been? We've been looking all over for you. We have to leave. The concert is canceled. The roof on the arena is coming apart." He had to yell, so I could hear him. No wonder I thought my name was whispered. I sniffle and wipe my face again.

"Hey are you crying?" He asks me.

"No," I sniffle again.

"Yes, you are, what's wrong?" He leans in close, so he can hear me.

"I got scared, I couldn't find anyone. And…And, " I hiccup. "Usually Eric would be the one to find me. And now he's not here and there's no one to find me." And I start to cry all over again. I've never really, have ever, let Cam, see me cry, like this before. But the water works wont shut off. I feel like all the glue that has been holding me together for the past month is now coming unglued.

"I found you," he says, his voice is gentle, his touch is gentle on my cheek. "I'll always be here to find you." He puts his finger under my chin, and makes me look at him. His touch ignites sparks on my skin. It makes me shudder.

I sniffle. "Thanks Cam," his blue eyes look dark in the dim light. I reach out to touch his face. I trace his lips with my finger, he takes my hand and kisses it. "Come on we gotta go."

He pulls me up off the floor. He holds me there, his face so close to mine. I'm still trembling and he holds me tightly against him. I can feel his strength, and his warmth. Just like Eric's, used to be.

"Everything will be alright, Janie you'll see." He says, his arms around me.

"It doesn't feel like it will, Cam, ever." I say against his shirt.

"It will, I promise," he says in my hair.

I turn my head up to look at him. I want that kiss, that's waiting for me on his lips. But instead he kisses my forehead.

"Come on their waiting for us, grab your suitcase, leave the rest, will be back tomorrow, lock the door." He has a flashlight, which he shined in the room.

He takes my hand. "Cam?" Someone is calling. "Where are you? We're ready to leave."

"We're coming," he yells above the wind.

We hurry to the exit. Everyone is in the bus. Rob, Matt, Dale, and Hawk-Tom, Cam's body guard. I hand Carl my suitcase and climb in, Cam in behind me, he slams the door closed. The bus is park, just inside the arenas tunnel, so we don't have to go out into the storm. Its still pounding out. Carl climbs in, starts the bus. As Carl pulls out, a big part of the roof flies past us, he looks both ways, to make sure nothing else is coming our way. The wind is whipping around us. And things are flying in the air. Hitting the side of the bus. Another part of the roof from the arena, comes crashing down a few feet from us.

"Where are we going?" I ask Carl.

"To the hotel." He says.

"This is more dangerous than staying in the arena?" Cam says a little sarcastically.

"They wanted us out of there in case, the roof caves in." Rob says.

The hotel isn't to far. The traffic lights are out. The street lights are out. All of the city is dark. There isn't any vehicles on the road, except for us. Carl has to dodge all kinds of things, being thrown into the road. Carl is a good driver. So I wasn't worried. I eased back into the seat next to Cam. He has his arm around the back of the seat. I reach up and pull his arm around my shoulder. And hang onto his fingers. He doesn't let go. He moves closer to me. I can lean against him. And I do. Our hips and legs touching. So close there's no air between us. I worry about my boys, back at home on the farm.

Carl drives slow. But steady. Where almost there to the hotel. The water pelts the windshield. Its really hard to see.

Carl pulls up to the front doors of the hotel. They have lights, miraculously. Maybe a generator. We get out and sprint through the doors.

There are a few rooms left. We have to share. We go to the fourth floor, were the rooms are. You can hear the wind, trying to loosen the roof off of the hotel. We all look up at the ceiling as if we can see it happen.

Everyone goes to their rooms. I stand outside, where do I go? Cam opens the door and pulls me in. Closes the door behind him.

"This looks okay," he says, looking around.

"I guess, looks like any other hotel room," I say. I get the feeling Cam is up to something, maybe?

He turns on the TV. The news about the storm. He orders some dinner from room service. There's only one bed, a big king size bed. That's okay. All is I want to do, besides eat, is curl up in his arms and go to sleep.

We eat dinner, while we watch TV. Cam finds a movie. A comedy. I tell him I'm worried about the boys. He says he'll call them now. There's no signal on his cell phone and we try the hotel phone. No phone either. I guess will have to wait until the morning.

I lay in the bed curled up. My eyes are getting heavy. I nod in and out of sleep. Until I finally let sleep over take me.

During the night the wind and rain pound the window. The pounding wakes me up. Cam is laying next to me. He put the blanket over me. I use the bathroom. I look out the window. You can hardly see anything. There's pieces of leaves and debris stuck to the window.

I hope my kids are alright. I'm not sure if the storm was in Hanna. I'll call first thing in the morning. I look at the time, its early morning. Still dark out. Its gonna be a crummy day if this storm still continues.

I climb back into bed. I don't move any closer to Cam. It just isn't right, it hasn't been since Eric died. It hasn't been that long. I have this yearning to be held, though, especially now. I want to be held for a long time.

I miss Eric so much. How we used to sleep in each others arms. Passing the morning away, talking about some silly thing. Until the boys would come running into our room and jump into the bed with us. Then it was laughs and giggles.

I should stop thinking about this before I start crying again. I curl up on my side, my back facing Cam. It's a big bed. But I feel him move, I must of woke him up.

"Did I wake you?" I ask him.

"No," he says. "Is everything alright?"

"Yes, the storm woke me up, I'm worried about the boys."

"They said Hanna is okay, it wasn't in the direct path of the storm, they should be fine, Janie, don't worry." I knew he moved closer to me, I can feel him, his warmth on my back. And Cam is always warm.

"Janie?" He says.

"Yeah?" I whisper.

"Can I put my arm around you?" He asks me, his breath is warm in my hair.

"Yes," I say and turn to face him. I move into his warm embrace. He wears no shirt. His skin on my face. I take a deep breath and I shudder, when I let it out. He laughs. He pulls the blankets up around us. We go back to sleep. The storm raging outside, us together safe inside.

I call Anne and my kids later in the morning. Nothing major happened on the farm. Eric Jr. gets on the phone and gives me a full detailed list of everything that happened on the farm. The horses were afraid of the thunder, and the wind. But he wasn't, he had to console Cameron. I told him he was a brave little boy. "I'm not little, Mom," he says, "I'm almost seven." He makes me laugh, and I miss them all the time. They gave the horses carrots and sugar cubes to calm them down. The alpaca's weren't scared at all, and the dogs ran into the bathroom to hide. Yeah that sounded just like Duke and Harlow. I told them I would see them the next weekend. Or sooner. "Bye, Mommy I love you," Eric Jr. says.

"Bye honey, I love you guys too." I hung up, and laughed again about what he said.

He has his fathers sense of humor too.

"Everything alright?" Cam asks me after I hang up.

"Everything is good," I tell him.

We went back to the arena, once the storm ended. And everyone started to come outside to see the damage. Carl still had to drive around all the debris that was in the road. The city had started to clean up immediately.

The crew had covered all of the equipment with tarps. So everything was okay.

However, the extent of the damage done to the arena roof, would postpone the concerts for at least two weeks or more. So it gave me and everyone else some time off. I went home. I brought my trunk home too. I had to do a better job of cleaning it all out. And make sure no one snuck anything into it. Put some new locks on it.

The bags of dresses and things were by the door, where I told Anne to leave them. I wanted to go through it all, and pack it away, if it had happy memories attached to it. If not then it was gone.

I still have Eric's clothes in the closet and in the dresser. His shoes, where he left them. His toothbrush still in the bathroom. Everything that was his. I haven't had the heart to get rid of any of it. And do I have to? Is there a law that says I have to?

I remember my grandmother, once told me a story about when her mother died. The relatives, or friends or maybe even neighbors, took all of her mothers belongings away. My grandmother said she had nothing of her mothers left, nothing to even remember her by. That was what they did, a long time ago. She said she wanted to talk about her mother to someone, anyone, even her father. And no one wanted to talk about her. How strange people were about death then. I talk a lot about my Dad, there isn't a day that goes by that I don't think about him, either. There isn't a moment ever, that I don't think of Eric. He's constantly in my thoughts every waking second of my day.

I wear Eric's wedding ring around my neck on a chain. Under my shirt. It hangs there with mine. Tied in a knot. Forever tied together. Close to my heart. Someday I hope to let the not so important things go. But right now everything is important to me and I cant let them go.

I see his shoes under the hall desk and it feels like he's here. Our wedding pictures are everywhere. I look at them and sometimes its as if I don't really see them. As if it was so long ago, so long ago…… And then other days it only feels like yesterday.

I meet the guitar teacher who answered Anne's ad. He went to school with Cam. Didn't everyone go to school with Cam? He said he had a band too. But I guess it wasn't high on his list as a career. He's a good teacher and has a lot of patience. And the boys like him, they've learned a lot from him.

I can tell he wants to ask me about Cam and his band. I don't mind talking about Cam. Or the band. When he talks about them, he seems just a tiny bit remorseful, that he didn't make it big like Cam.

I have a huge herb garden and vegetable garden. Luckily a lot of the plants like the cold. I've been working on getting that organized.

For two weeks now, I've been outside, weeding and thinning, on my hands and knees most of the time. When I work I really get into it. And the entire world goes away. All the outside world disappears, all the problems, all the pain, everything. I let Geronimo out of his fenced in pen, he wont run, he's to old to care. He roams around, eating all the sweet grass. While I was weeding, he came up behind me, and nuzzled me with his nose, in the back of my head, breathing hot air into my hair. He always did that to me, when Eric would bring him for our ride together. I closed my eyes, it sent goose-bumps all over me. For just that one moment, it felt like Eric was here. And I was here with Eric, in our own little world together, nothing from the outside world could come in.

That's why I didn't hear the car pull up. Or hear my name called, or even see the person standing in the shade of the big oak tree until he was almost standing right in front of me. The sun in my eyes, as I squinted to see who it was. I'm sure I looked a mess. I'm wearing the most raggedy clothes, I probably have dirt all over my face. I know my hair is a big mess. I put it up in a big clip, but its fallen out of the clip and its all around my face. I have no shoes on. I kicked them off long ago.

The dogs are sleeping in the grass, "some watch dogs, you are," I say to them, Duke lifts up his head and looks at me, then lays back down again. So they didn't even bark when the person came up in front of me. Geronimo chewing the grass, around the dogs.

I shield my eyes as I look up. "Can I help you?" I ask.

He clears his throat, and says, "Cant you see me, Janie? Its me Cam."

"Oh Cam, I'm sorry, no the sun is in my eyes. What a nice surprise, what are you doing here?"

"I came to visit, I've missed you. My big house is pretty lonely," he sighs.

"What's the matter, that cat of yours isn't any company?" I tease.

"The house is so big, half the time I cant find the damn cat." He laughs.

"Any news about the arena yet? When can we get back to work?" I ask him, as I try to fix my hair, and brush some of the dirt off of me.

“They say at least another week, we should really book another arena, but I think everyone needed a rest.” He says.

“Yeah, I sure did. I’ve caught up on all my work, around here and then some. I met the kids guitar teacher too.” I get up and dust myself off, its useless, I’m just to dirty. The dogs get up and come over to Cam. Wagging their tails, Duke puts his nose in Cam’s hand. Harlow brings a ball for Cam to throw. And drops it at his feet, Cam picks it up and throws it, they go off running and barking after the ball.

“Some watch dogs, uh?” I say.

“Yeah they are funny, so are you finished here? I came to take you out to dinner.” He says.

“Oh…I guess, I’m done. I have to take a shower and get dressed. Are you pressed for time?” I ask him.

“No take your time.” He says. We walk towards the house. I feel so tiny standing next to Cam without my shoes on. Six foot one is a nice height for a man. I can wear my four inch heels and be almost the same height as him. Nice for kissing. With that thought. I get that awkward and shy feeling again. Like I’m some stupid little school girl and the guy shes crushing on just found out.

“Come to the house, the boys should be home from school soon, they’ll be happy to see you.”

“So how are the guitar lessons coming?” Cam asks.

“Good, you should hear the boys play, its amazing. The teacher said he went to school with you.”

“Oh yeah, who is it?” He asks.

“Rob Smith, do you remember him? I ask, I open the back door to the kitchen. We walk in, just before the door slams shut, Duke and Harlow barrel in.

“I have to feed these two monkeys,” I say. “Make yourself at home. Do you want something to drink?”

“A beer, if you got one.” He says. He looks around, touches things. I hand him a beer, Eric’s beer. Feed the dogs.

“You have a nice house Janie.” Cam says. It’s the first time Cam has ever been here. At my new house.

“Thanks, I’ll go and take a shower and get dressed. Would you mind getting the boys off the school bus?”

“No, no problem?” He says.

CHAPTER 50

He goes outside and sits on the porch swing, takes his beer with him. I look in the hall mirror. Oh good god, I look an awful mess. My nose is even peeling. I run upstairs to the bathroom to take a shower. The dogs following me. I see the school bus coming up the long driveway, from the bathroom window. Cam goes out to meet the bus. I can hear the excited voice of the bus driver. "Oh my god, Cam Konner, oh my god, can I have a picture with you?" She asks him.

I laugh, I guess I would have the same reaction too, I use to didn't I. She's a doll anyway.

I take a shower. Use my favorite smelling shampoo and soap. The best smelling stuff, like every flower in the desert. I forgot to ask Cam where we are going. I look out the window again. Their still standing outside talking. I open the window. "Hi guys," I yell down to them.

"Hi, mommy," they yell back.

"Hey, Cam? Where are we going for dinner, what should I wear?"

"Not to dressy," he says, "Casual."

"Okay, I'll be down soon. Hi Karen," I yell to the bus driver. And wave to her. She waves back. I close the window. Go to my room and throw open the closet door. I have a closet full of beautiful clothes, but its always a delimia what to pick out and wear. Eric bought me clothes, every time we went to a different city. Sexy, lacy things. Its amazing he ever found the time. And he got over feeling funny about buying woman's clothes, once he found out just how sexy some of them were. And that he could go into a little shop and no one would look at him. I find a pretty white lacy blouse, pink dress pants and my vera wang pink patent leather pumps. A little jewelry. Pearl necklace. Pearl earrings. A little makeup, my face is sunburned. My nose peeling. Freckles dot my face, just like when I was a little kid. And I hated them.

I take a long look at myself in the mirror. How strange things have turned out. I think. And it all started with an obsession. I close the door. Walk outside.

Cam looks at me and smiles. "Hi mommy, you look pretty." Eric Jr. says.

"Thanks honey, how was school today?"

"Good," he says, "Jeremy got in trouble again, for eating the glue." Cam makes a funny face. "Yeah, that Jeremy, sounds like quite a kid." I laugh. Cam chuckles.

We walk them over to Anne's house. "You have to go to Grandma's house tonight, Uncle Cam wants to take Mommy out for dinner. Okay?"

"Okay," they both say. Besides going to Grandmas house, is like camping out. And she spoils them. Up late, lots of snacks, and movies, games, and new toys. She spoils them.

I knock on the door. "Hi Anne, could you watch the boys tonight, Cam is taking me out."

"Oh hi Cam," she says. She smiles at Cam and says sure, lets the boys in. I kiss them both.

"Bye Uncle Cam, bye Mommy," they yell back.

"Be good for Grandma," I tell them. "Thanks Anne."

"I'll see you guys later, be good."

Cam puts his arm around my waist as we walk back towards his hummer. I feel uncomfortable with Anne watching us.

We walk to the hummer, he opens the door for me. I get in. He gets in the drivers side. It's the hummer from now on. I know he'd rather drive something fast. And dangerous.

"Where are we going?" I ask.

"Back to Edmondton, to a nice little restaurant." He says, with a smile.

It'll take a while to get there. Its early. Were quiet as we drive down the dirt road onto the main road, out of Hanna. I notice he barely looks at the small town as we pass through it. I thought he always had fond memories of this town.

I want to ask him so many things. Like how is he feeling about us. If there is an us. Could there be an us? Maybe its to soon, to ask, to soon for me anyway. So I don't ask.

"The boys look good," he breaks the long silence.

"Oh yeah, their doing good. Jeff fills in a lot, as a father figure. He does look like Eric…but its not the same…. You never answered me about the music teacher, Rob Smith, if you remember him?"

"I knew him…we were sort of like rivals. I had my band, he had his band. We competed for gigs in town. At one point, he wanted to join my band, but I didn't want him to. So I told him, no."

"Oh, he never acted like anything happened between you guys, I wont bring it up anymore." I give him a lame nervous smile.

"Its in the past, it doesn't matter anymore. He pauses. "Look theres no easy way to say this, so I'm just gonna say it. I've been wanting to ask you…how have you been feeling since Eric died?"

"You can ask…I've been wanting to ask you the same after Melissa died…I have my moments, you know." He shakes his head, like he knows exactly what I'm talking about.

"Sometimes I'm okay and I think about all the good things we had together, and then sometimes…like late at night, when I'm alone in bed, it overwhelms me and hits me like a ton of rocks, that Eric is really gone. And this heavy lonliness falls over me like a blanket. Sometimes it makes me feel like I'm suffocating. I have to throw the covers off and sit up in bed. I cant cry to much anymore, although I do, but just for a second or two, then its over. My crying gets the boys upset, so I try not to do it to often. So I'll do it in the shower or when I'm alone." I look over at him. The hummer has bucket seats. I want to sit next to him.

"What about you?" I ask.

"Something about the same. I relive certain moments with her. How I could have changed things or maybe I could have done more. Sometimes I feel like its all my fault."

"No Cam, its not, never was, it was something that was out of your hands. Same thing with Eric. If I had known he had a heart condition. I would have made him go to the doctor and get it fixed. But he kept it a secret. So don't blame yourself." He grabs my hand and squeezes it.

"I know, sometimes its hard though, like you said, especially when your alone."

"Well maybe we shouldn't be alone. Then we wont have time to think about such things."

"Maybe." He says. We get to Edmondton quicker than I thought we would. We talked most of the way. Once Cam broke the silence.

He parks downtown. "You don't mind walking, do you?"

"No me, walking, it's a nice night for a walk. Are you sure you can? You have no body guard with you." He gives me a smirk. As I tease him about his shadow.

"I don't always need a body guard, just some sunglasses, a hoodie, and a girlfriend on my arm, no one will know who I am." He threads his arm through mine as we walk downtown to the restaurant.

When he says girlfriend, it made my heart jump all over the place. He takes my hand and we walk passed the shops. There still open.

"You know what?" I say. "I wish I could find that pink dress I had, the one I ruined. I loved that dress."

"We could shop," he says.

We pass a jewelry store. I pause at the window display. I love diamonds and gold and shiney things. That sparkle. Cam watches me. "Diamonds are a girls best friend." He says.

"Something like that," I say and sigh. "Eric bought me my ring here."

"Really, that's funny, I bought Melissa's ring here too."

"Hum…"I say. We walk further down. Theres a dress shop. But it doesn't have any thing close to the pink dress I want. Or any that I even like, only because I'm looking for that one pink dress.

That pink one, the only pink one. Eric's pink dress.

"The restaurant is up ahead," he says. "I made reservations." We go in. There is no one here. I look around confused.

"Cam is it closed?"

"No, I booked it just for us," he says. Of course he did, cause he's Cam Konner.

"Oh," the owner comes over to us, happy that were here. I bet. Sits us at a cozy table, by the window.

"All of the food you requested is ready, for you to eat, Mr. Konner." The man says.

"Hungry?" Cams asks me.

"Yes, always." I smile at him.

"Okay bring it out then."

"Very good Mr. Konner," he bows and walks to the kitchen. Theres some music playing softly in the back ground.

"You want to dance?" Cam asks me.

I smile at him. "You dance?" Oh yeah that's right you do, at the Italian restaurant you did, a little. And at my wedding, you did, a little." I tease.

"What, what are you saying? That I cant dance?" He puts his hand over his heart. "Oh you wound me Janie." He pouts.

I laugh, he holds out his hand to me. I take his hand and he walks me over to a little clearing in the room. Puts his arm around my waist and pulls me to him. I lean my head against his shoulder. We move to the music. He's breathing in my hair. I love the smell of him. I close my eyes tight. Its just like when I first met him. How I wanted to remember his scent. How I inhaled his smell off of that tee shirt I took from him. Every single day and night before I went to bed.

He drops my hand and wraps his arms around my back. I put mine behind him. I stick my hands in his back pockets of his pants. He sort of moans a little. "Cam? Are you okay?" I ask him.

"More than okay, I like the way your hands feel on my butt."

"I thought something was wrong, the way you moaned." I tease. Of course I knew why he moaned. It was always easy to get Cam to moan and groan. We hear an, "a hum." The waiter has come with the food. Everything you could want. Cam ordered.

Lobster, steak, chicken, tons of veggies, all kind of side dishes. I'll try not to eat to much, dessert is more my thing.

We sat and ate for a long time. Until almost all the food and dessert were gone. We thanked the owner of the restaurant for the great food. He was more than happy, I'm sure Cam paid him well.

"That was great, thank you," I say.

"Diffenetly," he says.

We walk some more past the shops on the other side of the street. Most are closed now. Theres another jewelry shop. I pause at. But don't stand there long.

We walk back to the hummer. We get in. Drive back to my house. Its late now. I call Anne and ask her if the boys are asleep. She says yes. They can stay the night. I say thanks. But I don't tell Cam that my house will be empty. It would be so easy.

I do ask him if he wants to stay, in fact I insist he stay, cause its late. He can stay in the guest room. I don't want him traveling again.

He says sure, with a little to much enthusiasium. I pretend to get the boys, this way he thinks they are in the house and we arent alone.

I show him the guest room. He says good night. Doesn't attempt to kiss me. In fact I didn't get one single kiss from him all night. I'm very disappointed.

"Night Cam," I say at my bedroom door.

"Night Janie," he says. We both linger at our doors. I want to run over to him and grab him and smother him with kisses, pull him into my room, push him on the bed and take advantage of him.

But I don't. And he doesn't either. I turn the knob and close the door, behind me. I'm all hot and bothered now.

I want him to, I want it more than anything. I want him. I lean against the door and look at my bed. Its Eric's and my bed. It's a scared place. No way is any other man going to be in it. I could go to his room, though. No…just go to bed. By myself.

CAM

For two torturous weeks, I paced around, wrote some songs. Did this and that. And couldn't get Janie out of my mind. And then I decided I had to see her before it drove me insane.

The arena was being fixed, but there might be another week of work. So I had to leave my big empty house. As I drove down the driveway, and then out onto the dirt road, I felt giddy.

I'm glad I came. I watched her for a while, working in her garden. Before she even realized anyone was there. She made me smile, my smiles were never faked, when ever I smiled at her. What I feel for her in my heart isn't faked either. It feels like the real thing.

The sun made her hair shine. The way she rubbed dirt on her face, every time she brushed her hair out of her eyes. She looked so sexy in grungy old clothes. Her hair put up in a wild mess. Watching her, like a light bulb exploding in my head, I realized I wanted her, I needed her, I… loved… her. Then the next question, did she still feel the same about me? She once did. But so many things have happened to us. Still her company would be better than this lonliness.

I drove with a million things to say to her. A million things to ask her. Then when I had my chance I asked her only one of these questions. Am I the biggest chicken or what? But it was the most important question I wanted to ask her. I wanted to know how she felt about me. Sometimes I'm not sure. Sometimes I catch her looking at me. The way she used to. Then I'm not sure if its something else I see, like sadness in her eyes. Or loneliness, but its something, I'm not sure.

I love the boys too. I never thought I would love kids, but I do. They really are great. And make everything fun. I wonder what would have happened if the first baby Janie lost, lived. And then we found out it was mine. I wonder if things would have been different.

So I took a chance, that she was at home, alone. And that she would be happy to see me. She was surprised to see me. I think she was happy to see me. She was all for going out. Two lonely people nothing wrong with that.

I felt like I was invading her home though, with all of Eric's stuff all around. It's a process we all have to go through, when we mourn the loss of someone. For some people it takes a long time.

I lay in the bed, debating if I should go to her room or not. I decide maybe it's not a good idea.

I stayed the rest of the week. I helped out on the farm, I haven't done work like this since I was a kid. Or a teen trying to make some extra money. We laughed a lot, we ate good food, we even went to the movies.

It was time to get back to work. I left on the weekend. The arena was finished. Janie waited for me to come to her to say good-bye. She tilted her head up at me. I think she was waiting for a kiss. I kissed her forehead instead, "see you soon." I told her. I smiled to myself, as I looked at her in the rearview mirror, she looked utterly disappointed and flabbergasted.

JANIE

I packed my now cleaned out trunk up with new dresses and shoes. As I was packing, I remembered how Cam left me, all miserable, he didn't even kiss me good-bye. Kissed me instead on my forehead. I saw that hint of a smile on his face. I knew he was teasing me. But he left me all……ya know, hot and bothered.

I had a whole new wardrobe of scarfs, just for Cam. Jewelry, and thongs for Cam. My other suitcase with my everyday clothes. This time I put a lock on the trunk and suitcase. I was ready to go and waited for the limo.

Kissed the boys good-bye. The driver put the trunk in the trunk, no pun intended. The suitcase had to come inside with me. The boys waved good bye. I waved back. I was excited. And felt like a teenager again. All excited to see the guy I loved. The guy I loved. There it was, my true feelings for Cam, I did love him. And it hit me. Again like a train wreck. I did love him. More than I knew I did. And I was truly surprised, by this. I thought it was only an obsession. But I did love him.

I would be with Cam again. The week we spent at the house was relaxing and fun. He didn't kiss my lips, not one single time he was here. Instead he kissed my forehead, like I was a little kid. I think my mouth was hanging open when he drove off.

The ride was short, because my mind was filled with Cam. I was so lost in my thoughts that I didn't even hear the driver ask me if I wanted to go to the hotel first.

There's a new guy, who helps me out now. My body guard? He carries my bags to the dressing room. He's no Eric, that's for sure. He's not friendly at all. And he isn't good looking at all, either. Kind of grunts when he works. Like he's pissed off, that he has to to this for me.

I tell him to tell Cam I'm here. He tells me, Cam already knows. And practice is in half an hour.

"The driver told him," he says. As if I asked the question.

I make my way to the center of the arena. The last time I was here. I was terrified. The raging storm outside, the overwhelming lonliness without Eric to protect me.

Theres a new stage. Its brightly lit. I wave to Cam. He waves back, and his face lights up when he sees me.

He comes running over to me. "Hey," he says. And picks me up off the floor, in a big bear hug. "How was your trip? I'm so glad your here, Janie," he says against my neck..

"My trip was good, and I'm very glad to be here with you Cam." He's kind of closing off the air in my lungs. He lets me go. And looks at me. Brushes the hair out of my eyes. His eyes are so incredibly blue, and intense as he looks at me. Then he gives me a big grin.

"Good," he says. "I want to show you the new stage they designed for us. Its really big, and everyone in the audience can have a good view of the stage." He walks me over to the stage.

His hand on my back, that same tingly feeling when he touches me.

His touch on my back sends shivers all over me. His nearness, he presses his shoulder against mine. I lean into him. We are both very much aware of each other and of what we do to each other. But yet we are both fighting it. He shows me where he says to come in for my dance. The back stage is designed all differently too.

I know he really wants to get rid of the song, from the play list, but theres nothing else for me to dance too. So he keeps it just for me.

"How do you like the new guy? He asks me.

"He's alright, not very friendly, certainly not good looking, that's for sure."

"He's not suppose to be," he grins.

We walk around the arena, his arm around my waist. I look up at the ceiling. You can see the reinforced steel beams they put in the roof. Scary to think it could have all come crashing down on us.

Matt calls him to do a sound check. "I'll see you later," he whispers in my ear and kisses my cheek. His hand runs down my back, to my butt. And he squeezes it. He's driving me crazy.

And he knows he is. Why is he taking his time letting me know what he wants?

I haven't done my usual workout in about a month. Theres a couple of hours to kill, so I guess I'll get back into the intense workout, I always put myself through. I have some thinking to do, anyway, and it's a good way to clear my head and to figure things out.

I notice, I'm getting strange looks from everyone I pass. Well, not strange, but a lot of smiles and nods. Everyone is paying a little to much attention to me. Like when I first started the tour. Then they all got used to me, and I was just another one of the crew. So I shrugged it off, and continued running up and down the stairs. I have a good work out, and realize I actually missed doing it.

We eat dinner. I get ready for the concert. Fans talking, the excitement building as it gets closer to the start of the show. I pick out a new dark blue sequined dress to wear. It makes my eyes look a darker green.

Cam is doing my song, second tonight. I wait backstage. The arena is packed, like it always is, to a sold out crowd. Fans screaming as they walk on stage. Piros blasting. I always plug my ears. The first song finished. Cam looks back at me. I always get the jitters, but when he looks at me, a calm washes over me. I give him the nod.

I used to have Eric to lean on, back stage, giving me support, now I do it myself. Cam plays the first cord, I skip out. Then dance my way around Matt and Rob. Do my usual dancing, on the deck with Dale. The finish I stand next to Cam and slowly sliding down his side, down his leg to the floor. Its easier then banging my knees on the floor. I feel every muscle in Cam's leg as I slide down. I sit on the floor at his feet. I still have my arms wrapped around his leg. I sit for a minute, to catch my breath. Then Cam offers me his hand.

He helps me up, I usually leave quickly, so the show can go on. But this time he stops me from leaving. He holds onto my hand. He took off his guitar from around his shoulder. And put it on the floor. I'm confused. Because he's never done this before. I look around at all the guys, and back to Cam. No one is giving me a clue.

He has my hand in his, and wont let go of it. I look again at Rob and Matt, they both shrug, and I look at Dale, he's still sitting behind his drums, and throws up his hands.

I feel the blood rising up my neck to my face. While I was looking at Dale, and pleading with him, with my eyes to help me out, Cam got down on his knees.

He's looking up at me. "Cam," I say between my teeth, "What are you doing?" I can hear the crowd. Everyone is wondering whats going on.

He's got the mic in his other hand. He talks into it. And he says, "This is Janie everyone," and he looks up at me and smiles, "and I'm going to ask her to be my wife." The audience screams. I don't know if it was girls, that screamed or what.

Then he asks me, "Janie, will you marry me?" And he pulls out a box with a ring in it. My eyes must be as big as the moon, I feel like I'm having an outer body experience, again, always do with Cam. I feel the air rushing through my ears, it sounds like rushing water.

I have one hand in Cam's strong hand, and the other is at my neck, cause I think I'm gonna pass out. I'm so stunned, I cant speak. My heart pounds hard in my chest. Making it echo in my head. Sweat starts to trickle down my back.

He's still looking up at me, waiting for my answer. I have my hand on my chest, to keep my heart from coming through my skin. I look at the audience, who have started chanting, "say yes, say yes."

This is what I've always wanted, tears have welled in my eyes and escape, sliding down my cheeks.

CHAPTER 51

"Janie?" He says. I'm gonna start blubbering in one minute.

I manage to say a strangled, "YES," and I shake my head up and down to confirm my answer. And I start crying. He puts the ring on my finger and jumps up to hug and kiss me, in front of thousands of fans. Everyone is clapping, and cheering, whistling, even his brother, and Rob. Dale comes down from the drum deck, to join us.

I wipe my face off, with the back of my hand. Dale gives me a big hug, swinging me around, Rob and Matt even hug me. Cam kisses me again. The show must go on though. I don't even remember what happened next. I'm walking like a zombie. I've got a ridiculous smile on my face. I feel so light, I could float away. I know I have to do something, but I cant remember what it is. I laugh, how silly I am.

Hell, Cam just asked me to marry him, I look at the ring. Its beautiful. A square diamond, surrounded by tiny diamonds all along the whole band and around the big diamond too. WOW!

I am still in shock, never in a million years did I expect this. I thought he was so unsure about us, that's the way he acted. Or at least that's what I was led to believe.

I have to stop and stand still for a few minutes. I cant breathe, I'm a little dizzy. Breathe, Janie, Breathe. My head says, "Yeah but Cam just asked me to marry him." I say back.

I lean against the wall to steady myself. Cam was way to cool today. I'm a wreck. I look at the ring again. Its beautiful and one I saw in the jewelry store window. So that's why we stopped in front of the stores. He wanted to see what I liked. How in the world can he be so calm out there?

I laugh and I cry at the same time. I may be in shock, but it's a great feeling. I stand in the same spot through five more songs. That's half the show. That's when Cam comes back stage to change his shirt. Wipe the sweat off and get a drink. He comes over to me and hugs me. I close my eyes. And fall into him.

"Janie, I love you," he says kissing my neck. I take a deep breath and shudder against him.

"I love you too, Cam, I've been waiting to say that to you forever."

He changes his shirt and runs back out. Rob is playing, so is Dale. Its slowly sinking in.

I run to change my clothes, for the sign songs. The ring isn't to big, but I take it off for a minute to get undressed and dressed again in my casual clothes. I slip the ring back on my finger. It's a perfect fit. I move my hand around so it catches the light. The diamond sparkles brilliantly.

Its old fashion looking, but so exquisite.

I have just enough time to make it back to the stage. My stool is next to Cam's, already waiting for me. He starts to play softly, I come out on stage, walking towards him trying to keep my composure. Sit down next to him.

"Janie, are you ready?" He asks.

I nod to him, and smile, my heart is about to explode. I love him so much. How do I tell him that, how do I tell him my heart is going to explode.

He starts to play and sing. I have to concentrate on the words and not on his sexy voice, or the way is mouth is moving, or his lips. Or even the fact that I'm going to marry him.

We do three songs. He thanks me. I take a bow and walk off stage. I wait for the show to finish.

He has two more oncore songs to sing. Then he adds, “Janie likes this song.” And sings “Mistake.” Only none of this is a mistake. He even sings the song he wrote for me.

The end of the show has been changed, since we first did it, for Melissa. Were we all come out, every crew member, every person that is involved with putting the show together. Theres so many of us, that we fill up the whole stage. Everyone waves at the crowd and we all bow together. Cam says goodnight.

I want to scream, to cry and to laugh and jump into his arms, smother his face with kisses. And tell him I’ll love him forever.

I find him up front of the mass of people. I jump into his arms. And hug and kiss him, like I’ve never been allowed to kiss him before. Long and hard, soft and gentle.

“Hey man, get a room,” someone yells. I’m to happy to care what we look like. People leave the stage, were still wrapped up in each other.

“I never want to let you go,” I tell him.

“Then don’t,” he says. “I hope their both happy for us,” he says looking up towards the heavens.

“I’m sure they are.” I feel so dreamy, I’ve got my dream right here. The guy, that’s been in my dreams for so long.

“Next month,” he says, “we take a break, will get married then. On the Greek isle, have our honeymoon there. How does that sound to you?”

“Next month? I have to get a dress and bridesmaids and flowers, a caterer, photographer, oh my god, theres so many things to do. Its not enough time.” I squeek.

“Shhh,” he says, “Everything is taken care of. You just need to pick out your dress. And she’s coming for you tomorrow. She’ll meet you here.”

“Oh my god, Cam thank you, this is happening so fast.” I have to sit down, I sit on the floor.

He sits too, puts his arm around me. “You have nothing to think about or do. But just relax.”

“Who will give me away?” I ask.

“Eric Jr. wants to.”

“Oh, you already talked to him? They know already?”

“Yup they do.” He grins.

"So everyone knew?"

"Yup," he gives me another devilish grin.

"I cant believe my kids are that good at keeping a secret. I'm stunned. They've never kept secrets from me before."

"Well this one was special, they even helped me pick out the ring." He says.

The next day the seamstress comes to the arena. I pick out something vintage. Not quite white, with lots of lace. Low cut, short train, it swishes nicely around my legs. Its light enough for the Greek isles heat.

I even get to buy some honeymoon clothes. I want them to be extra special, and extra sexy. I wait on the bathing suit though, because I can get a really awesome one on the isle.

My dress will be ready in time to pack it safely in my trunk. Cam and the boys are going to wear the traditional white shirt and pants. Bridemaids are Rob's, and Matt's wives, and Dale's wife. Anyone that wishes to come, can.

We have three weeks of concerts to do. Its amazing to me that I can concentrate at all. I have a mental list in my head of things I have to do. But I write it down anyway. Since were moving in with Cam, I give the house to Jeff and his wife. I ask them to keep Erics things like his shoes by the door. Just for a while. They say they will, I'm sure they wont. But they pack everything up in boxes and put it out in the barn or up in the attic.

I take one of Eric's favorite red flannel shirts with me. It still smells like him. The rest they can pack away with the rest of his stuff.

I'm not sure how Cam will feel about some of Eric's things, coming with me. I don't know what he did with Melissa's things.

Three weeks seems like an eternity away. Everything is set for the wedding, according to Cam. He wont tell me anything. Everything is packed for the wedding, except for my dress. Which I'm getting nervous about. I have to go to several fittings. The woman keeps making excuses why its taking so long. I better find something as a back up. I find a beautiful simple, but elegant dress, with a long straight skirt that goes to the floor. Simple strap sleeves, with a cap sleeve that hangs down over my shoulder, and its white. So I buy that one, I think I saw Taylor Swift wear it at some awards show.

One week is gone. Two weeks are gone. One more week to go. We finish up the concerts. The crew packs everything away.

I have my trunk packed and waiting by the door. The boys too. I haven't seen Cam all week. I don't know where he is or what he's been doing. All is I know is its making me extremely anxious, nervous and out of sorts. I do a lot of pacing around, the dress maker calls me two days before we are going to leave, I tell her to forget it. She's furious, that I didn't cancel before she went to all this trouble, I tell her to bad. She made me a nervous wreck and I had to go out and buy another dress.

I drive back to the dress store and buy it anyway. I could wear one for the honeymoon dress.

The dress is beautiful anyway. It's a little longer than I wanted. Who cares. It's the least of my problems.

I call Cam, he's not answering his cell phone, I call his house, no answer. I ask everyone if they know where he is. No one knows or aren't saying.

Its time for us to get on the plane, passports in hand, as well as birth certificate's. And I'm not sure if I should go or not. Is he ditching me? Is he running away? Did he change his mind? All these stupid thoughts and questions keep popping up in my head, my thoughts are swamped with these horrible ideas.

We wanted to write our own vows. Of course Cam's will be perfect poetic and amazingly beautiful. Mine… I'm having a hard time putting my feelings down in the right way I want to say them. I know I love him. And I want to make him happy. I will love him no matter what. So how do you make it sound all so poetic? I'm fretting over this way to much, and its giving me a headache.

The boys are excited. I invited Eric's family, but they opted out. I can understand that. But still their grandchildren will be in the wedding party. But I know, it just will hurt to much.

We land in Greece. I still haven't heard from Cam and I'm getting very upset. We take the boat to the isle. There's always plenty of people to help you out, to large men take the luggage, up to the villa.

We got off the boat and I stood on the dock, looking up at the house, bathed in sunlight. Its white exterior shining like a pearl in the ocean.

I can see decorations waving in the breeze. White tulling hanging from the veranda, with flowers flowing down the sides of the poles. I could see people scurrying all over.

"Come on Mommy, lets go up to the house." Eric Jr. grabbed my hand and pulled me to the stairs that led up to the house. Cameron was already at the top. Waving for us to join him.

Everything that had a surface, was decorated with flowers or streamers, or ribbons. Nothing was left untouched. Flowers were in tall vases and filled the air with fragmented smell of Jasmine, wisteria are floating in the air. I stand at the bottom of the stairs looking up at everything. I climbed the stairs. One step at a time. The sun in my eyes. The beautiful view of the water. The white house in the gleaming sun. People running passed me. Its all so wonderful. I forget that I'm upset. And reach the top of the stairs, someone besides my son is standing there.

Cam is waiting for me. I'm so surprised, I almost full backwards down the stairs. Cam reaches out for me and catches me. I'm in his strong arms and he's holding me tight, against his chest, I know I'm safe.

"Cam, where have you been?" I whisper in his ear. I see Rob and his wife. Matt and his wife. Dale and his wife. He gives me a wave. Some of the crew too. Local people setting things up.

"I've been here Janie, making sure this day would be special for us." He kisses me.

"But why didn't you tell me," I know I hate it when I whine. "I've been frantic with worry….I though maybe you backed out of this, I wasn't even sure if I should come." I whisper, so I don't sound so hysterical, which I'm beginning to feel I am becoming.

"I'm sorry, but I had to leave rather quickly, and I wanted you to stay there while I fixed everything here. Someone should have told you." He says.

"No… no one said a word." I hiccup.

"Well…you're here now, come and see all that's been done." He takes my hand. I should be mad at him, but I'm not. He's done all this for me, for us.

I unpack, hang both dresses up. I'll decide the day of the wedding which dress I want to wear. I cant wait to wear them. Tomorrow is the big day. So the girls through a little party for me. The guys take Cam away. I'm so nervous, I get a little bombed. I never drink, never have. I laugh a lot. Then I'm down for the count.

Its quiet now. I wake up early and stare out the window from my room. Its still dark out, but you can see just a hint of the sun coming up over the horizon. A hint of a pink sky. Some fishermen are out in their boats already. I still have a few hours. I fall asleep easily. A soft breeze blowing through the open window.

I wake up, with the boys jumping on my bed. "Wake up Mommy." They both say together.

"Today is the big day," Eric Jr. says, with a big smile.

"Did Cam put you up to this?" I ask him, with one eye open.

"No Mommy, we want to go to the beach, please?"

"I guess we can," I tell them. "Go get your suits on. Did you eat breakfast?"

"No, we're to excited to eat breakfast." They both say.

Just then one of the ladies from the village, knocks and comes in with a tray of breakfast food. She places it on the night stand by the bed, nods and smiles to me, and leaves.

"Come on and eat with Mommy," there's a note on the tray. I open it, its from Cam.

My special girl,

Enjoy your breakfast, our wedding is at 8:00. I hope you like a night wedding. I wont see you today. I'll be waiting for you at the alter. Cant wait! I love you, Cam.

I hadn't even thought about the time for our wedding. But a night wedding would be perfect. So we have most of the day to play at the beach. I take the boys to the beach with a picnic basket. I bask in the sun. The boys play in the sand and water. I look up at the house every so often. There's still a lot of activity up there, I cant imagine what else there is to do. And I think I can see Cam's dirty blonde curls every so often too.

As time grows closer to the evening. I'm starting to get nervous and excited. I tell the boys its time to go. We have to get ready for tonight.

Everyone gets a bath. I dress the boys first in their white clothes. They get a little flower in the pocket. They run out and leave me alone. I know everyone is taking care of their own things to do. So I just have to worry about myself. I picked a pale yellow for the girls to wear. The guys all in white.

I soak in a hot bath. I notice the time. Stunned that time has sped up.

I dry off and start to get dressed. My dress I decide, is the second one I bought, which is the simple white dress. Its so simple, that it looks so elegant. Light and airy for the warm night. Even though the sun has gone down, its still very warm. The gentle breeze blows through my window, and gives me a tranquil feeling. This is perfect, this is going to be perfect.

I fix my hair in some soft curls, something that Cam tries to get rid of all the time. I try to get, because my hair is so straight. And his is so curly. I pile it on my head. I'm no hairdresser. I never was a hairdresser. I slid my dress over my head. Its silky coolness caresses my skin. I look at my shoes. Some how they don't seem to fit the atmosphere of the Greek isle, or my dress, or the way I feel. I think I'll go barefoot. My nails are done nicely anyway.

I put on some very light makeup. Some light perfume, and jewelry, Cam gave me. Especially my ring.

I take off my wedding rings from Eric, kiss them and put it lovingly away in my suitcase. I hope Eric approves of this.

I look out the window at the water. I wonder if Cam is as nervous as I am. I'm ready. I've closed the old chapter of my life and a new chapter begins. I'm ready for new beginnings, for a long and happy life with Cam. It amazes me, to be loved by two wonderful men. Some never get to love at all.

Eric Jr. comes in, he has a small box. He hands it to me. I open it. "Its Cam's wedding ring," he says. "Cam told me to hold it for you." He smiles.

"Its beautiful," I close the box and give it back to him.

"Cam says its time, Mommy. I have to walk you out." He offers me his hand.

"Okay honey," I take a deep breath. I start to think how this all started. I zone out for a few minutes. It all started with an obsession.

"Mommy," Eric Jr. is tugging on my dress. "Mommy, come on, are you scared?" He asks.

"No honey, just thinking about something, that's all," I say.

"About Daddy?" He asks.

"Yeah about Daddy, but Daddy is happy for us." I take his hand. We walk out through the double doors, to the veranda. There's a carpet stretched out to the alter. I see everyone standing by the alter.

The girls in yellow on the left. The guys on the right in white. Then my eyes fall on Cam. And like always my breath catches in my throat. He looks so handsome. There's a light shining all around him, not like a spot light, but like an inner light that's shining through. His eyes sparkle blue like the water below. They light up when he sees me, standing just inside the doors.

Eric Jr. takes my hand. Cam nods to the string trio, to play the music. Its one of his songs, the one he wrote for me. I bite my upper lip to keep it from quivering and to keep me from crying. If I bite hard enough, it will remind me not to cry.

We walk slowly down, the carpet to the beat of the music. I cant believe how many people are here. Even my busy brother. Most of the crew and their wives or girlfriends. I see them, but my eyes are only focused on Cam. He's smiling his beautiful smile at me. I smile back. Eric Jr. hands me over to him. I kiss Eric, Jr. before he stands next to his brother, who is standing by Cam.

He knows he's named after Cam. So he feels pretty special.

Cam takes my hand in his. In my hand is a crumpled piece of paper with my wedding vows on it. Just like with Eric, its funny what you think of. But I doubt I can even see it, much less read it. It wasn't any good anyway, my vows.

Cam says his vows and there so beautiful, he looks at me with such love in his eyes, that I know for sure that this is for real. I have to bite my lip again. He says his vows so perfect. His voice steady and sure. Then its my turn. I cant remember anything that I wrote. So I say what's in my heart. His eyes get misty, as do mine. I might as well let it happen. Cause my heart is about to explode.

We exchange rings. Mine is incrusted with little diamonds to match my engagement ring. His is a solid gold band. The inscription on the inside of his band says, "to my obsession, forever in my heart. Love Janie." I don't know what mine says, yet.

The minister says we are married and to kiss the bride. It's a passionate kiss. Everyone claps and yahoos. Everyone throws flowers at us.

We have the reception here. Of course, that's why Cam wanted everything to be perfect.

The place is big enough that we can go off some place private. Pictures. I take some myself. We gave everyone a camera, too. Its interesting to see what everyone else will take.

The party goes on long into the night. Cam and I sneak off to one of the guest houses in a secluded place by the beach. The boys will stay with Rob, his wife and kids.

CHAPTER 52

Its what I've always wanted, but yet I feel so, again that stupidly shy feeling. The place is beautiful. A big beautiful bed, white silky netting draped around it from the ceiling to the floor. Flowers thrown over the top of the sheets. There's champagne and food. There's a soft glow from the candles.

I'm cemented to the spot, I stopped at, when I walked through the door to the guest house.

Cam walks over to me and takes my hand. He pulls me in. And into his arms. "Janie," he whispers, so sensuously in my ear. He kisses me and I kiss him back, with such intensity that surprises even me. I remember everything I love about him.

"You look so beautiful." he says. His voice is low and sexy. "You take my breath away."

He lowers one side of my dress, then the other until my dress is on the floor. I have his shirt off, one button at a time. Then his pants. He picks me up in his arms, and puts me on the bed. He's gentle and loving. Tender and intense. He brings out the best in me. And he whispers in my ear, something that he once said to me before, "Take all of me Janie, please take all of me." And I will. "I'm yours Janie Newton, Edwards, Konner." He looks tenderly into my eyes. When he said, "Janie Konner," my heart pounds a mile a minute. Chills over my entire body, I'm Janie Konner! I want everything, everything of Cam, and more. I want more of this life, more of what life has to offer. And this is the start of a new chapter of my life.

We stay for another week, I call my kids every day, just to let them know I haven't abandoned them. Their okay with all of this. Rob and his wife are making sure they are having a lot of fun.

We sight see in Greece. Something I've always wanted to do. The ruins, because I like that stuff. Eric and I never went here, when we were on our honeymoon, we spent to much time in the hotel room. No one expects Cam to be here. So there is no paparazzi. We have a wonderful time, together. Cam can be himself, and doesn't have to worry about crazy fans, ah, uhmmmm… remind you of someone?

Its over way to quickly. We go back to the Greek isle to pack, and get the kids.

Cam is already on his cell phone for our next concerts. "It went to quick, Cam." I say. He agrees.

We move into Cam's mansion. I hope I don't have to clean this place. I only bring some of my sentimental furniture with me. The kids toys and stuff. The dogs stay on the farm with Jeff. We settle in for a short time.

We are going to the states for the next set of concerts. I'm not feeling to good. I think the jet lag is finally catching up with me. I sleep a lot. We pack our bags. My trunk is by the door, where it seems to have a home there now, its just to heavy to drag around. Maybe it should stay out in the garage.

The boys go to their grandmother's, Anne's house. I'm going to have to think of a more permanent solution to this. I miss them and they miss me. Plus we want to be a family.

Always before we go on tour again, we have physicals. I go for mine. Tell the doctor, I 'm feeling tired.

"Anything else?" He asks.

I tell him, I don't think so, why? He gives me that look, he once gave me several years ago.

"Oh no….," I say. "Not that."

"Let's see," he says, he hands me the stick. I hand it back to him. Two minutes later.

"Yup, just as I thought." He says, " its positive." He smiles, "Congratulations."

"Oh great," I say. I leave his office in shock to say the least. I guess. Then I'm happy. Except that Cam didn't want children, oh well. He'll have to know. How exactly do I tell him?

"Your awfully quiet tonight," Cam says to me, we sit at the dinner table, I pick at my food. Everything that I try to eat tastes disgusting. Even the smell of food makes me nauseous. Especially pork and the smell of coffee.

Were traveling in the tour bus. We have our own now.

"Anything wrong?" He asks me.

"No.... just miss the boys." I poke at my food.

He smiles and pats my leg. "Will figure something out for them."

"Okay, then....you'll have to figure out something else too." I say.

"Like what?" He shoves a piece of steak in his mouth. And waits for my answer.

"I'm pregnant." I look at his face to see his reaction. He puts his fork down, really slowly, wipes his mouth off with the napkin and swallows his food.

He's mad. I knew it. He goes a little pale and his face goes blank for a minute. I swallow thinking he's not happy about this at all......

So I quickly say, like its my fault. "I'm sorry, I know you didn't want any children. I honestly thought I couldn't have anymore. Cause Eric and I were trying to have another, and it never happened. So I just thought...your mad aren't you?" I blink back tears.

"Shhhh...." He says, he puts his finger to my lips. "I think its wonderful. I never thought I wanted to be a father. But I love the boys like their my own. And it love it. I'm not mad. I'm thrilled." He hugs and kisses me and cradles me in his arms.

"So your happy?" I say against his shoulder.

"Yes!" He laughs. "I cant wait, I cant wait to tell everyone. As a matter of fact, hang on." He takes out his cell phone and starts to call everyone.

"Yeah a father, me, yeah can you believe it?" Over and over, until he calls all the most important people on his cell phone.

"Can you dance?" He asks. "No, never mind, no you know what, you aren't going to. You can sign if you want. But we aren't taking any chances like the first time." He says.

"The first time?" I ask.

"Yeah my first baby. The one you lost." He says.

"You knew about that?"

"I heard you tell me, when I was out in the hospital. I remember it, I thought I was dreaming. I counted the days, since our shower together. It all seemed possible, I had my suspicions." He smiles.

I'm shocked. "So you really can hear things around you?"

"I guess you can. I remember it so clearly, like I was actually there, talking to you. I could see you and smell your perfume. I could feel you touching me. It was the weirdest thing. I could feel all of these things, but yet I couldn't respond." He says.

Everyone congratulations us and watches me grow, and waddle around. I see Dr. Harris. She'll be around when I need her. Cam is going to send me home before my due date. In fact he's going to postpone the tour when I'm closer to the date. Fine by me. I'm so big, its hard for me to move. I still try to walk, but get winded fast. If it goes like the other two, it'll be early.

I go home a month before I'm due. The boys come home, and they're happy too. I'm going to home school them, for one thing the mansion is out in the middle of no where. So going on a school bus would take forever for them to get to school. Cam suggests a tutor for now.

I go into the hospital three weeks early. Cam jumps on the next flight home. Another C-section for me. And he's allowed to come in with me. Of course your mostly covered up, like a tent draped over your stomach. I'm awake.

He so proud, he could burst.

It's a month now. And I'm going with him on tour. I don't want him to miss, one minute of his baby. The boys come too.

He's into about three songs, during the concert. He talks to the audience. And tells them to "shhhh... please be quiet for a few minutes, I have something important to tell you."

It takes a while for the entire arena to quiet down, but they do.

He calls me out, "Janie come on out." I walk out with the baby in my arms. Everyone is watching, not quite understanding what's going on.

He puts his arm around my shoulder.

"This is my wife, Janie, she used to be the dancer, she'll be back, if she wants to." He smiles at me. I smile back. That one will have to think about.

"And this," he says. Taking the baby out of my arms and holds her in his arms. "And this is our new baby, Melissa Erica, I'm a daddy."

You hear everyone go, "Aweeeee." And they clap. Then someone starts singing, "Happy Birthday." And soon the whole arena is singing. "Happy Birthday."

We smile at each other. What a nice gesture by the fans.

He kisses her on the head, and she moves her tiny arms and hands in the air. Her little lips pursed together. Then he kisses me and hands her back to me.

"Thank you," he says. "Are you ready to rock?" He yells into the mic. I hurry off stage, she's gonna be use to the noise soon, anyway.

Everyone screams. I go back to the tour bus, and put her to sleep, the boys are in the arena with the crew.

She's sleeping now. I watch her in amazement. The boys will hang out with Cam, until every thing is taken care of. It may not be a healthy life style for now. But its our life. Her name, Melissa after Cam's first wife and Erica after Eric. We thought it was fitting, a way to remember them both.

In our living room, we have pictures. On one side is Cam and Melissa, on the other side is Eric and me. And a picture of our family. Our new family. Its so we wont forget them. Cause, "Love never dies."

Cam still donates to the breast cancer foundation. Its become his crusade.

I take pictures and video everyday, of the baby, so Cam wont miss a minute of her growing up. I laugh when I think about the poor guy who will want to go out with her. He'll have to go through Cam first. Every chance he gets he comes to the tour bus. Its not a great place for kids right now. When the boys finish school, they can join Cams band or go to collage.

My life has been an incredible adventure. Some obsessed idea, I had. That had no hope of going anywhere. I'm amazed. I want my life filled with laughter, and happy endings. With lots of love and understanding.

I hope the next chapter of my life is just as amazing. I want it all, I want everything and more!

THE END

To all the rockers, that I have met and love.

Three Days Grace, Buckcherry, Daughtry, Nickelback, Papa Roach, Saving Abel, and Hinder, Hoobastank. And Sammy Hagar. Lifehouse.
And to one rocker especially, whom shall remain nameless, who I love dearly, for inspiring this story.

YOUR OBSESSED FAN, JANIE

This is the song that Janie wrote, when she was mad about Cam ignoring her at all the concerts.

I wanted you
But you had no clue
For years I followed you
And still you had no clue
Then one day, you looked my way, and still you couldn't see how I wanted you

Your smile teased me
Your eyes deceived me
Your laugh enticed me
Your voice it drew me in

Till I was nothing more than a crumpled piece of paper
So when you looked my way that one fateful day
that's when I followed you home

You tried to slam the door in my face
And that was quite the mistake
All I wanted to do was to talk to you
For you to notice me
For maybe even care
So its come down to this
I had to do something quick
Before you got away

I tied you up, and put a gag in you mouth
So you would listen to what I had to say
Cause I just wanted you

I wanted you to notice me
Now look what you've made me do
You tried to slap my face
And that was a mistake
You tried to run

Anything to stop you
From leaving this place
So stop and listen to me
Look at me and notice me
Cause I just wanted to say, notice me.

If any part of this story, whether person, place or thing, has any similarities to a real person place or thing, its purely coincidental. Jill

ACKNOWLEDGMENTS

And a special thanks to my two sons, Andrew and Aaron Keller, for their support, and technical advise. For my brother, Harry Nolan, for his support. And cover design. Thanks to Clark Angelo, my agent for answering all of my questions and getting things started and to all at Trafford Publishing for all their help. And especially to Dawn Lani, for being the first person to read my book. For your courageous battle with breast cancer. Keep on fighting. For telling me that the book was good, that you couldn't put it down. For giving me some pointers, on ways to make it better. Thanks Dawn. I really appreciate your honesty.

Jill A. Nolan Jan.
2011

JILL A. NOLAN

Was born in Bayshore, Long Isand, New York. She grew up in Smithtown until the age of 21, then moved to Mastic, New York. She's an avid reader, and admits that Stephanie Meyers got her reading again. She also admits that she loves vampire books and romance novels the most.

Writing is a hobbie, as is photography, tons of crafts, rock stars and concerts, and NASCAR racing, her favorite driver is, Tony Stewart. She works as a professional driver. And she is a published photographer. She's been writing since she was nine years old. This is her first published book, she has written eight others and hopes to have them published soon.

She lives with one of her sons, while the other lives in North Carolina. She says writing this book was a healing process for her, after her father died. She said it helped to heal the pain. Her mother passed away after the book was written.